INTO AND OUT OF THE PRIMITIVE

INTO AND OUT OF THE PRIMITIVE

ROBERT AMES BENNET

ILLUSTRATED BY
ALLEN T. TRUE

POPULAR PUBLICATIONS · 2024

TABLE OF CONTENTS

INTO THE PRIMITIVE

To the man and to the beast;
To the girl, the snake, the blossom;
To fever and fire and fear;
To hurricane blast and storm within;
To bloody fang and venomed tooth;
To love, to hate, to pain, to joy,—
For of such is Life,
In the Primitive—and out.

1

WAVE-TOSSED AND CASTAWAY

THE BEGINNING WAS at Cape Town, when Blake and Winthrope boarded the steamer as fellow passengers with Lady Bayrose and her party.

This was a week after Winthrope had arrived on the tramp steamer from India, and her Ladyship had explained to Miss Leslie that it was as well for her not to be too hasty in accepting his attentions. To be sure, he was an Englishman, his dress and manners were irreproachable, and he was in the prime of ripened youth. Yet Lady Bayrose was too conscientious a chaperon to be fully satisfied with her countryman's bare assertion that he was engaged on a diplomatic mission requiring reticence regarding his identity. She did not see why this should prevent him from confiding in *her*.

Notwithstanding this, Winthrope came aboard ship virtually as a member of her Ladyship's party. He was so quick, so thoughtful of her comfort, and paid so much more attention to her than to Miss Leslie, that her Ladyship had decided to tolerate him, even before Blake became a factor in the situation.

From the moment he crossed the gangway the American engineer entered upon a daily routine of drinking and gambling, varied only by attempts to strike up an off-hand acquaintance with Miss Leslie. This was Winthrope's opportunity, and his clever frustration of what Lady Bayrose termed "that low bounder's impudence" served to install him in the good graces of her Ladyship as well as in the favor of the American heiress.

Such, at least, was what Winthrope intimated to the persistent engineer with a superciliousness of tone and manner that would have stung even a British lackey to resentment. To Blake it was supremely galling. He could not rejoin in kind, and the slightest attempt at physical retort would have meant irons and confinement. It was a British ship. Behind Winthrope was Lady Bayrose; behind her Ladyship, as a matter of course, was all the despotic authority of the captain. In the circumstances, it was not surprising that the American drank heavier after each successive goading.

Meantime the ship, having touched at Port Natal, steamed on up the East Coast, into the Mozambique Channel.

On the day of the cyclone, Blake had withdrawn into his stateroom with a number of bottles, and throughout that fearful afternoon was blissfully unconscious of the danger. Even when the steamer went on the reef, he was only partially roused by the shock.

He took a long pull from a quart flask of whiskey, placed the flask with great care in his hip pocket, and lurched out through the open doorway. There he reeled headlong against the mate, who had rushed below with three of the crew to bring up Miss Leslie. The mate cursed him virulently, and in the same breath ordered two of the men to fetch him up on deck.

The sea was breaking over the steamer in torrents; but between waves Blake was dragged across to the side and flung over into the bottom of the one remaining boat. He served as a cushion to break the fall of Miss Leslie, who was tossed in after him. At the same time, Winthrope, frantic with fear, scrambled into the bows and cut loose. One of the sailors leaped, but fell short and went down within arm's length of Miss Leslie.

She and Winthrope saw the steamer slip from the reef and sink back into deep water, carrying down in the vortex the mate and the few remaining sailors. After that all was chaos to them. They were driven ashore before the terrific gusts of the cyclone, blinded by the stinging spoondrift to all else but the hell of breakers and coral reefs in whose midst they swirled so dizzily. And through it all Blake lay huddled on the bottom boards, gurgling blithely of spicy zephyrs and swaying hammocks.

There came the seemingly final moment when the boat went spinning stern over prow....

Half sobered, Blake opened his eyes and stared solemnly about him. He was given little time to take his bearings. A smother of broken surf came seething up from one of the great breakers, to roll him over and scrape him a little farther up the muddy shore. There the flood deposited him for a moment, until it could gather force to sweep back and drag him down again toward the roaring sea that had cast him up.

Blake objected,—not to the danger of being drowned, but to interference with his repose. He had reached the obstinate stage. He grunted a protest.... Again the flood seethed up the shore, and rolled him away from the danger.

This was too much! He set his jaw, turned over, and staggered to his feet. Instantly one of the terrific wind-blasts struck his broad back and sent him spinning for yards. He brought up in a shallow pool, beside a hummock.

Under the lee of the knoll lay Winthrope and Miss Leslie. Though conscious, both were draggled and bruised and beaten to exhaustion. They were together because they had come ashore together. When the boat capsized, Miss Leslie had been flung against the Englishman, and they had held fast to each other with the desperate clutch of drowning persons. Neither of them ever recalled how they gained the shelter of the hummock.

Blake, sitting waist-deep in the pool, blinked at them benignly with his pale blue eyes, and produced the quart flask, still a third full of whiskey.

"I shay, fren's," he observed, "ha' one on me. Won' cos' you shent—notta re' shent!"

"You fuddled lout!" shouted Winthrope. "Come out of that pool."

"Wassama'er pool! Pool's allri'!"

The Englishman squinted through the driving scud at the intoxicated man with an anxious frown. In all probability he felt no commiseration for the American; but it was no light matter to be flung up barehanded on the most unhealthful and savage stretch of the Mozambique coast, and Blake might be able to help them out of their predicament. To leave him in the pool was therefore not to be thought of. So soon as he had drained his bottle, he would lie down, and that would be the end of him. As any attempt to move him forcibly was out of the question, the situation demanded that Winthrope justify his intimations of diplomatic training. After considering the problem for several minutes, he met it in a way that proved he was at least not lacking in shrewdness and tact.

"See here, Blake," he called, in another lull between the shrieking gusts, "the lady is fatigued. You're too much of a gentleman to ask her to come over there."

It required some moments for this to penetrate Blake's fuddled brain. After a futile attempt to gain his feet, he crawled out of the pool on all fours, and, with tears in his eyes, pressed his flask upon Miss Leslie. She shrank away from him, shuddering, and drew herself up in a huddle of flaccid limbs and limp garments. Winthrope, however, not only accepted the flask, but came near to draining it.

Blake squinted at the diminished contents, hesitated, and cast a glance of maudlin gallantry at Miss Leslie. She lay coiled, closer than before, in a draggled heap. Her posture suggested sleep. Blake stared at her, the flask extended waveringly before him. Then he brought it to his lips, and drained out the last drop.

"Time turn in," he mumbled, and sprawled full length in the brackish ooze. Immediately he fell into a drunken stupor.

Winthrope, invigorated by the liquor, rose to his knees, and peered around. It was impossible to face the scud and spoondrift from the furious sea; but to leeward he caught a glimpse of a marsh flooded with salt water, its reedy vegetation beaten flat by the storm. He himself was beaten down by a terrific gust. Panting and trembling, he waited for the wind to lull, in hope that he might obtain a clearer view of his surroundings. Before he again dared rise to his feet, darkness swept down with tropical suddenness and blurred out everything.

The effect of the whiskey soon passed, and Winthrope huddled between his companions, drenched and exhausted. Though he could hear Miss Leslie moaning, he was too miserable himself to inquire whether he could do anything for her.

Presently he became aware that the wind was falling. The centre of the cyclone had passed before the ship struck, and they were now in the outermost circle of the vast whirl-wind. With the consciousness of this change for the better, Winthrope's fear-racked nerves relaxed, and he fell into a heavy sleep.

2

WORSE THAN WILDERNESS

A WAIL FROM Miss Leslie roused the Englishman out of a dream in which he had been swimming for life across a sea of boiling oil. He sat up and gazed about him, half dazed. The cyclone had been followed by a dead calm, and the sun, already well above the horizon, was blazing upon them over the glassy surfaces of the dying swells with fierce heat.

Winthrope felt about for his hat. It had been blown off when, at the striking of the steamer, he had rushed up on deck. As he remembered, he straightened, and looked at his companions. Blake lay snoring where he had first outstretched himself, sleeping the sleep of the just—and of the drunkard. The girl, however, was already awake. She sat with her hands clasped in her lap, while the tears rolled slowly down her cheeks.

"My—ah—dear Miss Genevieve, what is the matter?" exclaimed Winthrope.

"Matter? Do you ask, when we are here on this wretched coast, and may not get away for weeks? Oh, I did so count on the London season this year! Lady Bayrose promised that I should be among those presented."

"Well, I—ah—fancy, Lady Bayrose will do no more

presenting—unless it may be to the heavenly choir, you know."

"Why, what do you mean, Mr. Winthrope? You told me that she and the maids had been put in the largest boat—"

"My dear Miss Genevieve, you must remember that I am a diplomat. It was all quite sufficiently harrowing, I assure you. They were, indeed, put into the largest boat—Beastly muddle!—While they waited for the mate to fetch you, the boat was crushed alongside, and all in it drowned."

"Drowned!—drowned! Oh, dear Lady Bayrose! And she'd travelled so much—oh, oh, it is horrible! Why did she persuade me to visit the Cape? It was only to be with her— And then for us to start off for India, when we might have sailed straight to England! Oh, it is horrible! *horrible!* And my maid, and all— It cannot be possible!"

"Pray, do not excite yourself, my dear Miss Genevieve. Their troubles are all over. Er— Gawd has taken them to Him, you know."

"But the pity of it! To be drowned—so far from home!"

"Ah, if that's all you're worrying about!—I must say I'd like to know how we'll get a snack for breakfast. I'm hungry as a—er—groom."

"Eating! How can you think of eating, Mr. Winthrope— and all the others drowned? This sun is becoming dreadfully hot. It is unbearable! Can you not put up some kind of an awning?"

"Well, now, I must say, I was never much of a hand at such things, and really I can't imagine what one could rig up. There might have been a bit of sail in the boat, but one can't see a sign of it. I fancy it was smashed."

Miss Leslie ventured a glance at Blake. Though still

lying as he had sprawled in his drunkenness, there was a comforting suggestion of power in his broad shoulders and square jaw.

"Is he still—in that condition?"

"Must have slept it off by this time, and there's no more in the flask," answered Winthrope. Reaching over with his foot, he pushed against Blake's back.

"Huh! All right," grunted the sleeper, and sat up, as had Winthrope, half dazed. Then he stared around him, and rose to his feet. "Well, what in hell! Say, this is damn cheerful!"

"I fancy we are in a nasty fix. But I say, my man, there is a woman present, and your language, you know—"

Blake turned and fixed the Englishman with a cold stare.

"Look here, you bloomin' lud," he said, "there's just one thing you're going to understand, right here and now. I'm not your man, and we're not going to have any of that kind of blatter. Any fool can see we're in a tight hole, and we're like to keep company for a while—probably long as we last."

"What—ah—may I ask, do you mean by that?"

Blake laughed harshly, and pointed from the reef-strewn sea to the vast stretches of desolate marsh. Far inland, across miles of brackish lagoons and reedy mud-flats, could be seen groups of scrubby, half-leafless trees; ten or twelve miles to the southward a rocky headland jutted out into the water; otherwise there was nothing in sight but sea and swamp. If it could not properly be termed a sea-view, it was at least a very wet landscape.

"Fine prospect," remarked Blake, dryly. "We'll be in luck if the fever don't get the last of us inside a month; and as for you two, you'd have as much show of lasting a month as a toad with a rattlesnake, if it wasn't for Tom Blake,—that's my name—Tom Blake,—and as long as this shindy lasts, you're welcome to call me Tom or Blake, whichever suits. But understand, we're not going to have any more of your bloody, bloomin' English condescension. Aboard ship you had the drop on me, and could pile on dog till the cows came home. Here I'm Blake, and you're Winthrope."

"Believe me, Mr. Blake, I quite appreciate the—ah—situation. And now, I fancy that, instead of wasting time—"

"It's about time you introduced me to the lady," interrupted Blake, and he stared at them half defiantly, yet with a twinkle in his eyes.

Miss Leslie flushed. Winthrope swore softly, and bit his lip. Aboard ship, backed by Lady Bayrose and the captain, he had goaded the American at pleasure. Now, however, the situation was reversed. Both title and authority had been swept away by the storm, and he was left to shift for himself against the man who had every reason to hate him for his overbearing insolence. Worse still, both he and Miss Leslie were now dependent upon the American, in all probability for life itself. It was a bitter pill and hard to swallow.

Blake was not slow to observe the Englishman's hesitancy. He grinned.

"Every dog has his day, and I guess this is mine," he said. "Take your time, if it comes hard. I can imagine it's a pretty stiff dose for your ludship. But why in—why in frozen hades an American lady should object to an introduction to a countryman who's going to do his level best to save her pretty little self from the hyenas—well, it beats me."

Winthrope flushed redder than the girl.

"Miss Leslie, Mr. Blake," he murmured, hoping to put an end to the situation.

But yet Blake persisted. He bowed, openly exultant.

"You see, Miss," he said, "I know the correct thing quite as much as your swells. I knew all along you were Jenny Leslie. I ran a survey for your dear papa when he was manipulating the Q.T. Railroad, and he did me out of my pay."

"Oh, but Mr. Blake, I am sure it must be a mistake; I am sure that if it is explained to papa—"

"Yes; we'll cable papa to-night. Meantime, we've something else to do. Suppose you two get a hustle on yourselves, and scrape up something to eat. I'm going out to see what's left of that blamed old tub."

"Surely you'll not venture to swim out so far!" protested Winthrope. "I saw the steamer sink as we cast off."

"Looks like a mast sticking up out there. Maybe some of the rigging is loose."

"But the sharks! These waters swarm with the vile creatures. You must not risk your life!"

"'Cause why? If I do, the babes in the woods will be left without even the robins to cover them, poor things! But cheer up!—maybe the mud-hens will do it with lovely water-lilies."

"Please, Mr. Blake, do not be so cruel!" sobbed Miss Leslie, her tears starting afresh. "The sun makes my head ache dreadfully, and I have no hat or shade, and I'm becoming so thirsty!"

"And you think you've only to wait, and half a dozen stewards will come running with parasols and ice water.

Neither you nor Winthrope seem to 've got your eyes open. Just suppose you get busy and do something. Winthrope, chase yourself over the mud, and get together a mess of fish that are not too dead. Must be dozens, after the blow. As for you, Miss Jenny, I guess you can pick up some reeds, and rig a headgear out of this handkerchief— Wait a moment. Put on my coat, if you don't want to be broiled alive through the holes of that peek-a-boo."

"But I say, Blake—" began Winthrope.

"Don't say—do!" rejoined Blake; and he started down the muddy shore.

Though the tide was at flood, there was now no cyclone to drive the sea above the beach, and Blake walked a quarter of a mile before he reached the water's edge. There was little surf, and he paused only a few moments to peer out across the low swells before he commenced to strip.

Winthrope and Miss Leslie had been watching his movements; now the girl rose in a little flurry of haste, and set to gathering reeds. Winthrope would have spoken, but, seeing her embarrassment, smiled to himself, and began strolling about in search of fish.

It was no difficult search. The marshy ground was strewn with dead sea-creatures, many of which were already shrivelling and drying in the sun. Some of the fish had a familiar look, and Winthrope turned them over with the tip of his shoe. He even went so far as to stoop to pick up a large mullet; but shrank back, repulsed by its stiffness and the unnatural shape into which the sun was warping it.

He found himself near the beach, and stood for half an hour or more watching the black dot far out in the water,— all that was to be seen of Blake. The American, after wading off-shore another quarter of a mile, had reached swimming depth, and was heading out among the reefs with steady, vigorous strokes. Half a mile or so beyond him Winthrope could now make out the goal for which he was aiming,— the one remaining topmast of the steamer.

"By Jove, these waters are full of sharks!" murmured Winthrope, staring at the steadily receding dot until it disappeared behind the wall of surf which spumed up over one of the outer reefs.

A call from Miss Leslie interrupted his watch, and he hastened to rejoin her. After several failures, she had contrived to knot Blake's handkerchief to three or four reeds in the form of a little sunshade. Her shoulders were protected by Blake's coat. It made a heavy wrap, but it shut out the blistering sun-rays, which, as Blake had foreseen, had quickly begun to burn the girl's delicate skin through her open-work bodice.

Thus protected, she was fairly safe from the sun. But the sun was by no means the worst feature of the situation. While Winthrope was yet several yards distant, the girl began to complain to him. "I'm so thirsty, Mr. Winthrope! Where is there any water? Please get me a drink at once, Mr. Winthrope!"

"But, my dear Miss Leslie, there is no water. These pools are all sea-water. I must say, I'm deuced dry myself. I can't see why that cad should go off and leave us like this, when we need him most."

"Indeed, it is a shame— Oh, I'm so thirsty! Do you think it would help if we ate something?"

"Make it all the worse. Besides, how could we cook

anything? All these reeds are green, or at least water-soaked."

"But Mr, Blake said to gather some fish. Had you not best—"

"He can pick up all he wants. I shall not touch the beastly things."

"Then I suppose there is nothing to do but wait for him."

"Yes, if the sharks do not get him."

Miss Leslie uttered a little moan, and Winthrope, seeing that she was on the verge of tears, hastened to reassure her. "Don't worry about him, Miss Genevieve! He'll soon return, with nothing worse than a blistered back. Fellows of that sort are born to hang, you know."

"But if he should be—if anything should happen to him!"

Winthrope shrugged his shoulders, and drew out his silver cigarette case. It was more than half full, and he was highly gratified to find that neither the cigarettes nor the vesta matches in the cover had been reached by the wet.

"By Jove, here's luck!" he exclaimed, and he bowed to Miss Leslie. "Pardon me, but if you have no objections—"

The girl nodded as a matter of form, and Winthrope hastened to light the cigarette already in his fingers. The smoke by no means tended to lessen the dryness of his mouth; yet it put him in a reflective mood, and in thinking over what he had read of shipwrecked parties, he remembered that a pebble held in the mouth is supposed to ease one's thirst.

To be sure, there was not a sign of a pebble within miles of where they sat; but after some reflection, it occurred to him that one of his steel keys might do as well. At first

Miss Leslie was reluctant to try the experiment, and only the increasing dryness of her mouth forced her to seek the promised relief. Though it failed to quench her thirst, she was agreeably surprised to find that the little flat bar of metal eased her craving to a marked degree.

Winthrope now thought to rig a shade as Miss Leslie had done, out of reeds and his handkerchief, for the sun was scorching his unprotected head. Thus sheltered, the two crouched as comfortably as they could upon the half-dried crest of the hummock, and waited impatiently for the return of Blake.

3

THE WORTH OF FIRE

THOUGH THE SEA within the reefs was fast smoothing to a glassy plain in the dead calm, they did not see Blake on his return until he struck shallow water and stood up to wade ashore. The tide had begun to ebb before he started landward, and though he was a powerful swimmer, the long pull against the current had so tired him that when he took to wading he moved at a tortoise-like gait.

"The bloomin' loafer!" commented Winthrope. He glanced quickly about, and at sight of Miss Leslie's arching brows, hastened to add: "Beg pardon! He—ah—reminds me so much of a navvy, you know."

Miss Leslie made no reply.

At last Blake was out of the water and toiling up the muddy beach to the spot where he had left his clothes. While dressing he seemed to recover from his exertions in the water, for the moment he had finished, he sprang to his feet and came forward at a brisk pace.

As he approached, Winthrope waved his fifth cigarette at him with languid enthusiasm, and called out as heartily as his dry lips would permit: "I say, Blake, deuced glad the sharks didn't get you!"

"Sharks?—bah! All you have to do is to splash a little, and they haul off."

"How about the steamer, Mr. Blake?" asked Miss Leslie, turning to face him.

"All under but the maintopmast—curse it!—wire rigging at that! Couldn't even get a bolt."

"A bolt?"

"Not a bolt; and here we are as good as naked on this infernal— Hey, you! what you doing with that match? Light your cigarette—light it!— Damnation!"

Heedless of Blake's warning cry, Winthrope had struck his last vesta, and now, angry and bewildered, he stood staring while the little taper burned itself out. With an oath, Blake sprang to catch it as it dropped from between Winthrope's fingers. But he was too far away. It fell among the damp rushes, spluttered, and flared out.

For a moment Blake knelt, staring at the rushes as though stupefied; then he sprang up before Winthrope, his bronzed face purple with anger.

"Where's your matchbox? Got any more?" he demanded.

"Last one, I fancy—yes; last one, and there are still two cigarettes. But look here, Blake, I can't tolerate your talking so deucedly—"

"You idiot! you—you— Hell! and every one for cigarettes!"

From a growl Blake's voice burst into a roar of fury, and he sprang upon Winthrope like a wild beast. His hands closed upon the Englishman's throat, and he began to shake him about, paying no heed to the blows his victim showered upon his face and body, blows which soon began to lessen in force.

Terror-stricken, Miss Leslie put her hands over her eyes, and began to scream—the piercing shriek that will unnerve the strongest man. Blake paused as though transfixed, and as the half-suffocated Englishman struggled in his grasp, he flung him on the ground, and turned to the screaming girl.

"Stop that squawking!" he said. The girl cowed down. "So; that's better. Next time keep your mouth shut."

"You—you brute!"

"Good! You've got a little spunk, eh?"

"You coward—to attack a man not half your strength!"

"Steady, steady, young lady! I'm warm enough yet; I've still half a mind to wring his fool neck."

"But why should you be so angry! What has he done, that you—"

"Why—why? Lord! what hasn't he done! This coast fairly swarms with beasts. We've not the smell of a gun; and now this idiot—this dough-head—has gone and thrown away our only chance—fire—and on his measly cigarettes!" Blake choked with returning rage.

Winthrope, still panting for breath, began to creep away, at the same time unclasping a small penknife. He was white with fear; but his gray eyes—which on shipboard Blake had never seen other than offensively supercilious— now glinted in a manner that served to alter the American's mood.

"That'll do," he said. "Come here and show me that knife."

"I'll show it you where it will do the most good," muttered Winthrope, rising hastily to repel the expected attack.

"So you've got a little sand, too," said Blake, almost good-naturedly. "Say, that's not so bad. We'll call it quits on the matches. Though how you could go and throw them away—"

"Deuce take it, man! How should I know? I've never before been in a wreck."

"Neither have I—this kind. But I tell you, we've got to keep our think tanks going. It's a guess if we see to-morrow, and that's no joke. Now do you wonder I got hot?"

"Indeed, no! I've been an ass, and here's my hand to it—if you really mean it's quits."

"It's quits all right, long as you don't run out of sand," responded Blake, and he gripped the other's soft hand until the Englishman winced. "So; that's settled. I've got a hot temper, but I don't hold grudges. Now, where're your fish?"

"I—well, they were all spoiled."

"Spoiled?"

"The sun had shrivelled them."

"And you call that spoiled! We're like to eat them rotten before we're through with this picnic. How about the pools?"

"Pools? Do you know, Blake, I never thought of the pools. I stopped to watch you, and then we were so anxious about you—"

Blake grunted, and turned on his heel to wade into the half-drained pool in whose midst he had been deposited by the hurricane.

Two or three small fish lay faintly wriggling on the surface. As Blake splashed through the water to seize them, his foot struck against a living body which floundered violently and flashed a brilliant forked tail above the muddy water. Blake sprang over the fish, which was entangled in the reeds, and with a kick, flung it clear out upon the ground.

"A coryphene!" cried Winthrope, and he ran forward to stare at the gorgeously colored prize.

"Coryphene?" repeated Blake, following his example. "Good to eat?"

"Fine as salmon. This is only a small one, but—"

"Fifteen pounds, if an ounce!" cried Blake, and he thrust his hand in his pocket. There was a moment's silence, and Winthrope, glancing up, saw the other staring in blank dismay.

"What's up!" he asked.

"Lost my knife."

"When?—in the pool? If we felt about—"

"No; aboard ship, or in the surf—"

"Here is my knife."

"Yes; almost big enough to whittle a match! Mine would have done us some good."

"It is the best steel."

"All right; let's see you cut up the fish."

"But you know, Blake, I shouldn't know how to go about it. I never did such a thing."

"And you, Miss Jenny? Girls are supposed to know about cooking."

"I never cooked anything in all my life, Mr. Blake, and it's alive,—and—and I am very thirsty, Mr. Blake!"

"Lord!" commented Blake. "Give me that knife."

Though the blade was so small, the American's hand was strong. After some little haggling, the coryphene was killed and dressed. Blake washed both it and his hands in the pool, and began to cut slices of flesh from the fish's tail.

"We have no fire," Winthrope reminded him, flushing at the word.

"That's true," assented Blake, in a cheerful tone, and he offered Winthrope two of the pieces of raw flesh. "Here's your breakfast. The trimmed piece is for Miss Leslie."

"But it's raw! Really, I could not think of eating raw fish. Could you, Miss Leslie?"

Miss Leslie shuddered. "Oh, no!—and I'm so thirsty I could not eat anything."

"You bet you can!" replied Blake. "Both of you take that fish, and go to chewing. It's the stuff to ease your thirst while we look for water. Good Lord!—in a week you'll be glad to eat raw snake. Finnicky over clean fish, when you swallow canvas-back all but raw, and beef running blood, and raw oysters with their stomachs full of disintegrated animal matter, to put it politely! You couldn't tell rattle-snake broth from chicken, and dog makes first-rate veal—when you've got to eat it. I've had it straight from them that know, that over in France they eat snails and fish-worms. It's all a matter of custom or the style."

"To be sure, the Japanese eat raw fish," admitted Winthrope.

"Yes; and you'd swallow your share of it if you had an invite to a swell dinner in Tokio. Go on now, both of you. It's no joke, I tell you. You've got to eat, if you expect to get to water before night. Understand? See that headland south? Well, it's a hundred to one we'll not find water short of there, and if we make it by night, we'll be doing better than I figure from the look of these bogs. Now go to chewing. That's it! That's fine, Miss Jenny!"

Miss Leslie had forced herself to take a nibble of the raw fish. The flavor proved less repulsive than she had expected, and its moisture was so grateful to her parched mouth that she began to eat with eagerness. Not to be outdone, Winthrope promptly followed her lead. Blake had already cut himself a second slice. After he had cut more for his companions, he began to look them over with a closeness that proved embarrassing to Miss Leslie.

"Here's more of the good stuff," he said. "While you're chewing it, we'll sort of take stock. Everybody shell out everything. Here's my outfit—three shillings, half a dozen poker chips, and not another blessed— Say, what's become of that whiskey flask? Have you seen my flask?"

"Here it is, right beside me, Mr. Blake," answered Miss Leslie. "But it is empty."

"Might be worse! What you got?—hair-pins, watch? No pocket, I suppose?"

"None; and no watch. Even most of my pins are gone," replied the girl, and she raised her hand to her loosely coiled hair.

"Well, hold on to what you've got left. They may come in for fish-hooks. Let's see your shoes."

Miss Leslie slowly thrust a slender little foot just beyond the hem of her draggled white skirt.

"Good Lord!" groaned Blake, "slippers, and high heels at that! How do you expect to walk in those things?"

"I can at least try," replied the girl, with spirit.

"Hobble! Pass 'em over here, Winnie, my boy."

The slippers were handed over. Blake took one after the other, and wrenched off the heel close to its base.

"Now you've at least got a pair of slippers," he said, tossing them back to their owner. "Tie them on tight with a couple of your ribbons, if you don't want to lose them in the mud. Now, Winthrope, what you got beside the knife?"

Winthrope held out a bunch of long flat keys and his cigarette case. He opened the latter, and was about to throw away the two remaining cigarettes when Blake grasped his wrist.

"Hold on! even they may come in for something. We'll at least keep them until we need the case."

"And the keys!"

"Make arrow-heads, if we can get fire."

"I've heard of savages making fire by rubbing wood."

"Yes; and we're a long way from being savages,—at present. All the show we have is to find some kind of quartz or flint, and the sooner we start to look the better. Got your slippers tied, Miss Jenny?"

"Yes; I think they'll do."

"Think! It's knowing's the thing. Here, let me look."

The girl shrank back; but Blake stooped and examined first one slipper and then the other. The ribbons about both were tied in dainty bows. Blake jerked them loose and twisted them firmly over and under the slippers and about the girl's slender ankles before knotting the ends.

"There; that's more like. You're not going to a dance," he growled.

He thrust the empty whiskey flask into his hip pocket, and went back to pass a sling of reeds through the gills of the coryphene.

"All ready now," he called. "Let's get a move on. Keep my coat closer about your shoulders, Miss Jenny, and keep your shade up, if you don't want a sunstroke."

"Thank you, Blake, I'll see to that," said Winthrope. "I'm going to help Miss Leslie along. I've fastened our two shades together, so that they will answer for both of us."

"How about yourself, Mr. Blake?" inquired the girl. "Do you not find the sun fearfully hot?"

"Sure; but I wet my head in the sea, and here's another souse."

As he rose with dripping head from beside the pool, he slung the coryphene on his back, and started off without further words.

4

A JOURNEY IN DESOLATION

MORNING WAS WELL advanced, and the sun beat down upon the three with almost overpowering fierceness. The heat would have rendered their thirst unendurable had not Blake hacked off for them bit after bit of the moist coryphene flesh.

In a temperate climate, ten miles over firm ground is a pleasant walk for one accustomed to the exercise. Quite a different matter is ten miles across mud-flats, covered with a tangle of reeds and rushes, and frequently dipping into salt marsh and ooze. Before they had gone a mile Miss Leslie would have lost her slippers had it not been for Blake's forethought in tying them so securely. Within a little more than three miles the girl's strength began to fail.

"Oh, Blake," called Winthrope, for the American was some yards in the lead, "pull up a bit on that knoll. We'll have to rest a while, I fancy. Miss Leslie is about pegged."

"What's that?" demanded Blake. "We're not half-way yet!"

Winthrope did not reply. It was all he could do to drag the girl up on the hummock. She sank, half-fainting, upon the dry reeds, and he sat down beside her to protect her with the shade. Blake stared at the miles of swampy flats which yet lay between them and the out-jutting headland of gray rock. The base of the cliff was screened by a belt of trees; but the nearest clump of green did not look more than a mile nearer than the headland.

"Hell!" muttered Blake, despondently. "Not even a short four miles. Mush and sassiety girls!"

Though he spoke to himself, the others heard him. Miss Leslie flushed, and would have risen had not Winthrope put his hand on her arm.

"Could you not go on, and bring back a flask of water for Miss Leslie?" he asked. "By that time she will be rested."

"No; I don't fetch back any flasks of water. She's going when I go, or you can come on to suit yourselves."

"Mr. Blake, you—you won't go, and leave me here! If you have a sister—if your mother—"

"She died of drink, and both my sisters did worse."

"My God, man! do you mean to say you'll abandon a helpless young girl?"

"Not a bit more helpless than were my sisters when you rich folks' guardians of law and order jugged me for the winter, 'cause I didn't have a job, and turned both girls into the street—onto the street, if you know what that means— one only sixteen and the other seventeen. Talk about help- less young girls— Damnation!"

Miss Leslie cringed back as though she had been struck. Blake, however, seemed to have vented his anger in the curse, for when he again spoke, there was nothing more than impatience in his tone. "Come on, now; get aboard. Winthrope couldn't lug you a half-mile, and long's it's the only way, don't be all day about it. Here, Winthrope, look to the fish."

"But, my dear fellow, I don't quite take your idea, nor does Miss Leslie, I fancy," ventured Winthrope.

"Well, we've got to get to water, or die; and as the lady can't walk, she's going on my back. It's a case of have-to."

"No! I am not—I am not! I'd sooner die!"

"I'm afraid you'll find that easy enough, later on, Miss Jenny. Stand by, Winthrope, to help her up. Do you hear? Take the knife and fish, and lend a hand."

There was a note in Blake's voice that neither Winthrope nor Miss Leslie dared disregard. Though scarlet with mortification, she permitted herself to be taken pick-a-back upon Blake's broad shoulders, and meekly obeyed his command to clasp her hands about his throat. Yet even at that moment, such are the inconsistencies of human nature, she could not but admire the ease with which he rose under her weight.

Now that he no longer had the slow pace of the girl to consider, he advanced at his natural gait, the quick, tireless stride of an American railroad-surveyor. His feet, trained to swamp travel in Louisiana and Panama, seemed to find the firmest ground as by instinct, and whether on the half-dried mud of the hummocks or in the ankle-deep water of the bogs, they felt their way without slip or stumble.

Winthrope, though burdened only with the half-eaten coryphene, toiled along behind, greatly troubled by the mud and the tangled reeds, and now and then flung down by some unlucky misstep. His modish suit, already much damaged by the salt water, was soon smeared afresh with a coating of greenish slime. His one consolation was that Blake, after jeering at his first tumble, paid no more attention to him. On the other hand, he was cut by the seeming

indifference of Miss Leslie. Intent on his own misery, he
failed to consider that the girl might be suffering far greater
discomfort and humiliation.

More than three miles had been covered before Blake
stopped on a hummock. Releasing Miss Leslie, he stretched
out on the dry crest of the knoll, and called for a slice of
the fish. At his urging, the others took a few mouthfuls,
although their throats were now so parched that even the
moist flesh afforded scant relief. Fortunately for them all,
Blake had been thoroughly trained to endure thirst. He
rested less than ten minutes; then, taking Miss Leslie up
again like a rag doll, he swung away at a good pace.

The trees were less than half a mile distant when he
halted for the second time. He would have gone to them
without a pause though his muscles were quivering with
exhaustion, had not Miss Leslie chanced to look around
and discover that Winthrope was no longer following
them. For the last mile he had been lagging farther and
farther behind, and now he had suddenly disappeared. At
the girl's dismayed exclamation, Blake released his hold,
and she found herself standing in a foot or more of mud
and water. The sweat was streaming down Blake's face. As
he turned around, he wiped it off with his shirtsleeves.

"Do you—can it be, Mr. Blake, that he has had a
sunstroke?" asked Miss Leslie.

"Sunstroke? No; he's just laid down, that's all. I thought
he had more sand—confound him!"

"But the sun is so dreadfully hot, and I have his shade."

"And he's been tumbling into every other pool. No; it's
not the sun. I've half a mind to let him lie—the paper-

legged swell! It would no more than square our aboard-ship accounts."

"Surely, you would not do that, Mr. Blake! It may be that he has hurt himself in falling."

"In this mud?—bah! But I guess I'm in for the pack-mule stunt all around. Now, now; don't yowl, Miss Jenny. I'm going. But you can't expect me to love the snob."

As he splashed away on the return trail, Miss Leslie dabbed at her eyes to check the starting tears.

"Oh, dear— Oh, dear!" she moaned; "what have I done, to be so treated? Such a brute, Oh, dear!—and I am so thirsty!"

In her despair she would have sunk down where she stood had not the sliminess of the water repelled her. She gazed longingly at the trees, in the fore of which stood a grove of stately palms. The half-mile seemed an insuper-able distance, but the ride on Blake's back had rested her, and thirst goaded her forward.

Stumbling and slipping, she waded on across the inun-dated ground, and came out upon a half-baked mud-flat, where the walking was much easier. But the sun was now almost directly overhead, and between her thirst and the heat, she soon found herself faltering. She tottered on a few steps farther, and then stopped, utterly spent As she sank upon the dried rushes, she glanced around, and was vaguely conscious of a strange, double-headed figure following her path across the marsh. All about her became black.

The next she knew, Blake was splashing her head and face with brackish water out of the whiskey flask. She raised her hand to shield her face, and sat up, sick and dizzy.

"That's it!" said Blake. He spoke in a kindly tone, though

his voice was harsh and broken with thirst. "You're all right now. Pull yourself together, and we'll get to the trees in a jiffy."

"Mr. Winthrope—?"

"I'm here, Miss Genevieve. It was only a wrenched ankle. If I had a stick, Blake, I fancy I could make a go of it over this drier ground."

"And lay yourself up for a month. Come, Miss Jenny, brace up for another try. It's only a quarter-mile, and I've got to pack him."

The girl was gasping with thirst; yet she made an effort, and assisted by Blake managed to gain her feet. She was still dizzy; but as Blake swung Winthrope upon his back, he told her to take hold of his arm. Winthrope held the shade over her head. Thus assisted, and sheltered from the direct beat of the sun-rays, she tottered along beside Blake, half unconscious.

Fortunately the remaining distance lay across a stretch of bare dry ground, for even Blake had all but reached the limit of endurance. Step by step he labored on, staggering under the weight of the Englishman, and gasping with a thirst which his exertions rendered even greater than that of his companions. But through the trees and brush which stretched away inland in a wall of verdure he had caught glimpses of a broad stream, and the hope of fresh water called out every ounce of his reserve strength.

At last the nearest palm was only a few paces distant. Blake clutched Miss Leslie's arm, and dragged her forward with a rush, in a final outburst of energy. A moment later all three lay gasping in the shade. But the river was yet another hundred yards distant. Blake waited only to regain his breath; then he staggered up and went on. The others, unable to rise, gazed after him in silent misery.

Soon Blake found himself rushing through the jungle along a broad trail pitted with enormous footprints; but he was so near mad with thirst that he paid no heed to the spoor other than to curse the holes for the trouble they gave him. Suddenly the trail turned to the left and sloped down a low bank into the river. Blind to all else, Blake ran down the slope, and dropping upon his knees, plunged his head into the water.

At first his throat was so dry that he could no more than rinse his mouth. With the first swallow, his swollen tongue mocked him with the salt, bitter taste of sea-water. The tide was flowing! He rose, sputtering and choking and gasping. He stared around. There was no question that he was on the bank of a river and would be certain of fresh water with the ebb tide. But could he endure the agony of his thirst all those hours?

He thought of his companions.

"Good God!" he groaned, "they're goners anyway!"

He stared dully up the river at the thousands of water-fowl which lined its banks. Within close view were herons and black ibises, geese, pelicans, flamingoes, and a dozen other species of birds of which he did not know the names. But he sat as though in a stupor, and did not move even when one of the driftwood logs on a mud-shoal a few yards up-stream opened an enormous mouth and displayed two rows of hooked fangs. It was otherwise when the noon-time stillness was broken by a violent splashing and loud snortings down-stream. He glanced about, and saw six or eight monstrous heads drifting towards him with the tide.

"What in—Whee! a whole herd of hippos!" he muttered. "That's what the holes mean."

The foremost hippopotamus was headed directly for him. He glared at the huge head with sullen resentment. For all his stupor, he perceived at once that the beast intended to land; and he sat in the middle of its accustomed path. His first impulse was to spring up and yell at the creature. Then he remembered hearing that a white hunter had recently been killed by these beasts on one of the South African lakes. Instead of leaping up, he sank down almost flat, and crawled back around the turn in the path. Once certain that he was hidden from the beasts, he rose to his feet and hastened back through the jungle.

He was almost in view of the spot where he had left Winthrope and Miss Leslie, when he stopped and stood hesitating.

"I can't do it," he muttered; "I can't tell her,—poor girl!"

He turned and pushed into the thicket. Forcing a way through the tangle of thorny shrubs and creepers, until several yards from the path, he began to edge towards the face of the jungle, that he might peer out at his companions, unseen by them.

There was more of the thicket before him than he had thought, and he was still fighting his way through it, when he was brought to a stand by a peculiar cry that might have been the bleat of a young lamb: "Ba—ba!"

"What's that!" he croaked.

He stood listening, and in a moment he again heard the cry, this time more distinctly: "Blak!—Blak!"

There could be no mistake. It was Winthrope calling for him, and calling with a clearness of voice that would have been physically impossible half an hour since. Blake's sunken eyes lighted with hope. He burst through the last screen of jungle, and stared towards the palm under which he had left his companions. They were not there.

Another call from Winthrope directed his gaze more seaward. The two were seated beside a fallen palm, and Miss Leslie had a large round object raised to her lips. Winthrope was waving to him.

"Cocoanuts!" he yelled. "Come on!"

Three of the palms had been overthrown by the hurricane, and when Blake came up, he found the ground strewn with nuts. He seized the first he came to; but Winthrope held out one already opened. He snatched it from him, and placed the hole to his swollen lips. Never had champagne tasted half so delicious as that cocoanut milk. Before he could drain the last of it through the little opening, Winthrope had the husks torn from the ends of two other nuts, and the convenient germinal spots gouged open with his penknife.

Blake emptied the third before he spoke. Even then his voice was hoarse and strained. "How'd you strike 'em?"

"I couldn't help it," explained Winthrope. "Hardly had you disappeared when I noticed the tops of the fallen palms, and thought of the nuts. There was one in the grass not twenty feet from where we lay."

"Lucky for you—and for me, too, I guess," said Blake. "We were all three down for the count. But this settles the first round in our favor. How do you like the picnic, Miss Jenny?"

"Miss Leslie, if you please," replied the girl, with hauteur.

"Oh, say, Miss Jenny!" protested Blake, genially. "We

live in the same boarding-house now. Why not be folksy? You're free to call me Tom. Pass me another nut, Winthrope. Thanks! By the way, what's your front name? Saw it aboard ship—Cyril—"

"Cecil," corrected Winthrope, in a low tone.

"Cecil—Lord Cecil, eh?—or is it only The Honorable Cecil?"

"My dear sir, I have intimated before that, for reasons of—er—State—"

"Oh, yes; you're travelling incog., in the secret service. Sort of detective—"

"Detective!" echoed Winthrope, in a peculiar tone.

Blake grinned. "Well, it is rawther a nawsty business for your honorable ludship. But there's nothing like calling things by their right names."

"Right names—er—I don't quite take you. I have told you distinctly, my name is Cecil Winthrope!"

"O-h-h! how lovely!—See-sill! See-seal!—Bet they called you Sissy at school. English, chum of mine told me your schools are corkers for nicknames. What'll we make it—Sis or Sissy?"

"I prefer my patronymic, Mr. Blake," replied Winthrope.

"All right, then; we'll make it Pat, if that's your choice. I say, Pat, this juice is the stuff for wetness, but it makes a fellow remember his grub. Where'd you leave that fish?"

"Really, I can't just say, but it must have been where I wrenched my ankle."

"You cawn't just say! And what are we going to eat?"

"Here are the cocoanuts."

"Bright boy! go to the head of the class! Just take some more husk off those empty ones."

Winthrope caught up one of the nuts, and with the aid of his knife, stripped it of its husk. At a gesture from Blake, he laid it on the bare ground, and the American burst it open with a blow of his heel. It was an immature nut, and the meat proved to be little thicker than clotted cream. Blake divided it into three parts, handing Miss Leslie the cleanest.

Though his companions began with more restraint, they finished their shares with equal gusto. Winthrope needed no further orders to return to his husking. One after another, the nuts were cracked and divided among the three, until even Blake could not swallow another mouthful of the luscious cream.

Toward the end Miss Leslie had become drowsy. At Winthrope's urging, she now lay down for a nap, Blake's coat serving as a pillow. She fell asleep while Winthrope was yet arranging it for her. Blake had turned his back on her, and was staring moodily at the hippopotamus trail, when Winthrope hobbled around and sat down on the palm trunk beside him.

"I say, Blake," he suggested, "I feel deuced fagged myself. Why not all take a nap?"

"'And when they awoke, they were all dead men,'" remarked Blake.

"By Jove, that sounds like a joke," protested the Englishman. "Don't rag me now."

"Joke!" repeated Blake. "Why, that's Scripture, Pat, Scripture! Anyway, you'd think it no joke to wake up and find yourself going down the throat of a hippo."

"Hippo?"

"Dozens of them over in the river. Shouldn't wonder if they've all landed, and 're tracking me down by this time."

"But hippopotami are not carnivorous—they're not at all dangerous, unless one wounds them, out in the water."

"That may be; but I'm not taking chances. They've got mouths like sperm whales—I saw one take a yawn. Another thing, that bayou is chuck full of alligators, and a fellow down on the Rand told me they're like the Central American gavials for keenness to nip a swimmer."

"They will not come out on this dry land."

"Suppose they won't—there're no other animals in Africa but sheep, eh?"

"What can we do? The captain told me that there are both lions and leopards on this coast."

"Nice place for them, too, around these trees," added Blake. "Lucky for us, they're night-birds mostly,—if that Rand fellow didn't lie. He was a Boer, so I guess he ought to know."

"To be sure. It's a nasty fix we're in for to-night. Could we not build some kind of a barricade?"

"With a penknife! Guess we'll roost in a tree."

"But cannot leopards climb? It seems to me that I have heard—"

"How about lions?"

"They cannot; I'm sure of that."

"Then we'll chance the leopards. Just stretch out here, and nurse that ankle of yours. I don't want to be lugging you all year. I'm going to hunt a likely tree."

5

THE RE-ASCENT OF MAN

AFTERNOON WAS FAR advanced, and Winthrope was beginning to feel anxious, when at last Blake pushed out from among the close thickets. As he approached, he swung an unshapely club of green wood, pausing every few paces to test its weight and balance on a bush or knob of dirt.

"By Jove!" called Winthrope; "that's not half bad! You look as if you could bowl over an ox."

Blake showed that he was flattered.

"Oh, I don't know," he responded; "the thing's blamed unhandy. Just the same, I guess we'll be ready for callers to-night."

"How's that?"

"Show you later, Pat, me b'y. Now trot out some nuts. We'll feed before we move camp."

"Miss Leslie is still sleeping."

"Time, then, to roust her out. Hey, Miss Jenny, turn out! Time to chew."

Miss Leslie sat up and gazed around in bewilderment.

"It's all right, Miss Genevieve," reassured Winthrope. "Blake has found a safe place for the night, and he wishes us to eat before we leave here."

"Save lugging the grub," added Blake. "Get busy, Pat."

As Winthrope caught up a nut, the girl began to arrange her disordered hair and dress with the deft and graceful movements of a woman thoroughly trained in the art of self-adornment. There was admiration in Blake's deep eyes as he watched her dainty preening. She was not a beautiful girl—at present she could hardly be termed pretty; yet even in her draggled, muddy dress she retained all the subtle charms of culture which appeal so strongly to a man. Blake was subdued. His feelings even carried him so far as an attempt at formal politeness, when they had finished their meal.

"Now, Miss Leslie," he began, "it's little more than half an hour to sundown; so, if you please, if you're quite ready, we'd best be starting."

"Is it far?"

"Not so very. But we've got to chase through the jungle. Are you sure you're quite ready?"

"Quite, thank you. But how about Mr. Winthrope's ankle?"

"He'll ride as far as the trees. I can't squeeze through with him, though."

"I shall walk all the way," put in Winthrope.

"No, you won't. Climb aboard," replied Blake, and catching up his club, he stooped for Winthrope to mount his back. As he rose with his burden, Miss Leslie caught sight of his coat, which still lay in a roll beside the palm trunk.

"How about your coat, Mr. Blake?" she asked. "Should you not put it on?"

"No; I'm loaded now. Have to ask you to look after it. You may need it before morning, anyway. If the dews here

are like those in Central America, they are d-darned liable
to bring on malarial fever."

Nothing more was said until they had crossed the open
space between the palms and the belt of jungle along
the river. At other times Winthrope and Miss Leslie
might have been interested in the towering screw-palms,
festooned to the top with climbers, and in the huge ferns
which they could see beneath the mangroves, in the
swampy ground on their left. Now, however, they were
far too concerned with the question of how they should
penetrate the dense tangle of thorny brush and creepers
which rose before them like a green wall. Even Blake hesitated as he released Winthrope, and looked at Miss Leslie's
costume. Her white skirt was of stout duck; but the flimsy
material of her waist was ill-suited for rough usage.

"Better put the coat on, unless you want to come out on
the other side in full evening dress," he said. "There's no
use kicking; but I wish you'd happened to have on some
sort of a jacket when we got spilled."

"Is there no path through the thicket?" inquired
Winthrope.

"Only the hippo trail, and it don't go our way. We've got
to run our own line. Here's a stick for your game ankle."

Winthrope took the half-green branch which Blake
broke from the nearest tree, and turned to assist Miss
Leslie with the coat. The garment was of such coarse cloth
that as Winthrope drew the collar close about her throat
Miss Leslie could not forego a little grimace of repug-
nance. The crease between Blake's eyes deepened, and the
girl hastened to utter an explanatory exclamation: "Not so
tight, Mr. Winthrope, please! It scratches my neck."

"You'd find those thorns a whole lot worse," muttered Blake.

"To be sure; and Miss Leslie fully appreciates your kindness," interposed Winthrope.

"I do indeed, Mr. Blake! I'm sure I never could go through here without your coat."

"That's all right. Got the handkerchief?"

"I put it in one of the pockets."

"It'll do to tie up your hair."

Miss Leslie took the suggestion, knotting the big square of linen over her fluffy brown hair.

Blake waited only for her to draw out the kerchief, before he began to force a way through the jungle. Now and then he beat at the tangled vegetation with his club. Though he held to the line by which he had left the thicket, yet all his efforts failed to open an easy passage for the others. Many of the thorny branches sprang back into place behind him, and as Miss Leslie, who was the first to follow, sought to thrust them aside, the thorns pierced her delicate skin, until her hands were covered with blood. Nor did Winthrope, stumbling and hobbling behind her, fare any better. Twice he tripped headlong into the brush, scratching his arms and face.

Blake took his own punishment as a matter of course, though his tougher and thicker skin made his injuries less painful. He advanced steadily along the line of bent and broken twigs that marked his outward passage, until the thicket opened on a strip of grassy ground beneath a wild fig-tree.

"By Jove!" exclaimed Winthrope, "a banyan!"

"Banyan? Well, if that's British for a daisy, you've hit it," responded Blake. "Just take a squint up here. How's that for a roost?"

Winthrope and Miss Leslie stared up dubiously at the edge of a bed of reeds gathered in the hollow of one of the huge flattened branches at its junction with the main trunk of the banyan, twenty feet above them.

"Will not the mosquitoes pester us, here among the trees?" objected Winthrope.

"Storm must have blown 'em away. I haven't seen any yet."

"There will be millions after sunset."

"Maybe; but I bet they keep below our roost"

"But how are we to get up so high?" inquired Miss Leslie.

"I can swarm this drop root, and I've a creeper ready for you two," explained Blake.

Suiting action to words, he climbed up the small trunk of the air root, and swung over into the hollow where he had piled the reeds. Across the broad limb dangled a rope-like creeper, one end of which he had fastened to a branch higher up. He flung down the free end to Winthrope.

"Look lively, Pat," he called. "The sun's most gone, and the twilight don't last all night in these parts. Get the line around Miss Leslie, and do what you can on a boost."

"I see; but, you know, the vine is too stiff to tie."

Blake stifled an oath, and jerked the end of the creeper up into his hand. When he threw it down again, it was looped around and fastened in a bowline knot.

"Now, Miss Leslie, get aboard, and we'll have you up in a jiffy," he said.

"Are you sure you can lift me?" asked the girl, as Winthrope slipped the loop over her shoulders.

Blake laughed down at them. "Well, I guess yes! Once hoisted a fellow out of a fifty-foot prospect hole—big fat Dutchman at that. You don't weigh over a hundred and twenty."

He had stretched out across the broadest part of the branch. As Miss Leslie seated herself in the loop, he reached down and began to haul up on the creeper, hand over hand. Though frightened by the novel manner of ascent, the girl clung tightly to the line above her head, and Blake had no difficulty in raising her until she swung directly beneath him. Here, however, he found himself in a quandary. The girl seemed as helpless as a child, and he was lying flat. How could he lift her above the level of the branch?

"Take hold the other line," he said. The girl hesitated. "Do you hear? Grab it quick, and pull up hard, if you don't want a tumble!"

The girl seized the part of the creeper which was fastened above, and drew herself up with convulsive energy. Instantly Blake rose to his knees, and grasping the taut creeper with one hand, reached down with the other, to swing the girl up beside him on the branch.

"All right, Miss Jenny," he reassured her as he felt her tremble. "Sorry to scare you, but I couldn't have made it without. Now, if you'll just hold down my legs, we'll soon hoist his ludship."

He had seated her in the broadest part of the shallow hollow, where the branch joined the main trunk of the fig. Heaped with the reeds which he had gathered during the afternoon, it made such a cozy shelter that she at once forgot her dizziness and fright. Nestling among the reeds, she leaned over and pressed down on his ankles with all her strength.

The loose end of the creeper had fallen to the ground when Blake lifted her upon the branch, and Winthrope was already slipping into the loop. Blake ordered him to take it off, and send up the club. As the creeper was again flung down, a black shadow swept over the jungle.

"Hello! Sunset!" called Blake. "Look sharp, there!"

"All ready," responded Winthrope.

Blake drew in a full breath, and began to hoist. The position was an awkward one, and Winthrope weighed thirty or forty pounds more than Miss Leslie. But as the Englishman came within reach of the descending loop, he grasped it and did what he could to ease Blake's efforts. A few moments found him as high above the ground as Blake could raise him. Without waiting for orders, he swung himself upon the upper part of the creeper, and climbed the last few feet unaided. Blake grunted with satisfaction as he pulled him in upon the branch.

"You may do, after all," he said. "At any rate, we're all aboard for the night; and none too soon. Hear that!"

"What?"

"Lion, I guess—Not that yelping. Listen!"

The brief twilight was already fading into the darkness of a moonless night, and as the three crouched together in their shallow nest, they were soon made audibly aware of the savage nature of their surroundings. With the gathering night the jungle wakened into full life. From all sides came the harsh squawking of birds, the weird cries of monkeys and other small creatures, the crash of heavy

animals moving through the jungle, and above all the yelp
and howl and roar of beasts of prey.

After some contention with Winthrope, Blake conceded
that the roars of his lion might be nothing worse than the
snorting of the hippopotami as they came out to browse for
the night. In this, however, there was small comfort, since
Winthrope presently reasserted his belief in the climbing
ability of leopards, and expressed his opinion that, whether
or not there were lions in the neighborhood, certain of the
barking roars they could hear came from the throats of the
spotted climbers. Even Blake's hair bristled as his imagina-
tion pictured one of the great cats creeping upon them in
the darkness from the far end of their nest limb, or leaping
down out of the upper branches.

The nerves of all three were at their highest tension when
a dark form swept past through the air within a yard of
their faces. Miss Leslie uttered a stifled scream, and Blake
brandished his club. But Winthrope, who had caught a
glimpse of the creature's shape, broke into a nervous laugh.

"It's only a fruit bat," he explained. "They feed on the
banyan figs, you know."

In the reaction from this false alarm, both men relaxed,
and began to yield to the effects of the tramp across the
mud-flats. Arranging the reeds as best they could, they
stretched out on either side of Miss Leslie, and fell asleep
in the middle of an argument on how the prospective leopard was most likely to attack.

Miss Leslie remained awake for two or three hours
longer. Naturally she was more nervous than her companions, and she had been refreshed by her afternoon's nap.
Her nervousness was not entirely due to the wild beasts.

Though Blake had taken pains to secure himself and his companions in loops of the creeper, fastened to the branch above, Winthrope moved about so restlessly in his sleep that the girl feared he would roll from the hollow.

At last her limbs became so cramped that she was compelled to change her position. She leaned back upon her elbow, determined to rise again and maintain her watch the moment she was rested. But sleep was close upon her. There was a lull in the louder noises of the jungle. Her eyes closed, and her head sank lower. In a little time it was lying upon Winthrope's shoulder, and she was fast asleep.

As Blake had asserted, the mosquitoes had either been blown away by the cyclone, or did not fly to such a height. None came to trouble the exhausted sleepers.

6

MAN AND GENTLEMAN

NIGHT HAD ALMOST passed, and all three, soothed by the refreshing coolness which preceded the dawn, were sleeping their soundest, when a sudden fierce roar followed instantly by a piercing squeal caused even Blake to start up in panic. Miss Leslie, too terrified to scream, clung to Winthrope, who crouched on his haunches, little less overcome.

Blake was the first to recover and puzzle out the meaning of the crashing in the jungle and the ferocious growls directly beneath them.

"Lie still," he whispered. "We're all right. It's only a beast that's killed something down below us."

All sat listening, and as the noise of the animals in the thicket died away, they could hear the beast beneath them tear at the body of its victim.

"The air feels like dawn," whispered Winthrope. "We'll soon be able to see the brute."

"And he us," rejoined Blake.

In this both were mistaken. During the brief false dawn they were puzzled by the odd appearance of the ground. The sudden flood of full daylight found them staring down into a dense white fog.

"So they have that here!" muttered Blake—"fever-fog!"

"Beastly shame!" echoed Winthrope. "I'm sure the creature has gone off."

This assertion was met by an outburst of snarls and yells that made all start back and crouch down again in their sheltering hollow. As before, Blake was the first to recover.

"Bet you're right," he said. "The big one has gone off, and a pack of these African coyotes are having a scrap over the bones."

"You mean jackals. It sounds like the nasty beasts."

"If it wasn't for that fog, I'd go down and get our share of the game."

"Would it not be very dangerous, Mr. Blake?" asked Miss Leslie. "What a fearful noise!"

"I've chased coyotes off a calf with a rope; but that's not the proposition. You don't find me fooling around in that sewer gas of a fog. We'll roost right where we are till the sun does for it. We've got enough malaria in us already."

"Will it be long, Blake?" asked Winthrope.

"Huh? Getting hungry this quick? Wait till you've tramped around a week, with nothing to eat but your shoes."

"Surely, Mr. Blake, it will not be so bad!" protested Miss Leslie.

"Sorry, Miss Jenny; but cocoanut palms don't blow over every day, and when those nuts are gone, what are we going to do for the next meal?"

"Could we not make bows?" suggested Winthrope. "There seems to be no end of game about."

"Bows—and arrows without points! Neither of us could hit a barn door, anyway."

"We could practise."

"Sure—six weeks' training on air pudding. I can do better with a handful of stones."

"Then we should go at once to the cliffs," said Miss Leslie.

"Now you're talking—and it's Pike Peak or bust, for ours. Here's one night to the good; but we won't last many more if we don't get fire. It's flints we're after now."

"Could we not make fire by rubbing sticks?" said Winthrope, recalling his suggestion of the previous morning. "I've heard that natives have no trouble—"

"So've I, and what's more, I've seen 'em do it. Never could make a go of it myself, though."

"But if you remember how it is done, we have at least some chance—"

"Give you ten to one odds! No; we'll scratch around for a flint good and plenty before we waste time that way."

"The mist is going," observed Miss Leslie.

"That's no lie. Now for our coyotes. Where's my club?"

"They've all left," said Winthrope, peering down. "I can see the ground clearly, and there is not a sign of the beasts."

"There are the bones—what's left of them," added Blake. "It's a small deer, I suppose. Well, here goes."

He threw down his club, and dropped the loose end of the creeper after it. As the line straightened, he twisted the upper part around his leg, and was about to slide to the ground, when he remembered Miss Leslie.

"Think you can make it alone?" he asked.

The girl held up her hands, sore and swollen from the lacerations of the thorns. Blake looked at them, frowned, and turned to Winthrope.

"Um! you got it, too, and in the face," he grunted. "How's your ankle?"

Winthrope wriggled his foot about, and felt the injured ankle.

"I fancy it is much better," he answered. "There seems to be no swelling, and there is no pain now."

"That's lucky; though it will tune up later. Take a slide, now. We've got to hustle our breakfast, and find a way to get over the river."

"How wide is it?" inquired Winthrope, gazing at his swollen hands.

"About three hundred yards at high tide. May be narrower at ebb."

"Could you not build a raft?" suggested Miss Leslie.

Blake smiled at her simplicity. "Why not a boat? We've got a penknife."

"Well, then, I can swim."

"Bully for you! Guess, though, we'll try something else. The river is chuck full of alligators. What you waiting for, Pat? We haven't got all day to fool around here."

Winthrope twisted the creeper about his leg and slid to the ground, doing all he could to favor his hands. He found that he could walk without pain, and at once stepped over beside Blake's club, glancing nervously around at the jungle.

Blake jerked up the end of the creeper, and passed the loop about Miss Leslie. Before she had time to become frightened, he swung her over and lowered her to the ground lightly as a feather. He followed, hand under hand, and stood for a moment beside her, staring at the dew-dripping foliage of the jungle. Then the remains of the night's quarry caught his eye, and he walked over to examine them.

"Say, Pat," he called, "these don't look like deer bones. I'd say—yes; there's the feet—it's a pig."

"Any tusks?" demanded Winthrope.

Miss Leslie looked away. A heap of bones, however cleanly gnawed, is not a pleasant sight. The skull of the animal seemed to be missing; but Blake stumbled upon it in a tuft of grass, and kicked it out upon the open ground. Every shred of hide and gristle had been gnawed from it by the jackals; yet if there had been any doubt as to the creature's identity, there was evidence to spare in the savage tusks which projected from the jaws.

"Je-rusalem!" observed Blake; "this old boar must have been something of a scrapper his own self."

"In India they have been known to kill a tiger. Can you knock out the tusks?"

"What for?"

"Well, you said we had nothing for arrow points—"

"Good boy! We'll cinch them, and ask questions later."

A few blows with the club loosened the tusks. Blake handed them over to Winthrope, together with the whiskey flask, and led the way to the half-broken path through the thicket. A free use of his club made the path a little more worthy of the name, and as there was less need of haste than on the previous evening, Winthrope and Miss Leslie came through with only a few fresh scratches. Once on open ground again, they soon gained the fallen palms.

At a word from Blake, Miss Leslie hastened to fetch nuts for Winthrope to husk and open. Blake, who had plucked three leaves from a fan palm near the edge of the jungle, began to split long shreds from one of the huge leaves of a cocoanut palm. This gave him a quantity of coarse, stiff fibre, part of which he twisted in a cord and used to tie one of the leaves of the fan palm over his head.

"How's that for a bonnet?" he demanded.

The improvised head-gear bore so grotesque a resemblance to a recent type of picture hat that Winthrope could not repress a derisive laugh. Miss Leslie, however, examined the hat and gave her opinion without a sign of amusement. "I think it is splendid, Mr. Blake. If we must go out in the sun again, it is just the thing to protect one."

"Yes. Here's two more I've fixed for you. Ready yet, Winthrope?"

The Englishman nodded, and the three sat down to their third feast of cocoanuts. They were hungry enough at the start, and Blake added no little keenness even to his own appetite by a grim joke on the slender prospects of the next meal, to the effect that, if in the meantime not eaten themselves, they might possibly find their next meal within a week.

"But if we must move, could we not take some of the nuts with us?" suggested Winthrope.

Blake pondered over this as he ate, and when, fully satisfied, he helped himself up with his club, he motioned the others to remain seated.

"There are your hats and the strings," he said, "but you won't need them now. I'm going to take a prospect along the river; and while I'm gone, you can make a try at stringing nuts on some of this leaf fibre."

"But, Mr. Blake, do you think it's quite safe?" asked Miss Leslie, and she glanced from him to the jungle.

"Safe?" he repeated. "Well, nothing ate you yesterday, if that's anything to go by. It's all I know about it."

He did not wait for further protests. Swinging his club on his shoulder, he started for the break in the jungle which marked the hippopotamus path. The others looked at each other, and Miss Leslie sighed.

"If only he were a gentleman!" she complained.

Winthrope turned abruptly to the cocoanuts.

7

AROUND THE HEADLAND

IT WAS MID morning before Blake reappeared. He came from the mangrove swamp where it ran down into the sea. His trousers were smeared to the thigh with slimy mud; but as he approached, the drooping brim of his palm-leaf hat failed to hide his exultant expression.

"Come on!" he called. "I've struck it. We'll be over in half an hour."

"How's that?" asked Winthrope.

"Bar," answered Blake, hurrying forward. "Sling on your hats, and get into my coat again, Miss Jenny. The sun's hot as yesterday. How about the nuts?"

"Here they are. Three strings; all that I fancied we could carry," explained Winthrope.

"All right. The big one is mine, I suppose. I'll take two. We'll leave the other. Lean on me, if your ankle is still weak."

"Thanks; I can make it alone. But must we go through mud like that?"

"Not on this side, at least. Come on! We don't want to miss the ebb."

Blake's impatience discouraged further inquiries. He had turned as he spoke, and the others followed him, walking close together. The pace was sharp for Winthrope, and his ankle soon began to twinge. He was compelled to accept Miss Leslie's invitation to take her arm. With her help, he managed to keep within a few yards of Blake.

Instead of plunging into the mangrove wood, which here was undergrown with a thicket of giant ferns, Blake skirted around in the open until they came to the seashore. The tide was at its lowest, and he waved his club towards a long sand spit which curved out around the seaward edge of the mangroves. Whether this was part of the river's bar, or had been heaped up by the cyclone would have been beyond Winthrope's knowledge, had the question occurred to him. It was enough for him that the sand was smooth and hard as a race track.

Presently the party came to the end of the spit, where the river water rippled over the sand with the last feeble out-suck of the ebb. On their right they had a sweeping view of the river, around the flank of the mangrove screen. Blake halted at the edge of the water, and half turned.

"Close up," he said. "It's shallow enough; but do you see those logs over on the mud-bank? Those are alligators."

"Mercy!—and you expect me to wade among such creatures?" cried Miss Leslie.

"I went almost across an hour ago, and they didn't bother me any. Come on! There's wind in that cloud out seaward. Inside half an hour the surf'll be rolling up on this bar like all Niagara."

"If we must, we must, Miss Genevieve," urged Winthrope. "Step behind me, and gather up your skirts. It's best to keep one's clothes dry in the tropics."

The girl blushed, and retained his arm.

"I prefer to help you," she replied.

"Come on!" called Blake, and he splashed out into the water.

The others followed within arm's-length, nervously conscious of the rows of motionless reptiles on the mud-flat, not a hundred yards distant.

In the centre of the bar, where the water was a trifle over knee-deep, some large creature came darting downstream beneath the surface, and passed with a violent swirl between Blake and his companions. At Miss Leslie's scream, Blake whirled about and jabbed with his club at the supposed alligator.

"Where's the brute? Has he got you?" he shouted.

"No, no; he went by!" gasped Winthrope. "There he is!"

A long bony snout, fringed on either side by a row of lateral teeth, was flung up into view.

"Sawfish!" said Blake, and he waded on across the bar, without further comment.

Miss Leslie had been on the point of fainting. The tone of Blake's voice revived her instantly.

There were no more scares. A few minutes later they waded out upon a stretch of clean sand on the south side of the river. Before them the beach lay in a flattened curve, which at the far end hooked sharply to the left, and appeared to terminate at the foot of the towering limestone cliffs of the headland. A mile or more inland the river jungle edged in close to the cliffs; but from there to the beach the forest was separated from the wall of rock by a little sandy plain, covered with creeping plants and small palms. The greatest width of the open space was hardly more than a quarter of a mile.

Blake paused for a moment at high-tide mark, and Winthrope instantly squatted down to nurse his ankle.

"I say, Blake," he said, "can't you find me some kind of a crutch? It is only a few yards around to those trees."

"Good Lord! you haven't been fool enough to overstrain that ankle— Yes, you have. Dammit! why couldn't you tell me before?"

"It did not feel so painful in the water."

"I helped the best I could," interposed Miss Leslie. "I think if you could get Mr. Winthrope a crutch—"

"Crutch!" growled Blake. "How long do you think it would take me to wade through the mud? And look at that cloud! We're in for a squall. Here!"

He handed the girl the smaller string of cocoanuts, flung the other up the beach, and stooped for Winthrope to mount his back. He then started off along the beach at a sharp trot. Miss Leslie followed as best she could, the heavy cocoanuts swinging about with every step and bruising her tender body.

The wind was coming faster than Blake had calculated. Before they had run two hundred paces, they heard the roar of rain-lashed water, and the squall struck them with a force that almost overthrew the girl. With the wind came torrents of rain that drove through their thickest garments and drenched them to the skin within the first half-minute.

Blake slackened his pace to a walk, and plodded sullenly along beneath the driving down-pour. He kept to the lower edge of the beach, where the sand was firmest, for the force of the falling deluge beat down the waves and held in check the breakers which the wind sought to roll up the beach.

The rain storm was at its height when they reached the

foot of the cliffs. The gray rock towered above them, thirty or forty feet high. Blake deposited Winthrope upon a wet ledge, and straightened up to scan the headland. Here and there ledges ran more than half-way up the rocky wall; in other places the crest was notched by deep clefts; but nowhere within sight did either offer a continuous path to the summit. Blake grunted with disgust.

"It'd take a fire ladder to get up this side," he said. "We'll have to try the other, if we can get around the point. I'm going on ahead. You can follow, after Pat has rested his ankle. Keep a sharp eye out for anything in the flint line—quartz or agate. That means fire. Another thing, when this rain blows over, don't let your clothes dry on you. I've got my hands full enough, without having to nurse you through malarial fever. Don't forget the cocoanuts, and if I don't show up by noon, save me some."

He stooped to drink from a pool in the rock which was overflowing with the cool, pure rainwater, and started off at his sharpest pace. Winthrope and Miss Leslie, seated side by side in dripping misery, watched him swing away through the rain, without energy enough to call out a parting word.

Beneath the cliff the sand beach was succeeded by a talus of rocky debris which in places sloped up from the water ten or fifteen feet. The lower part of the slope consisted of boulders and water-worn stones, over which the surf, reinforced by the rising tide, was beginning to break with an angry roar.

Blake picked his way quickly over the smaller stones near the top of the slope, now and then bending to snatch up a fragment that seemed to differ from the others. Finding nothing but limestone, he soon turned his attention solely to the passage around the headland. Here he had expected to find the surf much heavier. But the shore was protected by a double line of reefs, so close in that the channel between did not show a whitecap. This was fortunate, since in places the talus here sank down almost to the level of low tide. Even a moderate surf would have rendered farther progress impracticable.

Another hundred paces brought Blake to the second corner of the cliff, which jutted out in a little point. He clambered around it, and stopped to survey the coast beyond. Within the last few minutes the squall had blown over, and the rain began to moderate its down-pour. The sun, bursting through the clouds, told that the storm was almost past, and its flood of direct light cleared the view.

Along the south side of the cliff the sea extended in twice as far as on the north. From the end of the talus the coast trended off four or five miles to the south-southwest in a shallow bight, whose southern extremity was bounded by a second limestone headland. This ridge ran inland parallel to the first, and from a point some little distance back from the shore was covered with a growth of leafless trees.

Between the two ridges lay a plain, open along the shore, but a short distance inland covered with a jungle of tall yellow grass, above which, here and there, rose the tops of scrubby, leafless trees and the graceful crests of slender-shafted palms. Blake's attention was drawn to the latter by that feeling of artificiality which their exotic appearance so often wakens in the mind of the Northern-bred man even after long residence in the tropics. But in a moment

he turned away, with a growl. "More of those darned feath-
er-dusters!" He was not looking for palms.

The last ragged bit of cloud, with its showery accom-
paniment, drifted past before the breeze which followed
the squall, and the end of the storm was proclaimed by a
deafening chorus of squawks and screams along the higher
ledges of the cliff. Staring upward, Blake for the first time
observed that the face of the cliff swarmed with seafowl.

"That's luck!" he muttered. "Guess I haven't forgot how
to rob nests. Bet our fine lady'll shy at sucking them raw!
All the same, she'll have to, if I don't run across other rock
than this, poor girl!"

He advanced again along the talus, and did not stop
until he reached the sand beach. There he halted to make
a careful examination, not only of the loose debris, but of
the solid rock above. Finding no sign of flint or quartz,
he growled out a curse, and backed off along the beach,
to get a view of the cliff top. From a point a little beyond
him, outward to the extremity of the headland, he could
see that the upper ledges and the crest of the cliff, as well,
were fairly crowded with seafowl and their nests. His smile
of satisfaction broadened when he glanced inland and saw,
less than half a mile distant, a wooded cleft which apparently ran up to the summit of the ridge. From a point
near the top a gigantic baobab tree towered up against the
skyline like a Brobdingnagian cabbage.

"Say, we may have a run for our money, after all," he
murmured. "Shade, and no end of grub, and, by the green
of those trees, a spring—limestone water at that. Next
thing, I'll find a flint!"

He slapped his leg, and both sound and feeling reminded him that his clothes were drenched.

"Guess we'll wait about that flint," he said, and he made for a clump of thorn scrub a little way inland.

As the tall grass did not grow here within a mile of the shore, there was nothing to obstruct him. The creeping plants which during the rainy season had matted over the sandy soil were now leafless and withered by the heat of the dry season. Even the thorn scrub was half bare of leaves.

Blake walked around the clump to the shadiest side, and began to strip. In quick succession, one garment after another was flung across a branch where the sun would strike it. Last of all, the shoes were emptied of rainwater and set out to dry. Without a pause, he then gave himself a quick, light rub-down, just sufficient to invigorate the skin without starting the perspiration.

Physically the man was magnificent. His muscles were wiry and compact, rather than bulky, and as he moved, they played beneath his white skin with the smoothness and ease of a tiger's.

After the rub-down, he squatted on his heels, and spent some time trying to bend his palm-leaf hat back into shape. When he had placed this also out in the sun, he found himself beginning to yawn. The dry, sultry air had made him drowsy. A touch with his bare foot showed him that the sand beneath the thorn bush had already absorbed the rain and offered a dry surface. He glanced around, drew his club nearer, and stretched himself out for a nap.

8

THE CLUB AGE

IT WAS PAST two o'clock when the sun, striking in where Blake lay outstretched, began to scorch one of his legs. He stirred uneasily, and sat upright. Like a sailor, he was wide awake the moment he opened his eyes. He stood up, and peered around through the half leafless branches.

Over the water thousands of gulls and terns, boobies and cormorants were skimming and diving, while above them a number of graceful frigate birds—those swart, scarlet-throated pirates of the air,—hung poised, ready to swoop down and rob the weaker birds of their fish. All about the headland and the surrounding water was life in fullest action. Even from where he stood Blake could hear the harsh clamor of the seafowl.

In marked contrast to this scene, the plain was apparently lifeless. When Blake rose, a small brown lizard darted away across the sand. Otherwise there was neither sight nor sound of a living creature. Blake pondered this as he gathered his clothes into the shade and began to dress.

"Looks like the siesta is the all-round style in this God-forsaken hole," he grumbled. "Haven't seen so much as a rabbit, nor even one land bird. May be a drought—no; must be the dry season— Whee, these things are hot! I'm thirsty as a shark. Now, where's that softy and her Lady-ship? 'Fraid she's in for a tough time!"

He drew on his shoes with a jerk, growled at their stiff-ness, and club in hand, stepped clear of the brush to look for his companions. The first glance along the foot of the cliff showed him Winthrope lying under the shade of the overhanging ledges, a few yards beyond the sand beach. Of Miss Leslie there was no sign. Half alarmed by this, Blake started for the beach with his swinging stride. Winthrope was awake, and on Blake's approach, sat up to greet him.

"Hello!" he called. "Where have you been all this time?"

"Sleep. Where's Miss Leslie?"

"She's around the point."

Blake grinned mockingly. "Indeed! But I fawncy she won't be for long."

He would have passed on, but Winthrope stepped before him.

"Don't go out there, Blake," he protested. "I—ah—think it would be better if I went."

"Why?" demanded Blake.

Winthrope hesitated; but an impatient movement by Blake forced an answer: "Well, you remember, this morn-ing, telling us to dry our clothes."

"Yes; I remember," said Blake. "So you want to serve as lady's valet?"

Winthrope's plump face turned a sickly yellow.

"I—ah—valet?—What do you mean, sir? I protest—I do not understand you!" he stammered. But in the midst, catching sight of Blake's bewildered stare, he suddenly flushed crimson, and burst out in unrestrained anger:

"You—you bounder—you beastly cad! Any man with an ounce of decency—"

Blake uttered a jeering laugh— "Wow! Hark, how the British lion r-r-ro-ars when his tail's twisted!"

"You beastly cad!" repeated the Englishman, now purple with rage.

Blake's unpleasant pleasantry gave place to a scowl. His jaw thrust out like a bulldog's, and he bent towards Winthrope with a menacing look. For a moment the Englishman faced him, sustained by his anger. But there was a steely light in Blake's eyes that he could not withstand. Winthrope's defiant stare wavered and fell. He shrank back, the color fast ebbing from his cheeks.

"Ugh!" growled Blake. "Guess you won't blat any more about cads! You damned hypocrite! Maybe I'm not on to how you've been hanging around Miss Leslie just because she's an heiress. Anything is fair enough for you swells. But let a fellow so much as open his mouth about your exalted set, and it's perfectly dreadful, you know!"

He paused for a reply. Winthrope only drew back a step farther, and eyed him with a furtive, sidelong glance. This brought Blake back to his mocking jeer. "You'll learn, Pat, me b'y. There's lots of things'll show up different to you before we get through this picnic. For one thing, I'm boss here—president, congress, and supreme court. Understand?"

"By what right, may I ask?" murmured Winthrope.

"Right!" answered Blake. "That hasn't anything to do with the question—it's might. Back in civilized parts, your little crowd has the drop on my big crowd, and runs things to suit themselves. But here we've sort of reverted to primitive society. This happens to be the Club Age, and I'm the Man with the Big Stick. See?"

"I myself sympathize with the lower classes, Mr. Blake. Above all, I think it barbarous the way they punish one who is forced by circumstances to appropriate part of the ill-gotten gains of the rich upstarts. But do you believe, Mr. Blake, that brute strength—"

"You bet! Now shut up. Where're the cocoanuts?"

Winthrope picked up two nuts and handed them over.

"There were only five," he explained.

"All right. I'm no captain of industry."

"Ah, true; you said we had reverted to barbarism," rejoined Winthrope, venturing an attempt at sarcasm.

"Lucky for you!" retorted Blake. "But where's Miss Leslie all this time? Her clothes must have dried hours ago."

"They did. We had luncheon together just this side of the point."

"Oh, you did! Then why shouldn't I go for her?"

"I—I—there was a shaded pool around the point, and she thought a dip in the salt water would refresh her. She went not more than half an hour ago."

"So that's it. Well, while I eat, you go and call her—and say, you keep this side the point. I'm looking out for Miss Leslie now."

Winthrope hurried away, clenching his fists and almost weeping with impotent rage. Truly, matters were now very different from what they had been aboard ship. Fortunately he had not gone a dozen steps before Miss Leslie appeared around the corner of the cliff. He was scrambling along over the loose stones of the slope without the slightest consideration for his ankle. The girl, more thoughtful, waved to him to wait for her where he was.

As she approached, Blake's frown gave place to a look that made his face positively pleasant. He had already drained the cocoanuts; now he proceeded to smash the shells into small bits, that he might eat the meat, and at the same time keep his gaze on the girl. The cliff foot being well shaded by the towering wall of rock, she had taken off his coat, and was carrying it on her arm; so that there was nothing to mar the effect of her dainty openwork waist, with its elbow sleeves and graceful collar and the filmy veil of lace over the shoulders and bosom. Her skirt had been washed clean by the rain, and she had managed to stretch it into shape before drying.

Refreshed by a nap in the forenoon and by her salt-water dip, she showed more vivacity than at any time that Winthrope could remember during their acquaintance. Her suffering during and since the storm had left its mark in the dark circles beneath her hazel eyes, but this in no wise lessened their brightness; while the elasticity of her step showed that she had quite recovered her well-bred ease and grace of movement.

She bowed and smiled to the two men impartially. "Good-afternoon, gentlemen."

"Same to you, Miss Leslie!" responded Blake, staring at her with frank admiration. "You look fresh as a daisy."

Genial and sincere as was his tone, the familiarity jarred on her sensitive ear. She colored as she turned from him.

"Is there anything new, Mr. Winthrope?" she asked.

"I'm afraid not, Miss Genevieve. Like ourselves, Blake took a nap."

"Yes; but Blake first took a squint at the scenery. Just see if you've got everything, and fix your hats. We'll be in the sun for half a mile or so. Better get on the coat, Miss Leslie. It's hotter than yesterday."

"Permit me," said Winthrope.

Blake watched while the Englishman held the coat for the girl and rather fussily raised the collar about her neck and turned back the sleeves, which extended beyond the tips of her fingers. The American's face was stolid; but his glance took in every little look and act of his companions. He was not altogether unversed in the ways of good society, and it seemed to him that the Englishman was somewhat over-assiduous in his attentions.

"All ready, Blake," remarked Winthrope, finally, with a last lingering touch.

"'Bout time!" grunted Blake. "You're fussy as a tailor. Got the flask and cigarette case and the knife?"

"All safe, sir—er—all safe, Blake."

"Then you two follow me slow enough not to worry that ankle. I don't want any more of the pack-mule in mine."

"Where are we going, Mr. Blake?" exclaimed Miss Leslie. "You will not leave us again!"

"It's only a half-mile, Miss Jenny. There's a break in the ridge. I'm going on ahead to find if it's hard to climb."

"But why should we climb?"

"Food, for one thing. You see, this end of the cliff is covered with sea-birds. Another thing, I expect to strike a spring."

"Oh, I hope you do! The water in the rain pools is already warm."

"They'll be dry in a day or two. Say, Winthrope, you

might fetch some of those stones—size of a ball. I used to be a fancy pitcher when I was a kid, and we might scare up a rabbit or something."

"I play cricket myself. But these stones—"

"Better'n a gun, when you haven't got the gun. Come on. We'll go in a bunch, after all, in case I need stones."

With due consideration for Winthrope's ankle,—not for Winthrope,—Blake set so slow a pace that the half-mile's walk consumed over half an hour. But his smouldering irritation was soon quenched when they drew near the green thicket at the foot of the cleft. In the almost deathlike stillness of mid-afternoon, the sound of trickling water came to their ears, clear and musical.

"A spring!" shouted Blake. "I guessed right. Look at those green plants and grass; there's the channel where it runs out in the sand and dries up."

The others followed him eagerly as he pushed in among the trees. They saw no running water, for the tiny rill that trickled down the ledges was matted over with vines. But at the foot of the slope lay a pool, some ten yards across, and overshadowed by the surrounding trees. There was no underbrush, and the ground was trampled bare as a floor.

"By Jove," said Winthrope; "see the tracks! There must have been a drove of sheep about."

"Deer, you mean," replied Blake, bending to examine the deeper prints at the edge of the pool. "These ain't sheep tracks. A lot of them are larger."

"Could you not uncover the brook?" asked Miss Leslie. "If animals have been drinking here, one would prefer cleaner water."

"Sure," assented Blake. "If you're game for a climb, and

can wait a few minutes, we'll get it out of the spring itself. We've got to go up anyway, to get at our poultry yard."

"Here's a place that looks like a path," called Winthrope, who had circled about the edge of the pool to the farther side.

Blake ran around beside him, and stared at the tunnel-like passage which wound up the limestone ledges beneath the over-arching thickets.

"Odd place, is it not?" observed Winthrope. "Looks like a fox run, only larger, you know."

"Too low for deer, though—and their hoofs would have cut up the moss and ferns more. Let's get a close look."

As he spoke, Blake stooped and climbed a few yards up the trail to an overhanging ledge, four or five feet high. Where the trail ran up over this break in the slope the stone was bare of all vegetation. Blake laid his club on the top of the ledge, and was about to vault after it, when, directly beneath his nose, he saw the print of a great catlike paw, outlined in dried mud. At the same instant a deep growl came rumbling down the "fox run." Without waiting for a second warning, Blake drew his club to him, and crept back down the trail. His stealthy movements and furtive backward glances filled his companions with vague terror. He himself was hardly less alarmed.

"Get out of the trees—into the open!" he exclaimed in a hoarse whisper, and as they crept away, white with dread of the unknown danger, he followed at their heels, looking backward, his club raised in readiness to strike.

Once clear of the trees, Winthrope caught Miss Leslie by the hand, and broke into a run. In their terror, they paid no heed to Blake's command to stop. They had darted off so unexpectedly that he did not overtake them short of a hundred yards.

"Hold on!" he said, gripping Winthrope roughly by the shoulder. "It's safe enough here, and you'll knock out that blamed ankle."

"What is it? What did you see?" gasped Miss Leslie.

"Footprint," mumbled Blake, ashamed of his fright.

"A lion's?" cried Winthrope.

"Not so large—'bout the size of a puma's. Must be a leopard's den up there. I heard a growl, and thought it about time to clear out."

"By Jove, we'd better withdraw around the point!"

"Withdraw your aunty! There's no leopard going to tackle us out here in open ground this time of day. The sneaking tomcat! If only I had a match, I'd show him how we smoke rat holes."

"Mr. Winthrope spoke of rubbing sticks to make fire," suggested Miss Leslie.

"Make sweat, you mean. But we may as well try it now, if we're going to at all. The sun's hot enough to fry eggs. We'll go back to a shady place, and pick up sticks on the way."

Though there was shade under the cliff within some six hundred feet, they had to go some distance to the nearest dry wood—a dead thorp-bush. Here they gathered a quantity of branches, even Miss Leslie volunteering to carry a load.

All was thrown down in a heap near the cliff, and Blake squatted beside it, penknife in hand. Having selected the dryest of the larger sticks, he bored a hole in one side and dropped in a pinch of powdered bark. Laying the stick in the full glare of the sun, he thrust a twig into the hole, and began to twirl it between his palms. This movement he kept up for several minutes; but whether he was unable to twirl the twig fast enough, or whether the right kind of wood or tinder was lacking, all his efforts failed to produce a spark.

Unwilling to accept the failure, Winthrope insisted upon trying in turn, and pride held him to the task until he was drenched with sweat. The result was the same.

"Told you so," jeered Blake from where he lay in the shade. "We'd stand more chance cracking stones together."

"But what shall we do now?" asked Miss Leslie. "I am becoming very tired of cocoanuts, and there seems to be nothing else around here. Indeed, I think this is all such a waste of time. If we had walked straight along the shore this morning we might have reached a town."

"We might, Miss Jenny, and then, again, we mightn't. I happened to overhaul the captain's chart—Quilimane, Mozambique—that's all for hundreds of miles. Towns on this coast are about as thick as hens'-teeth."

"How about native villages?" demanded Winthrope.

"Oh, yes; maybe I'm fool enough to go into a wild nigger town without a gun. Maybe I didn't talk with fellows down on the Rand."

"But what shall we do?" repeated Miss Leslie, with a little frightened catch in her voice. She was at last beginning to realize what this rude break in her sheltered, pampered life might mean. "What shall we do? It's—it's absurd to think of having to stay in this horrid country for weeks or perhaps months—unless some ship comes for us!"

"Look here, Miss Leslie," answered Blake, sharply yet not unkindly; "suppose you just sit back and use your thinker a bit. If you're your daddy's daughter, you've got brains somewhere down under the boarding-school stuff."

"What do you mean, sir?"

"Now, don't get huffy, please! It's a question of think, not of putting on airs. Here we are, worse off than the people of the Stone Age. They had fire and flint axes; we've got nothing but our think tanks, and as to lions and leopards and that sort of thing, it strikes me we've got about as many on hand as they had."

"Then you and Mr. Winthrope should immediately arm yourselves."

"How?—But we'll leave that till later. What else?"

The girl gazed at the surrounding objects, her forehead wrinkled in the effort at concentration. "We must have water. Think how we suffered yesterday! Then there is shelter from wild beasts, and food, and—"

"All right here under our hands, if we had fire. Understand?"

"I understand about the water. You would frighten the leopard away with the fire; and if it would do that, it would also keep away the other animals at night. But as for food, unless we return for cocoanuts—"

"Don't give it up! Keep your thinker going on the side, while Pat tells us our next move. Now that he's got the fire sticks out of his head—"

"I say, Blake, I wish you would drop that name. It is no harder to say Winthrope."

"You're off, there," rejoined Blake. "But look here, I'll make it Win, if you figure out what we ought to do next."

"Really, Blake, that would not be half bad. They—er—they called me Win at Harrow."

"That so? My English chum went to Harrow—Jimmy Scarbridge."

"Lord James!—your chum?"

"He started in like you, sort of top-lofty. But he chummed all right—after I took out a lot of his British starch with a good walloping."

"Oh, really now, Blake, you can't expect any one with brains to believe that, you know!"

"No; I don't know, you know,—and I don't know if you've got any brains, you know. Here's your chance to show us. What's our next move?"

"Really, now, I have had no experience in this sort of thing—don't interrupt, please! It seems to me that our first concern is shelter for the night. If we should return to your tree nest, we should also be near the cocoa palms."

"That's one side. Here's the other. Bar to wade across— sharks and alligators; then swampy ground—malaria, mosquitoes, thorn jungle. Guess the hands of both of you are still sore enough, by their look."

"If only I had a pot of cold cream!" sighed Miss Leslie.

"If only I had a hunk of jerked beef!" echoed Blake.

"I say, why couldn't we chance it for the night around on the seaward face of the cliff?" asked Winthrope. "I noticed a place where the ledges overhang—almost a cave. Do you think it probable that any wild beast would venture so close to the sea?"

"Can't say. Didn't see any tracks; so we'll chance it for to-night. Next!"

"By morning I believe my ankle will be in such shape that I could go back for the string of cocoanuts which we dropped on the beach."

"I'll go myself, to-day, else we'll have no supper. Now we're getting down to bedrock. If those nuts haven't been washed away by the tide, we're fixed for to-night; and for two meals, such as they are. But what next? Even the rain pools will be dried up by another day or so."

"Are not sea-birds good to eat?" inquired Miss Leslie.

"Some."

"Then, if only we could climb the cliff—might there not be another place?"

"No; I've looked at both sides. What's more, that spotted tomcat has got a monopoly on our water supply. The river may be fresh at low tide; but we've got nothing to boil water in, and such bayou stuff is just concentrated malaria."

"Then we must find water elsewhere," responded Miss Leslie. "Might we not succeed if we went on to the other ridge?"

"That's the ticket! You've got a headpiece, Miss Jenny! It's too late to start now. But first thing to-morrow I'll take a run down that way, while you two lay around camp and see if you can twist some sort of fish-line out of cocoanut fibre. By braiding your hair, Miss Jenny, you can spare us your hair-pins for hooks."

"But, Mr. Blake, I'm afraid—I'd rather you'd take us with you. With that dreadful creature so near—"

"Well, I don't know. Let's see your feet?"

Miss Leslie glanced at him, and thrust a slender foot from beneath her skirt.

"Um-m—stocking torn; but those slippers are tougher than I thought. Most of the way will be good walking, along the beach. We'll leave the fishing to Pat—er—beg pardon—Win! With his ankle—"

"By Jove, Blake, I'll chance the ankle. Don't leave me behind. I give you my word, you'll not have to lug me."

"Oh, of course, Mr. Winthrope must go with us!"

"'Fraid to go alone, eh?" demanded Blake, frowning.

His tone startled and offended her; yet all he saw was a politely quizzical lifting of her brows.

"Why should I be afraid, Mr. Blake?" she asked.

Blake stared at her moodily. But when she met his gaze with a confiding smile, he flushed and looked away.

"All right," he muttered; "well move camp together. But don't expect me to pack his ludship, if we draw a blank and have to trek back without food or water."

9

THE LEOPARDS' DEN

WHILE BLAKE MADE a successful trip for the abandoned cocoanuts, his companions levelled the stones beneath the ledges chosen by Winthrope, and gathered enough dried sea-weed along the talus to soften the hard beds.

Soothed by the monotonous wash of the sea among the rocks, even Miss Leslie slept well. Blake, who had insisted that she should retain his coat, was wakened by the chilliness preceding the dawn. Five minutes later they started on their journey.

The starlight glimmered on the waves and shed a faint radiance over the rocks. This and their knowledge of the way enabled them to pick a path along the foot of the cliff without difficulty. Once on the beach, they swung along at a smart gait, invigorated by the cool air.

Dawn found them half way to their goal. Blake called a halt when the first red streaks shot up the eastern sky. All stood waiting until the quickly following sun sprang forth from the sea. Blake's first act was to glance from one headland to the other, estimating their relative distances. His grunt of satisfaction was lost in Winthrope's exclamation, "By Jove, look at the cattle!"

Blake and Miss Leslie turned to stare at the droves of

animals moving about between them and the border of the tall grass. Miss Leslie was the first to speak. "They can't be cattle, Mr. Winthrope. There are some with stripes. I do believe they're zebras!"

"Get down!" commanded Blake. "They're all wild game. Those big ox-like fellows to the left of the zebras are eland. Whee! wouldn't we be in it if we owned that water hole? I'll bet I'd have one of those fat beeves inside three days."

"How I should enjoy a juicy steak!" murmured Miss Leslie.

"Raw or jerked?" questioned Blake.

"What is 'jerked'?"

"Dried."

"Oh, no; I mean broiled—just red inside."

"I prefer mine quite rare," added Winthrope.

"That's the way you'll get it, damned rare— Beg your pardon, Miss Jenny! Without fire, we'll have the choice of raw or jerked."

"Horrors!"

"Jerked meat is all right. You cut your game in strips—"

"With a penknife!" laughed Miss Leslie.

Blake stared at her glumly. "That's so. You've got it back on me— Butcher a beef with a penknife! We'll have to take it raw, and dog-fashion at that."

"Haven't I heard of bamboo knives?" said Winthrope.

"Bamboo?"

"I'm sure I can't say, but as I remember, it seems to me that the varnish-like glaze—"

"Silica? Say, that would cut meat. But where in—where in hades are the bamboos?"

"I'm sure I can't say. Only I remember that I have seen them in other tropical places, you know."

"Meantime I prefer cocoanuts, until we have a fire to broil our steaks," remarked Miss Leslie.

"Ditto, Miss Jenny, long's we have the nuts and no meat. I'm a vegetarian now—but maybe my mouth ain't watering for something else. Look at all those chops and roasts and stews running around out there!"

"They are making for the grass," observed Winthrope. "Hadn't we better start?"

"Nuts won't weigh so much without the shells. We'll eat right here."

There were only a few nuts left. They were drained and cracked and scooped out, one after another. The last chanced to break evenly across the middle.

"Hello," said Blake, "the lower part of this will do for a bowl, Miss Jenny. When you've eaten the cream, put it in your pocket. Say, Win, have you got the bottle and keys and—"

"All safe—everything."

"Are you sure, Mr. Winthrope?" asked Miss Leslie. "Men's pockets seem so open. Twice I've had to pick up Mr. Blake's locket."

"Locket?" echoed Blake.

"The ivory locket. Women may be curious, Mr. Blake, but I assure you, I did not look inside, though—"

"Let me—give it here—quick!" gasped Blake.

Startled by his tone and look, Miss Leslie caught an oval object from the side pocket of the coat, and thrust it into Blake's outstretched hand. For a moment he stared at it, unable to believe his eyes; then he leaped up, with a yell that sent the droves of zebras and antelope flying into the tall grass.

"Oh! oh!" screamed Miss Leslie. "Is it a snake? Are you bitten?"

"Bitten?—Yes, by John Barleycorn! Must have been fuzzy drunk to put it in my coat. Always carry it in my fob pocket. What a blasted infernal idiot I've been! Kick me, Win,—kick me hard!"

"I say, Blake, what is it? I don't quite take you. If you would only—"

"Fire!—*fire!* Can't you see? We've got all hell beat! Look here."

He snapped open the slide of the supposed locket, and before either of his companions could realize what he would be about, was focussing the lens of a surveyor's magnifying-glass upon the back of Winthrope's hand. The Englishman jerked the hand away—

"*Ow!* That burns!"

Blake shook the glass in their bewildered faces.

"Look there!" he shouted, "there's fire; there's water; there's birds' eggs and beefsteaks! Here's where we trek on the back trail. We'll smoke out that leopard in short order!"

"You don't mean to say, Blake—"

"No; I mean to do! Don't worry. You can hide with Miss Jenny on the point, while I engineer the deal. Fall in."

The day was still fresh when they found themselves back at the foot of the cliff. Here arose a heated debate between the men. Winthrope, stung by Blake's jeering words, insisted upon sharing the attack, though with no great enthusiasm. Much to Blake's surprise, Miss Leslie came to the support of the Englishman.

"But, Mr. Blake," she argued, "you say it will be perfectly safe for us here. If so, it will be safe for myself alone."

"I can play this game without him."

"No doubt. Yet if, as you say, you expect to keep off the leopard with a torch, would it not be well to have Mr. Winthrope at hand with other torches, should yours burn out?"

"Yes; if I thought he'd be at hand after the first scare."

Winthrope started off, almost on a run. At that moment he might have faced the leopard single-handed. Blake chuckled as he swung away after his victim. Within ten paces, however, he paused to call back over his shoulder: "Get around the point, Miss Jenny, and if you want something to do, try braiding the cocoanut fibre."

Miss Leslie made no response; but she stood for some time gazing after the two men. There was so much that was characteristic even in this rear view. For all his anger and his haste, the Englishman bore himself with an air of well-bred nicety. His trim, erect figure needed only a fresh suit to be irreproachable. On the other hand, a careless observer, at first glance, might have mistaken Blake, with his flannel shirt and shouldered club, for a hulking navvy. But there was nothing of the navvy in his swinging stride or in the resolute poise of his head as he came up with Winthrope.

Though the girl was not given to reflection, the contrast between the two could not but impress her. How well her countryman—coarse, uncultured, but full of brute strength and courage—fitted in with these primitive surroundings. Whereas Winthrope... and herself....

She fell into a kind of disquieted brown study. Her eyes had an odd look, both startled and meditative,—such a look as might be expected of one who for the first time is peering beneath the surface of things, and sees the naked Realities of Life, the real values, bared of masking conventions. It may have been that she was seeking to ponder the meaning of her own existence—that she had caught a glimpse of the vanity and wastefulness, the utter futility of her life. At the best, it could only have been a glimpse. But was not that enough?

"Of what use are such people as I?" she cried. "That man may be rough and coarse,—even a brute; but he at least does things—I'll show him that I can do things, too!"

She hastened out around the corner of the cliff to the spot where they had spent the night. Here she gathered together the cocoanut husks, and seating herself in the shade of the overhanging ledges, began to pick at the coarse fibre. It was cruel work for her soft fingers, not yet fully healed from the thorn wounds. At times the pain and an overpowering sense of injury brought tears to her eyes; still more often she dropped the work in despair of her awkwardness. Yet always she returned to the task with renewed energy.

After no little perseverance, she found how to twist the fibre and plait it into cord. At best it was slow work, and she did not see how she should ever make enough cord for a fish-line. Yet, as she caught the knack of the work and her fingers became more nimble, she began to enjoy the novel pleasure of producing something.

She had quite forgot to feel injured, and was learning to endure with patience the rasping of the fibre between her fingers, when Winthrope came clambering around the corner of the cliff.

"What is it?" she exclaimed, springing up and hurrying to meet him. He was white and quivering, and the look in his eyes filled her with dread.

Her voice shrilled to a scream, "He's dead!"

Winthrope shook his head.

"Then he's hurt!—he's hurt by that savage creature, and you've run off and left him—"

"No, no, Miss Genevieve, I must insist! The fellow is not even scratched."

"Then why—?"

"It was the horror of it all. It actually made me ill."

"You frightened me almost to death. Did the beast chase you?"

"That would have been better, in a way. Really, it was horrible! I'm still sick over it, Miss Genevieve."

"But tell me about it. Did you set fire to the bushes in the cleft, as Mr. Blake—"

"Yes; after we had fetched what we could carry of that long grass—two big trusses. It grows ten or twelve feet tall, and is now quite dry. Part of it Blake made into torches, and we fired the bush all across the foot of the cleft. Really, one would not have thought there was that much dry wood in so green a dell. On either side of the rill the grass and brush flared like tinder, and the flames swept up the cleft far quicker than we had expected. We could hear them crackling and roaring louder than ever after the smoke shut out our view."

"Surely, there is nothing so very horrible in that."

"No, oh, no; it was not that. But the beast—the leopard! At first we heard one roar; then it was that dreadful snarling and yelling—most awful squalling!... The wretched thing came leaping and tumbling down the path, all singed and blinded. Blake fired the big truss of grass, and the brute rolled right into the flames. It was shocking—dreadfully shocking! The wretched creature writhed and leaped about till it plunged into the pool.... When it sought to crawl out, all black and hideous, Blake went up and killed it with his club—crushed in its skull— Ugh!"

Miss Leslie gazed at the unnerved Englishman with calm scrutiny.

"But why should you feel so about it?" she asked. "Was it not the beast's life against ours?"

"But so horrible a death!"

"I'm sure Mr. Blake would have preferred to shoot the creature, had he a gun. Having nothing else than fire, I think it was all very brave of him. Now we are sure of water and food. Had we not best be going?"

"It was to fetch you that Blake sent me."

Winthrope spoke with perceptible stiffness. He was chagrined, not only by her commendation of Blake, but by the indifference with which she had met his agitation.

They started at once, Miss Leslie in the lead. As they rounded the point, she caught sight of the smoke still rising from the cleft. A little later she noticed the vultures which were streaming down out of the sky from all quarters other than seaward. Their focal point seemed to be the trees at the foot of the cleft. A nearer view showed that they were alighting in the thorn bushes on the south border of the wood.

Of Blake there was nothing to be seen until Miss Leslie, still in the lead, pushed in among the trees. There they found him crouched beside a small fire, near the edge of the pool. He did not look up. His eyes were riveted in a hungry stare upon several pieces of flesh, suspended over the flames on spits of green twigs.

"Hello!" he sang out, as he heard their footsteps. "Just in time, Miss Jenny. Your broiled steak'll be ready in short order."

"Oh, build up the fire! I'm simply ravenous!" she exclaimed, between impatience and delight.

Winthrope was hardly less keen; yet his hunger did not altogether blunt his curiosity.

"I say, Blake," he inquired, "where did you get the meat?"

"Stow it, Win, my boy. This ain't a packing house. The stuff may be tough, but it's not—er—the other thing. Here you are, Miss Jenny. Chew it off the stick."

Though Winthrope had his suspicions, he took the piece of half-burned flesh which Blake handed him in turn, and fell to eating without further question. As Blake had surmised, the roast proved far other than tender. Hunger, however, lent it a most appetizing flavor. The repast ended when there was nothing left to devour. Blake threw away his empty spit, and rose to stretch. He waited for Miss Leslie to swallow her last mouthful, and then began to chuckle.

"What's the joke?" asked Winthrope.

Blake looked at him solemnly.

"Well now, that was downright mean of me," he drawled; "after robbing them, to laugh at it!"

"Robbing who?"

"The buzzards."

"You've fed us on leopard meat! It's—it's disgusting!"

"I found it filling. How about you, Miss Jenny?"

Miss Leslie did not know whether to laugh or to give way to a feeling of nausea. She did neither.

"Can we not find the spring of which you spoke?" she asked. "I am thirsty."

"Well, I guess the fire is about burnt out," assented Blake. "Come on; we'll see."

The cleft now had a far different aspect from what it had presented on their first visit. The largest of the trees, though scorched about the base, still stood with unwithered foliage, little harmed by the fire. But many of their small companions had been killed and partly destroyed by the heat and flames from the burning brush. In places the fire was yet smouldering.

Blake picked a path along the edge of the rill, where the moist vegetation, though scorched, had refused to burn. After the first abrupt ledge, up which Blake had to drag his companions, the ascent was easy. But as they climbed around an outjutting corner of the steep right wall of the cleft, Blake muttered a curse of disappointment. He could now see that the cleft did not run to the top of the cliff, but through it, like a tiny box canyon. The sides rose sheer and smooth as walls. Midway, at the highest point of the cleft, the baobab towered high above the ridge crest, its gigantic trunk filling a third of the breadth of the little gorge. Unfortunately it stood close to the left wall.

"Here's luck for you!" growled Blake. "Why couldn't the blamed old tree have grown on the other side? We might have found a way to climb it. Guess we'll have to smoke out another leopard. We're no nearer those birds' nests than we were yesterday."

"By Jove, look here!" exclaimed Winthrope. "This is our

chance for antelope! Here by the spring are bamboos—real bamboos,—and only half the thicket burned."

"What of them?" demanded Blake.

"Bows—arrows—and did you not agree that they would make knives?"

"Umph—we'll see. What is it, Miss Jenny?"

"Isn't that a hole in the big tree?"

"Looks like it. These baobabs are often hollow."

"Perhaps that is where the leopard had his den," added Winthrope.

"Shouldn't wonder. We'll go and see."

"But, Mr. Blake," protested the girl, "may there not be other leopards?"

"Might have been; but I'll bet they lit out with the other. Look how the tree is scorched. Must have been stacks of dry brush around the hole, 'nough to smoke out a fireman. We'll look and see if they left any soup bones lying around. First, though, here's your drink, Miss Jenny."

As he spoke, Blake kicked aside some smouldering branches, and led the way to the crevice whence the spring trickled from the rock into a shallow stone basin. When all had drunk their fill of the clear cool water, Blake took up his club and walked straight across to the baobab. Less than thirty steps brought him to the narrow opening in the trunk of the huge tree. At first he could make out nothing in the dimly lit interior; but the fetid, catty odor was enough to convince him that he had found the leopards' den.

He caught the vague outlines of a long body, crouched five or six yards away, on the far side of the hollow. He sprang back, his club brandished to strike. But the expected attack did not follow. Blake glanced about as though considering the advisability of a retreat. Winthrope and Miss Leslie were staring at him, white-faced. The sight of their terror seemed to spur him to dare-devil bravado; though his actions may rather have been due to the fact that he realized the futility of flight, and so rose to the requirements of the situation—the grim need to stand and face the danger.

"Get behind the bamboos!" he called, and as they hurriedly obeyed, he caught up a stone and flung it in at the crouching beast.

He heard the missile strike with a soft thud that told him he had not missed his mark, and he swung up his club in both hands. Given half a chance, he would smash the skull of the female leopard as he had crushed her blinded mate.... One moment after another passed, and he stood poised for the shock, tense and scowling.... Not so much as a snarl came from within. The truth flashed upon him.

"Smothered!" he yelled.

The others saw him dart in through the hole. A moment later two limp grayish bodies were flung out into the open. Immediately after, Blake reappeared, dragging the body of the mother leopard.

"It's all right; they're dead!" cried Winthrope, and he ran forward to look at the bodies.

Miss Leslie followed, hardly less curious.

"Are they all dead, Mr. Blake?" she inquired.

"Wiped out—whole family. The old cat stayed by her kittens, and all smothered together—lucky for us! Get busy with those bamboos, Win. I'm going to have these skins, and the sooner we get the cub meat hung up and curing, the better for us."

"Leopard meat again!" rejoined Winthrope.

"Spring leopard, young and tender! What more could you ask? Get a move on you."

"Can I do anything, Mr. Blake?" asked Miss Leslie.

"Hunt a shady spot."

"But I really mean it."

"Well, if that's straight, you might go on along the gully, and see if there's any place to get to the top. You could pick up sticks on the way back, if any are left. We'll have to fumigate this tree hole before we adopt it for a residence."

"Will it be long before you finish with your—with the bodies?"

"Well, now, look here, Miss Jenny; it's going to be a mess, and I wouldn't mind hauling the carcasses clear down the gully, out of sight, if it was to be the only time. But it's not, and you've got to get used to it, sooner or later. So we'll start now."

"I suppose, if I must, Mr. Blake— Really, I wish to help."

"Good. That's something like! Think you can learn to cook?"

"See what I did this morning."

Blake took the cord of cocoanut fibre which she held out to him, and tested its strength.

"Well, I'll be—blessed!" he said. "This is something like. If you don't look out, you'll make quite a camp-mate, Miss Jenny. But now, trot along. This is hardly arctic weather, and our abattoir don't include a cold-storage plant. The sooner these lambs are dressed, the better."

10

PROBLEMS IN WOODCRAFT

IT WAS NO pleasant sight that met Miss Leslie's gaze upon her return. The neatest of butchering can hardly be termed aesthetic; and Blake and Winthrope lacked both skill and tools. Between the penknife and an improvised blade of bamboo, they had flayed the two cubs and haggled off the flesh. The ragged strips, spitted on bamboo rods, were already searing in the fierce sun-rays.

Miss Leslie would have slipped into the hollow of the baobab with her armful of fagots and brush; but Blake waved a bloody knife above the body of the mother leopard, and beckoned the girl to come nearer.

"Hold on a minute, please," he said. "What did you find out?"

Miss Leslie drew a few steps nearer, and forced herself to look at the revolting sight. She found it still more difficult to withstand the odor of the fresh blood. Winthrope was pale and nauseated. The sight of his distress caused the girl to forget her own loathing. She drew a deep breath, and succeeded in countering Blake's expectant look with a half-smile.

"How well you are getting along!" she exclaimed.

"Didn't think you could stand it. But you've got grit all

right, if you *are* a lady," Blake said admiringly. "Say, you'll make it yet! Now, how about the gully?"

"There is no place to climb up. It runs along like this, and then slopes down. But there is a cliff at the end, as high as these walls."

"Twenty feet," muttered Blake. "Confound the luck! It isn't that jump-off; but how in—how are we going to get up on the cliff? There's an everlasting lot of omelettes in those birds' nests. If only that bloomin'—how's that, Win, me b'y?—that bloomin', blawsted baobab was on t' other side. The wood's almost soft as punk. We could drive in pegs, and climb up the trunk."

"There are other trees beyond it," remarked Miss Leslie.

"Then maybe we can shin up—"

"I fear the branches that overhang the cliff are too slender to bear any weight."

"And it's too infernally high to climb up to this overhanging baobab limb."

"I say," ventured Winthrope, "if we had a axe, now, we might cut up one of the trees, and make a ladder."

"Oh, yes; and if we had a ladder, we might climb up the cliff!"

"But, Mr. Blake, is there not some way to cut down one of the trees? The tree itself would be a ladder if it fell in such a way as to lean against the cliff."

"There's only the penknife," answered Blake. "So I guess we'll have to scratch eggs off our menu card. Spring leopard for ours! Now, if you really want to help, you might scrape the soup bones out of your boudoir, and fetch a lot more brush. It'll take a big fire to rid the hole of that cat smell."

"Will not the tree burn?"

"No; these hollow baobabs have green bark on the inside as well as out. Funny thing, that! We'd have to keep a fire going a long time to burn through."

"Yet it would burn in time?"

"Yes; but we're not going to—"

"Then why not burn through the trunk of one of those small trees, instead of chopping it down?"

"By—heck, Miss Jenny, you've got an American headpiece! Come on. Sooner we get the thing started, the better."

Neither Winthrope nor Miss Leslie was reluctant to leave the vicinity of the carcasses. They followed close after Blake, around the monstrous bole of the baobab. A little beyond it stood a group of slender trees, whose trunks averaged eight inches thick at the base. Blake stopped at the second one, which grew nearest to the seaward side of the cleft.

"Here's our ladder," he said. "Get some firewood. Pound the bushes, though, before you go poking into them. May be snakes here."

"Snakes?—oh!" cried Miss Leslie, and she stood shuddering at the danger she had already incurred.

The fire had burnt itself out on a bare ledge of rock between them and the baobab, and the clumps of dry brush left standing in this end of the cleft were very suggestive of snakes, now that Blake had called attention to the possibility of their presence.

He laughed at his hesitating companions. "Go on, go on! Don't squeal till you're bit. Most snakes hike out, if you give them half a chance. Take a stick, each of you, and pound the bushes."

Thus urged, both started to work. But neither ventured into the thicker clumps. When they returned, with large armfuls of sticks and twigs, they found that Blake had used his glass to light a handful of dry bark, out in the sun, and was nursing it into a small fire at the base of the tree, on the side next the cliff.

"Now, Miss Jenny," he directed, "you're to keep this going—not too big a fire—understand? Same time you can keep on fetching brush to fumigate your cat hole. It needs it, all right."

"Will not that be rather too much for Miss Leslie?" asked Winthrope.

"Well, if she'd rather come and rub brains on the skins,— Indian tan, you know,—or—"

"How can you mention such things before a lady?" protested Winthrope.

"Beg your pardon, Miss Leslie! you see, I'm not much used to ladies' company. Anyway, you've got to see and hear about these things. And now I'll have to get the strings for Win's bamboo bows. Come on, Win. We've got that old tabby to peel, and a lot more besides."

Miss Leslie's first impulse was to protest against being left alone, when at any moment some awful venomous serpent might come darting at her out of the brush or the crevices in the rocks. But her half-parted lips drew firmly together, and after a moment's hesitancy, she forced herself to the task which had been assigned her. The fire, once started, required little attention. She could give most of her time to gathering brush for the fumigation of the leopard den.

She had collected quite a heap of fuel at the entrance of

the hollow, when she remembered that the place would first have to be cleared of its accumulation of bones. A glance at her companions showed that they were in the midst of tasks even more revolting. It was certainly disagreeable to do such things; yet, as Mr. Blake had said, others had to do them. It was now her time to learn. She could see him smile at her hesitation.

Stung by the thought of his half contemptuous pity, she caught up a forked stick, and forced herself to enter the tree-cave. The stench met her like a blow. It nauseated and all but overpowered her. She stood for several moments in the centre of the cavity, sick and faint. Had it been even the previous day, she would have run out into the open air.

Presently she grew a little more accustomed to the stench, and began to rake over the soft dry mould of the den floor with her forked stick. Bones!—who had ever dreamed of such a mess of bones?—big bones and little bones and skulls; old bones, dry and almost buried; mouldy bones; bones still half-covered with bits of flesh and gristle—the remnants of the leopard family's last meal.

At last all were scraped out and flung in a heap, three or four yards away from the entrance. Miss Leslie looked at the result of her labor with a satisfied glance, followed by a sigh of relief. Between the heat and her unwonted exercise, she was greatly fatigued. She stepped around to a shadier spot to rest.

With a start, she remembered the fire.

When she reached it there were only a few dying embers left. She gathered dead leaves and shreds of fibrous inner bark, and knelt beside the dull coals to blow them into life.

She could not bear the thought of having to confess her carelessness to Blake.

The hot ashes flew up in her face and powdered her hair with their gray dust; yet she persisted, blowing steadily until a shred of bark caught the sparks and flared up in a tiny flame. A little more, and she had a strong fire blazing against the tree trunk.

She rested a short time, relaxing both mentally and physically in the satisfying consciousness that Blake never should know how near she had come to failing in her trust.

Soon she became aware of a keen feeling of thirst and hunger. She rose, piled a fresh supply of sticks on the fire, and hastened back through the cleft towards the spring. Around the baobab she came upon Winthrope, working in the shade of the great tree. The three leopard skins had been stretched upon bamboo frames, and he was resignedly scraping at their inner surfaces with a smooth-edged stone. Miss Leslie did not look too closely at the operation.

"Where is—he?" she asked.

Winthrope motioned down the cleft.

"I hope he hasn't gone far. I'm half famished. Aren't you?"

"Really, Miss Genevieve, it is odd, you know. Not an hour since, the very thought of food—"

"And now you're as hungry as I am. Oh, I do wish he had not gone off just at the wrong time!"

"He went to take a dip in the sea. You know, he got so messed up over the nastiest part of the work, which I positively refused to do—"

"What's that beyond the bamboos?— There's something alive!"

"Pray, don't be alarmed. It is—er—it's all right, Miss Genevieve, I assure you."

"But what is it? Such queer noises, and I see something alive!"

"Only the vultures, if you must know. Nothing else, I assure you."

"Oh!"

"It is all out of sight from the spring. You are not to go around the bamboos until the—that is, not to-day."

"Did Mr. Blake say that?"

"Why, yes—to be sure. He also said to tell you that the cutlets were on the top shelf."

"You mean—?"

"His way of ordering you to cook our dinner. Really, Miss Genevieve, I should be pleased to take your place, but I have been told to keep to this. It is hard to take orders from a low fellow,—very hard for a gentleman, you know."

Miss Leslie gazed at her shapely hands. Three days since she could not have conceived of their being so rough and scratched and dirty. Yet her disgust at their condition was not entirely unqualified.

"At least I have something to show for them," she murmured.

"I beg pardon," said Winthrope.

"Just look at my hands—like a servant's! And yet I am not nearly so ashamed of them as I would have fancied. It is very amusing, but do you know, I actually feel proud that I have done something—something useful, I mean."

"Useful?—I call it shocking, Miss Genevieve. It is simply vile that people of our breeding should be compelled to do such menial work. They write no end of romances about

castaways; but I fail to see the romance in scraping skins
Indian fashion, as this fellow Blake calls it."

"I suppose, though, we should remember how much
Mr. Blake is doing for us, and should try to make the best
of the situation."

"It has no best. It is all a beastly muddle," complained
Winthrope, and he resumed his nervous scraping at the
big leopard skin.

The girl studied his face for a moment, and turned away.
She had been trying so hard to forget.

He heard her leave, and called after, without looking up:
"Please remember. He said to cook some meat."

She did not answer. Having satisfied her thirst at the
spring, she took one of the bamboo rods, with its haggled
blackening pieces of flesh, and returned to the fire. After
some little experimenting, she contrived a way to support
the rod beside the fire so that all the meat would roast
without burning.

At first, keen as was her hunger, she turned with disgust
from the flabby sun-seared flesh; but as it began to roast,
the odor restored her appetite to full vigor. Her mouth
fairly watered. It seemed as though Winthrope and Blake
would never come. She heard their voices, and took the
bamboo spit from the fire for the meat to cool. Still they
failed to appear, and unable to wait longer, she began to eat.
The cub meat proved far more tender than that of the old
leopard. She had helped herself to the second piece before
the two men appeared.

"Hold on, Miss Jenny; fair play!" sang out Blake. "You've
set to without tooting the dinner-horn. I don't blame you,
though. That smells mighty good."

Both men caught at the hot meat with eagerness, and Winthrope promptly forgot all else in the animal pleasure of satisfying his hunger. Blake, though no less hungry, only waited to fill his mouth before investigating the condition of the prospective tree ladder. The result of the attempt to burn the trunk did not seem encouraging to the others, and Miss Leslie looked away, that her face might not betray her, should he have an inkling of her neglect. She was relieved by the cheerfulness of his tone.

"Slow work, this fire business—eh? Guess, though, it'll go faster this afternoon. The green wood is killed and is getting dried out. Anyway, we've got to keep at it till the tree goes over. This spring leopard won't last long at the present rate of consumption, and we'll need the eggs to keep us going till we get the hang of our bows."

"What is that smoke back there?" interrupted Miss Leslie. "Can it be that the fire down the cleft has sprung up again?"

"No; it's your fumigation. You had plenty of brush on hand, so I heaved it into the hole, and touched it off. While it's burning out, you can put in time gathering grass and leaves for a bed."

"Would you and Mr. Winthrope mind breaking off some bamboos for me?"

"What for?"

Miss Leslie colored and hesitated. "I—I should like to divide off a corner of the place with a wall or screen."

Winthrope tried to catch Blake's eye; but the American was gazing at Miss Leslie's embarrassed face with a puzzled look. Her meaning dawned upon him, and he hastened to reply.

"All right, Miss Jenny. You can build your wall to suit yourself. But there'll be no hurry over it. Until the rains begin, Win and I'll sleep out in the open. We'll have to take turn about on watch at night, anyway. If we don't keep up a fire, some other spotted kitty will be sure to come nosing up the gully."

"There must also be lions in the vicinity," added Winthrope.

Miss Leslie said nothing until after the last pieces of meat had been handed around, and Blake sprang up to resume work.

"Mr. Blake," she called, in a low tone; "one moment, please. Would it save much bother if a door was made, and you and Mr. Winthrope should sleep inside?"

"We'll see about that later," replied Blake, carelessly.

The girl bit her lip, and the tears started to her eyes. Even Winthrope had started off without expressing his appreciation. Yet he at least should have realized how much it had cost her to make such an offer.

By evening she had her tree-cave—house, she preferred to name it to herself—in a habitable condition. When the purifying fire had burnt itself out, leaving the place free from all odors other than the wholesome smell of wood smoke, she had asked Blake how she could rake out the ashes. His advice was to wet them down where they lay.

This was easier said than done. Fortunately, the spring was only a few yards distant, and after many trips, with her palm-leaf hat for bowl, the girl carried enough water to sprinkle all the powdery ashes. Over them she strewed the leaves and grass which she had gathered while the fire was burning. The driest of the grass, arranged in a far corner, promised a more comfortable bed than had been her lot for the last three nights.

During this work she had been careful not to forget the fire at the tree. Yet when, near sundown, she called the others to the third meal of leopard meat, Blake grumbled at the tree for being what he termed such a confounded tough proposition.

"Good thing there's lots of wood here, Win," he added. "We'll keep this fire going till the blamed thing topples over, if it takes a year."

"Oh, but you surely will not stay so far from the baobab to-night!" exclaimed Miss Leslie.

"Hold hard!" soothed Blake. "You've no license to get the jumps yet a while. We'll have another fire by the baobab. So you needn't worry."

A few minutes later they went back to the baobab, and Winthrope began helping Miss Leslie to construct a bamboo screen in the narrow entrance of the tree-cave, while Blake built the second fire.

As Winthrope was unable to tell time by the stars, Blake took the first watch. At sunset, following the engineer's advice, Winthrope lay down with his feet to the small watch-fire, and was asleep before twilight had deepened into night. Fagged out by the mental and bodily stress of the day, he slept so soundly that it seemed to him he had hardly lost consciousness when he was roused by a rough hand on his forehead.

"What is it?" he mumbled.

"'Bout one o'clock," said Blake. "Wake up! I ran over-time, 'cause the morning watch is the toughest. But I can't keep 'wake any longer."

"I say, this is a beastly bore," remarked Winthrope, sitting up.

"Um-m," grunted Blake, who was already on his back.

Winthrope rubbed his eyes, rose wearily, and drew a blazing stick from the fire. With this upraised as a torch, he peered around into the darkness, and advanced towards the spring.

When, having satisfied his thirst, he returned somewhat hurriedly to the fire, he was startled by the sight of a pale face gazing at him from between the leaves of the bamboo screen.

"My dear Miss Genevieve, what is the matter?" he exclaimed.

"Hush! Is he asleep?"

"Like a top."

"Thank Heaven!... Good-night."

"Good-night—er—I say, Miss Genevieve—"

But the girl disappeared, and Winthrope, after a glance at Blake's placid face, hurried along the cleft to stack the other fire. When he returned he noticed two bamboo rods which Blake had begun to shape into bow staves. He looked them over, with a sneer at Blake's seemingly unskilful workmanship; but he made no attempt to finish the bows.

11

A DESPOILED WARDROBE

SOON AFTER SUNRISE Miss Leslie was awakened by the snap and dull crash of a falling tree. She made a hasty toilet, and ran out around the baobab. The burned tree, eaten half through by the fire, had been pushed over against the cliff by Blake and Winthrope. Both had already climbed up, and now stood on the edge of the cliff.

"Hello, Miss Jenny!" shouted Blake. "We've got here at last. Want to come up?"

"Not now, thank you."

"It's easy enough. But you're right. Try your hand again at the cutlets, won't you? While they're frying, we'll get some eggs for dessert How does that strike you?"

"We have no way to cook them."

"Roast 'em in the ashes. So long!"

Miss Leslie cooked breakfast over the watch-fire, for the other had been scattered and stamped out by the men when the tree fell. They came back in good time, walking carefully, that they might not break the eggs with which their pockets bulged. Between them, they had brought a round dozen and a half. Blake promptly began stowing all in the hot ashes, while Winthrope related their little adventure with unwonted enthusiasm.

"You should have come with us, Miss Genevieve," he began. "This time of day it is glorious on the cliff top. Though the rock is bare, there is a fine view—"

"Fine view of grub near the end," interpolated Blake.

"Ah, yes; the birds—you must take a look at them, Miss Genevieve! The sea end of the cliff is alive with them—hundreds and thousands, all huddled together and fighting for room. They are a sight, I assure you! They're plucky, too. It was well we took sticks with us. As it was, one of the gannets—boobies, Blake calls them—caught me a nasty nip when I went to lift her off the nest."

"Best way is to kick them off," explained Blake. "But the point is that we've hopped over the starvation stile. Understand? The whole blessed cliff end is an omelette waiting for our pan. Pass the leopardettes, Miss Jenny."

When the last bit of meat had disappeared, Blake raked the eggs from the ashes, and began to crack them, solemnly sniffing at each before he laid it on its leaf platter. Some were a trifle "high." None, however, were thrown away.

When it was all over, Winthrope contemplated the scattered shells with a satisfied air.

"Do you know," he remarked, "this is the first time I have felt—er—replenished since we found those cocoanuts."

"How about one of 'em now to top off on?" questioned Blake.

Miss Leslie sighed. "Why did you speak of them! I am still hungry enough to eat more eggs—a dozen—that is, if we had a little salt and butter."

"And a silver cup and napkins!" added Blake. "About the salt, though, we'll have to get some before long, and some kind of vegetable food. It won't do to keep up this whole meat menu."

"If only those little bamboo sprouts were as good as they look—like a kind of asparagus!" murmured Miss Leslie.

"I've heard that the Chinese eat them," said Winthrope.

"They eat rats, too," commented Blake.

"We might at least try them," persisted Miss Leslie.

"How? Raw?"

"I have heard papa tell of roasting corn when he was a boy."

"That's so; and roasting-ears are better than boiled. Win, I guess we'll have a sample of bamboo asparagus *à la* Les-lee!"

Winthrope took the penknife, and fetched a handful of young sprouts from the bamboo thicket. They were heated over the coals on a grill of green branches, and devoured half raw.

"Say," mumbled Blake, as he ruminated on the last shoot, "we're getting on some for this smell hole of a coast: house and chicken ranch, and vegetables in our front yard— We've got old Bobbie Crusoe beat, hands down, on the start-off, and he with his shipful of stuff for handicap!"

"Then you believe that the situation looks more hopeful, Mr. Blake?"

"Well, we've at least got an extension on our note for a week or two. But I'm not going to coddle you with a lot of lies, Miss Jenny. There's the fever coming, sure as fate. I may stave it off a while; you and Win, ten to one, will be down in a few days—and not a smell of quinine in our commissary. Then there'll be dysentery and snakes and wild beasts— No; we're not out of the woods yet, not by a—considerable."

"By Jove, Blake," muttered Winthrope, "I must say, you're not very encouraging."

"Didn't say I was trying to be."

"But, Mr. Blake, I am sure papa will offer a large reward when the steamer is reported as lost. There will be ships searching for us—"

"We're not in the British Channel, and I'll bet what few boats do coast along here don't nose about much among these coral reefs."

"I fancy it would do no harm to erect a signal," said Winthrope.

"Only thing that would make a show is Miss Leslie's skirt," replied Blake.

"There is the big leopard skin," persisted Winthrope. To his surprise the engineer took the suggestion under serious consideration.

"Well, I don't know," he said. "If we had a water background, now. But against the rock and trees,—no; what we want is white. I'll tell you—when Miss Jenny sets to and makes herself a dress of that skin, I'll fly her skirt to the zephyrs."

"Mr. Blake! I really think that is cruel of you!"

"Oh, come now; that's not fair! I wouldn't have said a word, but you said you wanted to help."

"I beg your pardon, Mr. Blake. I—I did not quite understand you. I really do want to help—to do my share—"

"Now you're talking! You see, it's not only a question of the signal, but of clothes. We've got to figure anyway on needing new ones before long. Look at my pants and vest, and Win's too. Inside a month we'll all be in hide—or in hiding. That's a joke, Win, me b'y; see?"

"But in the meantime—"began Miss Leslie.

"In the meantime we're like to miss a chance or two of being picked up, just because we've failed to stick out a signal that'd catch the eye twice as far off as any other color than scarlet. Do you suppose I worked my way up from axeman to engineer, and didn't learn anything about flags?"

"But it is all really too absurd! I do not know the first thing about sewing, and I have neither thread nor needle."

"It's up to you, though, if you want to help. My sisters sewed mighty soon after they learned to toddle. 'Bout time you learned— There, now; I didn't mean to hurt your feelings. You've made a fair stagger at cooking, and I bet you win out on the dressmaking. For needle you can use one of these long slim thorns—poke a hole, and then slip the thread through, like a shoemaker."

"Ah, yes; but the thread?" put in Winthrope.

"The cocoanut fibre would hardly do," said Miss Leslie, forgetting to dry her eyes.

"No. We could get fairly good fibres out of the palm leaves; but catgut will be a whole lot better. I'll slit up a lot for you, fine enough to sew with. And now, let's get down to tacks. No offence—but did either of you ever learn to do anything useful in all your blessed little lives?"

"Why, Mr. Blake, of course I—"

"Of course what?" demanded Blake, as Miss Leslie hesitated. "We know all about your cooking and sewing. What else?"

"I—I see what you meant. I fear that nothing of what I learned would be of service now."

"Boarding-school rot, eh? And you, Winthrope?"

"If you would kindly name over what you have in mind."

"Um!" grunted Blake. "Well, it's first of all a question of a practical—practical, mind you,—knowledge of metallurgy, ceramics, and how to stick an arrow through a beef roast."

"I—ah—I believe I intimated that I have some knowledge of archery. But I doubt—"

"Cut it out! You'll have enough else to do. Get busy over those bows and arrows, and don't quit till you've got them in shape. Leave my bow good and stiff. I can pull like a mule can kick. Well, Miss Jenny; what is it?"

"Is not—has not ceramics something to do with burning china?"

"Sure!—china, pottery, and all that. Know anything about it?"

"Why, I have a friend who amuses herself by painting china, and I know it has to be burned."

"And that's all!" grunted Blake. "Well, let me tell you. When I was a little kid I used to work in a pottery. All I can remember is that they'd take clay, shape it into a pot, dry it, and bake the thing in a kiln. We've got to work the same game somehow. This kind of eating will mean dysentery in short order. So there's going to be a bean-pot for our stews, or Tom Blake'll know the reason why. Nurse up that ankle of yours, Win. We'll trek it to-morrow—cocoanuts, and maybe something else. There's clay on the far bank of the river, and across from it I saw a streak that looked like brown hæmatite."

12

SURVIVAL OF THE FITTEST

THE NEXT FOUR days slipped by almost unheeded. Blake saw to it that not only himself but his companions had work to occupy every hour of daylight. When not engaged in cooking and fuel gathering, Miss Leslie was learning by painful experience the rudiments of dressmaking.

At the start she had all but ruined the beautiful skin of the mother leopard before Blake chanced to see her and took over the task of cutting it into shape for a skirt. But when it came to making a waist of the cub fur, he said that she would have to puzzle out the pattern from her other one. Between cooking three meals a day over an open fire, gathering several armfuls of wood, and making a dress with penknife, thorn, and catgut, the girl had little time to think of other matters than her work.

Winthrope had been gazetted as hunter in ordinary. His task was to keep Miss Leslie supplied with fresh eggs and each day to kill as many of the boobies and cormorants as he could skin and split for drying. Blake had changed his mind about taking him when he went for cocoanuts. Instead, he had gone alone on several trips, bringing three or four loads of nuts, then a little salt from the seashore, dirty but very welcome, and last of all a great lump of clay, wrapped in palm fronds.

With this clay he at once began experiments in the art of pottery. Having mixed and beaten a small quantity, he moulded it into little cups and bowls, and tried burning them over night in the watch-fire. A few came out without crack or flaw. Vastly elated by this success, he fashioned larger vessels from his clay, and within the week could brag of two pots suitable for cooking stews, and four large nondescript pieces which he called plates. What was more, all had a fairly good sand glaze, for he had been quick to observe a glaze on the bottoms of the first pots, and had reasoned out that it was due to the sand which had adhered while they stood drying in the sun.

He next turned his attention to metallurgy. The first move was to search the river bank for the brown bog iron ore which he believed he had seen from the farther side. After a dangerous and exhausting day's work in the mire and jungle, he came back with nothing more to show for his pains than an armful of creepers. Late in the afternoon, he had located the hæmatite, only to find it lying in a streak so thin that he could not hope to collect enough for practical purposes.

"Lucky we've got something to fall back on," he added, after telling of his failure. "Pass over those keys of yours, Win. Good! Now untangle those creepers. To-night we'll take turns knotting them up into some sort of a rope-ladder. I'm getting mighty weary of hoofing it all around the point every time I trot to the river. After this I'll go down the cliff at that end of the gully."

Winthrope, who had become very irritable and

depressed during the last two days, turned on his heel, with the look of a fretful child.

To cover this undiplomatic rudeness, Miss Leslie spoke somewhat hurriedly. "But why should you return again to the river, Mr. Blake? I'm sure you are risking the fever; and there must be savage beasts in the jungle."

"That's my business," growled Blake. He paused a moment, and added, rather less ungraciously, "Well, if you care, it's this way—I'm going to keep on looking for ore. Give me a little iron ore, and we'll mighty soon have a lot of steel knives and arrow-heads that'll amount to something. How're we going to bag anything worth while with bamboo tips on our arrows? Those boar tusks are a fizzle."

"So you will continue to risk your life for us? I think that is very brave and generous, Mr. Blake!"

"How's that?" demanded Blake, not a little puzzled. He was fully conscious of the risk; but this was the first intimation he had received or conceived that his motives were other than selfish— "Um-m! So that's the ticket. Getting generous, eh?"

"Not getting—you *are* generous! When I think of all you have done for us! Had it not been for you, I am sure we should have died that first day ashore."

"Well, don't blame me. I couldn't have let a dog die that way; and then, a fellow needs a Man Friday for this sort of thing. As for you, I haven't always had the luck to be favored with ladies' company."

"Thank you, Mr. Blake. I quite appreciate the compliment. But now, I must put on supper."

Blake followed her graceful movements with an intentness which, in turn, drew Winthrope's attention to himself.

The Englishman smiled in a disagreeable manner, and resumed his work on the bows, with the look of one mentally preoccupied. After supper he found occasion to spend some little time among the bamboos.

When at sunset Miss Leslie withdrew into the baobab, Winthrope somewhat officiously insisted upon helping her set up her screen in the entrance. As he did so, he took the opportunity to hand her a bamboo knife, and to draw her attention to several double-pointed bamboo stakes which he had hidden under the litter.

"What is it?" she asked, troubled by his furtive glance back at Blake.

"Merely precaution, you know," he whispered. "The ground in there is quite soft. It will be no trouble, I fancy, to put up the stakes, with their points inclined towards the entrance."

"But why—"

"Not so loud, Miss Genevieve! It struck me that if any one should seek to enter in the night, he would find these stakes deucedly unpleasant. Be careful how you handle them. As you see, the sharper points, which are to be set uppermost, run off into a razor edge. Put them up now, before it grows too dark. You know how ninepins are set— that shape. Good-night! You see, with these to guard the entrance, you need not be afraid to go to sleep at once."

"Thank you," she whispered, and began to thrust the stakes into the ground as he had directed.

He had not been mistaken. The vague doubts and fears which she already entertained would have kept her awake throughout the night, but thanks to the sense of security afforded by the sword-bayonets of her silent little sentries, the girl was soon able to calm herself, and was fast asleep long before Blake wakened Winthrope.

Immediately after breakfast, Blake—who had spent his watch in grinding the edges from a stone and experimenting with split and bent twigs—put Winthrope's keys in the fire, and began an attempt to shape them into a knife-blade. To heat the steel to the required temperature, he used a bamboo blowpipe, with his lungs for bellows.

Winthrope turned away with an indifferent bearing; but Miss Leslie found herself compelled to stop and admire his dexterous use of his rude tools.

One after another, the keys were welded together, end to end, in a narrow ribbon of steel. The thinnest one, however, was not fastened to the tip until it had been used to burn a groove in the edge of a rib, selected from among the bones which Miss Leslie had thrown out of the baobab. The last key was then fastened to the others; the blade ground sharp, tempered, and inserted in the groove. Finally, pieces of the key-ring were fitted in bands around the bone, through notches cut in the ends of the steel blade. The result was a bone-handled, bone-backed knife, with a narrow cutting edge of fine steel.

Long before it was finished Miss Leslie had been forced away by the requirements of her own work. In fact, Blake did not complete his task until late in the afternoon. At the end, he spent more than an hour grinding the handle into shape. When he came to show the completed knife to Miss Leslie, he was fairly aglow with justifiable pride.

"How's that for an Eskimo job?" he demanded. "Bunch of keys and a bone, eh?"

"You are certainly very ingenious, Mr. Blake!"

"Nixy! There's little of the inventor in my top piece—only some hustle and a good memory. I was up in Alaska, you know. Saw a sight of Eskimo work."

"Still, it is very skilfully done."

"That may be— Look out for the edge! It'd do to shave. No more bamboo splinters for me—dull when you hit a piece of bone. I'm ready now to skin a rhinoceros."

"If you can catch one!"

"Guess we could find enough of them around here, all right. But we'll start in on some of Win's sheep and cattle."

"Oh, do! One grows tired of eggs, and all these sea-birds are so tough and fishy, no matter how I cook them."

"We'll sneak down to the pool, and make a try with the bows this evening. I'll give odds, though, that we draw a blank. Win's got the aim, but no drive; I've got the drive, but no aim. Even if I hit an antelope, I don't think a bamboo-pointed arrow would bother him much."

"Don't the savages kill game without iron weapons?"

"Sure; but a lot have flint points, and a lot of others use poison. I know that the Apaches and some of those other Southern Indians used to fix their arrows with rattlesnake poison."

"How horrible!"

"Well, that depends on how you look at it. I guess they thought guns more horrible when they tackled the whites and got the daylight let through 'em. At any rate, they swapped arrows for rifles mighty quick, and any one who knows Apaches will tell you it wasn't because they thought bullets would do less damage."

"Yet the thought of poison—"

"Yes; but the thought of self-preservation! Sooner than

starve, I'd poison every animal in Africa—and so would you."

"I—I— You put it in such a horrible way. One must consider others, animals as well as people; and yet—"

"Survival of the fittest. I've read some things, and I'm no fool, if I do say it myself. For instance, I'm the boss here, because I'm the fittest of our crowd in this environment; but back in what's called civilized parts, where the law lets a few shrewd fellows monopolize the means of production, a man like your father—"

"Mr. Blake, it is not my fault if papa's position in the business world—"

"Nor his, either—it's the cussed system! No; that's all right, Miss Jenny. I was only illustrating. Now, I take it, both you and Win would like to get rid of a boss like me, if you could get rid of Africa at the same time. As it is, though, I guess you'd rather have me for boss, and live, than be left all by your lonesomes, to starve."

"I—I'm sure there is no question of your leadership, Mr. Blake. We have both tried our best to do what you have asked of us."

"*You* have, at least. But I know. If a ship should come to-morrow, it'd be Blake to the back seat. 'Papa, give this—er—person a check for his services, while I chase off with Winnie, to get my look-in on 'Is Ri-yal 'Ighness.'"

Miss Leslie flushed crimson— "I'm sure, Mr. Blake—"

"Oh, don't let that worry you, Miss Jenny. It don't me. I couldn't be sore with you if I tried. Just the same, I know what it'll be like. I've rubbed elbows enough with snobs and big bugs to know what kind of consideration they

give one of the mahsses—unless one of the mahsses has
the drop on them. Hello, Win! What's kept you so late?"

"None of your business!" snapped Winthrope.

Miss Leslie glanced at him, even more puzzled and startled by this outbreak than she had been by Blake's strange
talk. But if Blake was angered, he did not show it.

"Say, Win," he remarked gravely, "I was going to take
you down to the pool after supper, on a try with the bows.
But I guess you'd better stay close by the fire."

"Yes; it is time you gave a little consideration to those
who deserve it," rejoined Winthrope, with a peevishness of
tone and manner which surprised Miss Leslie. "I tell you,
I'm tired of being treated like a dog."

"All right, all right, old man. Just draw up your chair,
and get all the hot broth aboard you can stow," answered
Blake, soothingly.

Winthrope sat down; but throughout the meal, he
continued to complain over trifles with the peevishness of
a spoiled child, until Miss Leslie blushed for him. Greatly
to her astonishment, Blake endured the nagging without
a sign of irritation, and in the end took his bow and arrows
and went off down the cleft, with no more than a quiet
reminder to Winthrope that he should keep near the fire.

When, shortly after dark, the engineer came groping
his way back up the gorge, he was by no means so calm.
Out of six shots, he had hit one antelope in the neck and
another in the haunch; yet both animals had made off all
the swifter for their wounds.

The noise of his approach awakened Winthrope, who
turned over, and began to complain in a whining falsetto.
Miss Leslie, who was peering out through the bars of her

screen, looked to see Blake kick the prostrate man. His frown showed only too clearly that he was in a savage temper. To her astonishment, he spoke in a soothing tone until Winthrope again fell asleep. Then he quietly set about erecting a canopy of bamboos over the sleeper.

Just why he should build this was a puzzle to the girl. But when she caught a glimpse of Blake's altered expression, she drew a deep breath of relief, and picked her way around the edge of her bamboo stakes, to lie down without a trace of the fear which had been haunting her.

13

THE MARK OF THE BEAST

MORNING FOUND WINTHROPE more irritable and peevish than ever. Though he had not been called on watch by Blake until long after midnight, he had soon fallen asleep at his post and permitted the fire to die out. Shortly before dawn, Blake was roused by a pack of jackals, snarling and quarrelling over the half-dried seafowl. To charge upon the thieves and put them to flight with a few blows of his club took but a moment. Yet daylight showed more than half the drying frames empty.

Blake was staring glumly at them, with his broad back to Winthrope, when Miss Leslie appeared. The sudden cessation of Winthrope's complaints brought his companion around on the instant. The girl stood before him, clad from neck to foot in her leopard-skin dress.

"Well, I'll be—dashed!" he exclaimed, and he stood staring at her open-mouthed.

"I fear it will be warm. Do you think it becoming?" she asked, flushing, and turning as though to show the fit of the costume.

"Do I?" he echoed. "Miss Jenny, you're a peach!"

"Thank you," she said. "And here is the skirt. I have ripped it open. You see, it will make a fine flag."

"If it's put up. Seems a pity, though, to do that, when we're getting on so fine. What do you say to leaving it down, and starting a little colony of our own?"

Miss Leslie raised the skirt in her outstretched hands. Behind it her face became white as the cloth.

"Well?" demanded Blake soberly, though his eyes were twinkling.

"You forget the fever," she retorted mockingly, and Blake failed to catch the quaver beneath the light remark.

"Say, you've got me there!" he admitted. "Just pass over your flag, and scrape up some grub. I'll be breaking out a big bamboo. There are plenty of holes and loose stones on the cliff. We'll have the signal up before noon."

Miss Leslie murmured her thanks, and immediately set about the preparation of breakfast.

When Blake had the bamboo ready, with one edge of the broad piece of white duck lashed to it with catgut as high up as the tapering staff would bear, he called upon Winthrope to accompany him.

"You can go, too, Miss Jenny," he added. "You haven't been on the cliff yet, and you ought to celebrate the occasion."

"No, thank you," replied the girl. "I'm still unprepared to climb precipices, even though my costume is that of a savage."

"Savage? Great Scott! that leopard dress would win out against any set of Russian furs a-going, and I've heard they're considered all kinds of dog. Come on. I can swing you into the branches, and it's easy from there up."

"You will excuse me, please."

"Yes, you can go alone," interposed Winthrope. "I am

An evening at baobab home.

indisposed this morning, and, what is more, I have had enough of your dictation."

"You have, have you?" growled Blake, his patience suddenly come to an end. "Well, let me tell you, Miss Leslie is a lady, and if she don't want to go, that settles it. But as for you, you'll go, if I have to kick you every step."

Winthrope cringed back, and broke into a childish whine. "Don't—don't do it, Blake— Oh, I say, Miss Genevieve, how can you stand by and see him abuse me like this?"

Blake was grinning as he turned to Miss Leslie. Her face was flushed and downcast with humiliation for her friend. It seemed incredible that a man of his breeding should betray such weakness. A quick change came over Blake's face.

"Look here," he muttered, "I guess I'm enough of a sport to know something about fair play. Win's coming down with the fever, and's no more to blame for doing the baby act than he'll be when he gets the delirium, and gabbles."

"I will thank you to attend to your own affairs," said Winthrope.

"You're entirely welcome. It's what I'm doing.— Do you understand, Miss Jenny?"

"Indeed, yes; and I wish to thank you. I have noticed how patient you have been—"

"Pardon me, Miss Leslie," rasped Winthrope. "Can you not see that for a fellow of this class to talk of fair play and patience is the height of impertinence? In England, now, such insufferable impudence—"

"That'll do," broke in Blake. "It's time for us to trot along."

"But, Mr. Blake, if he is ill—"

"Just the reason why he should keep moving. No more of your gab, Win! Give your jaw a lay-off, and try wiggling your legs instead."

Winthrope turned away, crimson with indignation. Blake paused only for a parting word with Miss Leslie. "If you want something to do, Miss Jenny, try making yourself a pair of moccasins out of the scraps of skin. You can't stay in this gully all the time. You've got to tramp around some, and those slippers must be about done for."

"They are still serviceable. Yet if you think—"

"You'll need good tough moccasins soon enough. Singe off the hair, and make soles of the thicker pieces. If you do a fair job, maybe I'll employ you as my cobbler, soon as I get the hide off one of those skittish antelope."

Miss Leslie nodded and smiled in response to his jesting tone. But as he swung away after Winthrope, she stood for some time wondering at herself. A few days since she knew she would have taken Blake's remark as an insult. Now she was puzzled to find herself rather pleased that he should so note her ability to be of service.

When she roused herself, and began singeing the hair from the odds and ends of leopard skin, she discovered a new sensation to add to her list of unpleasant experiences. But she did not pause until the last patch of hair crisped close to the half-cured surface of the hide. Fetching the penknife and her thorn and catgut from the baobab, she gathered the pieces of skin together, and walked along the cleft to the ladder-tree. There had been time enough for Blake and Winthrope to set up the signal, and she was curious to see how it looked.

She paused at the foot of the tree, and gazed up to where the withered crown lay crushed against the edge of the cliff. The height of the rocky wall made her hesitate; yet the men, in passing up and down, had so cleared away the twigs and leaves and broken the branches on the upper side of the trunk, that it offered a means of ascent far from difficult even for a young lady.

The one difficulty was to reach the lower branches. She could hardly touch them with her finger-tips. But her barbaric costume must have inspired her. She listened for a moment, and hearing no sound to indicate the return of the men, clasped the upper side of the trunk with her hands and knees, and made an energetic attempt to climb. The posture was far from dignified, but the girl's eyes sparkled with satisfaction as she found herself slowly mounting.

When, flushed and breathless, she gained a foothold among the branches, she looked down at the ground, and permitted herself a merry little giggle such as she had not indulged in since leaving boarding-school. She had actually climbed a tree! She would show Mr. Blake that she was not so helpless as he fancied.

At the thought, she clambered on up, finding that the branches made convenient steps. She did not look back, and the screen of tree-tops beneath saved her from any sense of giddiness. As her head came above the level of the cliff, she peered through the foliage, and saw the signal-flag far over near the end of the headland. The big piece of white duck stood out bravely against the blue sky, all the more conspicuous for the flocks of frightened seafowl which wheeled above and around it.

Surprised that she did not see the men, Miss Leslie

started to draw herself up over the cliff edge. She heard
Winthrope's voice a few yards away on her left. A sudden
realization that the Englishman might consider her exploit
ill-bred caused her to sink back out of sight.

She was hesitating whether to descend or to climb on
up, when Winthrope's peevish whine was cut short by a
loud and angry retort from Blake. Every word came to the
girl's ears with the force of a blow.

"You do, do you? Well, I'd like to know where in hell you
come in. She's not your sister, nor your mother, nor your
aunt, and if she's your sweetheart, you've both been damned
close-mouthed over it."

There was an irritable, rasping murmur from Winthrope,
and again came Blake's loud retort.

"Look here, young man, don't you forget you called me
a cad once before. I can stand a good deal from a sick man;
but I'll give it to you straight, you'd better cut that out. Call
me a brute or a savage, if that'll let off your steam; but,
understand, I'm none of your English kinds."

Again Winthrope spoke, this time in a fretful whine.

Blake replied with less anger: "That's so; and I'm going
to show you that I'm the real thing when it comes to being
a sport. Give you my word, I'll make no move till you're
through the fever and on your legs again. What I'll do
then depends on my own sweet will, and don't you forget
it. I'm not after her fortune. It's the lady herself that takes
my fancy. Remember what I said to you when you called
me a cad the other time. You had your turn aboard ship.
Now I can do as I please; and that's what I'm going to do,
if I have to kick you over the cliff end first, to shut off your
pesky interference."

The girl crouched back into the withered foliage, dazed with terror. Again she heard Blake speak. He had dropped into a bitter sneer.

"No chance? It's no nerve, you mean. You could brain me, easy enough, any night—just walk up with a club when I'm asleep. Trouble is, you're like most other under dogs—'fraid that if you licked your boss, there'd be no soup bones. So I guess I'm slated to stay boss of this colony—grand Poo Bah and Mikado, all in one. Understand? You mind your own business, and don't go to interfering with me any more!… Now, if you've stared enough at the lady's skirt—"

The threat of discovery stung the girl to instant action. With almost frantic haste, she scrambled down to the lower branches, and sprang to the ground. She had never ventured such a leap even in childhood. She struck lightly but without proper balance, and pitched over sideways. Her hands chanced to alight upon the remnants of leopard skin. Great as was her fear, she stopped to gather all together in the edge of her skirt before darting up the cleft.

At the baobab she turned and gazed back along the cliff edge. Before she had time to draw a second breath, she caught a glimpse of Blake's palm-leaf hat, near the crown of the ladder tree.

"O-o-h!—he didn't see me!" she murmured. Her frantic strength vanished, and a deathly sickness came upon her. She felt herself going, and sought to kneel to ease the fall.

She was roused from the swoon by Blake's resonant shout: "Hey, Miss Jenny! where are you? We've got your laundry on the pole in fine shape!"

The girl's flaccid limbs grew tense, and her body quivered with a shudder of dread and loathing. Yet she set her little white teeth, and forced herself to rise and go out to face the men. Both met her look with a blank stare of consternation.

"What is it, Miss Genevieve?" cried Winthrope. "You're white as chalk!"

"It's the fever!" growled Blake. "She's in the cold stage. Get a pot on. We'll—"

"No, no; it's not that! It's only—I've been frightened!"

"Frightened?"

"By a—a dreadful beast!"

"Beast!" repeated Blake, and his pale eyes flashed as he sprang across to where his bow and arrows and his club leaned against the baobab. "I'll have no beasts nosing around my dooryard! Must be that skulking lion I heard last night. I'll show him!" He caught up his weapons and stalked off down the cleft.

"By Jove!" exclaimed Winthrope; "the man really must be mad. Call him back, Miss Genevieve. If anything should happen to him—"

"If only there might!" gasped the girl.

"Why, what do you mean?"

She burst into a hysterical laugh. "Oh! oh! it's such a joke—such a joke! At least he's not a hyena—oh, no; a brave beast! Hear him shout! And he actually thinks it's a lion! But it isn't—it's himself! Oh, dear! oh, dear! what shall I do?"

"Miss Genevieve, what do you mean? Be calm, pray, be calm!"

"Calm!—when I heard what he said? Yes; I heard every word! In the top of the tree—"

"In the tree? Heavens! Miss—er—Miss Genevieve!"

stammered Winthrope, his face paling. "Did you—did you hear all?"

"Everything—everything he said! What shall I do? I am so frightened! What shall I do?"

"Everything *he* said?" echoed Winthrope.

"You spoke too low for me to hear; but I'm sure you faced him like a gentleman—I must believe it of you—"

Winthrope drew in a deep breath. "Ah, yes; I did, Miss Genevieve—I assure you. The beast! Yet you see the plight I am in. It is a nasty muddle—indeed it is! But what can I do? He is strong as a gorilla. Really, there is only one way—no doubt you heard him taunt me over it. I assure you I should not be afraid—but it would be so horrid—so cold-blooded. As a gentleman, you know—"

"No; it is not that!" broke in the girl. "He is right. Neither of us has the courage—even when he is asleep."

"My dear Miss Genevieve, this beast instinct to kill—"

"Yes; but think of him. If he is a beast, he is at least a brave one. While we—we haven't the courage of rabbits. I thought you called yourself an English gentleman. Are you going to stand by, and not lift a finger?"

"Really, now, Miss Genevieve, to murder a man—"

"Self-defence is not a crime—self-preservation. If you have a spark of manhood—"

"My dear—"

"For Heaven's sake, if you can't do anything, at least keep still! Oh, I'm sure I shall go mad! If only I had been drowned!"

"Ah, yes, to be sure. But really now, what you ask is a good deal for a man to risk. The fellow might wake up and murder me! Should I take the risk, might I—er—expect some manifestation of your gratitude, Miss Genevieve?"

"Of course! of course! I should always—"

"I—ah—refer to the—the—bestowal of your hand."

"My hand? I— Would you bargain for my esteem? I thought you a gentleman!"

"To be sure—to be sure! Who says I am not? But all is fair in love and war, you know. Your choice is quite free. I take it, you will not consider his—er—proposals. But if you do not wish my aid, you have another way of escape—that is—at least other women have done it."

The girl gazed at him, her eyes dilating with horror as she realized his meaning.

"No, no; not that!" she gasped. "I want to live—I've a right to live! Why, I'm only just twenty-two—I—"

"Hush!" cautioned Winthrope. "He's coming back. Be calm! There will be time until I get over this vile malaria. It may be that he himself will have the fever."

"He will not have the fever," replied the girl, in a hopeless tone, and she leaned back listlessly against the baobab, as Blake swung himself up, frowning and sullen, and flung his weapons from him.

"Bah!" he grumbled, "I told you that brute was a sneak. I've chased clean down to the pool and into the open, and not a smell of him. Must have hiked off into the tall grass the minute he heard me."

"If only he had gone off for good!" murmured Miss Leslie.

"Maybe he has; though you never can count on a sneak. Even you might be able to shoo him off next time; but, like as not, he'd come along when we were all out calling, and clean out our commissary. Guess I'll set to and run up a barricade down there where the gully is narrowest. There're shoals of dead thorn-brush to the right of the pool."

"Ah, yes; I fancy the vultures will be so vexed when they find your hedge in the way," remarked Winthrope.

"My! how smart we're getting!" retorted Blake. "Don't worry, though. We'll stow the stuff in Miss Jenny's boudoir, and I guess the birdies'll be polite enough to keep out."

"I must say, Blake, I do not see why you should wish to drag us away from here."

"There're lots of things you don't see, Win, me b'y— jokes, for instance. But what could you expect?—you're English. Now, don't get mad. Worst thing in the world for malaria."

"One would fancy you could see that I am not angry. I've a splitting headache, and my back hurts. I am ill."

Blake looked him over critically, and nodded. "That's no lie, old man. You're entitled to a hospital check all right. Miss Jenny, we'll appoint you chief nurse. Make him comfortable as you can, and give him hot broth whenever he'll take it. You can do your sewing on the side. Whenever you need help, call on me. I'm going to begin that barricade."

14

FEVER AND FIRE AND FEAR

BY NIGHTFALL WINTHROPE was tossing and groaning on the bed of leaves which Miss Leslie had heaped beneath his canopy. Though not delirious, his high temperature, coupled with the pains which racked every nerve and bone in his body, rendered him light-headed. He would catch himself up in the midst of some rambling nonsense to inquire anxiously whether he had said anything silly or strange. On being reassured upon this, he would relax again, and, as likely as not, break into a babyish wail over his aches and pains.

Blake shook his head when he learned that the attack had not been preceded by a chill.

"Guess he's in for a hot time," he said. "There is more'n one kind of malarial fever. Some are a whole lot like typhus."

"Typhus? What is that?" asked Miss Leslie.

"Sort of rapid fire, double action typhoid. Not that I think Win's got it—only malaria. What gets me is that we've only been here these few days, and yet it looks like he's got the continuous, no-chill kind."

"Then you think he will be very ill?"

"Well, I guess he'll think so. It ought to run out in a week or ten days, though. We've had good water, and it usually takes time for malaria to soak in deep. Now, don't worry, Miss Jenny. It'll do him no good, and you a lot of harm. Take things easy as you can, for you've got to keep up your strength. If you don't, you'll be down yourself before Win is up."

"Ill while he is helpless and unable—? Oh, no; that cannot be! I must not give way to the fever until—"

"Don't worry. You'll likely stave it off for a couple of weeks or so. You're lively yet, and that's a good sign. I knew Win was in for it when he began to grouch and loaf and do the baby act. I haven't much use for dudes in general, and English dudes in particular; but I'll admit that, while Win's soft enough in spots, he's not all mush and milk."

"Thank you, Mr. Blake."

"You're welcome. I couldn't say less, seeing that Win can't speak for himself. Now you tumble in and get a good sleep. I'll go on as night nurse, and work at the barricade same time. You're not going to do any night-nursing. I can gather the thorn-brush in the afternoons, and pile it up at night."

In the morning Miss Leslie found that Blake had built a substantial canopy over the invalid, in place of the first ramshackle structure.

"It's best for him to be out in the air," he explained; "so I fixed this up to keep off the dew. But whenever it rains, we'll have to tote him inside."

"Ah, yes; to be sure. How is he?" murmured the girl.

"He's about the same this morning. But he got a little sleep. Keep him dosed with all the hot broth he'll take. And

say, roust me out at noon. I've had my breakfast. Now I'll
have a snooze. So long!"

He nodded, and crawled under the shade of the nearest
bush, too drowsy to observe her look of dismay.

At noon, having learned that Winthrope's condition
showed little change, Blake ate a hearty meal, and at once
set off down the cleft. He did not reappear until nightfall;
though at intervals Miss Leslie had heard his step as he
came up the ravine with his loads of thorn-brush.

This course of action became the routine for the following ten days. It was broken only by three incidents, all relating to the important matter of food supply. Winthrope had
soon tired of broth, and showed such an insatiable craving for cocoanut milk that the stock on hand had become
exhausted within the week.

The day after, Blake took the rope ladder, as he called the
tangle of knotted creepers, and went off towards the north
end of the cleft. When he returned, a little before dark, the
lower part of his trousers was torn to shreds, and the palms
of his hands were blistered and raw; but he carried a heavy
load of cocoanuts. After a vain attempt to climb the giant
palms on the far side of the river, he had found another
grove near at hand, in the little plain, and had succeeded
in reaching the tops of two of the smaller palms.

Under his directions, Miss Leslie clarified a bowl of bird
fat—goose-grease, Blake called it,—and dressed his hands.
Yet even with the bandages which she made of soft inner
bark and the handkerchiefs, he was unable to handle the
thorn-brush the following day. Unfortunately for him, he
was not content to sit idle. During the night he had cut
a bamboo fishing-pole and lengthened Miss Leslie's line

of plaited cocoanut-fibre with a long catgut leader. In the afternoon he completed his outfit with a hairpin hook and a piece of half-dried meat.

He was back an hour earlier than usual, and he brought with him a dozen or more fair-sized fish. His mouth was watering over the prospective feast, and Miss Leslie showed herself hardly less eager for a change from their monotonous diet. As the fish were already dressed, she raked up the coals and quickly contrived a grill of green bamboos.

When the odor of the broiling fish spread about in the still air, even Winthrope sniffed and turned over, while Blake watched the crisping delicacies with a ravenous look. Unable to restrain himself, he caught up the smallest fish, half cooked, and bolted it down with such haste that he burnt his mouth. He ran over to the spring for a drink, and Winthrope cackled derisively.

Miss Leslie was too absorbed in her cooking to observe the result of Blake's greediness. She had turned the fish for the last time, and was about to lift them off the fire, when Blake came running back, and sent grill and all flying with a violent kick.

"Salt!" he gasped—"where's the salt? I'm poisoned!"

"Poisoned?"

"Poison fish! Don't eat! God!—Where's the salt?"

The girl stared at him. His agony was so great that beads of sweat were rolling down his face. He writhed, and stretched out a quivering hand—"Salt, quick!—warm water—salt!"

"But there's none left! You remember, yesterday—"

"God!" groaned Blake, and for a moment he sank down,

overcome by a racking convulsion. Then his jaw closed like a bulldog's, and gritting his teeth with the effort, he staggered up and rushed off down the cleft.

"Stop! stop, Mr. Blake! Where are you going?" screamed the girl.

She started to run after him, but was halted by an outburst of delirious laughter. Winthrope was sitting upright and waving his fever-blotched hands—"Hi, hi! look at 'im run! 'E's got w'at'll do for 'im! Run, you swine; you—"

There followed a torrent of cockney abuse so foul that Miss Leslie blushed scarlet with shame as she sought to quiet him. But the excitement had so heightened his fever that he was in a raving delirium. It was close upon midnight before his temperature fell, and he sank into a death-like torpor. In her ignorance, she supposed that he had fallen asleep.

Her relief was short-lived, for soon she remembered Blake. She could see him lying beside the pool or out on the bare plain, his resolute eyes cold and glassy, his powerful body contorted in the death agony. The vision filled her with dismay. With all his coarseness, the man had showed himself so resourceful, so indomitable, that when she sought to dwell upon her reasons to fear him, she found herself admiring his virile manliness. He might be a brute, but he did not belong among the jackals and hyenas. Indeed, as she called to mind his strong face and frank, blunt speech she all but disbelieved what her own ears had heard.

And anyway, without his aid, what should she do? Winthrope had already become as weak as a child. The emaciation of his jaundiced features was a mockery of their former plumpness. Blake had said that the fever might run on for another week, and that even if Winthrope recovered, he would probably be helpless for several days besides.

What was no less serious, though she had concealed the fact from Blake, she herself had been troubled the past week with the depression and lassitude which had preceded Winthrope's attack. If Blake was dead, and she should fall ill before Winthrope recovered, they would both die from lack of care. And if they did not die of the fever, what of their future, here on this desolate savage coast!

But the very keenness of her mental anguish so exhausted and numbed the girl's brain that she at last fell into a heavy sleep. The fire burned low, and shadowy forms began to creep from behind the bamboos and the trees and rocks down the gorge. There was no sound; but greedy, wolfish eyes gleamed in the starlight.

Only the day before Blake had told Miss Leslie to store the last rack of cured meat inside the baobab. The two sleepers lay between the fire and the entrance to the hollow. Slowly the embers of the fire died away into gray ashes, and slowly the night prowlers drew nearer. The boldest of the pack crept close to Miss Leslie, and, with teeth bared and back bristling, sniffed at the edge of her skirt. Whether because of her heavy breathing or the odor of the leopard skin, the beast drew away, with an uneasy whine.

There was a pause; then, backed by three others, the leader approached Winthrope. He was still lying in the death-like torpor, and he lacked the protection which, in all likelihood, the leopard skin had given Miss Leslie. The cowardly brutes took him for dead or dying. They sniffed at him from head to foot, and then, with a ferocious outburst of snarls and yells, flung themselves upon him.

Had it not chanced that Winthrope was lying upon his side, with one arm thrown up, he would have been fatally wounded by the first slashing bites of his assailants. The two which sought to tear him were baffled by the thick folds of Blake's coat, while their leader's slash at the victim's throat was barred by the upraised arm. With a savage snap, the beast's jaws closed on the arm, biting through to the bone. At the same instant the fourth jackal tore ravenously at one of the outstretched legs.

With a shriek of agony, Winthrope started up from his torpor, and struck out frantically in a fury of pain and terror. Startled by the violence of this unexpected resistance, the jackals leaped back—only to spring in again as the remainder of the pack made a rush to forestall them.

Winthrope was staggering to his feet, when the foremost brute leaped upon him. He fell heavily against one of the main supports of his bamboo canopy, and the entire structure came down with a crash. Two of the jackals, caught beneath the roof, howled with fear as they sought to free themselves. The others, with brute dread of an unknown danger, drew away, snarling and gnashing their teeth.

Wakened by the first ferocious yelps of Winthrope's assailants, Miss Leslie had started up and stared about in the darkness. On all sides she could see pairs of fiery eyes and dim forms like the phantom creatures of a nightmare. Winthrope's shriek, instead of spurring her to action, only confused her the more and benumbed her faculties. She thought it was his death cry, and stood trembling, transfixed with horror.

Then came the fall of the canopy. His cries as he sought to throw it off showed that he was still alive. In a flash her bewilderment vanished. The stagnant blood surged again through her arteries in a fiery, stimulating torrent. With a cry, to which primeval instinct lent a menacing note, she groped her way to the fallen canopy, and stooped to lift up one side.

"Quick!—into the tree!" she called.

Still frantic with terror, Winthrope struggled to his feet. She thrust him towards the baobab, and followed, dragging the mass of interwoven bamboos. Emboldened by the retreat of their quarry, the snarling pack instantly began to close in. Fortunately they were too cowardly to rush at once, and fear spurred their intended victims to the utmost haste. Groping and stumbling, the two felt their way to the baobab, and Miss Leslie pushed Winthrope headlong through the entrance. As he fell, she turned to face the pack.

The foremost beasts were at the rear edge of the bamboo framework, their eyes close to the ground. Instinct told her that they were crouching to leap. With desperate strength she caught up the canopy before her like a great shield, and drew it in after her until the ends of the cross-bars were wedged fast against the sides of the opening. Though it seemed so firm, she clung to it with a convulsive grasp as she felt the pack leaders fling themselves against the outer side.

But Blake had lashed the bamboos securely together, and none of the beasts was heavy enough to snap the supple bars. Finding that they could not break down the barrier, they began to scratch and tear at the thatch which covered the frame. Soon a pair of lean jaws thrust in and snapped at the girl's skirt. She sprang back, with a cry: "Help! Quick, Mr. Winthrope! They're breaking through!"

Winthrope made no response. She stooped, and found him lying inert where he had fallen. She had only herself to depend upon. A screen of sharp sticks which she had made for the entrance was leaning against the inner wall, within easy reach. To grasp it and thrust it against the other framework was the work of an instant.

Still she trembled, for the eager beasts had ripped the thatch from the canopy, and their inthrust jaws made short work of the few leaves on her screen. Unaware that even a lion or a tiger is quickly discouraged by the knife-like splinters of broken bamboo, she expected every moment that the jackals would bite their way through her frail barrier.

She remembered the stakes given her by Winthrope, hidden under the leaves and grass of her bed. She groped her way across the hollow, and uncovered one of the stakes. In her haste she cut her hand on its razor-like edge. All unheeding, she sprang back towards the entrance. She was none too soon. One of the smaller jackals had forced its head and one leg between the bars, and was struggling to enlarge the opening.

Fearful that the whole pack was about to burst in upon her, the girl grasped the bamboo stake in both hands, and began stabbing and lunging at the beast with all her strength. The jackal squirmed and snarled and snapped viciously. But the girl was now frantic. She pressed nearer, and though the white teeth grazed her wrist, she drove home a thrust that changed the beast's snarls into a howl of pain. Before she could strike again, it had struggled back out of the hole, beyond reach.

Tense and panting with excitement, she leaned forward, ready to stab at the next beast. None appeared, and presently she became aware that the pack had been daunted by the experience of their unlucky fellow. Their snarls and yells had subsided to whines, which seemed to be coming from a greater distance. Still she waited, with the bamboo stake upraised ready to strike, every nerve and muscle of her body tense with the strain.

So great was the stress of her fear and excitement that she had not heeded the first gray lessening of the night. But now the glorious tropical dawn came streaming out of the east in all its red effulgence. Above and through the bamboo barrier glowed a light such as might have come from a great fire on the cliff top. Still tense and immovable, the girl stared out up the cleft. There was not a jackal in sight. She leaned forward and peered around, unable to believe such good fortune. But the night prowlers had slunk off in the first gray dawn.

The girl drew in a deep, shuddering sigh, and sank back. Her hand struck against Winthrope's foot. She turned about quickly and looked at him. He was lying upon his face. She hastened to turn him upon his side, and to feel his forehead. It was cool and moist. He was fast asleep and drenched with sweat. The great shock of his pain and fear and excitement had broken his fever.

With the relief and joy of this discovery, the girl completely relaxed. Not observing Winthrope's wounds, which had bled little, she sought to force a way out through the entrance. It was by no means an easy task to free the wedged framework, and when, after much pulling and pushing, she at last tore the mass loose, she found herself perspiring no less freely than Winthrope.

She was far too preoccupied, however, to consider what this might mean. Her first thought was of the fire. She ran to her rude stone fireplace and raked over the ashes. They were still warm, but there was not a live ember among them. Yet she realized that Winthrope must have hot food when he wakened, and Blake had carried with him the magnifying glass. For a little she stood hesitating. But the defeat of the jackals had given her courage and resolution such as she had never before known. She returned into the cave, and chose the sharpest of her stakes. Having made certain that Winthrope was still asleep, she set off boldly down the cleft.

At the first turn she came upon Blake's thorn barricade. It stretched across the narrowest part of the cleft in an impenetrable wall, twelve feet high. Only in the centre was a gap, which could have been filled by Blake in less than two hours' work. The girl's eyes brightened. She herself could gather the thorn-brush and fill the gap before night. They no longer need fear the jackals or even the larger beasts of prey. None the less, they must have fire.

Spurred on by the thought, she was about to spring through the barricade when she heard the tread of feet on the path beyond. She crouched down, and peered through the tangle of brush in the edge of the gap. Less than ten paces away Blake was plodding heavily up the trail. She stepped out before him.

"You—you! Are you alive?" she gasped.

"'Live? You bet your boots!" came back the grim

response. "You bet I'm alive—though I had to go Jonah one better to do it. The whale heaved him up; I heaved up the whale—and it took about a barrel of sea-water to do it."

"Sea-water?"

"Sure… I tumbled over twice on the way. But I made the beach. Lord! how I pumped in the briny deep! Guess I won't go into details—but if you think you know anything about seasickness— *Whew!* Lucky for yours truly, the tide was just starting out, and the wind off shore. I'd fallen in the water, and the Jonah business laid me out cold. Didn't know anything until the tide came up again and soused me."

"I am very glad you're not dead. But how you must have suffered! You are still white, and your face is all creased."

Blake attempted a careless laugh. "Don't worry about me. I'm here, O.K., all that's left,—a little wobbly on my pins, but hungry as a shark. But say, what's up with you? You're sweating like a— Good thing, though. It'll stave off your spell of fever a while. How'd you happen to be coming down here so early?"

"I was starting to find you."

"Me!"

"Not you—that is, I thought you were dead. I was going to make certain, and to—to get the burning-glass."

"Um-m. I see. Let the fire go out, eh?"

"Do not blame me, Mr. Blake! I was so ill and worn out, and I've paid for it twice over, really I have. Didn't those awful beasts attack you?"

"Beasts? How's that?" he demanded.

"Oh, but you must have heard them! The horrid things

tried to kill us!" she cried, and she poured out a half inco-
herent account of all that had happened since he left.

Blake listened intently, his jaw thrust out, his eyes glowing upon her with a look which she had never before seen
in any man's eyes. But his first comment had nothing to
do with her conduct.

"How's that?—sorry Win got rousted out of his nice
little snooze— Snooze! Why, don't you know, we'd been
all alone in our glory by to-night if it hadn't been for those
brutes. He was in the stupor, and that would have been the
end of him if the beasts hadn't stirred him up so lively. I've
heard of such a thing before, but I always thought it was a
fake. Here you are sweating, too."

"I feel much better than yesterday. I did not tell you, but
I have felt ill for nearly a week."

"'Fraid to tell, eh?—and you were so scared over the
beasts— Scared! By Jiminy, you've got grit, little woman!
There's two kinds of scaredness; you've got the Stone-
wall Jackson kind. If anybody asks you, just refer them to
Tommy Blake."

"Thank you, Mr. Blake. But should we not hasten back
now to prepare something for Mr. Winthrope?"

"Ditto for yours truly. I'm like that sepulchre you read
about—white outside, and within nothing but bare bones
and emptiness."

15

WITH BOW AND CLUB

THE FIRE WAS soon re-lit, and a pot of meat set on to stew. It had ample time to simmer. Winthrope was wrapped in a life-giving sleep, out of which he did not waken until evening, while Blake, unable to wait for the pot to boil, and nauseated by the fishy odor of the dried seafowl, hunted out the jerked leopard meat, and having devoured enough to satisfy a native, fell asleep under a bush.

The sun was half down the sky when he sat up and looked around, wide awake the moment he opened his eyes. Miss Leslie was quietly placing an armful of sticks on the fuel heap beside the baobab.

"Hello, Miss Jenny! Hard at it, I see," he called cheerfully.

"Hush!" she cautioned. "Mr. Winthrope is still asleep."

"Good thing for him. He'll need all of that he can get."

"Then you think—?"

"Well, between you and me, I don't believe Win was built for the tropics. This fever of his, coming on so soon, wouldn't have hit nine men in ten half so hard. He's bound to have another spell in a month or two, and—"

"But cannot we possibly get away from here before then? Is there no way? Surely, you are so resourceful—"

"Nothing doing, Miss Jenny! Give me tools, and I'd

engage to turn out a seagoing boat. But as it is, the only thing I could do would be to fire-burn a log. That would take two or three months, and in the end we'd have a lop-sided canoe that'd live about half a second in one of these tropic squalls."

"Do not the natives sail in canoes?"

"Maybe they do—and they make fire by rubbing sticks. We don't."

"But what can we do?"

"Take our medicine, and wait for a ship to show up."

"But we have no medicine."

"Have no— Say, Miss Jenny, you really ought to have stayed home from boarding-school and England long enough to learn your own language. I meant, we've got to take what's coming to us, without laying down or grouching. Both are the worst thing out for malaria."

"You mean that we must resign ourselves to this intolerable situation—that we must calmly sit here and wait until the fever—"

"No; I'll take care we don't sit around very much. We'll go on the hike, soon as Win can wobble. Which reminds me, I've got a little hike on hand now. I'm going to close up that barricade before dark. Me for a quiet night!"

Without waiting for a reply, he took his weapons, and swung briskly away down the cleft.

He returned a few minutes before sunset, with what appeared to be a large fur bag upon his back. Miss Leslie was pouring a bowl of broth from the stew-pot, and did not notice him until he sang out to her: "Hey, Miss Jenny, spill over that stuff! No more of that in ours!"

"It's for Mr. Winthrope. He has just wakened," she replied, still intent on her pouring.

"And you'd kill him with that slop! Heave it over. He's going to have beef juice."

"Oh! what's that on your back? You've killed an antelope!"

"Sure! Bushbuck, I guess they call him. Sneaked up when he was drinking, and stuck an arrow into his side. He jumped off a little way, and turned to see what'd bit him. I hauled off and put the second arrow right through his eye, into his brain. Neatest thing you ever saw."

"You surely are becoming a splendid archer!"

"Yes; Jim dandy! I could do it again about once in ten thousand shots. All the same, I've raked in this peacherino. Trot out your grill and we'll have something fit to eat."

"You spoke of beef juice."

"I've a dozen steaks ready to broil. Slap 'em on the fire, and I'll squeeze out enough juice with my fist to do Win for to-night."

He made good his assertion, using several of the steaks, which, having lost less than half their juices in the process, were eaten with great relish by Miss Leslie and himself.

Winthrope, after drinking the stimulating beef juice and a quantity of hot water, turned over and fell asleep again while Blake was dressing his wounds. None of these was serious of itself; but Blake knew the danger of infection in the tropics, and carefully washed out the gashes before applying the tallow salve which Miss Leslie had tried out from the antelope fat.

The dressing was completed by torchlight. Blake then rolled the sleeper into a comfortable position, took the torch from Miss Leslie, and left the cave, pausing at the entrance to mutter a gruff good-night. The girl murmured a response, but watched him anxiously as he passed out. A step beyond the entrance he paused and turned again. In the red glare of the torch, his face took on an expression that filled her with fright. Shrouded by the gloom of the hollow, she drew back to her bed, and without turning her eyes away from him, groped for one of her bamboo stakes.

But before she could arm herself, she saw Blake stoop over and grasp with his free hand the mass of interwoven bamboos. He straightened himself, and the framework swung lightly up and over, until it stood on end across the cave entrance. The girl stole around and peered out at him. He had spread open the antelope skin, and was beginning to slice the meat for drying. Though his forehead was furrowed, his expression was by no means sinister. Relieved at the thought that the light must have deceived her, she returned to her bed and was soon sleeping as soundly as Winthrope.

Blake strung the greater part of the meat on the drying racks, built a smudge fire beneath, and stretched the antelope skin on a frame. This done, he took his club and a small piece of bloody meat, and walked stealthily down the cleft to the barricade. Quiet as was his approach, it was met by a warning yelp on the farther side of the thorny wall, and he could hear the scurry of fleeing animals.

He kept on until the barricade loomed up before him in the starlight. From cliff to cliff the wall now stretched across the gorge without hole or gap. But Blake grasped the trunk of a young date-palm which projected from the barricade near the bottom, and pushed it out. The displacement of the spiky fronds disclosed the low passage which he had made in the centre of the barricade. He placed the piece of meat on one side, two or three feet from the hole, and squatted down across from it, with his club balanced on his shoulder.

Half an hour passed—an hour; and still he waited, silent and motionless as a statue. At last stealthy footsteps sounded on the outer side of the thorn wall, and an animal began to creep through the wall, sniffing for the bait. Blake waited with the immobility of an Eskimo. The delay was brief.

With a boldness for which Blake had not been prepared, the beast leaped through and seized the meat. Even in the dim light, Blake could see that he had lured an animal larger than any jackal. But this only served to lend greater force to his blow. As he struck, he leaped to his feet The brute fell as though struck by lightning and lay still.

Blake prodded the inert form warily; then knelt and passed his hands over it. The beast had whirled about just in time to meet the descending club, and the blow had crushed in its skull. Chuckling at the success of his ruse, he drew the palm back into the opening, and swung his prize over his shoulder. When he came to the fire, a glance showed him that he had killed a full-grown spotted hyena.

In the morning, when Miss Leslie appeared, there were two hides stretched on bamboo frames, and the air was dark with vultures streaming down into the cleft near the barricade. Blake was sleeping the sleep of the just, and did not waken until she had built the fire and begun to broil the steaks which he had saved.

Again they had a feast of the fresh antelope meat. But

with repletion came more of fastidiousness, and Blake agreed with Miss Leslie when she remarked that salt would have added to the flavor. He set off presently, and spent half a day on the talus of the headland, gathering salt from the rock crannies.

For the next three days he left the cleft only to gather eggs. The greater part of his time was spent in tanning the hyena and antelope skins. Meantime Miss Leslie continued to nurse Winthrope and to gather firewood. Under Blake's directions, she also purified the salt by dissolving it in a pot of water, and allowing the dirt to settle, when the clarified solution was poured off and evaporated over the fire in one of the earthenware pans.

At first Winthrope had been too weak to sit up. But treated to a liberal diet of antelope broth, raw eggs, hot water, and cocoanut milk, he gained strength faster than Blake had expected. On the fourth day Blake set him to work on the final rubbing of the new skins; on the fifth, he ordered him to go for eggs.

Much to Miss Leslie's surprise, Winthrope started off without a word of protest. All his peevish irritability and childishness had gone with the fever, and the girl was gratified to see the quiet manner in which he set about a task which seemed an imposition upon his half-regained strength. But the very motive which, seemingly, prevented him from protesting, impelled her to speak for him.

"Mr. Blake!" she exclaimed, "Mr. Winthrope is going off without a word; but I can't endure it! You have no right to send him on such an errand. It will kill him!"

Blake met her indignant look with a sober stare.

"What if it does!" he said. "Better for him to die in the

gallant service of his fellows, than to sit here and rot. Eh, Win?"

"Do not trouble yourself, Miss Genevieve. I hope I shall pull through all right. If not—"

"No, you shall not! I'll go myself!"

"See here, Miss Leslie," said Blake, somewhat sternly; "who's got the responsibility of keeping you two alive for the next month or so? I've been in the tropics before, and I know something of the way people have to live to get out again. I'm trying to do my best, and I tell you straight, if you won't mind me, I'm going to make you, no matter how much it hurts your feelings. You see how nice and meek Win takes his orders. I explained matters to him last night—"

"I assure you, Blake, you shall have no cause for complaint as to my conduct," muttered Winthrope. "I should like to observe, however, that in speaking to Miss Leslie—"

"There you are again, with your everlasting talk. Cut it out, and get busy. To-morrow we all go on a hike to the river."

As Winthrope started off, Blake turned to Miss Leslie, with a good-natured grin.

"You see, it's this way, Miss Jenny—" he began. He caught her look of disdain, and his face darkened. "Mad, eh? So that's the racket!"

"Mr. Blake, I will not have you talk to me in that way. Mr. Winthrope is a gentleman, but nothing more to me than a friend such as any young woman—"

"That settles it! I'll take your word for it, Miss Jenny," broke in Blake, and springing up, he set about his work, whistling.

The girl gazed at his broad back and erect head, uncertain whether she should feel relieved or anxious. The more she thought the matter over, the more uncertain she became, and the more she wondered at her uncertainty. Could it be possible that she was becoming interested in a man who, if her ears had not deceived her— But no! That could not be possible!

Yet what a ring there was to his voice!—so clear and tonic after Winthrope's precise, modulated drawl. And her countryman's firmness! He could be rude if need be; but he would make her do what he thought was best for her health. Was it not possible that she had misunderstood his words on the cliff, and so misjudged—wronged—him?— that Winthrope, so eager to stipulate for her hand— But then Winthrope had more than confirmed her dreadful conclusions taken from Blake's words, and Winthrope was an English gentleman. It could not be possible that an English gentleman—

She ended in a state of utter bewilderment.

16

THE SAVAGE MANIFEST

AS WINTHROPE HAD succeeded in dragging himself to and from the headland without a collapse, the following morning, as soon as the dew was dry, Blake called out all hands for the expedition. He was in the best of humors, and showed unexpected consideration by presenting Winthrope with a cane, which he had cut and trimmed during the night.

Having sent Miss Leslie to fill the whiskey flask with spring water, he dropped three cocoanut-shell bowls, a piece of meat and a lump of salt into one of the earthenware pots, and slung all over his shoulder in the antelope skin. With his bow hung over the other shoulder, knife and arrows in his belt, and his big club in hand, he looked ready for any contingency.

"We'll hit first for the mouth of the river," he said. "I'm going on ahead. If I'm not in sight when you come up, pick a tree where the ground is dry, and wait."

"But I say, Blake," replied Winthrope, "I see animals over in the coppices, and you should know that I am physically unable—"

"Nothing but antelope," interrupted Blake. "I've seen them enough now to know them twice as far off. And you can bet on it they'd not be there if any dangerous beast was in smelling distance."

"That is so clever of you, Mr. Blake," remarked Miss Leslie.

"Simple enough when you happen to think of it," responded Blake. "Yes; the only thing you've got to look out for's the ticks in the grass. They'll keep you interested. They bit me up in great shape."

He scowled at the recollection, nodded by way of emphasis, and was off like a shot. The edge of the plain beneath the cliff was strewn with rocks, among which, even with Miss Leslie's help, Winthrope could pick his way but slowly. Before they were clear of the rough ground, they saw Blake disappear among the mangroves.

The ticks proved less annoying than they had apprehended after Blake's warning. But when they approached the mouth of the river, they were alarmed to hear, above the roar of the surf, loud snorting, such as could only be made by large animals. Fearful lest Blake had roused and angered some forest beast, they veered to the right, and ran to hide behind a clump of thorns. Winthrope sank down exhausted the moment they reached cover; but Miss Leslie crept to the far end of the thicket and peered around.

"Oh, look here!" she cried. "It's a whole herd of elephants trying to cross the river mouth where we did, and they're being drowned, poor things!"

"Elephants?" panted Winthrope, and he dragged himself forward beside her. "Why, so there are; quite a drove of the beasts. Yet, I must say, they appear smaller—ah, yes; see their heads. They must be the hippos Blake saw."

"Those ugly creatures? I once saw some at the zoo. Just the same, they will be drowned. Some are right in the surf!"

"I can't say, I'm sure, Miss Genevieve, but I have an idea that the beasts are quite at home in the water. I fancy they enjoy surf bathing as keenly as ourselves."

"I do believe you are right. There is one going in from the quiet water. But look at those funny little ones on the backs of the others!"

"Must be the baby hippos," replied Winthrope, indifferently. "If you please, I'll take a pull at the flask. I am very dry."

When he had half emptied the flask, he stretched out in the shade to doze. But Miss Leslie continued to watch the movements of the snorting hippos, amused by the ponderous antics of the grown ones in the surf, and the comic appearance of the barrel-like infants as they mounted the backs of their obese mothers.

Presently Blake came out from among the mangroves, and walked across to the beach, a few yards away from the huge bathers. To all appearances, they paid as little attention to him as he to them. Miss Leslie glanced about at Winthrope. He was fast asleep. She waited a few moments to see if the hippopotami would attack Blake. They continued to ignore him, and gaining courage from their indifference, she stepped out from behind the thicket, and advanced to where Blake was crouched on the beach. When she came up, she saw beside him a heap of oysters, which he was opening in rapid succession.

"Hello! You're just in time to help," he called. "Where's Win!"

"Asleep behind those bushes."

"Worst thing he could do. But lend a hand, and we'll shuck these oysters before rousting him out. You can rinse those I've opened. Fill the pot with water, and put them in to soak."

"They look very tempting. How did you chance to find them?"

"Saw 'em on the mangrove roots at low tide, first time I nosed around here. Tide was well up to-day; but I managed to get these all right with a little diving. Only trouble, the skeets most ate me alive."

Miss Leslie glanced at her companion's dry clothing, and came back to the oysters themselves. "These look very tempting. Do you like them raw?"

"Can't say I like them much any way, as a rule. But if I did, I wouldn't eat this mess raw."

"Yes?"

"This must be the dry season here, and the river is running mighty clear. Just the same, it's nothing more than liquid malaria. We'll not eat these oysters till they've been pasteurized."

"If the water is so dangerous, I fear we will suffer before we can return," replied Miss Leslie, and she held up the flask.

"What!" exclaimed Blake. "Half gone already? That was Winthrope."

"He was very thirsty. Could we not boil a potful of the river water?"

"Yes, when the ebb gets strong, if we run too dry. First, though, we'll make a try for cocoanuts. Let's hit out for the nearest grove now. The main thing is to keep moving."

As he spoke, Blake caught up the pot and his club, and

started for the thorn clump, leaving the skin, together with the meat and the salt, for Miss Leslie to carry. Winthrope was wakened by a touch of Blake's foot, and all three were soon walking away from the seashore, just within the shady border of the mangrove wood.

At the first fan-palm Blake stopped to gather a number of leaves, for their palm-leaf hats were now cracked and broken. A little farther on a ruddy antelope, with lyrate horns, leaped out of the bush before them and dashed off towards the river before Blake could string his bow. As if in mockery of his lack of readiness, a troupe of large green monkeys set up a wild chattering in a tree above the party.

"I say, Miss Jenny, do you think you can lug the pot, if we go slow? It isn't far now."

"I'll try."

"Good for you, little woman! That'll give me a chance to shoot quick."

They moved on again for a hundred yards or more; but though Blake kept a sharp lookout both above and below, he saw no game other than a few small birds and a pair of blue wood-pigeons. When he sought to creep up on the latter, they flew into the next tree. In following them, he came upon a conical mound of hard clay, nearly four feet high.

"Hello; this must be one of those white anthills," he said, and he gave the mound a kick.

Instantly a tiny object whirred up and struck him in the face.

"Whee!" he exclaimed, springing back and striking out. "A hornet! No; it's a bee!"

"Did it sting you?" cried Miss Leslie.

"Sting? Keep back; there's a lot more of 'em. Sting? Oh, no; he only hypodermicked me with a red-hot darning needle! Shy around here. There's a whole swarm of the little devils, and they're hopping mad. Hear 'em buzz!"

"But where is their hive?" asked Winthrope, as all three drew back behind the nearest bushes.

"Guess they've borrowed that ant-hill," replied Blake, gingerly fingering the white lump which marked the spot where the bee had struck him.

"Wouldn't it be delightful if we had some honey?" exclaimed Miss Leslie.

"By Jove, that really wouldn't be half bad!" chimed in Winthrope.

"Maybe we can, Miss Jenny; only we'll need a fire to tackle those buzzers. Guess it'll be as well to let them cool off a bit also. The cocoanuts are only a little way ahead now. Here; give me the pot."

They soon came to a small grove of cocoanut palms, where Blake threw down his club and bow and handed his burning-glass to Miss Leslie.

"Here," he said; "you and Win start a fire. It's early yet, but I'm thinking we'll all be ready enough for oyster stew."

"How about the meat?" asked Miss Leslie.

"Keep that till later. Here goes for our dessert."

Selecting one of the smaller palms, Blake spat on his hands, and began to climb the slender trunk. Aided by previous experiences, he mounted steadily to the top. The descent was made with even more care and steadiness, for he did not wish to tear the skin from his hands again.

"Now, Win," he said, as he neared the bottom and sprang down, "leave the cooking to Miss Leslie, and husk some of those nuts. You won't more'n have time to do it before the stew is ready."

Winthrope's response was to draw out his penknife. Blake stretched himself at ease in the shade, but kept a critical eye on his companions. Although Winthrope's fingers trembled with weakness, he worked with a precision and rapidity that drew a grunt of approval from Blake. Presently Miss Leslie, who had been stirring the stew with a twig, threw in a little salt, and drew the pot from the fire.

"*En avant*, gentlemen! Dinner is served," she called gayly.

"What's that?" demanded Blake. "Oh; sure. Hold on, Miss Jenny. You'll dump it all."

He wrapped a wisp of grass about the pot, and filled the three cocoanut bowls. The stew was boiling hot; but they fished up the oysters with the bamboo forks that Blake had carved some days since. By the time the oysters were eaten, the liquor in the bowl was cool enough to drink. The process was repeated until the pot had been emptied of its contents.

"Say, but that was something like," murmured Blake. "If only we'd had pretzels and beer to go with it! But these nuts won't be bad."

When they finished the cocoanuts, Winthrope asked for a drink of water.

"Would it not be best to keep it until later?" replied Miss Leslie.

"Sure," put in Blake. "We've had enough liquid refreshments to do any one. If I don't look out, you'll both be drinking river water. Just bear in mind the work I'd have to carve a pair of gravestones. No; that flask has got to do you till we get home. I don't shin up any more telegraph poles to-day."

"Would it not be best for Mr. Winthrope to rest during the noon hours?"

"'Fraid not, Miss Jenny. We're not on t'other side of Jordan yet, and there's no rest for the weary this side."

"What odd expressions you use, Mr. Blake!"

"Just giving you the reverse application of one of those songs they jolly us with in the mission churches—"

"I'm sure, Mr. Blake—"

"Me, too, Miss Jenny! So, as that's settled, we'll be moving. Chuck some live coals in the pot, and come on."

He started off, weapons in hand. Winthrope made a languid effort to take possession of the pot. But Miss Leslie pushed him aside, and wrapping all in the antelope skin, slung it upon her back.

"The brute!" exclaimed Winthrope. "To leave such a load for you, when he knew that I can do so little!"

The girl met his outburst with a brave attempt at a smile. "Please try to look at the bright side, Mr. Winthrope. Really, I believe he thinks it is best for us to exert ourselves."

"He has other opinions with which we of the cultured class would hardly agree, Miss Leslie. Consider his command that we shall go thirsty until he permits us to return to the cliffs. The man's impertinence is intolerable. I shall go to the river and drink when I choose."

"Oh, but the danger of malaria!"

"Nonsense. Malaria, like yellow fever, comes only from the bite of certain species of mosquitoes. If we have the fever, it will be entirely his fault. We have been bitten repeatedly this morning, and all because he must compel us to come with him to this infected lowland."

"Still, I think we should do what Mr. Blake says."

"My dear Miss Genevieve, for your sake I will endeavor not to break with the fellow. Only, you know, it is deuced hard to keep one's temper when one considers what a bounder—what an unmitigated cad—"

"Stop! I will not listen to another word!" exclaimed the girl, and she hurried after Blake, leaving Winthrope staring in astonishment.

"My word!" he muttered; "can it be, after all I've done—and him, of all the low fellows—"

He stood for several moments in deep thought. The look on his sallow face was far from pleasant.

17

THE SERPENT STRIKES

WHEN WINTHROPE CAME up with the others, they were gathering green leaves to throw on the fire which was blazing close beside the ant-hill.

"Get a move on you!" called Blake. "You're slow. Grab a bunch of leaves, and get into the smoke, if you don't want to be stung."

Winthrope neither gathered any leaves nor hurried himself, until he was visited by a highly irritated bee. Then he obeyed with alacrity. Blake was far too intent on other matters to heed the Englishman. Leaping in and out of the thick of the smoke, he pounded the ant-hill with his club, until he had broken a gaping hole into the cavity. The smoke, pouring into the hive, made short work of the bees that had not already been suffocated.

Although the antelope skin was drawn into the shape of a sack, both it and the pot were filled to overflowing with honey, and there were still more combs left than the three could eat.

Blake caught Winthrope smiling with satisfaction as he licked his fingers.

"What's the matter with my expedition now, old man?" he demanded.

"I—ah—must admit, Blake, we have had a most enjoyable change of food."

"If you are sure it will agree with you," remarked Miss Leslie.

"But I am sure of that, Miss Genevieve. I could digest anything to-day. I'm fairly ravenous."

"All the more reason to be careful," rejoined Blake. "I guess, though, what we've had'll do no harm. We'll let it settle a bit, here in the shade, and then hit the home trail."

"Could we not first go to the river, Mr. Blake? My hands are dreadfully sticky."

"Win will take you. It's only a little way to the bank here and there's not much underbrush."

"If you think it's quite safe—" remarked Winthrope.

"It's safe enough. Go on. You'll see the river in half a minute. Only thing, you'd better watch out for alligators."

"I believe that—er—properly speaking, these are crocodiles."

"You don't say! Heap of difference it will make if one gets you."

Miss Leslie caught Winthrope's eye. He turned on his heel, and led the way for her through the first thicket. Beyond this they came to a little glade which ran through to the river. When they reached the bank, they stepped cautiously down the muddy slope, and bathed their hands in the clear water. As Miss Leslie rose, Winthrope bent over and began to drink.

"Oh, Mr. Winthrope!" she exclaimed; "please don't! In your weak condition, I'm so afraid—"

"Do not alarm yourself. I am perfectly well, and I am

*Miss Leslie stood rigid, her face ashy-gray, her
dilated eyes fixed upon the adder.*

quite as competent to judge what is good for me as your—ah—countryman."

"Mr. Winthrope, I am thinking only of your own good."

Winthrope took another deep draught, rinsed his fingers fastidiously, and arose.

"My dear Miss Genevieve," he observed, "a woman looks at these matters in such a different light from a man. But you should know that there are some things a gentleman cannot tolerate."

"You were welcome to all the water in the flask. Surely with that you could have waited, if only to please me."

"Ah, if you put it that way, I must beg pardon. Anything to please you, I'm sure! Pray forgive me, and forget the incident. It is now past."

"I hope so!" she murmured; but her heart sank as she glanced at his sallow face, and she recalled his languid, feeble movements.

Piqued by her look, Winthrope started back through the glade. Miss Leslie was turning to follow, when she caught sight of a gorgeous crimson blossom under the nearest tree. It was the first flower she had seen since being shipwrecked. She uttered a little cry of delight, and ran to pluck the blossom.

Winthrope, glancing about at her exclamation, saw her stoop over the flower—and in the same instant he saw a huge vivid coil, all black and green and yellow, flash up out of the bedded leaves and strike against the girl. She staggered back, screaming with horror, yet seemed unable to run.

Winthrope swung up his stick, and dashed across the glade towards her.

"What is it—a snake?" he cried.

The girl did not seem to hear him. She had ceased screaming, and stood rigid with fright, glaring down at the ground before her. In a moment Winthrope was near enough, to make out the brilliant glistening body, now extended full length in the grass. It was nearly five feet long and thick as his thigh. Another step, and he saw the hideous triangular head, lifted a few inches on the thick neck. The cold eyes were fixed upon the girl in a malignant, deadly stare.

"Snake! *snake!*" he yelled, and thrust his cane at the reptile's tail.

Again came a flashing leap of the beautiful ornate coil, and the stick was struck from Winthrope's hand. He danced backward, wild with excitement.

"Snake!—Hi, Blake! monster!— Run, Miss Leslie! I'll hold him—I'll get another stick!"

He darted aside to catch up a branch, and then ran in and struck boldly at the adder, which reared hissing to meet him. But the blow fell short, and the rotten wood shattered on the ground. Again Winthrope ran aside for a stick. There was none near, and as he paused to glance about, Blake came sprinting down the glade.

"Where?" he shouted.

"There—Hi! look out! You'll be on him!"

Blake stopped short, barely beyond striking distance of the hissing reptile.

"Wow!" he yelled. "Puff adder! I'll fix him."

He leaped back, and thrust his bow at the snake. The challenge was met by a vicious lunge. Even where he stood

Winthrope heard the thud of the reptile's head upon the ground.

"Now, once more, tootsie!" mocked Blake, swinging up his club.

Again the adder struck at the bow tip, more viciously than before. With the flash of the stroke, Blake's right foot thrust forward, and his club came down with all the drive of his sinewy arm behind it. The blow fell across the thickest part of the adder's outstretched body.

"Told you so! See him wiggle!" shouted Blake. "Broke his back, first lick— What's the matter, Miss Jenny? He can't do anything now."

Miss Leslie did not answer. She stood rigid, her face ashy-gray, her dilated eyes fixed upon the writhing, hissing adder.

"I—I think the snake struck her!" gasped Winthrope, suddenly overcome with horror.

"God!" cried Blake. He dropped his club, and rushed to the girl. In a moment he had knelt before her and flung up her leopard-skin skirt. Her stockings ripped to shreds in his frantic grasp. There, a little below her right knee, was a tiny red wound. Blake put his lips to it, and sucked with fierce energy.

Then the girl found her voice.

"Go away—go away! How dare you!" she cried, as her face flushed scarlet.

Blake turned, spat, and burst out with a loud demand of Winthrope: "Quick! the little knife—I'll have to slash it! Ten times worse than a rattlesnake— Lord! you're slow—I'll use mine!"

"Let go of me—let go! What do you mean, sir?" cried the girl, struggling to free herself.

"Hold still, you little fool!" he shouted. "It's death—sure death, if I don't get the poison from that bite!"

"I'm not bitten— Let go, I say! It struck in the fold of my skirt."

"For God's sake, Jenny, don't lie! It's certain death! I saw the mark—"

"That was a thorn. I drew it out an hour ago."

Blake looked up into her hazel eyes. They were blazing with indignant scorn. He freed her, and rose with clumsy slowness. Again he glanced at her quivering, scarlet face, only to look away with a sheepish expression.

"I guess you think I'm just a damned meddlesome idiot," he mumbled.

She did not answer. He stood for a little, rubbing a finger across his sun-blistered lips. Suddenly he stopped and looked at the finger. It was streaked with blood.

"Whew!" he exclaimed. "Didn't stop to think of that! It's just as well for me, Miss Jenny, that wasn't an adder bite. A little poison on my sore lip would have done for me. Ten to one, we'd both have turned up our toes at the same time. Of course, though, that'd be nothing to you."

Miss Leslie put her hands before her face, and burst into hysterical weeping.

Blake looked around, far more alarmed than when facing the adder.

"Here, you blooming lud!" he shouted; "take the lady away, and be quick about it. She'll go dotty if she sees any more snake stunts. Clear out with her, while I smash the wriggler."

Winthrope, who had been staring fixedly at the beautiful coloring and loathsome form of the writhing adder, started at Blake's harsh command as though struck.

"I—er—to be sure," he stammered, and darting around to the hysterical girl, he took her arm and hurried her away up the glade.

They had gone several paces when Blake came running up behind them. Winthrope looked back with a glance of inquiry. Blake shook his head.

"Not yet," he said. "Give me your cigarette case. I've thought of something— Hold on; take out the cigarettes. Smoke 'em, if you like."

Case in hand, Blake returned to the wounded adder, and picked up his club. A second smashing blow would have ended the matter at once; but Blake did not strike. Instead, he feinted with his club until he managed to pin down the venomous head. The club lay across the monster's neck, and he held it fast with the pressure of his foot.

When, half an hour later, he wiped his knife on a wisp of grass and stood up, the cigarette case contained over a tablespoonful of a crystalline liquid. He peered in at it, his heavy jaw thrust out, his eyes glowing with savage elation.

"Talk about your meat trusts and Winchesters!" he exulted; "here's a whole carload of beef in this little box— enough dope to morgue a herd of steers. Good God, though, that was a close shave for her!"

His face sobered, and he stood for several moments staring thoughtfully into space. Then his gaze chanced to fall upon the great crimson blossom which had so nearly lured the girl to her death.

"Hello!" he exclaimed; "that's an amaryllis. Wonder if

she wasn't coming to pick it—" He snapped shut the lid of the cigarette case, thrust it carefully into his shirt pocket, and stepped forward to pluck the flower. "Makes a fellow feel like a kid; but maybe it'll make her feel less sore at me."

He stood gazing at the flower for several moments, his eyes aglow with a soft blue light.

"Whew!" he sighed; "if only— But what's the use? She's 'way out of my class—a rough brute like me! All the same, it's up to me to take care of her. She can't keep me from being her friend—and she sure can't object to my picking flowers for her."

Amaryllis in hand, he gathered up his bow and club. Then he paused to study the skin of the decapitated adder. The inspection ended with a shake of his head.

"Better not, Thomas. It would make a dandy quiver; but then, it might get on her nerves."

When he came to the ant-hill, he found companions and honey alike gone. He went on to the cocoanuts. There he came upon Winthrope stretched flat beside the skin of honey. Miss Leslie was seated a little way beyond, nervously bending a palm-leaf into shape for a hat.

"I say, Blake," drawled Winthrope, "you've been a deuced long time in coming. It was no end of a task to lug the honey—"

Blake brushed past without replying, and went on until he stood before the girl. As she glanced up at him, he held out the crimson blossom.

"Thought you might like posies," he said, in a hesitating voice.

Instead of taking the flower, she drew back with a gesture of repulsion.

"Oh, take it away!" she exclaimed.

Blake flung the rejected gift on the ground, and crushed it beneath his heel.

"Catch me making a fool of myself again!" he growled.

"I—I did not mean it that way—really I didn't, Mr. Blake. It was the thought of that awful snake."

But Blake, cut to the quick, had turned away, far too angry to heed what she said. He stopped short beside the Englishman; but only to sling the skin of honey upon his back. The load was by no means a light one, even for his strength. Yet he caught up the heavy pot as well, and made off across the plain at a pace which the others could not hope to equal.

As Winthrope rose and came forward to join Miss Leslie, he looked about closely for the bruised flower. It was nowhere in sight.

"Er—beg pardon, Miss Genevieve, but did not Blake drop the bloom—er—blossom somewhere about here?"

"Perhaps he did," replied Miss Leslie. She spoke with studied indifference.

"I—ah—saw the fellow exhibit his impudence."

"Ye-es?"

"You know, I think it high time the bounder is taken down a peg."

"Ah, indeed! Then why do you not try it?"

"Miss Genevieve! you know that at present I am physically so much his inferior—"

"How about mentally?"

Though the girl's eyes were veiled by their lashes, she saw Winthrope cast after Blake a look that seemed to her almost fiercely vindictive.

"Well?" she said, smiling, but watching him closely.

"Mentally!—We'll soon see about that!" he muttered. "I must say, Miss Genevieve, it strikes me as deuced odd, you know, to hear you speak so pleasantly of a person who—not to mention past occurrences—has to-day, with the most shocking disregard of—er—decency—"

"Stop!—stop this instant!" screamed the girl, her nerves overwrought.

Winthrope smiled with complacent assurance.

"My dear young lady," he drawled, "allow me to repeat, 'All is fair in love and war.' Believe me, I love you most ardently."

"No gentleman would press his suit at such a time as this!"

"Really now, I fancy I have always comported myself as a gentleman—"

"A trifle too much so, truth to say!" she retorted.

"Ah, indeed. However, this is now quite another matter. Has it not occurred to you, my dear, that this entire experience of ours since that beastly storm is rather—er—compromising?"

"You—you dare say such a thing! I'll go this instant and tell Mr. Blake! I'll—"

"Begging your pardon, madam,—but are you prepared to marry that barbarous clodhopper?"

"Marry? What do you mean, sir?"

"Precisely that. It is a question of marriage, if you'll pardon me. And, you see, I flatter myself, that when it comes to the point, it will not be Blake, but myself—"

"Ah, indeed! And if I should prefer neither of you?"

"Begging your pardon,—I fancy you will honor me with

your hand, my dear. For one thing, you admit that I am a gentleman."

"Oh, indeed!"

"One moment, please! I am trying to intimate to you, as delicately as possible, how—er—embarrassing you would find it to have these little occurrences—above all, to-day's—noised abroad to the vulgar crowd, or even among your friends—"

"What do you mean? What do you want?" cried the girl, staring at him with a deepening fear in her bewildered eyes.

"Believe me, my dear, it grieves me to so perturb you; but—er—love must have its way, you know."

"You forget. There is Mr. Blake."

"Ah, to be sure! But really now, you would not ask, or even permit him to murder me; and one is not legally bound, you know, to observe promises—a pledge of silence, for example—when extorted under duress, under violence, you know."

Miss Leslie looked the Englishman up and down, her brown eyes sparkling with quick-returning anger. He met her scorn with a smile of smug complacency.

"Cad!" she cried, and turning her back upon him, she set out across the plain after Blake.

18

THE EAVESDROPPER CAUGHT

EVEN HAD IT not been for her doubts of Blake, the girl's modesty would have caused her to think twice before repeating to him the Englishman's insulting proposal. While she yet hesitated and delayed, Winthrope came down with a second attack of fever. Blake, who until then had held himself sullenly apart from him as well as from Miss Leslie, at once softened to a gentler, or, at least, to a more considerate mood. Though his speech and bearing continued morose, he took upon himself all the duties of night nurse, besides working and foraging several hours each day.

Much to Miss Leslie's surprise, she found herself tending the invalid through the daytime almost as though nothing had happened. But everything about this wild and perilous life was so strange and unnatural to her that she found herself accepting the most unconventional relations as a regular consequence of the situation. She was feverishly eager for anything that might occupy her mind; for she felt that to brood over the future might mean madness. The mere thought of the possibilities was far too terrifying to be calmly dwelt upon. Though slight, there had been some little comfort in the belief that she could rely on

Winthrope. But now she was left alone with her doubt and dread. Even if she had nothing to fear from Blake, there were all the savage dangers of the coast, and behind those, far worse, the fever.

Meantime Blake went about his share of the camp work, gruff and silent, but with the usual concrete results. He brought load after load of fresh cocoanuts, and took great pains to hunt out the deliciously flavored eggs of the frigate birds to tempt Winthrope's failing appetite. When Miss Leslie suggested that beef juice would be much better for the invalid than broth, he went out immediately in search of a gum-bearing tree, and that night, after heating a small quantity of gum in the cigarette case with the adder poison, he spent hours replacing his arrow-heads with small barbed tips that could be loosened from their sockets by a slight pull.

A little before dawn he dipped two of his new arrow-heads in the sticky contents of the cigarette case, fitted them carefully to their shafts, and stole away down the cleft. Dawn found him crouched low in the grass where the overflow from the pool ran out into the plain along its little channel. He could see large forms moving away from him; then came the flood of crimson light, and he made out that the figures were a drove of huge eland.

His eyes flashed with eagerness. It was a long shot; but he knew that no more was required than to pierce the skin on any part of his quarry's body. He put his fingers between his teeth, and sent out a piercing whistle. It was a trick he had tried more than once on deer and pronghorn antelope. As he expected, the eland halted and swung half around. Their ox-like sides presented a mark hard to miss.

He rose and shot as they were wheeling to fly. Before he could fit his second arrow to the string, the whole herd were running off at a lumbering gallop. He lowered his bow, and walked after the animals, smiling with grim anticipation. He had seen his arrow strike against the side of the young bull at which he had aimed.

A little beyond where the bull had stood, he came upon the headless shaft of his arrow. As he stooped and caught it up, he saw one of the fleeing animals fall. When he came up with the dead bull, his first act was to recover his arrowtip and cut out the flesh around the wound. Provided only with his weak-bladed knife, he found it no easy task to butcher so large a beast. Though he had now acquired considerable dexterity in the art, noon had passed before he brought the first load of meat up the cleft.

So great was the abundance of meat that Blake worked all the remainder of the day and all night stringing the flesh on the curing racks, and Miss Leslie tried out pot after pot of fat and tallow, until every spare vessel was filled, and she had to resort to a hollow in the rock beside the spring. Blake promised to make more pots as soon as he could fetch the clay, but he had first to dress the eland hide, and prepare a new stock of thread and cord from parts of the animal which he was careful not to let her see.

Whatever their concern for the future,—and even Blake's was keen and bitter,—the party, as a party, for the time being might have been considered extremely fortunate. They had a shelter secure alike from the weather and from wild beasts; an abundance of nutritious food, and, as material for clothing, the bushbuck, hyena, and eland hides. To obtain more skins and more meat Blake now knew would be a simple matter so long as he had enough poison left in the cigarette case to moisten the tips of his arrows.

Even Winthrope's relapse proved far less serious than might reasonably have been expected. The fever soon left him, and within a few days he regained strength enough to care for himself. Here, however, much to Blake's perplexity and concern, his progress seemed to stop, and all Blake's urging could do no more than cause him to move languidly from one shady spot to another. He would receive Blake's orders with a smile and a drawling "Ya-as, to be sure!"— and would then absolutely ignore the matter.

Only in two ways did the invalid exhibit any signs of energy. He could and did eat with a heartiness little short of that shown by Blake, and he would insist upon seeking opportunities to press his attentions upon Miss Leslie. He was careful to avoid all offensive remarks; yet the veriest commonplace from his lips was now an offence to the girl. While he needed her as nurse, she had endured his talk as part of her duty. But now she felt that she could no longer do so. Taking advantage of a time when the Englishman was, as she supposed, enjoying a noonday siesta down towards the barricade, she went to meet Blake, who had been up on the cliff for eggs.

"Hello!" he sang out, as he swung down the tree, one hand gripping the clay pot in which he had gathered the eggs. "What you doing out in the sun? Get into the shade."

She stepped into the shade, and waited until he had climbed down the pile of stones which he had built for steps at the foot of the tree.

"Mr. Blake," she began, "could not I do this work,— gather the eggs?"

"You could, if I'd let you, Miss Jenny. But it strikes me you've got quite enough to do. Tell you the truth, I'd like to make Win take it in hand again. But all my cussing won't budge him an inch, and you know, when it comes to the rub, I couldn't wallop a fellow who can hardly stand up."

"Is he really so weak?" she murmured.

"Well, you know how— Say, you don't mean that you think he's shamming?"

"I did not say that I thought so, Mr. Blake. I do not care to talk about him. What I wish is that you will let me attend to this work."

"Couldn't think of it, Miss Jenny! You're already doing your share."

"Mr. Blake,—if you must know,—I wish to have a place where I can go and be apart—alone."

Blake scowled. "Alone with that dude! He'd soon find enough strength to climb up with you on the cliff."

"I—ah—Mr. Blake, would he be apt to follow me, if I told you distinctly I should rather be alone?"

"Would he? Well, I should rather guess not!" cried Blake, making no attempt to conceal his delight. "I'll give him a hint that'll make his hair curl. From now on, nobody climbs up this tree but you, without first asking your permission."

"Thank you, Mr. Blake! You are very kind."

"Kind to let you do more work! But say, I'll help out all I can on the other work. You know, Miss Jenny,—a rough fellow like me don't know how to say it, but he can think it just the same,—I'd do anything in the world for you!"

As he spoke, he held out his rough, powerful hand. She shrank back a little, and caught her breath in sudden fright. But when she met his steady gaze, her fear left her as quickly as it had come. She impulsively thrust out her hand, and he seized it in a grip that brought the tears to her eyes.

"Miss Jenny! Miss Jenny!" he murmured, utterly unconscious that he was hurting her, "you know now that I'm your friend, Miss Jenny!"

"Yes, Mr. Blake," she answered, blushing and drawing her hand free. "I believe you are a friend—I believe I can trust you."

"You can, by—Jiminy! But say," he continued, blundering with dense stupidity, "do you really mean that? Can you forgive me for being so confounded meddlesome, the other day, after the snake—"

He stopped short, for upon the instant she was facing him, as on that eventful day, scarlet with shame and anger.

"How dare you speak of it?" she cried. "You're—you're not a gentleman!"

Before he could reply, she turned and left him, walking rapidly and with her head held high. Blake stared after her in bewilderment.

"Well, what in—what in thunder have I done now?" he exclaimed. "Ladies are certainly mighty funny! To go off at a touch—and just when I thought we were going to be chums! But then, of course, I've the whole thing to learn about nice girls—like her!"

"I—ah—must certainly agree with you there, Blake," drawled Winthrope, from beside the nearest bush.

Blake turned upon him with savage fury: "You dirty sneak!—you *gentleman!* You've been eavesdropping!"

The Englishman's yellow face paled to a sallow mottled

gray. He had seen the same look in Blake's eyes twice before, and this time Blake was far more angry.

"You sneak!—you sham gent!" repeated the American, his voice sinking ominously.

Winthrope dropped in an abject heap, as though Blake had struck him with his club.

"No, no!" he protested shrilly. "I am a real—I am—I'm a not—"

"That's it—you're a not! That's true!" broke in Blake, with sudden grim humor. "You're a nothing. A fellow can't even wipe his shoes on nothing!"

The change to sarcasm came as an immense relief to Winthrope.

"Ah, I say now, Blake," he drawled, pulling together his assurance the instant the dangerous light left Blake's eyes, "I say now, do you think it fair to pick on a man who is so much your—er—who is ill and weak?"

"That's it—do the baby act," jeered Blake. "But say, I don't know just how much eavesdropping you did; so there's one thing I'll repeat for the special benefit of your ludship. It'll be good for your delicate health to pay attention. From now on, the cliff top belongs to Miss Leslie. Gents and book agents not allowed. Understand? You don't go up there without her special invite. If you do, I'll twist your damned neck!"

He turned on his heel, and left the Englishman cowering.

19

AN OMINOUS LULL

THE THREE SAW nothing more of each other that day. Miss Leslie had withdrawn into the baobab, and Blake had gone off down the cleft for more salt. He did not return until after the others were asleep. Miss Leslie had gone without her supper, or had eaten some of the food stored within the tree.

When, late the next morning, she finally left her seclusion, Blake was nowhere in sight. Ignoring Winthrope's attempts to start a conversation, she hurried through her breakfast, and having gathered a supply of food and water, went to spend the day on the headland.

Evening forced her to return to the cleft. She had emptied the water flask by noon, and was thirsty. Winthrope was dozing beneath his canopy, which Blake had moved some yards down towards the barricade. Blake was cooking supper.

He did not look up, and met her attempt at a pleasant greeting with an inarticulate grunt. When she turned to enter the baobab, she found the opening littered with bamboos and green creepers and pieces of large branches with charred ends. On either side, midway through the entrance, a vertical row of holes had been sunk through the bark of the tree into the soft wood.

"What is this?" she asked. "Are you planning a porch?"

"Maybe," he replied.

"But why should you make the holes so far in? I know so little about these matters, but I should have fancied the holes would come on the front of the tree."

"You'll see in a day or two."

"How did you make the holes? They look black, as though—"

"Burnt 'em, of course—hot stones."

"That was so clever of you!"

He made no response.

Supper was eaten in silence. Even Winthrope's presence would have been a relief to the girl; yet she could not go to waken him, or even suggest that her companion do so. Blake sat throughout the meal sullen and stolid, and carefully avoided meeting her gaze. Before they had finished, twilight had come and gone, and night was upon them. Yet she lingered for a last attempt.

"Good-night, friend!" she whispered.

He sprang up as though she had struck him, and blundered away into the darkness.

In the morning it was as before. He had gone off before she wakened. She lingered over breakfast; but he did not appear, and she could not endure Winthrope's suave drawl. She went for another day on the headland.

She returned somewhat earlier than on the previous day. As before, Winthrope was dozing in the shade. But Blake was under the baobab, raking together a heap of rubbish. His hands were scratched and bleeding. To the girl's surprise, he met her with a cheerful grin and a clear, direct glance.

"Look here," he called.

She stepped around the baobab, and stood staring. The entrance, from the ground to the height of twelve feet, was walled up with a mass of thorny branches, interwoven with yet thornier creepers.

"How's that for a front door?" he demanded.

"Door?"

"Yes."

"But it's so big. I could never move it."

"A child could. Look." He grasped a projecting handle near the bottom of the thorny mass. The lower half of the door swung up and outward, the upper half in and downward. "See; it's balanced on a crossbar in the middle. Come on in."

She walked after him in under the now horizontal door. He gave the inner end a light upward thrust, and the door swung back in its vertical circle until it again stood upright in the opening. From the inside the girl could see the strong framework to which was lashed the facing of thorns. It was made of bamboo and strong pieces of branches, bound together with tough creepers.

"Pretty good grating, eh?" remarked Blake. "When those green creepers dry, they'll shrink and hold tight as iron clamps. Even now nothing short of a rhinoceros could walk through when the bars are fast. See here."

He stepped up to the novel door, and slid several socketed crossbars until their outer ends were deep in the holes in the tree trunk, three on each side.

"How's that for a set of bolts?" he demanded.

"Wonderful! Really, you are very, very clever! But why should you go to all this trouble, when the barricade—"

"Well, you see, it's best to be on the safe side."

"But it's absurd for you to go to all this needless work. Not that I do not appreciate your kind thought for my safety. Yet look at your hands!"

Blake hastened to put his bleeding hands behind him.

"They are no sight for a lady!" he muttered apologetically.

"Go and wash them at once, and I'll put on a dressing."

Blake glowed with frank pleasure, yet shook his head.

"No, thank you, Miss Jenny. You needn't bother. They'll do all right."

"You must! It would please me."

"Why, then, of course— But first, I want to make sure you understand fastening the door. Try the bars yourself."

She obeyed, sliding the bars in and out until he nodded his satisfaction.

"Good!" he said. "Now promise me you'll slide 'em fast every night."

"If you ask it. But why?"

"I want to make perfectly safe."

"Safe? But am I not secure with—"

"Look here, Miss Leslie; I'm not going to say anything about anybody."

"Perhaps you had better say no more, Mr. Blake."

"That's right. But whatever happens, you'll believe I've done my best, won't you?—even if I'm not a— Promise me straight, you'll lock up tight every night."

"Very well, I promise," responded the girl, not a little troubled by the strangeness of his expression.

He turned at once, swung open the door, and went out.

During supper he was markedly taciturn, and immediately afterwards went off to his bed.

That night Miss Leslie dutifully fastened herself in with all six bars. She wakened at dawn, and hastened out to prepare Blake's breakfast, but she found herself too late. There were evidences that he had eaten and gone off before dawn. The stretching frame of one of the antelope skins had been moved around by the fire, and on the smooth inner surface of the hide was a laconic note, written with charcoal in a firm, bold hand:—

"Exploring inland. Back by night, if can."

She bit her lip in her disappointment, for she had planned to show him how much she appreciated his absurd but well-meant concern for her safety. As it was, he had gone off without a word, and left her to the questionable pleasure of a *tête-à-tête* with Winthrope. Hoping to avoid this, she hurried her preparations for a day on the cliff. But before she could get off, Winthrope sauntered up, hiding his yawns behind a hand which had regained most of its normal plumpness. His eye was at once caught by the charcoal note.

"Ah!" he drawled; "really now, this is too kind of him to give us the pleasure of his absence all day!"

"Ye-es!" murmured Miss Leslie. "Permit me to add that you will also have the pleasure of my absence. I am going now."

Winthrope looked down, and began to speak very rapidly: "Miss Genevieve, I—I wish to apologize. I've thought it over. I've made a mistake—I—I mean, my conduct the other day was vile, utterly vile! Permit me to appeal to your considerateness for a man who has been unfortunate—who, I mean, has been—er—was carried away by his feelings. Your favoring of that bloom—er—that—er—bounder so angered me that I—that I—"

"Mr. Winthrope!" interrupted the girl, "I will have you to understand that you do not advance yourself in my esteem by such references to Mr. Blake."

"Aye! aye, that Blake!" panted Winthrope. "Don't you see? It's 'im, an' that blossom! W'en a man's daffy—w'en 'e's in love!—"

Miss Leslie burst into a nervous laugh; but checked herself on the instant.

"Really, Mr. Winthrope!" she exclaimed, "you must pardon me. I—I never knew that cultured Englishmen ever dropped their h's. As it happens, you know, I never saw one excited before this."

"Ah, yes; to be sure—to be sure!" murmured Winthrope, in an odd tone.

The girl threw out her hand in a little gesture of protest.

"Really, I'm sorry to have hurt—to have been so thought-less!"

Winthrope stood silent. She spoke again: "I'll do what you ask. I'll make allowances for your—for your feelings towards me, and will try to forget all you said the other day. Let me begin by asking a favor of you."

"Ah, Miss Genevieve, anything, to be sure, that I may do!"

"It is that I wish your opinion. When Mr. Blake finished that absurd door last evening, he would not tell me why he had built it—only a vague statement about my safety."

"Ah! He did not go into particulars?" drawled Winthrope.

"No, not even a hint; and he looked so—odd."

Winthrope slowly rubbed his soft palms on upon the other.

"Do you—er—really desire to know his—the motive which actuated him?" he murmured.

"I should not have mentioned it to you, if I did not," she answered.

"Well—er—" He hesitated and paused for a full minute. "You see, it is a rather difficult undertaking to intimate such a matter to a lady—just the right touch of delicacy, you know. But I will begin by explaining that I have known it since the first—"

"Known what?"

"Of that bound—of—er—Blake's trouble."

"Trouble?"

"Ah! Perhaps I should have said affliction; yes, that is the better word. To own the truth, the fellow has some good qualities. It was no doubt because he realised, when in his better moments—"

"Better moments? Mr. Winthrope, I am not a child. In justice both to myself and to Mr. Blake, I must ask you to speak out plainly."

"My dear Miss Leslie, may I first ask if you have not observed how strangely at times the fellow acts,—'looks odd,' as you put it,—how he falls into melancholia or senseless rages? I may truthfully state that he has three times threatened my life."

"I—I thought his anger quite natural, after I had so rudely—and so many people are given to brooding— But if he was violent to you—"

"My dear Miss Genevieve, I hold nothing against the miserable fellow. At such times he is not—er—responsible, you know. Let us give the fellow full credit—that is why he himself built your door."

"Oh, but I can't believe it! I can't believe it!" cried the girl. "It's not possible! He's so strong, so true and manly, so kind, for all his gruffness!"

"Ah, my dear!" soothed Winthrope, "that is the pity of it. But when a man must needs be his worst enemy, when he must needs lead a certain kind of life, he must take the consequences. To put it as delicately as possible, yet explain all, I need only say one word—paranoia."

Miss Leslie gathered up her day's outfit with trembling fingers, and went to mount the cliff.

After waiting a few minutes Winthrope walked hurriedly through the cleft, and climbed the tree-ladder with an agility that would have amazed his companions. But he did not draw himself up on the cliff. Having satisfied himself that Miss Leslie was well out toward the signal, he returned to the baobab, and proceeded to examine Blake's door with minute scrutiny.

That evening, shortly before dark, Blake came in almost exhausted by his journey. Few men could have covered the same ground in twice the time. It had been one continuous round of grass jungle, thorn scrub, rocks, and swamp. And for all his pains, he brought back with him nothing more than the discouraging information that the back-country was worse than the shore. Yet he betrayed no trace of depression over the bad news, and for all his fatigue, maintained a tone of hearty cheerfulness until, having eaten his fill, he suddenly observed Miss Leslie's frigid politeness.

"What's up now?" he demanded. "You're not mad 'cause I hiked off this morning without notice?"

"No, of course not, Mr. Blake. Nothing of the kind. But I—"

"Well,-what?" he broke in, as she hesitated. "I can't, for the world, think of anything else I've done—"

"You've done! Perhaps I might suggest that it is a question of what you haven't done." The girl was trembling on the verge of hysterics. "Yes, what you've not done! All these weeks, and not a single attempt to get us away from here, except that miserable signal; and I as good as put that up! You call yourself a man! But I—I—" She stopped short, white with a sudden overpowering fear.

Winthrope looked from her to Blake with a sidelong glance, his lips drawn up in an odd twist.

There followed several moments of tense silence; then Blake mumbled apologetically: "Well, I suppose I might have done more. I was so dead anxious to make sure of food and shelter. But this trip to-day—"

"Mr.—Mr. Blake, pray do not get excited—I—I mean, please excuse me. I'm—"

"You're coming down sick!" he said.

"No, no! I have no fever."

"Then it's the sun. Yet you ought to keep up there where the air is freshest. I'll make you a shade."

She protested, and withdrew, somewhat hurriedly, to her tree.

In the morning Blake was gone again; but instead of a note, beside the fire stood the smaller antelope skin, converted into a great bamboo-ribbed sunshade.

She spent the day as usual on the headland. There was no wind, and the sun was scorching hot. But with her big sunshade to protect her from the direct rays, the heat was at least endurable. She even found energy to work at a basket which she was attempting to weave out of long, coarse grass; yet there were frequent intervals when her hands sank idle in her lap, and she gazed away over the shimmering glassy expanse of the ocean.

In the afternoon the heat became oppressively sultry, and a long slow swell began to roll shoreward from beyond the distant horizon, showing no trace of white along its oily crests until they broke over the coral reefs. There was not a breath of air stirring, and for a time the reefs so checked the rollers that they lacked force to drive on in and break upon the beach.

Steadily, however, the swell grew heavier, though not so much as a cat's-paw ruffled the dead surfaces of the watery hillocks. By sunset they were rolling high over both lines of reefs and racing shoreward to break upon the beach and the cliff foot in furious surf. The still air reverberated with the booming of the breakers. Yet the girl, inland bred and unversed in weather lore, sat heedless and indifferent, her eyes fixed upon the horizon in a vacant stare.

Her reverie was at last disturbed by the peculiar behavior of the seafowl. Those in the air circled around in a manner strange to her, while their mates on the ledges waddled restlessly about over and between their nests. There was a shriller note than usual in their discordant clamor.

Yet even when she gave heed to the birds, the girl failed to realize their alarm or to sense the impending danger. It was only that a feeling of disquiet had broken the spell of her reverie; it did not obtrude upon the field of her conscious thought. She sighed, and rose to return to the cleft, idly wondering that the air should seem more sultry than at mid-day. The peculiar appearance of the sun and the western sky meant nothing more to her than an odd effect of color and light. She smilingly compared it with an attempt at a sunset painted by an artist friend of the impressionist school.

Neither Winthrope nor Blake was in sight when she reached the baobab, and neither appeared, though she delayed supper until dark. It was quite possible that they had eaten before her return and had gone off again, the Englishman to doze, and Blake on an evening hunt.

At last, tired of waiting, she covered the fire, and retired into her tree-cave. The air in the cleft was still more stifling than on the headland. She paused, with her hand upraised to close the swinging door. She had propped it open when she came out in the morning. After a moment's hesitation, she went on across the hollow, leaving the door wide open.

"I will rest a little, and close it later," she sighed. She was feeling weary and depressed.

An hour passed. An ominous stillness lay upon the cleft. Even the cicadas had hushed their shrill note. The only sound was a muffled reverberating echo of the surf roaring upon the seashore. Beneath the giant spread of the baobab all was blackness.

Something moved in a bush a little way down the cleft. A crouching figure appeared, dimly outlined in the starlight. The figure crept stealthily across into the denser night of the baobab. The darkness closed about it like a shroud.

A blinding flash of light pierced the blackness. The figure halted and crouched lower, though the flash had gone again in a fraction of a second. A dull rumbling mingled with the ceaseless boom of the surf.

A second flash lighted the cleft with its dazzling coruscation. This time the creeping figure did not halt.

Again and again the forked lightning streaked across the sky, every stroke more vivid than the one before. The rumble of the distant thunder deepened to a heavy rolling which dominated the dull roar of the breakers. The storm was coming with the on-rush of a tornado. Yet the leaves hung motionless in the still air, and there was no sound other than the thunder and the booming of the surf.

The lightning flared, one stroke upon the other, with a brilliancy that lit up the cave's interior brighter than at mid-day.

In the white glare the girl saw Winthrope, crouched beneath her upswung door; and his face was as the face of a beast.

20

THE HURRICANE BLAST

FOR A MOMENT that seemed a moment of eternity, she lay on her bed, staring into the blank darkness. The storm burst with a crashing uproar that brought her to her feet, with a shriek. Her giant tree creaked and strained under the impact of the terrific hurricane blasts that came howling through the cleft like a rout of shrieking fiends. The peals of thunder merged into one continuous roar, beneath which the solid ledges of rock jarred and quivered. The sky was a pall of black clouds, meshed with a dazzling network of forked lightning.

The girl stood motionless, stunned by the uproar, appalled by the blinding glare of the thunder-bolts; yet even more fearful of the figure which every flash showed her still lurking beneath the door. A gust-borne bough struck with numbing force against her upraised arm. But she took no heed. She was unaware of the swirl of rain and sticks and leaves that was driving in through the open entrance.

On a sudden the door shook free from its props and whirled violently around on its balance-bar. There was a shriek that pierced above the shrilling of the cyclone,—a single human shriek.

The girl sprang across the cave. The heavy door swished up before her and down again, its lower edge all but grazing her face. For a moment it stopped in a vertical position, and hung quivering, like a beast about to leap upon its prey. Too excited to comprehend the danger of the act, the girl sprang forward and shot one of the thick bars into its socket.

A fierce gust leaped against the outer face of the door and thrust in upon it, striving to burst it bodily from its bearings. The top and the free side of the bottom bowed in. But the branches were still green and tough, the bamboo like whalebone, and the shrunken creepers held the frame together as though the joints were lashed with wire rope. Failing to smash in the elastic structure, or to snap the crossbar, it were as if the blast flung itself alternately against the top and bottom in a fierce attempt to again whirl the frame about. The white glare streaming in through the interstices showed the girl her opportunity. She grasped another bar and shot it into its socket as the lower part of the door gave back with the shifting of the pressure to the top. It was then a simple matter to slide the remaining bars into the deep-sunk holes. Within half a minute she had made the door fast, from the first bar to the sixth.

A heavy spray was beating in upon her through the chinks of the framework. She drew back and sought shelter in a niche at the side. Narrow as was the slit above the top of the door, it let in a torrent of water, which spouted clear across and against the far wall of the cave. It gushed down upon her bed and was already flooding the cave floor.

She piled higher the cocoanuts stored in her niche, and perched herself upon the heap to keep above the water.

But even in her sheltered corner the eddying wind showered her with spray. She waded across for her skin-covered sunshade, and returned to huddle beneath it, in the still misery and terror of a hunted animal that has crept wounded into a hole.

During the first hurricane there had been companions to whom she could look for help and comfort, and she had been to a degree unaware of the greatness of the danger. But in the few short weeks since, she had caught more than one glimpse of Primeval Nature,—she of the bloody fang, blind, remorseless, insensate, destroying, ever destroying.

True, this was on solid land, while before there had been the peril of the sea. But now the girl was alone. Outside the straining walls of her refuge, the hurricane yelled and shrieked and roared,—a headless, formless monster, furious to burst in upon her, to overthrow her stanch old tree giant, that in his fall his shattered trunk might crush and mangle her. Or at any instant a thunder-bolt might rend open the great tower of living wood, and hurl her blackened body into the pool on the cave floor.

Once she fancied that she heard Blake shouting outside the door; but when she screamed a shrill response, the blast mocked her with echoing shrieks, and she dared not venture to free the door. If it were Blake, he did not shout again. After a time she began to think that the sound had been no more than a freak of the shifting wind. Yet the thought of him out in the full fury of the cyclone served to turn her thoughts from her own danger. She prayed aloud for his safety, beseeching her God that he be spared. She sought to pray even for Winthrope. But the vision of that beastly face rose up before her, and she could not—then.

Presently she became aware of a change in the storm. The terrific gusts blew with yet greater violence, the thunder crashed heavier, the lightning filled the air with a flame of dazzling white light. But the rain no longer gushed across on the spot where her bed had been. It was entering at a different angle, and its force was broken by the bend in the thick wall of the entrance. After a time the deluge dashed aslant the entrance, gushing down the door in a cataract of foam.

Another interval, and the driving downpour no longer struck even the edge of the opening. The wind was veering rapidly as the cyclone centre moved past on one side. The area of the hurricane was little more than thrice that of a tornado, and it was advancing along its course at great speed. An hour more, and the outermost rim of the huge whirl was passing over the cleft.

Quickly the hurricane gusts fell away to a gale; the gale became a breeze; the breeze lulled and died away, stifled by the torrential rain.

Within the baobab all was again dark and silent. Utterly exhausted, the girl had sunk back against the friendly wall of the tree, and fallen asleep.

She was wakened by a hoarse call: "Miss Jenny! Miss Jenny, answer me! Are you all right?"

She started up, barely saving herself from a fall as the big unhusked nuts rolled beneath her feet. The morning sunlight was streaming in over her door. She sprang down ankle-deep into the mire of the cave floor, and ran to loosen the bars. As the door swung up, she darted out, with a cry of delight: "You are safe—safe! Oh, I was so afraid for you!

But you're drenched! You must build a fire—dry yourself—at once!"

"Wait," said Blake. "I've got to tell you something."

He caught her outstretched hands, and pushed them
down with gentle force. His face was grave, almost solemn.

"Think you can stand bad news—a shock?"

"I— What is it? You look so strange!"

"It's about Winthrope,—something very bad—"

She turned, with a gasp, and hid her face in her hands,
shuddering with horror and loathing.

"Oh! oh!" she cried, "I know already—I know all!"

"All?" demanded Blake, staring blankly.

"Yes; all! And—and he made me think it was you!" She
gasped, and fell silent.

Blake's face went white. He spoke in a clear, vibrant
voice, tense as an overstrained violin string: "I am speaking
about Winthrope—understand me?—Winthrope. He has
been badly hurt."

"The door swung down and struck him, when he was
creeping in."

"God!" roared Blake. "I picked him up like a sick baby—
the beast!—'stead of grinding my heel in his face! God!
I'll—"

"Tom! don't—don't even speak it! Tom!"

"God! When a helpless girl—when a—!" He choked,
beside himself with rage.

She sprang to him, and caught his sleeve in a convulsive
grasp. "Hush, for mercy's sake! Tom Blake, remember—
you're a man!"

He calmed like a ferocious dog at the voice of its master;
but it was several minutes before he could bring himself

to obey her insistent urging that he should return to the injured man.

"I'll go," he at last growled. "Wouldn't do it even for you, but he's good as dead—lucky for him!"

"Dead!"

"Dying.... You stay away."

He went around the baobab and a few paces along the cleft to the place where a limp form lay huddled on the ledges, out of the mud. Slowly, as though drawn by the fascination of horror, the girl crept after him. When she saw the broken, storm-beaten thing that had been Winthrope, she stopped, and would have turned back. After all, as Blake had said, he was dying—

When she stood at the feet of the writhing figure, and looked down into the battered face, it required all her will-power to keep from fainting. Blake frowned up at her for an instant, but said nothing.

Winthrope was speaking, feebly and brokenly, yet distinctly: "Really, I did not mean any harm—at first— you know. But a man does not always have control—"

"Not a beast like you!" growled Blake.

"Ow! Don't 'it me! I say now, I'm done for! My legs are cold already—"

"Oh, quick, Mr. Blake! build a fire! It may be, some hot broth—"

"Too late," muttered Blake. "See here, Winthrope, there's no use lying about it. You're going out mighty soon. See if you can't die like a man."

"Die!... Gawd, but I can't die—I can't die—Ow! it burns!"

He flung up a hand, and sought to tear at his wounds.

"Hold hard!" cried Blake, catching the hand in an iron grip.

Something in his touch, or the tone of command, seemed to cower the wretched man into a state of abject submission.

"S'elp me, I'll confess!—I'll confess all!" he babbled. "The stones are sewed in the stomach pad; I 'ad to take 'em hout of their settings, and melt up the gold." He paused, and a cunning smile stole over his distorted features. "Ho, wot a bloomin' lark! Valet plays the gent, an' they never 'as a hinkling! Mr. Cecil Winthrope, hif you please, an' a 'int of a title—wot a lark! 'Awkings, me lad, you're a gay 'oaxer! Wot a lark! wot a lark!"

Again there was a pause. The breath of the wounded man came in labored gasps. There was an ominous rattling in his throat. Yet once again he rallied, and this time his eyes turned to Miss Leslie, bright with an agonized consciousness of her presence and of all his guilt and shame.

His voice shrilled out in quavering appeal: "Don't—don't look at me, miss! I tried to make myself a gentleman; God knows I tried! I fought my way up out of the East End— out of that hell—and none ever lifted finger to help me. I educated myself like a scholar—then the stock sharks cheated me of my savings—out of the last penny; and I had to take service. My God! a valet—his Grace's valet, and I a scholar! Do you wonder the devil got into me? Do you—"

Blake's deep voice, firm but strangely husky, broke in upon and silenced the cry of agony: "There, I guess you've said enough."

"Enough!—and last night—My God! to be such a beast! The devil tempted me—aye, and he's paid me out in my own coin! I'm done for! God ha' mercy on me!—God ha' mercy—"

Again came the gasping rattle; this time there was no rally.

Blake thrust himself between Miss Leslie and the crumpled figure.

"Get back around the tree," he said harshly.

"What are you going to do?"

"That's my business," he replied. He thrust his burning-glass into her hand. "Here; go and build a fire, if you can find any dry stuff."

"You're not going to— You'll bury him!"

"Yes. Whatever he may have been, he's dead now, poor devil!"

"I can't go," she half whispered, "not until—until I've learned— Do you—can you tell me just what is paranoia?"

Blake studied a little, and tapped the top of his head.

"Near as I can say, it's softening of the brain.—up there."

"Do you think that—" she hesitated—"that he had it?"

Again Blake paused to consider.

"Well, I'm no alienist. I thought him a softy from the first. But that was all in line with what he was playing on us—British dude. Fooled me, and I'd been chumming with Jimmy Scarbridge,—and Jimmy was the straight goods, fresh imported—monocle even—when I first ran up against him. No; this—this Hawkins, if that's his name, had brains all right. Still, he may have been cracked. When folks go dotty, they sometimes get extra 'cute. The best I can think of him is that losing his savings may have made him slip a cog, and then the scare over the way we landed here and his spells of fever probably hurried up the softening."

"Then you believe his story?"

"Yes, I do. But if you'll go, please."

"One thing more—I must know now! Do you remember the day when you set up the signal, and you—you quarrelled with him?"

Blake reddened, and dropped his gaze. "Did he go and tell you that? The sneak!"

"If you please, let us say nothing more about him. But would you care to tell me what you meant—what you said then?"

Blake's flush deepened; but he raised his head, and faced her squarely as he answered: "No; I'm not going to repeat any dead man's talk; and as for what I said, this isn't the time or place to say anything in that line—now that we're alone. Understand?"

"I'm afraid I do not, Mr. Blake. Please explain."

"Don't ask me, Miss Jenny. I can't tell you now. You'll have to wait till we get aboard ship. We'll catch a steamer before long. 'T isn't every one of them that goes ashore in these blows."

"Why did you build that door? Did you suspect—" She glanced down at the huddled figure between them.

Blake frowned and hesitated; then burst out almost angrily: "Well, you know now he was a sneak; so it's not blabbing to tell that much—I knew he was before; and it's never safe to trust a sneak."

"Thank you!" she said, and she turned away quickly that she might not again look at the prostrate figure.

21

WRECKAGE AND SALVAGE

ALL THE WOOD in the cleft was sodden from the fierce downpour that had accompanied the cyclone; all the cleft bottom other than the bare ledges was a bed of mud; everything without the tree-cave had been either blown away or heaped with broken boughs and mud-spattered rubbish. But the girl had far too much to think about to feel any concern over the mere damage and destruction of things. It was rather a relief to find something that called for work.

Not being able to find dry fuel, she gathered a quantity of the least sodden of the twigs and branches, and spread them out on a ledge in the clear sunshine. While her firewood was drying, she scraped away the mud and litter heaped upon her rude hearth. She then began a search for lost articles. When she dug out the pottery ware, she found her favorite stew-pot and one of the platters in fragments. The drying-frames for the meat had been blown away, and so had the antelope and hyena skins.

Catching sight of a bit of white down among the bamboos, she went to it, and was not a little surprised to see the tattered remnant of her duck skirt. It had evidently been torn from the signal staff by the first gust of the cyclone, whirled down into the cleft by some flaw or eddy in the wind, and wadded so tightly into the heart of the thick clump of stems that all the fury of the storm had failed to dislodge it. Its recovery seemed to the girl a special providence; for of course they must keep up a signal on the cliff.

Having started her fire and set on a stew, she hunted out her sewing materials from their crevice in the cave, and began mending the slits in the torn flag. While she worked she sat on a shaded ledge, her bare feet toasting in the sun, and her soggy, mud-smeared moccasins drying within reach. When Blake appeared, the moccasins were still where she had first set them; but the little pink feet were safely tucked up beneath the tattered flag. Fortunately, the sight of the white cloth prevented Blake from noticing the moccasins.

"Hello!" he exclaimed. "What's that?—the flag? Say, that's luck! I'll break out a bamboo right off. Old staff's carried clean away."

"Mr. Blake,—just a moment, please. What have you done with—with it?"

Blake jerked his thumb upward.

"You have carried him up on the cliff?"

"Best place I could think of. No animals—and I piled stones over.... But, I say, look here."

He drew out a piece of wadded cloth, marked off into little squares by crossing lines of stitches. One of the squares near the edge had been ripped open. Blake thrust in his finger, and worked out an emerald the size of a large pea.

"O-h-h!" cried Miss Leslie, as he held the glittering gem out to her in his rough palm.

He drew it back, and carefully thrust it again into its pocket.

"That's one," he said. "There's another in every square of this innocent, harmless rag—dozens of them. He must have made a clean sweep of the duke's—or, more like, the duchess's jewels. Now, if you please, I want you to sew this up tight again, and—"

"I cannot—I cannot touch it!" she cried.

"Say, I didn't mean to— It was confounded stupid of me," mumbled Blake. "Won't you excuse me?"

"Of course! It was only the—the thought that—"

"No wonder. I always am a fool when it comes to ladies. I'll fix the thing all right."

Catching up the nearest small pot, he crammed the quilted cloth down within it, and filled it to the brim with sticky mud.

"There! Guess nobody's going to run off with a jug of mud—and it won't hurt the stones till we get a chance to look up the owner. He won't be hard to find—English duke minus a pint of first-class sparklers! Will you mind its setting in the cave after things are fixed up?"

"No; not as it is."

He nodded soberly. "All right, then. Now I'll go for the new flag-staff. You might set out breakfast."

She nodded in turn, and when he came back from the bamboos with the largest of the great canes on his shoulder, his breakfast was waiting for him. She set it before him, and turned to go again to her sewing.

"Hold on," he said. "This won't do. You've got to eat your share."

"I do not—I am not hungry."

"That's no matter. Here!"

He forced upon her a bowl of hot broth, and she drank it because she could not resist his rough kindness.

"Good! Now a piece of meat," he said.

"Please, Mr. Blake!" she protested.

"Yes, you must!"

She took a bite, and sought to eat; but there was such a lump in her throat that she could not swallow. The tears gushed into her eyes, and she began to weep.

Blake's close-set lips relaxed, and he nodded.

"That's it; let it run out. You're overwrought. There's nothing like a good cry to ease off a woman's nerves—and I guess ladies aren't much different from women when it comes to such things."

"But I—I want to get the flag mended!" she sobbed.

"All right, all right; plenty of time!" he soothed. "I'm going to see how things look down the cleft."

He bolted the last of his meat, and at once left her alone to cry herself back to calmness over the stitching of the signal.

His first concern was for the barricade. As he had feared, he found that it had been blown to pieces. The greater part of the thorn branches which he had gathered with so much labor were scattered to the four corners of the earth. He stood staring at the wreckage in glum silence; but he did not swear, as he would have done the week before. Presently his face cleared, and he began to whistle in a plaintive minor key. He was thinking of how she had looked when she darted out of the tree at his call—of her concern for him. When he was so angered at Winthrope, she had called him Tom!

After a time he started on, picking his way over the remnant of the barricade, without a falter in his whistling. The deluge of rain had poured down the cleft in a torrent, tearing away the root-matted soil and laying bare the ledges in the channel of the spring rill. But aside from an occasional boggy hole, the water had drained away.

At the foot, about the swollen pool, was a wide stretch of rubbish and mud. He worked his way around the edge, and came out on the plain, where the sandy soil was all the firmer for its drenching. He swung away at a lively clip. The air was fresh and pure after the storm, and a slight breeze tempered the sun-rays.

He kept on along the cliff until he turned the point. It was not altogether advisable to bathe at this time of day; but he had been caught out by the cyclone in a corner of the swamp, across the river, where the soil was of clay. Only his anxiety for Miss Leslie had enabled him to fight his way out of the all but impassable morass which the storm deluge had made of the half-dry swamp. At dawn he had reached the river, and swam across, reckless of the crocodiles. The turbid water of the stream had rid him of only part of his accumulated slime and ooze. So now he washed out his tattered garments as well as he could without soap, and while they were drying on the sun-scorched rocks, swam about in the clear, tonic sea-water, quite as reckless of the sharks as he had been of the ugly crocodiles in the river.

For all this, he was back at the baobab before Miss Leslie had stitched up the last slit in the torn flag.

She looked up at him, with a brave attempt at a smile.

"I am afraid I'm not much of a needle-woman," she sighed. "Look at those stitches!"

"Don't fret. They'll hold all right, and that's what we want," he reassured her. "Give it me, now. I've got to get it up, and hurry back for a nap. No sleep last night—I was out beyond the river, in the swamp—and to-night I'll have to go on watch. The barricade is down."

"Oh, that is too bad! Couldn't I take a turn on watch?"

Blake shook his head. "No; I'll sleep to-day, and work rebuilding the barricade to-night. Toward morning I might build up the fire, and take a nap."

He caught up the flag and its new staff, and swung away through the cleft.

He returned much sooner than Miss Leslie expected, and at once began to throw up a small lean-to of bamboos over a ledge at the cliff foot, behind the baobab. The girl thought he was making himself a hut, in place of the canopy under which he had slept before the storm, which, like Winthrope's, had been carried away. But when he stopped work, he laconically informed her that all she had to do to complete her new house was to dry some leaves.

"But I thought it was for yourself!" she protested. "I will sleep inside the tree."

"Doc Blake says no!" he rejoined—"not till it's dried out."

She glanced at his face, and replied, without a moment's hesitancy: "Very well. I will do what you think best."

"That's good," he said, and went at once to lie down for his much needed sleep.

He awoke just soon enough before dark to see the results of her hard day's labor. All the provisions stored in the tree had been brought out to dry, and a great stack of fuel, ready for burning, was piled up against the baobab; while all about the tree the rubbish had been neatly gathered together in heaps. Blake looked his admiration for her industry. But then his forehead wrinkled.

"You oughtn't to've done so much," he admonished.

"I'll show you I can tote fair!" she rejoined. During the afternoon she had called to mind that odd expression of a Southern girl chum, and had been waiting her opportunity to banter him with it.

He stared at her open-eyed, and laughed.

"Say, Miss Jenny, you'd better look out. You'll be speaking American, first thing!"

Thereupon, they fell to chattering like children out of school, each happy to be able to forget for the moment that broken figure up on the cliff top and the haunting fear of what another day might bring to them.

When they had eaten their meal, both with keen appetites, Blake sprang up, with a curt "Good-night!" and swung off down the cleft. The girl looked after him, with a lingering smile.

"I wish he hadn't rushed off so suddenly," she murmured. "I was just going to thank him for—for everything!"

The color swept over her face in a deep blush, and she darted around to her tiny hut as though some one might have overheard her whisper.

Yet, after all, she had said nothing; or, at least, she had merely said "everything."

22

UNDERSTANDING AND MISUNDERSTANDING

IN THE MORNING she found Blake scraping energetically at the inner surfaces of a pair of raw hyena skins.

"So you've killed more game!" she exclaimed.

"Game? No; hyenas. I hated to waste good poison on the brutes; but nothing else showed up, and I need a new pair of pa—er—trousers."

"Was it not dangerous—great beasts like these!"

"Not even enough to make it interesting. I'd have had some fun, though, with that confounded lion when the moon came up, if he hadn't sneaked off into the grass."

"A lion?"

"Yes. Didn't you hear him? The skulking brute prowled around for hours before the moon rose, when it was pitch dark. It was mighty lonesome, with him yowling down by the pool. Half a chance, and I'd given him something to yowl about. But it wasn't any use firing off my arrows in the dark, and, as I said, he sneaked off before—"

"Tom—Mr. Blake!—you must not risk your life!"

"Don't you worry about me. I've learned how to look out for Tom Blake. And you can just bank on it I'm going to

look out for Miss Jenny Leslie, too!… But say, after breakfast, suppose we take a run out on the cliffs for eggs?"

"I do not wish any to-day, thank you."

He waited a little, studying her down-bent face.

"Well," he muttered; "you don't have to come. I know
I oughtn't to take a moment's time. I did quite a bit last
night; but if you think—"

She glanced up, puzzled. His meaning flashed upon her,
and she rose.

"Oh, not that! I will come," she answered, and hastened
to prepare the morning meal.

When they came to the tree-ladder, she found that the
heap of stones built up by Blake to facilitate the first part
of the ascent was now so high that she could climb into
the branches without difficulty. She surmised that Blake
had found it necessary to build up the pile before he could
ascend with his burden.

They were at the foot of the heap, when, with a sharp
exclamation, Blake sprang up into the branches, and
scrambled to the top in hot haste. Wondering what this
might mean, Miss Leslie followed as fast as she could.
When she reached the top, she saw him running across
towards an out-jutting point on the north edge of the cliff.

She had hurried after him for more than half the distance
before she perceived the vultures that were gathered in a
solemn circle about a long and narrow heap of stones, on a
ledge, down on the sloping brink of the cliff. While at the
foot of the tree Blake had seen one of the grewsome flock
descending to join the others, and, fearful of what might
be happening, had rushed on ahead.

At his approach, the croaking watchers hopped

awkwardly from the ledges, and soared away; only to wheel, and circle back overhead. Miss Leslie shrank down, shuddering. Blake came back near her, and began to gather up the pieces of loose rock which were strewn about beneath the ledges on that part of the cliff.

"I know I piled up enough," he explained, in response to her look. "All the same, a few more will do no harm."

"Then you are sure those awful birds have not—"

"Yes; I'm sure."

He carried an armful of rocks to lay on the mound. When he began to gather more, she followed his example. They worked in silence, piling the rough stones gently one upon another, until the cairn had grown to twice its former size. The air on the open cliff top was fresher than in the cleft, and Miss Leslie gave little heed to the absence of shade. She would have worked on under the burning sun without thought of consequences. But Blake knew the need of moderation.

"There; that'll do," he said. "He may have been—all he was; but we've no more than done our duty. Now, we'll stroll out on the point."

"I should prefer to return."

"No doubt. But it's time you learned how to go nesting. What if you should be left alone here? Besides, it looks to me like the signal is tearing loose."

She accompanied him out along the cliff crest until they stood in the midst of the bird colony, half deafened by their harsh clamor. She had never ventured into their concourse when alone. Even now she cried out, and would have retreated before the sharp bills and beating wings had not Blake walked ahead and kicked the squawking birds out of the path. Having made certain that the big white flag was still secure on its staff, he led the way along the seaward brink of the cliff, pointing out the different kinds of seafowl, and shouting information about such of their habits and qualities as were of concern to hungry castaways.

He concluded the lesson by descending a dizzy flight of ledges to rob the nest of a frigate bird. It was a foolhardy feat at best, and doubly so in view of the thousands of eggs lying all around in the hollows of the cliff top. But from these Blake had recently culled out all the fresh settings of the frigate birds, and none of the other eggs equalled them in delicacy of flavor.

"How's that?" he demanded, as he drew himself up over the edge of the cliff, and handed the big chalky-white egg into her keeping.

"I would rather go without than see you take such risks," she replied coldly.

"You would, eh!" he cried, quite misunderstanding her, and angered by what seemed to him a gratuitous rebuff. "Well, I'd rather you'd say nothing than speak in that tone. If you don't want the egg heave it over."

Unable to conceive any cause for his sudden anger, she was alarmed, and drew back, watching him with sidelong glances.

"What's the matter?" he demanded. "Think I'm going to bite you?"

She shrank farther away, and did not answer. He stared at her, his eyes hard and bright. Suddenly he burst into a harsh laugh, and strode away towards the cliff, savagely kicking aside the birds that came in his path.

When, an hour later, the girl crept back along the cleft to the baobab, she saw him hard at work building a little hut, several yards down towards the barricade. The moment she perceived what he was about her bearing became less guarded, and she took up her own work with a spirit and energy which she had not shown since the adventure with the puff adder.

At her call to the noon meal, Blake took his time to respond, and when he at last came to join her, he was morose and taciturn. She met him with a smile, and exerted all her womanly tact to conciliate him.

"You must help me eat the egg," she said. "I've boiled it hard."

"Rather eat beef," he mumbled.

"But just to please me—when I've cooked it your way!"

He uttered an inarticulate sound which she chose to interpret as assent. The egg was already shelled. She cut it exactly in half, and served one of the pieces to him with a bit of warm fat and a pinch of salt. As he took the dish, he raised his sullen eyes to her face. She met his gaze with a look of smiling insistence.

"Come now," she said; "please don't refuse. I'm sorry I was so rude."

"Well, if you feel that way about it!—not that I care for fancy dishes," he responded gruffly.

"It would be missing half the enjoyment to eat such a delicacy without some one to share it," she said.

Blake looked away without answer. But she could see that his face was beginning to clear. Greatly encouraged, she chatted away as though they were seated at her father's dinner-table, and he was an elderly friend from the business world whom it was her duty to entertain.

For a while Blake betrayed little interest, confining himself to monosyllables except when he commented on the care with which she had cooked the various dishes. When she least expected, he looked up at her, his lips parted in a broad smile. She stopped short, for she had been describing her first social triumphs, and his untimely levity embarrassed her.

"Don't get mad, Miss Jenny," he said, his eyes twinkling. "You don't know how funny it seems to sit here and listen to you talking about those things. It's like serving up ice cream and onions in the same dish."

"I'm sure, Mr. Blake—"

"Beats a burlesque all hollow—Mrs. Sint-Regis-Waldoff's chop-sooey tea and young Mrs. Vandam-Jones's auto-cotillon—with us sitting here like troglodytes, chewing snake-poisoned antelope, and you in that Kundry dress—"

"Do you—I was not aware that you knew about music."

"Don't know a note. But give me a chance to hear good music, and I'm there, if I have to stand in the peanut gallery."

"Oh, I'm so glad! I'm very, very fond of music! Have you been to Bayreuth?"

"Where's that?"

"In Germany. It is where his operas are given as staged by Wagner himself. It is indescribably grand and inspiring—above all, the Parsifal!"

"I'll most certainly take that in, even if I have to cut short my engagement in this gee-lorious clime—not but what, when it comes to leopard ladies—" He paused, and surveyed her with frank admiration.

The blood leaped into her face.

"Oh!" she gasped, "I never dreamed that even such a man as you would compare me with—with a creature like that!"

"Such a man as me!" repeated Blake, staring. "What do you mean? I know I'm not much of a ladies' man; but to be yanked up like this when a fellow is trying to pay a compliment—well, it's not just what you'd call pleasant."

"I beg your pardon, Mr. Blake. I misunderstood. I—"

"That's all right, Miss Jenny! I don't ask any lady to beg my pardon. The only thing is I don't see why you should flare out at me that way."

For a full minute she sat, with down-bent head, her face clouded with doubt and indecision. At last she bravely raised her eyes to meet his.

"Do you wonder that I am not quite myself?" she asked. "You should remember that I have always had the utmost comforts of life, and have been cared for— Don't you see how terrible it is for me? And then the death of—of—"

"I can't be sorry for that!"

"But even you felt how terrible it was… and then— Oh, surely, you must see how—how embarrassing—"

It was Blake's turn to look down and hesitate. She studied his face, her bosom heaving with quick-drawn breath; but she could make nothing of his square jaw and firm-set lips. His eyes were concealed by the brim of his leaf hat. When he spoke, seemingly it was to change the subject: "Guess you saw me making my hut. I'm fixing it so it'll do me even when it rains."

Had he been the kind of man that she had been educated

to consider as alone entitled to the name of gentleman, she could have felt certain that he had intended the remark for a delicately worded assurance. But was Tom Blake, for all his blunt kindliness, capable of such tact? She chose to consider that he was.

"It's a cunning little bungalow. But will not the rain flood you out?"

"It's going to have a raised floor. You're more like to have the rain drive in on you again. I'll have to rig up a porch over your door. It won't do to stuff up the hole. You've little enough air as it is. But that can wait a while. There's other work more pressing. First, there's the barricade. By the time that's done, those hyena skins will be cured enough to use. I've got to have new trousers soon, and new shoes, too."

"I can do the sewing, if you will cut out the pattern."

"No; I'll take a stagger at it myself first. I'd rather you'd go egging. You need to run around more, to keep in trim."

"I feel quite well now, and I am growing so strong! The only thing is this constant heat."

"We'll have to grin and bear it. After all, it's not so bad, if only we can stave off the fever. Another reason I want you to go for eggs is that you can take your time about it, and keep a look-out for steamers."

"Then you think—?"

"Don't screw up your hopes too high. We've little show of being picked up by a chance boat on a coast with reefs like this. But I figure that if I was in your daddy's shoes, it'd be high time for me to be cabling a ship to run up from Natal, or down from Zanzibar, to look around for jettison, et cetera."

"I'm sure papa will offer a big reward."

"Second the motion! I've a sort of idea I wouldn't mind coming in for a reward myself."

"You? Oh, yes; to be sure. Papa is generous, and he will be grateful to any one who—"

"You think I mean his dirty money!" broke in Blake, hotly.

Her confusion told him that he had not been mistaken. His face, only a moment since bright and pleasant, took on its sullenest frown.

Miss Leslie rose hurriedly, and started along the cleft.

"Hello!" he called. "Not going for eggs now, are you?"

She did not reply.

"Hang it all, Miss Jenny! Don't go off like that."

"May I ask you to excuse me, Mr. Blake? Is that sufficient?"

"Sufficient? It's enough to give a fellow a chill! Come now; don't go off mad. You know I've a quick temper. Can't you make allowances?"

"You've—you've no right to look so angry, even if I did misunderstand you. You misunderstood me!" She caught herself up with a half sob. His silence gave her time to recover her composure. She continued with excessive politeness, "Need I repeat my request to be excused, Mr. Blake?"

"No; once is enough! But honest now, I didn't mean to be nasty."

"Good-day, Mr. Blake."

"Oh, da-darn it, good-day!" he groaned.

When, a few minutes later, she returned, he was gone. He did not come back until some time after dark, when she had withdrawn to her lean-to for the night. His hands were bleeding from thorn scratches; but after a hasty supper, he went back down the cleft to build up the new wall of the barricade with the great stack of fresh thorn-brush that he had gathered during the afternoon.

23

THE END OF THE WORLD

IN THE MORNING he met Miss Leslie with a sullen bearing, which, however, did not altogether conceal his desire to be on friendly terms. Having regained her self-control, she responded to this with such tact that by evening each felt more at ease in the new relationship, and Blake had lost every trace of his moroseness. The fact that both were passionately fond of music proved an immense help. It gave them an impersonal source of mutual sympathy and understanding,—a common meeting-ground in the world of art and culture, apart from and above the plane of their material wants.

Yet for all his enjoyment of the girl's wide knowledge of everything relating to music, Blake took care that their talks and discussions did not interfere with the activities of their primitive mode of life. As soon as he had finished with the barricade, he devoted himself to his tailoring and shoe-making; while Miss Leslie, between her cooking and wood-gathering and daily visits to the cliff for eggs, had much to occupy both her thoughts and her hands.

At first every ascent of the cliff was embittered by a painful consciousness of the cairn upon the north edge. Fortunately it was not in sight from the direct path to the headland, and, as she refrained from visiting it, the new happenings of her wild life soon thrust Winthrope and his death out of the foreground of her thoughts. Each day she had to nerve herself to meet the beaks and wings of the despoiled nest-owners; each day she looked with greater hope for the expected rescue ship, only to be increasingly disappointed.

But the hours she spent on the cliff crest after gathering the day's supply of eggs were not spent merely in watching and longing. The inconvenience of carrying the eggs in a handkerchief or in one of the heavy jars suggested a renewal of her attempt at basket-making. Memory, perseverance, and a trace of inventiveness enabled her to produce a small but serviceable hamper of split bamboo.

Encouraged by this success she gathered a quantity of tough, wiry grass, and wove a hat to take the place of the flimsy palm-leaf makeshift. The result was by no means satisfactory with regard to style, its shape being intermediate between a Mexican sombrero and a funnel; but aside from its appearance, she could not have wished for a more comfortable head-cover. Before showing it to Blake, she wove a second one for him, so that they were able to cast aside the grotesque, palm-leaf affairs at the same time.

The following morning Blake appeared in an outfit to match her leopard-skin dress. He had singed off the hair of the hide out of which he had made his moccasins, and his hyena-skin trousers quite matched the bristling stubble on his face.

"Hey, Miss Jenny!" he hailed; "what d' you think of this for fancy needlework?"

"Splendid! You're the very picture of an Argentine vaquero."

"Greaser?—ugh! Let me get back to the Weary Willy pants!"

"I mean you are very picturesque."

"That's it, is it? Glad I've got something to call your leopardine gown that won't make you huffy."

"We can at least call our costumes serviceable, and mine has proved much cooler than I expected."

"But our new hats beat all for that—regular sunshades. What do you say?—there's a good breeze— Let's take a hike."

"Not to the river! The very thought of that dreadful snake—"

"No; just the other way. I've been thinking for some time that we ought to run down to that south headland, and take a squint at the coast beyond. Ten to one, it's another stretch of swamps, but—"

"You think there is a chance we may find a town?"

"About one chance in a million, even for a native village. The slave trade wiped the niggers off this coast, and I guess those that hit out upcountry ran so hard they haven't been able to get back yet."

"But it has been years since the slave trade was forbidden."

"And they don't sell beer in Kansas—oh, no! I'll bet the dhows still slip over from Madagascar when the moon is in the right quarter. At any rate, niggers are mighty scarce or mighty shy around here. I've kept a watch for smoke, and haven't seen a suspicion of it anywhere. Maybe the swamps swing around inland and cut off this strip of coast.

It looked that way to me when I made that trip along the ridge. But there's a chance it used to be inhabited, and we may run across an abandoned village."

"I do not see that the discovery would do us any good."

"How about the chance of grain or bananas still growing? But that's all a guess. We're going because we need a change."

She nodded, and hastened to prepare breakfast, while he packed a skin bag with food, and examined the slender tips of his arrows. As a matter of precaution, he had been keeping them in the cigarette case, where the points would be certain of a coat of the sticky poison and at the same time guarded against inflicting a chance wound. But as he was now about to set out on a journey, he fitted tips into the heads of his two straightest shafts.

The morning was still fresh when they closed the barricade behind them and descended to the pool. There was no game in sight, but Blake had no wish to hunt at the commencement of the trip. The steady southwest wind had blown the sky clear of its malarial haze, and gave promise of a day which should know nothing of sultry calm—a day on which game would be hard to stalk, but one perfectly suited for a long tramp.

Mindful of ticks, Blake headed obliquely across to the beach. Once on the smooth, hard sand, they swung along at a brisk pace, light-hearted and keen with the spirit of adventure. Never had they felt more companionable. Miss Leslie laughed and chatted and sang snatches of songs, while Blake beat time with his club, or sought to whistle grand opera—he had healed his blistered lips some time before by liberal applications of antelope tallow.

Gulls and terns circled about them, or hovered over the water, ready to swoop down upon their finny prey. Sandpipers ran along the beach within a stone's throw, but the curlews showed their greater knowledge of mankind by keeping beyond gunshot.

Once a great flock of geese drove high overhead, their leader honking the alarm as they swept above the suspicious figures on the beach. Like the curlews, they had knowledge of mankind. But the flock of white pelicans which came sailing along in stately leisure on their immense wings floated past so low that Blake felt certain he could shoot one. He raised his bow and took aim, but refrained from shooting, at the thought that it might be a sheer waste of his precious poison.

A little later a herd of large animals appeared on the border of the grass jungle, but wheeled and dashed back into cover so quickly that Blake barely had time to make out that they were buffaloes—the first he had seen on this coast, but easily recognized by their resemblance to the Cape variety. Their flight gave him small concern; for the time being he was more interested in topography than game.

The southern headland now lay close before them, its seaward face rearing up sheer and lofty, but the approach behind running down in broken terraces. Mid-morning found the explorers at the foot of the ridge. Blake squinted up at the boulder-strewn slopes and the crannies of the broken ledges.

"Likely place for snakes, Miss Jenny," he remarked. "Guess I'd better lead."

Eager as she was to look over into the country beyond,

"It can't be that you want to go back to all those
society shams, after you've seen real life!"

the girl dropped into second place, and made no complaint about the wary slowness of her companion's advance. She found the most difficult parts of the ascent quite easy after her training on the tree-ladder. Blake could have taken ledges and all at a run, but as he mounted each terrace, he halted to spy out the ground before him. Like Miss Leslie, he was looking for snakes, though for an exactly opposite reason. He wished to add to the contents of the cigarette case.

Greatly to his disappointment and the girl's relief, neither snake nor sign of snake was to be seen all the way up the ridge. As they neared the crest Blake turned to offer her his hand up the last ledges, and in the instant they gained the top.

The wind, now freshening to a gale, struck the girl with such force that she would have been blown back down the ledges had not Blake clutched her wrist. Heedless alike of the painful grip which held her and of the gusts which tore at her skirt, the girl stood gazing out across the desolate swamps which stretched away to the southwest as far as the eye could see. She did not speak until Blake led her down behind the shelter of the crest ledges.

"What's the matter?" he demanded. "Didn't I warn you?"

She looked away to hide the tears which sprang into her eyes.

"I can't explain—only, it makes me feel so—so lonely!"

"Oh, come now, little woman; don't take on so!" he urged. "It might be a lot worse, you know. We've gotten along pretty well, considering."

"You have been very kind, Mr. Blake, and as you say, matters might have been worse. I do not forget how far more terrible was our situation the morning after the storm. Yet you must realize how disappointing it is to lose even the slightest hope of escape."

"Well, I don't know. If it wasn't for the fever that's bound to come with the rains, I, for one, would just as leave stick to this camp right along, providing the company don't change."

She turned upon him with flashing eyes, all thought of caution lost in her anger. "How dare you say such a thing? You are contemptible! I despise you!"

"My, Miss Jenny, but you are pretty when you get mad!" he exclaimed.

The answer took her completely aback. He was neither angry nor laughing at her, but met her defiant glance with candid, sober admiration. There was something more than admiration in his glowing eyes; yet she could not but see that her alarm had been baseless. His manner had never been more respectful. Suddenly she found that she could no longer meet his gaze. She looked away and stammered lamely, "You—you shouldn't say such things, you know."

"Why not? Hasn't everything been running smooth the last few days? Haven't we been good chummy comrades? Of course you've got the worst of the deal. I know I'm not much on fancy talk; but I like to hear it when I've a chance. I've led a lonesome sort of life since they did for my sisters— No; I'm not going to rake that up again. I'm only trying to give you an idea what it means to a fellow to be with a lady like you. May be it isn't polite to tell you all this, but it's just what I feel, and I never did amount to shucks as a liar."

"I believe I understand you, Mr. Blake, and I really feel highly complimented."

"No, you don't, any such thing, Miss Jenny. Own up, now! If I met you to-morrow on your papa's doorstep, you'd cut me cold."

"I should if you continued to be so rude. Have you no regard for my feelings? But here we are, talking nonsense, when we should be going—"

"Is it nonsense?" he broke in. "What does life mean, anyway? Here we can be true friends and comrades,—real, free living people. It can't be that you want to go back to all those society shams, after you've seen real life! As for me, what have I to gain by going back to the everlasting grind? I don't mind work; but when a man has nothing ahead to work for but a bank account, when it's grind, grind, grind till your head goes stale and all the world looks black, then there's no choice but throw up your job and go on a drunk, if you want to keep from a gun accident. Maybe you don't understand it. But that's what I've had to go through, time and again. Do you wonder I like to fancy an everlasting picnic here, with a little partner who wouldn't let me come within shouting distance of her in the land of lavender—trousers and peek-a-boos?"

"Mr. Blake, really you are most unjust! I could not be so—so ungrateful, after all your kindness. I—we should certainly be glad to number you among our friends."

"Drink and all, eh?"

"A man of your will-power has no need whatever to give way to such a habit."

"Course not, if he's got anything in sight worth while. Guess, though, my folks must have been poor white trash.

I never could go after money just for the fun of the game. No family, no friends, no—what-you-call-it?—culture— What's the use? I have a fair head for figures; but all the mathematics that I know I've had to catch hot off the bat. It's true I grubbed my C.E. out of a correspondence school; but a fellow has to have an all-round, crack-up education to put him where it's worth while."

"You still have time to work up. You are not much over thirty."

"Twenty-seven."

"Twenty-seven! I should have thought— What a hard life you must have had!"

"Hard work? Well, I suppose Panama did do for me some. But it wasn't so much that. Few fellows could hit up the pace I've set and come out at all."

"I do not understand."

"Just what you might expect of a fellow in my fix—all kinds of gamble and drink and—the rest of it."

Miss Leslie looked away, visibly distressed. She had not been reared after the French method. Young as she was, she had fluttered at will about the borders of the garden of vice, knowing well that the gaudy blossoms were lures to entice one into the pitfall. Yet never before had she caught so clear a glimpse of the slimy depths.

"That's it!" growled Blake. "Throw me down cold, just because I'm square enough to tell you straight out. You make me tired! I'm not one of the work-ox sort, that can chew the cud all the year round, and cork the blood out of their brains. I've got to cut loose from the infernal grind once in a while, and barring a chance now and then at opera, there's never been anything but a spree—"

"Oh, but that's so dreadfully shocking, Mr. Blake!"

"And then like all the other little hypocrites, you'll go and marry one of those swell dudes who's made that sort of thing his business, and everybody knows it, but it's all politely understood to've been done sub rosa, so it's all right, because he knows how to part his name in the middle and—"

"Please, please stop, Mr. Blake! You don't know how cruel you are!"

"Cruel? Suppose I told you about the millionaire cur that— Oh, now, don't go and cry! Please don't cry, Miss Jenny! I wouldn't hurt your feelings for the world! I didn't mean anything out of the way, really I didn't! It's only that when I get to thinking of—of things, it sets me half crazy. And now, can't you see how it's going to be ten times worse for me after—with you so altogether beyond me—" He stopped short, flushed, and stammered lamely, "I—I didn't mean to say that!"

She looked down, no less embarrassed.

"Please let us talk of something else," she murmured. "It has been such a pleasant morning, until you—until we began this silly discussion."

"All right, all right! Only mop up the dewdrops, and we'll turn on the sun machine. I really didn't mean to rip out that way at all. But, you see, the thing's been rankling in me ever since we came aboard ship at the Cape, and Winthrope and Lady Bayrose had my seat changed so I couldn't see you— Not that I hold anything against them now—"

"Mr. Blake, I suppose you know that this African coast is particularly dangerous for women. So far I have escaped the fever. But you yourself said that the longer the attack is delayed, the worse it will be."

Blake's face darkened, and he turned to stare inland along the ridge. She had flicked him on the raw, and he thought that she had done so intentionally.

"You think I haven't tried—that I've been shamming!" he burst out bitterly. "You're right. There's the one chance— But I couldn't leave you till the barricade was finished, and it's been only a few days since— All the same, I oughtn't to've waited a day. I'll start it to-morrow."

"What! Start what?"

"A catamaran. I can rig one up, in short order, that, with a skin sail and an outrigger, will do fairly well to coast along inside the reefs—barring squalls. Worst thing is that it's all a guess whether the nearest settlement is up the coast or down."

"And you can think of going, and leaving me all alone here!"

"That's better than letting you risk two-to-one chances on feeding the sharks."

"But you'd be risking it!"

Blake uttered a short harsh laugh.

"What's the difference?" He paused a moment; then added, with grim humor, "Anyway, they'll have earned a meal by the time they get me chewed up."

"You sha'n't go!"

"Oh, I don't know. We'll see about it to-morrow. There's a grove of cocoanuts yonder. Come on, and I'll get some nuts. I can't see any water around here, and it would be dry eating, with only the flask."

24

A LION LEADS THEM

THE PALM GROVE stood under the lee of the ridge, on a stretch of bare ground. Other than seaward, the open space was hemmed in by grass jungle, interspersed with clumps of thorn-brush. On the north side a jutting corner of the tall, yellow spear-grass curved out and around, with the point of the hook some fifty yards from the palms. Elsewhere the distance to the jungle was nearly twice as far.

Blake dropped the bag and his weapons, flung down his hat, and started up a palm shaft. The down-pointing bristles of his skin trousers aided his grip. Though the lofty crown of the palm was swaying in the wind, he reached the top and was down again before Miss Leslie had arranged the contents of the lunch bag.

"Guess you're not extra hungry," he remarked.

She made no response.

"Mad, eh? Well, toss me the little knife. Mine has got too good a meat-edge to spoil on these husks."

"It was very kind of you to climb for the nuts, and the wind blowing so hard up there," she said, as she handed over the penknife. "I am not angry. It is only that I feel tired and depressed. I hope I am not going to be—"

"No; you're not going to have the fever, or any such

thing! You're played out, that's all. I'm a fool for bringing you so far. You'll be all right after you eat and rest. Here; drink this cocoa milk."

She drained the nut, and upon his insistence, made a pretence at eating. He was deceived until, with the satisfying of his first keen hunger, he again became observant.

"Say, that won't do!" he exclaimed. "Look at your bowl. You haven't nibbled enough to keep a mouse alive."

"Really, I am not hungry. But I am resting."

"Try another nut. I'll have one ready in two shakes."

He caught his hat, which was dragging past in a downward eddy of the wind, and weighted it with a cocoanut. He wedged another nut between his knees, and bent over it, tearing at the husk. It took him only a few moments to strip the fibre from the end and gouge open the germ hole. He held out the nut, and glanced up to meet her smile of acceptance.

She was staring past him, her eyes wide with terror, and the color fast receding from her face.

"What in— Another snake?" he demanded, twisting warily about to glare at the ground behind him.

"There—over in the grass!" she whispered, "It looked out at me with terrible, savage eyes!"

"Snake?—that far off?"

"No, no!—a monster—a huge, fierce beast!"

"Beast?" echoed Blake, grasping his bow and arrows. "Where is he? Maybe only one of these African buffaloes. How'd he look?—horns?"

"I—I didn't see any. It was all shaggy, and yellow like the grass, and terrible eyes— *Oh!*"

The girl's scream was met by a ferocious, snarling roar,

so deep and prolonged that the air quivered and the very ground seemed to shake.

"God!—a lion!" cried Blake, the hair on his bare head bristling like a startled animal's.

He turned squarely about toward the ridge, his bow half drawn. Had the lion shown himself then, Blake would have shot on the instant. As it was, the beast remained behind the screening border of grass, where he could watch his intended quarry without being seen in turn. The delay gave Blake time for reflection. He spoke sharply, as it were biting off his words: "Hit out. I'll stop the bluffer."

"I can't. Oh, I'm afraid!"

Again the hidden beast gave voice to his mighty rumbling challenge. Still he did not appear, and Blake attempted a derisive jeer: "Hey, there, louder! We've not run yet! It's all right, little woman. The skulking sneak is trying to bluff us. 'Fraid to come out if we don't stampede. He'll make off when he finds we don't scare. Lions never tackle men in the daytime. Just keep cool a while. He'll—"

"Look!—there to the right!—I saw him again! He's creeping around! See the grass move!"

"That's only the wind. It eddies down— God! he is stalking around. Trying to take us from behind—curse him! He may get me, but I'll get him too,—the dirty sneak!"

The blood had flowed back into Blake's face, and showed on each cheek in a little red patch. His broad chest rose and fell slowly to deep respirations; his eyes glowed like balls of white-hot steel. He drew his bow a little tauter, and wheeled slowly to keep the arrow pointed at the slight wave in the grass which marked the stealthy movements of the lion. Miss Leslie, more terrified with every added

"Tom!" she cried, struggling to her knees,—"Tom!"

moment of suspense, cringed around, that she might keep him between her and the hidden beast.

Minute after minute dragged by. Only a man of Blake's obstinate, sullen temperament could have withstood the strain and kept cool. Even he found the impulse to leap up and run all but irresistible. Miss Leslie crouched behind him, no more able to run than a mouse with which a cat has been playing.

Once they caught a glimpse of the sinuous, tawny form gliding among the leafless stems of a thorn clump. Blake took quick aim; but the outlines of the beast were indistinct and the range long. He hesitated, and the opportunity was lost.

Yard by yard they watched the slight swaying of the grass tops which betrayed the cautious advance of the grim stalker. The beast did not roar again. Having failed to flush his game, he was seeking to catch them off their guard, or perhaps was warily taking stock of the strange creatures, whose like he had never seen.

Now and then there was a pause, and the grass tops swayed only to the down-puffs of the heightening gale. At such moments the two grew rigid, watching and waiting in breathless suspense. They could see, as distinctly as though there had been no screening grass, the baleful eyes of the huge cat and the shaggy forebody as the beast stood still and glared out at them.

Then the sinuous wave would start on again around the grass border, and Blake would draw in a deep breath and mutter a word of encouragement to the girl: "Look, now—the dirty sneak! Trying to give us the creeps, is he? I'll creeps him! 'Fraid to show his pretty mug!"

Not until the beast had circled half around the glade did his purpose flash upon Blake. With the wariness of all savage hunters, the animal had marked out the spur of jungle on the north side, where he could creep closer to his quarry before leaping from cover.

"The damned sneak!" growled Blake. "You there, Jenny?"

She could not speak, but he heard her gasp.

"Brace up, little woman! Where's your grit? You're out of this deal, anyway. He'll choke to death swallowing me— But say; couldn't you manage to shin up a palm, twenty feet or so, and hang on for a couple of minutes!"

"I—can't move—I am—"

"Make a try! It'll give me a run for my money. I'll take the next elevator after you. That'll bring the bluffer out on the hot-foot. I slip a surprise between his ribs, and we view the scenery while he's passing in his checks. Come; make a spurt! He's around the turn, and getting nearer every step."

"I can't—Tom,—there is no need that both of us— You climb up—"

He turned about as the meaning of her whisper dawned upon him. Her eyes were shining with the ecstasy of self-sacrifice. It was only the glance of an instant; then he was again facing the jungle.

"God! You think I'd do that!"

She made no reply. There was a pause. Blake—crouched on one knee, tense and alert—waited until the sinister wave was advancing into the point of the incurved jungle. Then he spoke, in a low, even tone: "Feel if my glass is there."

Her hand reached around and pressed against the fob pocket which he had sewn in the belt of his skin trousers.

"Right. Now slip my club up under my elbow—big end. Lick on the nose'll stop a dog or a bull. It's a chance."

She thrust the club under his right elbow, and he gripped it against his side.

At that moment the lion bounded from cover, with a roar like a clap of thunder. Blake sprang erect. The beast checked himself in the act of leaping, and crouched with his great paws outstretched, every hooked claw thrust out, ready to tear and mangle. In two or three bounds he could have leaped upon Blake and crushed him with a single stroke of his paw. As he rose to repeat his deafening roar, it seemed to Blake that he stood higher than a horse—that his mouth gaped wide as the end of a hogshead. And yet the beast stood hesitating, restrained by brute dread of the unknown. Never before had any animal that he had hunted reared up to meet his attack in this strange manner.

"Lie flat!" commanded Blake; "lie flat, and don't move! I'm going to call his bluff. Keep still till the poison gets in its work. I'll keep him busy long as I can. When it's over, hit out for home along the beach. Keep inside the barricade, and watch all you can from the cliffs. Might light a fire up there nights. There's sure to be a steamer before long—"

"Tom!" she cried, struggling to her knees,—"Tom!"

But he did not pause or look around. He was beginning to circle slowly to the left across the open ground, in a spiral curve that would bring him to the edge of the jungle within thirty yards of the lion. There was red now showing in his eyes. His hair was bristling, no longer with fear, but with sheer brute fury; his lips were drawn back from the clenched teeth; his nostrils distended and quivering; his forehead wrinkled like that of an angry mastiff. His look was more ferocious than that of the snarling beast he faced. All the primeval in him was roused. He was become a man of the Cave Age. He went to meet death, his mind and body aflame with fierce lust to kill.

The lion stilled his roars, and crouched as if to spring, snarling and grinning with rage and uncertainty. His eyes, unaccustomed to the glare of the mid-day sun, blinked incessantly, though he followed the man's every movement, his snarls deepening into growls at the slightest change of attitude.

In his blind animal rage, Blake had forgotten that the purpose of his lateral advance was to place as great a distance as possible between him and the girl before the clash. Yet instinct kept him moving along his spiral course, on the chance that he might catch his foe off his guard.

Suddenly the lion half rose and stretched forward, sniffing. There was an uneasy whining note in his growls. Blake let the club slip from beneath his arm, and drew his bow until the arrow-head lay upon his thumb. His outstretched arm was rigid as a bar of steel. So tense and alert were all his nerves that he knew he could drive home both arrows, and still have time to swing his club before the beast was upon him.

A puff of wind struck against his back, and swept on to the nostrils of the lion, laden with the odor of man. The beast uttered a short, startled roar, and whirling about, leaped away into the jungle so quickly that Blake's arrow flashed past a full yard behind.

The second arrow was on the string before the first had struck the ground. But the lion had vanished in the grass. With a yell, Blake dashed on across to the nearest point of the jungle. As he ran, he drew the burning-glass from his fob, and flipped it open, ready for use. If the lion had turned behind the sheltering grass stems, he was too cowardly to charge out again. Within a minute the jungle border was a wall of roaring flame.

The grass, long since dead, and bone-dry with the days of tropical sunshine since the cyclone, flared up before the wind like gunpowder. Even against the wind the fire ate its way along the ground with fearful rapidity, trailing behind it an upwhirling vortex of smoke and flame. No living creature could have burst through that belt of fire.

A wave of fierce heat sent Blake staggering back, scorched and blistered. There was no exultance in his bearing. For the moment all thought of the lion was swallowed up in awe of his own work. He stared at the hell of leaping, roaring flames from beneath his upraised arm. To the north sparks and lighted wisps of grass driven by the gale had already fired the jungle half way to the farther ridge.

Step by step Blake drew back. His heel struck against something soft. He looked down, and saw Miss Leslie lying on the sand, white and still. She had fainted, overcome by fear or by the unendurable heat. The heat must have stupefied him as well. He stared at her, dull-eyed, wondering if she was dead. His brain cleared. He sprang over to where the flask lay beside the remnants of the lunch.

He was dashing the last drops of the tepid water in her face, when she moaned, and her eyelids began to flutter. He flung down the flask, and fell to chafing her wrist.

"Tom!" she moaned.

"Yes, Miss Jenny, I'm here. It's all right," he answered.

"Have I had a sunstroke? Is that why it seems so— I can hardly breathe—"

"It's all right, I tell you. Only a little bonfire I touched off. Guess you must have fainted, but it's all right now."

"It was silly of me to faint. But when I saw that dreadful thing leap—" She faltered, and lay shuddering. Fearful that she was about to swoon again, Blake slapped her hand between his palms with stinging force.

"You're it!" he shouted. "The joke's on you! Kitty jumped just the other way, and he won't come back in a hurry with that fire to head him off. Jump up now, and we'll do a jig on the strength of it."

She attempted a smile, and a trace of color showed in her cheeks. With an idea that action would further her recovery, he drew her to a sitting position, stepped quickly behind, and, with his hands beneath her elbows, lifted her upright. But she was still too weak and giddy to stand alone. As he released his grip, she swayed and would have fallen had he not caught her arm.

"Steady!" he admonished. "Brace up; you're all right."

"I'm—I'm just a little dizzy," she murmured, clinging to his shoulder. "It will pass in a minute. It's so silly, but I'm that way— Tom, I—I think you are the bravest man—"

"Yes, yes—but that's not the point. Leave go now, like a sensible girl. It's about time to hit the trail."

He drew himself free, and without a glance at her blushing face, began to gather up their scattered outfit. His hat lay where he had weighted it down with the cocoanut. He tossed the nut into the skin bag, and jammed the hat on his head, pulling the brim far down over his eyes. When he had fetched his club, he walked back past the girl, with his eyes averted.

"Come on," he muttered.

The scarlet in the girl's cheeks swept over her whole face in a burning wave, which ebbed slowly and left her color-less. Blake had started off without a backward glance. She gazed about with a bewildered look at the palms and the barren ridge and the fiery tidal wave of flame. Her gaze came back to Blake, and she followed him.

Within a short distance she found herself out of the shel-tering lee of the ridge. The first wind gust almost overthrew her. She could never have walked against such a gale; but with the wind at her back she was buoyed up and borne along as though on wings. Her sole effort was to keep her foothold. Had it been their morning trip, she could have cried out with joy and skipped along before the gusts like a school-girl. Now she walked as soberly as the wind would permit, and took care not to lessen the distance between herself and Blake.

Mile by mile they hastened back across the plain,—on their right the blue sea of water, with its white-caps and spray; on their left the yellow sea of fire, with its dun fog of smoke.

Once only had Blake looked back to see if the girl was following. After that he swung along, with down-bent head, his gaze upon the ground. Even when he passed in under the grove and around the pool to the foot of the cleft, he began the ascent without waiting to assist her up the break in the path. The girl came after, her lips firm, her eyes bright and expectant. She drew herself up the ledge as though she had been bred to mountain climbing.

Inside the barricade Blake was waiting to close the

opening. She crept through, and rose to catch him by the sleeve.

"Tom, look at me," she said. "Once I was most unjust to you in my thoughts. I wronged you. Now I must tell you that I think you are the bravest—the noblest man—"

"Get away!" he exclaimed, and he shook off her hand roughly. "Don't be a fool! You don't know what you're talking about."

"But I do, Tom. I believe that you are—"

"I'm a blackguard—do you hear?"

"No blackguard is brave. The way you faced that terrible beast—"

"Yes, blackguard—to've gone and shown to you that I— to've let you say a single word— Can't you see? Even if I'm not what you call a gentleman, I thought I knew how any man ought to treat a woman—but to go and let you know, before we'd got back among people!"

"But—but, Tom, why not, if we—"

"No!" he retorted harshly. "I'm going now to pile up wood on the cliff for a beacon fire. In the morning I'll start making that catamaran—"

"No, you shall not— You shall not go off, and leave me, and—and risk your life! I can't bear to think of it! Stay with me, Tom—dear! Even if a ship never came—"

He turned resolutely, so as not to see her blushing face.

"Come now, Miss Leslie," he said in a dry, even tone; "don't make it so awfully hard. Let's be sensible, and shake hands on it, like two real comrades—"

She struck frantically at his outstretched hand.

"Keep away—I hate you!" she cried.

Before he could speak, she was running up the cleft.

25

IN DOUBLE SALVATION

WHEN, AN HOUR or more after dawn the next morning, the girl slowly drew open her door and came out of
the cave, Blake was nowhere in sight. She sighed, vastly
relieved, and hastened across to bathe her flushed face in
the spring. Stopping every few moments to listen for his
step down the cleft, she gathered up a hamper of food and
fled to the tree-ladder.

As she drew herself up on the cliff, she noticed a thin
column of smoke rising from the last smouldering brands
of a beacon fire that had been built in the midst of the bird
colony, on the extreme outer edge of the headland. She
did not, however, observe that, while the smoke column
streamed up from the fire directly skyward, beyond it there
was a much larger volume of smoke, which seemed to have
eddied down the cliff face and was now rolling up into
view from out over the sea. She gave no heed to this, for
the sight of the beacon had instantly alarmed her with the
possibility that Blake was still on the headland, and would
imagine that she was seeking him.

She paused, her cheeks aflame. But the only sign of
Blake that she could see was the fire itself. She reflected
that he might very well have left before dawn. As likely as

not, he had descended at the north end of the cleft, and had gone off to the river to start his catamaran. At the thought all the color ebbed from her cheeks and left her white and trembling. Again she stood hesitating. With a sigh she started on toward the signal staff.

She was close upon the border of the bird colony, when Blake sat up from behind a ledge, and she found herself staring into his blinking eyes.

"Hello!" he mumbled drowsily. He sprang up, wide awake, and flushing with the guilty consciousness of what he had done. "Look at the sun—way up! Didn't mean to oversleep, Miss Leslie. You see I was up pretty late, tending the beacon. But of course that's no excuse—"

"Don't!" she exclaimed. There were tears in her eyes; yet she smiled as she spoke. "I know what you mean by 'pretty late.' You've been up all night."

"No, I haven't. Not all night—"

"To be sure! I quite understand, Mr. Thomas Blake!... Now, sit down, and eat this luncheon."

"Can't. Haven't time. I've got to get to the river and set to work. I'll get some jerked beef and eat it on the way. You see—"

"Tom!" she protested.

"It's for you," he rejoined, and his lips closed together resolutely.

He was stepping past her, when over the seaward edge of the cliff there came a sound like the yell of a raging sea-monster.

"Siren!" shouted Blake, whirling about.

The cloud of smoke beyond the cliff end was now rolling up more to the left. He dashed away towards the north edge of the cliff as though he intended to leap off into space. The girl ran after him as fast as she could over the loose stones. Before she had covered half the distance she saw him halt on the very brink of the cliff, and begin to wave and shout like a madman. A few steps farther on she caught sight of the steamer. It was lying close in, only a little way off the north point of the headland.

Even as she saw the vessel, its siren responded to Blake's wild gestures with a series of joyous screams. There could be no mistake. He had been seen. Already they were letting go anchor, and there was a little crowd of men gathering about one of the boats. Blake turned and started on a run for the cliff. But Miss Leslie darted before him, compelling him to halt.

"Wait!" she cried, her eyes sparkling with happy tears. "Tom, it's come now. You needn't—"

"Let me by! I'm going to meet them. I want to—"

But she put her hands upon his shoulders.

"Tom!" she whispered, "let it be now, before any one— anything can possibly come between us! Let it be a part of our life here—here, where I've learned how brave and true a real man can be!"

"And then have him prove himself a sneak!" he cried. "No; I won't, Jenny! I've got you to think of. Wait till I've seen your father. Ten to one, he'll not hear of it—he'll cut you off without a cent. Not but what I'd be glad myself; but you're used to luxuries, girlie, and I'm a poor man. I can't give them to you—"

She laid a hand on his mouth, and smiled up at him in tender mockery.

"Come, now, Mr. Blake; you're not very complimentary.

After surviving my cooking all these weeks, don't you think I might do, at a pinch, for a poor man's wife!"

"No, Jenny!" he protested, trying to draw back. "You oughtn't to decide now. When you get back among your friends, things may look different. Think of your society friends! Wait till you see me with other men—gentlemen! I'm just a rough, uncultured, ordinary—"

"Hush!" she cried, and she again placed her hand on his mouth. "You sha'n't say such cruel things about Tom—my Tom—the man I trust—that I—"

Her arms slipped about his neck, and her eyes shone up into his with tender radiance.

"Don't!" he begged hoarsely. "'T ain't fair! I—I can't stand it!"

"The man I love!" she whispered.

He crushed her to him in his great arms.

"My little girl!—dear little girl!" he repeated, and he pressed his lips to her hair.

She snuggled her face closer against his shoulder, and replied in a very small voice, "I—I suppose you know that ship captains can m-marry people."

"But I haven't even a job yet!" he exclaimed. "Suppose your father—"

"Please listen!" she pleaded. There was a sound like suppressed sobbing.

"What is it?" he ventured, and he listened, greatly perturbed. The muffled voice sounded very meek and plaintive: "I'll try to do my part, Mr. Blake,—really I will! I—I hope we can manage to struggle along—somehow. You know, I have a little of my own. It's only three—three million; but—"

"What!" he demanded, and he held her out at arm's length, to stare at her in frowning bewilderment. "If I'd known that, I'd—"

"You'd never have given me a chance to—to propose to you, you dear old silly!" she cried, her eyes dancing with tender mirth. "See here!"

She turned from him, and back again, and held up a withered, crumpled flower. He looked, and saw that it was the amaryllis blossom.

"You—kept it!"

"Because—because, even then, down in the bottom of my heart, I had begun to realize—to know what you were like—and of course that meant— Tom, tell me! Do you think I'm utterly shameless? Do you blame me for being the one to—to—"

"Blame you!" he cried. He paused to put a finger under her chin and raise her down-bent face. His eyes were very blue, but there was a twinkle in their depths. "Oh, yes; it was dreadful, wasn't it? But I guess I've no complaint to file just now."

OUT OF THE PRIMITIVE

To my friend James Collier

1

THE CASTAWAYS

THE SECOND NIGHT north of the Zambezi, as well as the first, the little tramp rescue steamer had run out many miles into the offing and laid-to during the hours of darkness. The vicinity of the coral reefs that fringe the southeast coast of Africa is decidedly undesirable on moonless nights.

When the Right Honorable the Earl of Avondale came out of his close, hot stateroom into the refreshing coolness that preceded the dawn, the position of the Southern Cross, scintillating in the blue-black sky to port, told him that the steamer was headed in for the coast. The black surface of the quiet sea crinkled with lines of phosphorescent light under the ruffling of the faint breeze, which crept offshore heavy with the stench of rotting vegetation. It was evident that the ship was already close in again to the Mozambique swamps.

Lord James sniffed the rank odor, and hastened to make his way forward to the bridge. As he neared the foot of the ladder, his resilient step and the snowy whiteness of his linen suit attracted the attention of the watcher above on the bridge.

"Good-morning, m' lord," the officer called down in a bluff but respectful tone. "You're on deck early."

"Hullo, Meggs! That you?" replied his lordship, mounting the steps with youthful agility. "It seems you're still earlier."

"Knowing your lordship's anxiety, I decided to run in, so that we could renew the search with the first glimmer of daylight," explained the skipper. "We're now barely under headway. According to the smell, we're as near those reefs as I care to venture in the dark."

"Right-o! We'll lose no time," approved the young earl. "D'you still think to-day is apt to tell the tale, one way or the other?"

"Aye, your lordship. I may be mistaken; but, as I told you, reckoning together all the probabilities, we should to-day cover the spot where the *Impala* must have been driven on the coral—that is, unless she foundered in deep water."

"But, man, you said that was not probable."

"A new boat should be able to stand the racking of half a dozen cyclones, m' lord, without straining a bottom plate. No; it's far more probable she shook off her screw, or something went wrong with the steering gear or in the engine room. I've recharted her probable course and that of the cyclone. It was as well for us to begin our search at the Zambezi, as I told your lordship. But if to-day we fail to find where she piled her bones on the coral, it's odds we'll not to-morrow. On beyond, at Port Mozambique, we got only the north rim of the storm. I put in there for shelter when the barometer dropped."

"That was on your run south. Glad I had the luck to chance on a man who knows the coast as you do," remarked

Lord James. "Look at those steamers Mr. Leslie chartered by cable—a good week the start of us, and still beating the coverts down there along Sofala! Wasting time! If only I'd not gone off on that shunt to India— And they six weeks in these damnable swamps—if they won ashore at all! You still believe they had a chance of that?"

"Aye. As I explained to your lordship, if the *Impala* hadn't lost all her boats before she struck, there's a fair probability that the water inside the reefs—"

"Yes, yes, to be sure! If there was the slightest chance for any one aboard—Lady Bayrose, Miss Leslie and their maids, the only women passengers, and a British ship! Everything must have been done to save them. While Tom—he'd be sure to make the shore, if that was within the bounds of possibility. Yet even if they were cast up alive—six weeks on the vilest stretch of coast between Zanzibar and the Zambezi! They may be dying of the fever now—this very hour! Deuce take it, man! d'you wonder I'm impatient?"

"Aye, m'lord! But here's the dawn, and McPhee is keeping up a full head of steam. We'll soon be doing seven knots."

As he spoke, the skipper turned to step into the pilot house. Lord James faced about to the eastern sky, where the gray dawn was beginning to lessen the star-gemmed blackness above the watery horizon. Swiftly the faint glow brightened and became tinged with pink. The day was approaching with the suddenness of the tropical sunrise. In quick succession, the pink shaded to rose, the rose to crimson and scarlet splendor; and then the sun came leaping above the horizon, to flood sea and sky with its dazzling effulgence.

Captain Meggs had entered the pilot house in the blackness of night. He came out in the full glare of day. Lord James had turned his back to the sun. He was staring at the bank of white mist that, less than two miles to westward, shrouded the swampy coast. Meggs had brought out two pairs of binoculars, one of which he handed to his charterer.

"Your lordship sees," he remarked. "We're none too far out from the reefs."

"Beastly mist!" complained Lord James, his handsome high-bred face creased with impatience and anxiety. "D'you fancy we're anywhere near the islet from which we put off last evening?"

"I've tried to hold our position, m'lord. But these Mozambique Channel currents are so strong, and shift so with the tides, we may have been either set back or ahead."

Already the bank of morning mist was beginning to break up and melt away under the fervent rays of the sun. The young earl raised his glasses and gazed southwards along the face of the dissolving curtain. Through and between the ghostly wreaths and wisps of vapor he could see the winged habitants of the swamps—flamingoes, cranes, pelicans, ibises, storks, geese, all the countless tropical waterfowl—swimming and wading about the reedy lagoons or circling up to fly to other feeding grounds. Opposite the steamer the glasses showed with startling distinctness a number of hideous crocodiles crawling out on a slimy mudbank to bask in the sunshine. But nowhere could the searcher discern a trace of man or of man's habitation.

"Gad! not a sign! Rotten luck!" he muttered.

He turned and swept the four-mile curve of coast around to the north-northeast. Suddenly he stiffened and held the glasses fixed.

"Look!" he cried. "Off there to the northwards—cliffs!"

"Cliffs? Aye, a headland," confirmed the skipper.

"Put about for it immediately," directed Lord James. "If they were cast up here, they'd not have lingered in these vile bogs—would have made for the high ground."

Meggs nodded, and called the order to the steersman. The ship's bows swung around, and the little steamer was soon scuttling upcoast towards the headland, along the outer line of reefs, at a speed of seven knots.

From the first, Lord James held his glasses fixed on the barren guano-whitened ledges of the headland. But though he could discern with quickly increasing distinctness the seabirds that soared about the cliff crest and nested in its crevices, he perceived no sign of any signal such as castaways might be expected to place on so prominent a height.

When, after a full half-hour's run, the steamer skirted along the edge of the reefs, close in under the seaward face of the headland, the searcher at last lowered his binoculars, bitterly disappointed.

"Not a trace—not a trace!" he complained. "If they've been here, they've either gone inland or—we're too late! Six weeks—starvation—fever!"

Meggs shook his head reassuringly. "The top of the headland may be inaccessible, m'lord. We may find that they—Heh! what's that?"

He leaned forward to peer through his glasses at a

second headland that was swinging into view around the corner of the cliffs.

"*Smoke!*" he cried. "*Smoke!—and a flag!*"

"Gad!" murmured Lord James, hastily bringing his own glasses to bear.

The second headland was about five miles away. The thin column of smoke that was ascending from its crest near the outer end, could plainly be seen with the naked eye. But a sunlit cloud beyond necessitated the full magnifying power of the binoculars to disclose the white signal flag that flapped lazily on a slender staff near the beacon.

Lord James drew in a deep breath, and his gray eyes glowed with hope. Here was evidence that not all aboard the wrecked or foundered *Impala* had been lost.

"Meggs," he cried, "you're the one and only skipper! It must be their signal—it is their signal! But which of them?—who went under and who escaped!—Miss Genevieve? Tom?"

"This Mr. Blake?" ventured Meggs. "I take it, he's some relation to your lordship."

"No; chum—American engineer. Gad! if he went down! But it's impossible— Most resourceful man I ever knew. He must have won ashore with the others. And the women—a British captain! It must be we'll find crew and all safe!"

"Not on this coast," replied Meggs. "They'd have lost most their boats before the *Impala* struck."

"In that event—Deuce take it! will we never get there? If I had my motor-boat now! By Jove, this stretch here between the headlands is not swamp. It's dry plain—and black. Been burnt over. There's a place—tree-trunks still

smouldering. The grass has been fired within the last day
or two."

"No one in sight as yet, on the cliffs," said the skipper,
who had continued to scrutinize the northern headland.
"No watch above; no sign of any one or any camp below.
Must all be around on the far side. We'll clear the point,
and run in through the first break in the reefs."

"If they fail to show up on this side," qualified Lord
James, slowly sweeping the cliffs from foot to crest and
inland along the dry fire-blackened plain.

About half a mile from the beach the wall of rock was
cleft by a wooded ravine that ran up through the cliff ridge.
At its foot was a grove of trees whose bright green foliage seemed to indicate an abundance of water. Above, a
gigantic baobab tree towered out of the cleft and upreared
its enormous cabbage-shaped crown high over the crest
of the ridge.

In the midst of the general barrenness and aridity, the
verdant oasis of the ravine appeared to be the most certain
place to look for the castaways. Lord James fancied that he
could discern a slight haze of smoke rising out of the cleft
beneath the baobab. But if there was a camp in the cleft
bottom, it was hidden from view by the trees and cliff walls.
The only certain sign of man within sight was the signal
flag and the smoke of the smouldering fire in the midst
of the seabird colony near the outer end of the cliff crest.

The steamer was gliding along, with slackened headway,
close in under the headland, when a breath of air opened
out the folds of the tattered white flag. Meggs had been
watching it through his binoculars. He lowered the glasses,

and remarked knowingly: "Thought so. That's no ship's canvas. It's linen or duck— A woman's skirt ripped open."

"What! Then at least one of the women got ashore!"

"Aye. But d' you make out how that cloth is lashed to the bamboo? It was knotted on by a landsman. We'll find neither officers nor crew among the survivors."

The steamer was now opposite the face of the headland, Meggs sprang into the pilot house. Within the next few moments the speed of the vessel fell off to less than a knot. Slowly the old steamer swung her bows around towards the shore and began feeling her way into a narrow gap through the half hidden barrier of the reefs, which here were merged into a single line.

For the time being all the attention of Meggs was concentrated upon the safe conning of his ship through the dangerous passage. It was otherwise with Lord James. The last two shiplengths before the turn had opened up the view around the north corner of the headland. From the flank of the cliff ridge a wedge of brush-dotted plain extended a quarter-mile or so to a dense high jungle bordering a small river. The first glance had shown his lordship that it was of no use to look beyond the river. The coast trended away northwards in another vast stretch of fetid swamps and slimy lagoons.

With almost feverish eagerness, he turned to scan the little plain. First to catch his eye were a dozen or more graceful animals dashing away from the shore in panic-stricken flight. He turned his glasses upon them and saw that they were antelope. This was not encouraging. That the timid animals had been feeding in the vicinity of a human habitation a full hour after dawn was not probable. Nor did a careful search of the plain through the glasses disclose any sign of a hut or tent or the smoke of a camp-fire.

An order from Meggs preparatory for letting go anchor roused Lord James from his momentary pause. He faced the skipper, who was leaning from a window of the pilot house.

"Sound your siren, man!" he exclaimed. "There's no camp in sight. Yet they must be within hearing."

Meggs nodded, called an order for the lowering of a boat, and drew back into the pilot house. As he reappeared in the doorway, to step out on the bridge, the tramp's siren shrilled a blast loud enough to carry for miles. It echoed and re-echoed along the cliff walls, and was flung back upon the little steamer in a deafening blare.

Lord James turned to sweep the border of the river jungle with his glasses. A herd of fat ungainly hippopotami, on the bar out beyond the mangroves of the river mouth, fixed his gaze. But a moment afterwards one of the sailors in the bows pointed upwards and yelled excitedly: "Hi! hi!—there aloft! Lookut th' bloomin' mad 'un!"

At last—one of the castaways! High above, on the very brink of the precipice, near the outer end of the headland, a man stood waving down to the ship in wild excitement.

Lord James hastily focussed his glasses upon the beckoner. Seen through their powerful lenses, he seemed to leap to within a few feet—so near that Lord James could see the heaving of his broad chest under the tattered flannel shirt as he flung his arms about his head and bellowed down at the steamer in half frantic joy.

The looker wasted no second glance on the rude trousers of spotted hyena skin or the big lean body of the castaway.

Neither the wild whirling of the sun-blackened arms nor the bristly stubble of a six weeks' growth of beard could prevent him from instantly recognizing the face of his friend.

"Tom!—Tom!" he hailed. "Hullo! hullo, old man! Come down!"

Even as he cried out he realized that he could neither be heard nor recognized at so great a distance. Though the binoculars enabled him to see his friend with such wonderful distinctness, the deep shouts that the other was uttering were hardly audible above the clatter aboard the steamer. But now the ship's siren began to answer the hails of the castaway with a succession of joyous shrieks.

In the same moment Lord James perceived that a second castaway—a woman—was running forward along the crest of the headland. Fearlessly she came darting down the broken ledges, to stand on the cliff edge close beside the man. Lord James stared wonderingly at her dainty girlish form, clad in a barbaric costume of leopard skin. Her bare arms, slender from privation and burned brown by the sun, were upraised in graceful greeting above the sensitive high-bred face and its crown of soft brown hair.

"Genevieve!" murmured the earl. "What luck! Gad! what luck! Even if Hawkins went to the bottom and took the jewels with him! She's safe—both of 'em safe! Hey! what's that? Signalling towards the far side— There he bolts, and she after him! Couldn't run that way if they had the fever!"

He whirled about and sprang to descend the ladder, but paused to direct the skipper. "I'll command the boat. Men are not to land. D'you take me? There's at least one of the ladies here. Have a sling ready, and tell the stewardess her services will soon be required."

Before Meggs could reply, he was down the ladder and darting across to the side. But there he turned and ran aft to the cabin. The stewardess, a buxom Englishwoman, stood at the head of the companionway, gazing towards the cliff top. At his order, she followed him below. After several minutes he reappeared with a lady's dust-coat folded over his arm. The boat was already lowered and manned. He swung himself outboard and went down the tackle hand under hand.

As he dropped lightly into the sternsheets beside the cockswain he signed the men to thrust off. The boat shot out across the still water, and headed shorewards on a slant for the south corner of the headland. Urged on by their impatient passenger, the rowers bent to their oars with a will, despite the broiling heat of the sun in the dead calm air under the lee of the cliffs.

They were well in to the shore before the cockswain discovered a submerged ledge that ran out athwart their course almost to the coral reefs. This compelled them to put about and follow the ledge until they could round its outer end. As the boat at last cleared the obstruction and headed in again for the shore, the south flank of the cliffs came into view.

A short distance inland, the two castaways that had appeared on the cliff top were running towards the beach, the girl clinging to the hand of the man.

"Give way! give way, men!" urged Lord James. "At least let's not keep them waiting!"

2

TWO–AND ONE

SPURRED TO THEIR utmost, the oarsmen drove the boat shorewards so swiftly that it was less than thirty yards out when the castaways came flying out the rocky slope of the cliff foot and scrambled down to the water's edge.

Lord James sprang up and waved his yachting cap.

"Miss Leslie!—Tom, old man!" he joyously hailed them. "You're safe!—both safe!"

"Good Lord! That you, Jimmy?" shouted back the man, "Well, of all the— Hey! down brakes! 'Ware rocks!"

At the warning, the boat's crew backed water and came on inshore with more caution. Without stopping to ask her permission, the man caught up the panting, excited girl in his arms, and waded out to meet the boat.

"That's near enough. Swing round," he ordered.

The boat came about and backed in a length, to where he stood thigh-deep in the still water, with the blushing girl upraised on his broad shoulder. Lord James again lifted his cap. His bow could not have been more formal and respectful had the meeting occurred in the queen's drawing-room.

"Miss Leslie! This is a very great pleasure, 'pon my word! But you've overheated yourself. You should not have run," he remonstrated. As Blake lifted her in over the stern, he deftly unfolded the silk dustcoat and held it open for her. "Permit me—No need of such haste, y'know. I assure you, we're not so strict as to our hour of sailing."

"I—I— Of course we—" stammered the girl.

"To be sure! Ah, no hat! I should have foreseen. Very stupid of me not to've brought a hat or parasol. But I dare say you'll make out till we get back aboard ship."

His conventional manner and quiet conversational tone alike tended to ease her of her embarrassment. By the time she had slipped on the coat and seated herself, the crimson blushes that had flooded her tanned cheeks were fast subsiding, and she was able to respond with a fair degree of composure: "That was extremely thoughtful of you, Lord Avondale!"

"Not at all, not at all," he disclaimed. "Cocks'n, if you'll be so kind as to go forward, I'll take the tiller. Tom, old man! don't stand there all day. You'll get your feet damp. Climb in!"

"No; pull out," replied Blake, his eyes hardening with sudden resolve.

"I forgot something. Got to go back to the cleft. You take Jen—Miss Leslie aboard at once."

"Oh, no, Tom!" hastily protested the girl. "We'll wait here for you."

"Here?" he demanded. "And without your hat?"

Miss Leslie put her scarred and begrimed little hands to her dishevelled hair.

Blake went on in an authoritative tone: "It won't do for you to get a sunstroke now—after all these weeks. Jimmy, take her straight aboard. I've got to go back, I tell you. We didn't stop for anything. There's a jarful of mud and so forth that we sure can't leave to the hyenas." He met the girl's appealing glance with firm decision. "You must get aboard, out of this sun, fast as they can take you."

"Yes, of course, if you think it best—Tom," she acquiesced.

Her ready docility would of itself have been sufficient to surprise Lord James. But, in addition, there was a soft note in her voice and a glow in her beautiful hazel eyes that caused him to glance quickly from her to his friend. Blake was already turning about to wade ashore. From what little could be seen of his bristly face, its expression was stern, almost morose. The powerful jaw was clenched.

Though puzzled and a trifle discomposed, Lord James quietly seated himself beside the girl, and signing the men to give way, took the tiller.

"My dear Miss Leslie," he murmured, "if you but knew my delight over having found both you and Tom safe and well!"

"Then you really know him?" she replied. "Yes, to be sure; he called you by your first name. Wait! I remember now. One day soon after we were cast ashore—the second day, when we were thinking how to get fire, to drive away the leopard—"

"Leopard? I say! So that's where you got this odd gown?"

"No—the mother leopard and the cubs. I was going to say, Tom remarked that James Scarbridge had been his chum."

"Had been? He meant *is!*"

"Then it's true! Oh, isn't it strange and—and splendid? You know, I did not connect the remark with you, Lord James. He had told me to try to think how we were to find food for the next meal. His reference to you was made quite casually in his talk with Winthrope."

"Winthrope!" exclaimed Lord James. "Then he, too, reached shore? Yet if so—"

The girl put her hand before her eyes, as if to shut out some terrible sight. Her voice sank to a whisper: "He—he was killed in the second cyclone—a few days ago."

"Ah!" muttered the young earl. After a pause, he asked in a tone of profound sympathy, "And the others—Lady Bayrose?"

"Don't ask! don't ask!" she cried, shuddering and trembling.

But quickly she regained her composure and looked up at him with a calm unwavering gaze that told him how much she had undergone and the strength of character she had gained during the fearful weeks that she had been marooned on this savage and desolate coast.

"How foolish of me to give way!" she reproached herself. "It is what you might have expected of me before—before I had been through all this, with his example to uplift me out of my helplessness and inefficiency. Believe me, Lord Avondale, I am a very different young woman from the shallow, frivolous girl you knew during those days on the Mediterranean."

"Shallow! frivolous!" he protested. "Anything but that, Miss Genevieve!

You must have known how vastly different were my—er—impressions. If Lady Bayrose hadn't so suddenly shunted you off at Aden to the Cape boat—Took me quite by surprise, I assure you. Had you kept on to India, I had hoped to—er—"

She gave him a glance that checked his fast-mounting ardor.

"I—I beg pardon!" he apologized. "This of course is hardly the time—About the others, if I may ask—that is, if it's not too painful for you. I infer that Lady Bayrose—that she did not—reach the shore."

The girl's thorn-scarred, sun-blistered hands clasped together almost convulsively. But she met his look of concern with unflinching braveness.

"Poor dear Lady Bayrose!" she murmured. "They had put her and the maids into one of the boats—there at the first, when the ship crashed on the reef. They ran back to fetch me, but before they could rush me across, a wave more terrible than all the others swept the ship. It tore loose the boat and whirled them away, over and over!"

"Gad!" he exclaimed.

"It also carried away the captain and most of the crew. Between the breakers, Winthrope and Tom and I were flung into the one remaining boat. Winthrope cut the rope before the sailors could follow, and then—then the steamer slipped back off the reef and went down."

"I say! Only the three of you left! The boat brought you safe ashore?"

"No, we were overturned in the breakers, but were washed up—flung up—how, I cannot tell. The wind was frightful. It must have blown us out of the surf and along with the water that was being driven up and over into the lagoon. The first I knew, I was behind a little knoll with Winthrope. Tom was near—in a pool. He—he crawled out. It was nearly dark. We were all so beaten and exhausted that we slept until morning. When we awoke, there was no sign of—of any one else, or of the boat—nothing; only the top of the highest mast sticking up above the water, out beside the reef. Tom swam out to it; but he couldn't get anything—even he couldn't."

"Swam out, you say? These waters swarm with sharks. They're keen to nip a swimmer!"

The girl's eyes flashed. "Do you believe he'd fear them?—that he'd fear anything?"

"Not he! I fancy I ought to know, if any one. Knocked about with him, half 'round the world. I dare say he's told you."

"Would it be like him to claim the credit of your friendship? No! Before, on the steamer, we had mistaken him to be—to be what he appears to strangers—rough, almost uncouth. Yet even that frightful morning—it was among the swamps, ten miles or more up the coast. He carried us safe out of them, me nearly all the way—out of the bog and water, safe to the palms; and he as much tortured with thirst as were we!"

"Fancy! No joke about that—thirst!"

"Yet it was only the beginning of what he did for us. Starvation and wild beasts and snakes and the fever—he saved us from all. Yet he had nothing to begin with—no tools or weapons, only his burning glass. Can you wonder that I—that I—"

She stopped and looked down, the color mounting swiftly under the dark coat of tan that covered the exquisite complexion he remembered so pleasantly.

"My word!" he remonstrated, amazed and disquieted. "Surely not that!

It's—it's impossible! It can't be possible!"

"Do you think so?" she whispered. "If you but knew the half—the tenth—of what he has done!"

The rusty side of the tramp loomed up above them. The boat crew flung up their oars, and Lord James steered in alongside, under the sling that was being lowered for the rescued lady. She pointed up at it, and met the reproachful, half-dazed glance of her companion with a look of compassionate regret for his disappointment. Yet she made no effort to conceal the love for his friend and rival that shone with tender radiance from her candid eyes.

"You should know him—his true, his real self!" she said. "Hasten back. Do not delay to come aboard with me. Hasten ashore and to the cleft. See for yourself."

She caught the descending sling with a dexterity that astonished him, and seated herself in it before he could rise to assist her.

"Haul away," she called in a clear voice that held no note of timidity. Those above at the tackle hastened to obey. As she was swung upwards, she looked down at the earl and waved him to put off.

"Hasten!" she urged. "Do not wait. I am all right now. Even if he is returning, go to the cleft and see."

He shook his head, and waited until she had been hauled up the ship's side. But as her little moccasined feet cleared the bulwarks and Meggs himself leaned out to draw her inboard, he signed the oarsmen to thrust off again.

Knowing the course, they made direct for the end of the sunken ledge. Blake had not returned, nor was he anywhere in sight. They skirted in along the rocky slope of the cliff foot to where it curved away into the sand beach of the plain. Lord James sprang ashore alone and hastened inland along the base of the cliffs.

A brisk walk of ten minutes over the sandy plain brought him to the grove at the foot of the cleft. In the midst of the trees was a pool, half choked with the dried mud and rubbish of a recent flood from the ravine. The wash had obliterated all tracks below; but there were traces of a trail leading up the ravine over a four-foot ledge. He took the rock at a bound, and hastened on upwards between the lofty walled sides of the cleft.

At the first turn he was brought to an abrupt halt. From side to side, between two outjutting corners of rock, the ravine had been barricaded with a twelve-foot *boma* of thorn scrub. It was a fence high enough and strong enough to stop even a hungry lion. In the centre was a low opening, partly masked by the dry spiky fronds of a small date palm.

"Gad!" murmured the Englishman. "Some of Tom's engineering! And she said he started without weapons or tools—on this coast!... Yet for him to have won her— No, no, it's impossible! impossible! American or not, she's a lady—thoroughbred! He's a true stone, but in the rough—uncut, unpolished! A girl of her breeding—He's worth it, 'pon my word, he is; though I never would have fancied that she, of all girls— She's so different. No! it's impossible! it can't be! Must be pure fancy on her part—gratitude. It can't be anything more!"

A heavy step sounded on the far side of the barrier, and a deep voice called out to him: "Hello, there! That you, Jimmy? Thought it about time you were due. What you doing?—telling yourself how to climb over? Abase yeh noble knee to the dust and crawl through, me lud."

Without pausing to reply, Lord James stooped and crept through the narrow passage under the thorny wall. As he straightened up on the inner side, Blake caught and gripped his hand in a big calloused palm.

"Jimmy!" he exclaimed, his pale blue eyes glistening with the soft light of deep friendship. "Jimmy boy! to think you beat 'em to it! I figured ten to one odds that it was a tramp chartered by Papa Leslie— And then to see you pop up in the sternsheets, spic and span as a laundry ad! When you sang out— Lord!"

"Ring off, bo! Those're my fingers you're mashing!" objected the victim.

As Blake released him, he stepped aside and ran his eye up and down the sinewy rag-and-skin-clad form of the engineer. He nodded approvingly.

"Lean, hard as nails, no sign of fever—and after six weeks on this beastly coast! How'd you do it, old man? You're fit—deuced fit!"

"Fit to give pointers to the Wild Man from Borneo," chuckled Blake. He drew out a silver cigarette case and snapped open the lid. "See those little beauties?— No! hands off! Good Lord! those're my arrow tips, soaking in snake poison! A scratch would do for you as sure as a drink of cyanide. Brought down an eland with one of those little points—antelope big as a steer."

"Poison! fancy now!" exclaimed Lord James.

"Yes; from a puff adder that almost got Miss Jenny— fellow big as my leg. Struck at her as she bent to pick an amaryllis. If it had so much as grazed her hand or arm— God!"

He looked away, his teeth clenched together and the

sweat starting out on his broad forehead. What he thought of Genevieve Leslie was plainly evident in his convulsed face and dilated eyes. If he could be so overwrought by the mere remembrance of a danger that she had escaped, he must love her, not as most men love, but with all the depth and strength of his powerful nature. Lord James's lips pressed together and his gray eyes clouded with pain.

"Close shave, heh?" he muttered.

"Yes," replied Blake. He drew in a deep breath, and added, "Not the first, though, nor the last. But a miss is as good as a mile, hey, Jimmy boy?"

"Gad, old man, that sounds natural! Can't say you look it, though—not altogether. Must get you aboard and into another style of fine raiment. Fur trousers not good form in this climate, y'know. You picked up that shirt at a remnant counter, I take it. Come aboard. Must mow that alfalfa patch before any one suspects you're trying to raise a beard."

The friendly banter seemed to have the contrary effect from that intended. Blake's face darkened.

"Good Lord, no!" he rumbled. "Go aboard with her? What d'you take me for?"

"Give you my word, I don't take you at all," replied the puzzled Englishman.

"What! Hasn't she told you? But of course she wouldn't—unless she saw you alone," muttered Blake. "Come on up the canon. I've thought it all out—just what must be done. But it'll take some time to explain. Wait! Did you come alone?—any one follow you?"

"No. Told 'em to stay near the boat."

"Just the same, I'll make sure," said Blake. He dived into the barricade passage, and quickly reappeared, dragging at the butt of the date palm. "There, me lud; the door is shut. Nobody is going to walk in on our private conference now. Come on."

3

LORD AND MAN

BLAKE TURNED ABOUT and swung away up the ravine. Lord James followed in the half-obliterated path, which led along the edge of a tiny spring rill. The cleft was here closed in on each side with sheer walls of rock from twenty to thirty feet high. At the point where this small box canon intersected the middle of the cliff ridge, the gigantic baobab that Lord James had seen from the steamer, towered skyward, its huge trunk filling a good third of the width of the gorge. Across from it and nearer at hand was a thicket of bamboos, around which the spring rill trickled from a natural basin in the rock.

But the visitor gave scant heed to the natural features of the place. His glance passed from a great antelope hide, drying on a frame, to the bamboo racks on which sun-seared strips of flesh were curing over a smudge fire. Looking to his left, he saw a hut hardly larger than a dog kennel but ingeniously thatched with bamboo leaves. Then his glance was caught and held by a curious contrivance of interwoven thorn branches and creepers, fitted into a high narrow opening in the trunk of the baobab.

"What's that?—hollow tree?" he asked.

"Yes," answered Blake, without turning. "Sixteen-foot

room inside. That's where the she-leopard and the cubs were smothered. Fired the gully to drive out the family. All stayed at home and got smothered 'cept old Mr. Leopard. He ran the gantlet. Lord, how he squalled, poor brute! But they'd have eaten us if we hadn't eaten them. He landed in the pool, too scorched to see. Settled him with my club."

"Clubbed him?—a leopard! I say now! A bit different, that, to snipe shooting."

"Well, yes, a trifle different, Jeems—a trifle," conceded Blake.

"My word! What haven't you been through!" burst out the Englishman.

"And to think she, too, went through it all—six weeks of it!"

"That's it!" enthused Blake. "She's the truest, grittiest little girl the sun ever had the good luck to shine on! If she thinks now I can't realize—that I'm not going to do the square thing by her! I've been thinking it all over, Jimmy. I've got it all mapped out what I'm going to do. Wait, though!"

He sprang ahead and pulled at the thorny contrivance that stopped the opening in the baobab trunk. It was balanced midway up, on a crossbar. Almost at a touch, the lower part swung up and outward and the upper half down and inward. He stepped in under it, hesitated a moment, and went on into the hollow, with an exclamation of relief: "No, 't isn't her room any more, thank God!"

Lord James stared. Well as he knew the sterling qualities of his friend, he had never suspected him of such delicacy. He gazed curiously around at the unshapely but flawless sand-glazed earthenware set on a bamboo rack beside the open stone fireplace, at the rough-woven but strong baskets piled together near the foot of the baobab, at the pouch of antelope skin, the grass sombreros, the bamboo spits and forks and spoons—all the many useful utensils that told of the ingenuity and resourcefulness of his friend.

But, most of all, he was interested in the weighty hard-wood club leaning against the tree trunk and the great bamboo bow hanging above in a skin sheath beside a quiver full of long feather-tipped arrows. He was balancing the club when Blake came out of the tree-cave, carrying a young cocoanut in one hand, and in the other a small pot seemingly full of dried mud. Lord James replaced the club, and waved his hand around at the camp.

"'Pon my word, Tom," he commented, "you've out-Crusoed old Robinson!"

"Sure!" agreed Blake. "He had a whole shipful of stuff as a starter, while we didn't have anything except my magnifying glass and Win's penknife and keys."

He pulled out a curious sheath-knife made of a narrow ribbon of steel set in a bone back. "How's that for a blade? Big flat British keys—good steel. I welded 'em together, end to end."

"Gad! the pater's private keys!" gasped Lord James. "You don't tell me the rascal was imbecile enough to keep those keys in his pocket?—certain means of identification if he'd been searched!"

"What!" shouted Blake. "Then the duke he cleaned out was your dad. *Whew!*"

He whirled the mud-stoppered jug overhead and dashed it down at his feet. From amidst the shattered fragments he caught up a dirty cloth that was quilted across in small squares. He held it out to Lord James.

"There you are, Jimmy—my compliments and more or less of your family heirlooms."

"My word!" murmured the earl, catching eagerly at the cloth. "You got the loot from him? That's like you, Tom!"

"Look out!" cautioned Blake. "I opened one square to see what it was he had hidden. You'll find he hadn't been too daffy to melt the settings—keys or no keys. Say, but it's luck to learn they're yours! Hope they're all there."

"All the good ones will be. He couldn't have sold or pawned any of the best stones after we cabled. Gad! won't the pater be tickled! Ah!"

From the open square of which Blake had spoken, his lordship drew out a resplendent ruby. "Centre stone of Lady Anne's brooch!"

He ran his immaculate finger-tips over the many squares in the cloth. "A stone in every one—must be all of the really valuable loot! The settings were out of date—small value. How'd you get it from him, Tom?"

Blake hesitated, and answered in a low tone: "He got hurt the night of the second cyclone. But he wasn't responsible—poor devil! He must have been dotty all along. It didn't show much before—but I felt uneasy. That's why I built that thorn door—so she could bar herself in."

Lord James stared in horrified surprise. "You really do not mean—?"

"Yes—and it almost happened! God!" Again Blake clenched his teeth and the cold sweat burst out on his forehead.

"My word! That's worse than the snake!" murmured Lord James.

"She—she'd left the door up—heat was stifling," explained Blake. "I had gone off north, exploring. The beast was crawling in— But I've got to remember he wasn't responsible—a paranoiac!"

"Ah, yes. And then?" questioned the Englishman, tugging nervously at the tip of his little blond mustache.

"Then—then—" muttered Blake. "He got what was coming to him. Cyclone struck like a tornado. Door whirled down and knocked him out of the opening—smashed him!"

"The end he had earned!"

"Yes—even if he wasn't responsible, he had become just that—a beast. She had saved his life, too—night I ran down to the beach after eating a poison fish. Barricade hadn't been finished. He was down with the fever. They were attacked—jackals, hyenas. She got him safe inside the tree, with the yelling curs jumping at her."

"My word! she did that?—she? Of all the young ladies I've ever known, she was the very last I should have expected—"

"What! you've met her before?" demanded Blake.

"Then she hasn't told you?" replied his friend. "Lady Bayrose was one of my old friends, y'know. Met 'em aboard ship—sailed on the same steamer, after my run home."

"You did?" muttered Blake, in blank astonishment. "You know her?"

"You must have heard me sing out to her from the boat. Yes, I—er—had the voyage with her through the Mediterranean and down the Red Sea. But Lady Bayrose got

tiffed at me, and at Aden shifted to a Cape boat. I had to
go on to India alone."

"India?" queried Blake.

"Trailing Hawkins. He first went to India. But he
doubled back and 'round to Cape Colony."

"So that's why you didn't get here sooner," said Blake.

"Yes. Didn't notice that the *Impala* was posted. Didn't
know either you or Miss Leslie was aboard her until after
I learned you'd thrown up the management of that Rand
mine. Traced you to Cape Town. Odd that you and she and
Hawkins should all have booked on the same steamer!"

"Think so?" said Blake. "I don't. Winthrope—Hawkins,
that is—was smooth enough to know he'd not be suspected
if travelling as a member of Lady Bayrose's party. He had
already wormed himself into her favor. As for me—well,
they had come to look at the mine, and I had shown Jenny
through the workings. Does that make it clear why I threw
up the job and followed them to Cape Town?"

"She had not given you any reason to—surely, not any
encouragement? No, I can't believe it!"

"Course not, you British doughhead! It was all the other
way 'round. Think I didn't realize? She, a lady, and me—
what I am! But I couldn't help it—I just couldn't help
myself, Jimmy. Knew her father, too—all about his millions
and how he made them! He did me—twice. You'd think
the very name would have turned me. Yet the minute I set
eyes on her—say!"

"You're certainly hard hit!" murmured the young earl. He
flushed, bit his lip, hesitated, and burst out with impulsive
generosity: "Gad, old man! If it's true—if she really—er—
has come to love you, I own that you've won her fair and

square—all this, y'know." He waved his hand around in a sweeping gesture. "Saved her from all this. Yes—if it's really true!"

Blake looked away, and spoke in a hushed voice: "It's—it's true, Jimmy! Only a little while ago, there on the cliff edge when we saw your steamer, she—she told me. It started yesterday after I bluffed off the lion. You see, she—"

"Lion?" ejaculated Lord James.

"Yes." Blake flung up his head in an impatient gesture. "The beast tried to stalk us. Jumped back into the grass when I circled out at him. I got the grass fired before he screwed up courage to tackle me.— Don't cut in!— It was then that Jenny—she—she tried to say something. But I streaked for home. This morning, though, when I saw we were safe, I was weak enough to let her—speak out."

Lord James hesitated just perceptibly, and then caught his friend's big, ill-used hand in a cordial clasp. "So—you're engaged! Congratulations!"

"If only it was just that!" cried Blake. He flushed red under his thick coat of tan. "I—I suppose I've got to tell you, Jimmy—I must. I need your help to carry out my plan."

"Your plan?" repeated the Englishman wonderingly.

"To save her from—from committing herself. It isn't fair to her to let her do it now. She ought to wait till she gets back home, among her own people. You see she wants to— She—she says that ship captains can—" He caught his breath, and bent nearer, but with his face half averted. His voice sank to an almost inaudible murmur—"that ship captains can marry people."

"Ah!" gasped Lord James. But he recovered on the

instant. "Gad! that is a surprise, old man. Always the lady's privilege, though, to name the day, y'know. I shipped a stewardess to wait on the women—had hoped they would all have been saved. She'll do for lady's maid. Also brought along some women's togs, in case of emergencies. As for yourself, between mine and Megg's and his own wardrobes, my man can rig you up a presentable outfit. Clever chap, that Wilton."

"You've gone back to a valet again!" reproached Blake, momentarily diverted. Then his fists clenched and his brows met in a frown of self-disgust. "Lord! for me to forget for a second! Look here, Jimmy, you're clean off. You don't savvy a little bit. Don't you see the point? I can't let her commit herself now—here! You know I can't. It wouldn't be fair to her, and you know it."

Lord James met his look with a clear and unfaltering gaze, and answered steadily: "That all depends on one thing, Tom. If she really loves you—"

"D'you think she's the kind to do it, if she didn't?" demanded Blake. "No, that's not the point, at all. I've tried to be square, so far. She saw what I'm like when I cut loose—there on the ship. I was two-thirds drunk when the cyclone flung us ashore. No excuse—except that all of them had turned me down from the first—there at Cape Town. Yes, she knows just what I'm like when the craving is on me. Yesterday, down there at the south headland, before the lion came around, I gave her some idea of what I've done—all that."

"You've lived a cleaner life than most who're considered eligible!" exclaimed Lord James. "I know that with respect to women, you're the cleanest—"

"Eligible!" broke in Blake. "No man is that, far as she's concerned, unless it's you, Jimmy."

"Chuck it! You're always knocking yourself. But about this plan that's bothering you? Out with it."

"That's talking! All right, here it is, straight—I want you to get back aboard and steam away, fast as you can hike. You can run into Port Mozambique, if you're going north, and arrange for a boat to call by for me."

"You're daft!" cried Lord James. "Daft! Mad as a hatter! Can you fancy for a moment I'd go off and leave you here?"

"Guess you can't help yourself, Jimmy. The most you can do is force me to take to the jungle. You can't get me aboard. I tell you, I've figured it all out. I won't go aboard and let her do—what she's planning to do. You ought to know. Jimmy, that when I say a thing, I mean it. She's not going to set eyes on me again until after she's back in America. Is that plain?"

"Tom—old man! that's like you!" cried the Englishman, and again he gripped the other's rough hand. "I see now what you're driving at. It's a thing few men would have the bigness to do. You're giving up a certainty, because your love for her is great enough, unselfish enough to consider only her good. D'you fancy I could do such a thing? You're risking everything. Shows you're fit, even for her!"

"It's little enough—for her!" put in Blake.

"That's like you to say it," rejoined his friend. "See here, old man. You've made a clean breast of it all. I should be no less candid. You know now that I met her before—was all those weeks with her aboard ship. Need I tell you that I, too, love her?"

"You?" growled Blake. "But of course! I don't blame you. You couldn't help it."

"It's been an odd shuffling of the cards," remarked his friend. "What if— Aren't you afraid there may be a new deal, Tom? If you don't come aboard, she and I will be together at least as far as Zanzibar, and probably all the way to Aden, before I can find some one else to take her on to England."

"What of that?" rejoined Blake. "Think I don't know you're square, after the months we roughed-it together?"

"Then— But I can't leave you here in this hell-hole! You've no right to ask me to do that, Tom. If I could bring my guns ashore and stay with you— But she'll never be more in need of some one, if you insist upon your plan. I say! I have it— We'll slip you aboard after dark. You can lie in covert till we reach Port Mozambique. I trust I'm clever enough to keep her diverted that long. Can put it that you're outfitting—all that, y' know."

"Say, that's not so bad," admitted Blake, half persuaded. "I could slip ashore, soon as we ran into harbor, leaving her a note to tell her why."

"Right-o, Tammas! But wait. I'll go you one better. You can write your note and give it out that you've shifted to another ship. But you'll stay aboard with us, under cover. Of all the steamers that touch at Aden, one will soon come along with parties whom either she or I know. Then off she goes to the tight little island, and we follow after in our little tramp or on another liner. Hey, Tammas?"

"Well, I don't know," hesitated Blake. "It sounds all right."

"It is all right," insisted the younger man. "You'll be

aboard the same steamer with her as far as Aden, to keep an eye on me, y'know."

"On you?"

"You'd better. My word, Tom! don't you realize? If you—er—put it off, I'm bound to try for myself. Can't help it!"

"Think you've got a show, do you?" rallied Blake.

"I fancied I had as much chance as any one, before all this occurred. I at least should have been in the running, had it not been for the wreck—and you."

Blake stood for several moments, with his head down-bent and eyes fixed upon the ground. When he looked up and spoke, his face was grave and his voice deep and low.

"It's all of a piece, Jimmy. I don't blame you. Fact is, it's all the better. I've had all the advantage here. She and I've been living in the Cave Age, and I've proved myself an A-1 cave-man, if I do say it myself. It may be hard for her to get the right perspective of things, even after she's back in her own environment. Understand?"

"I take it, you mean she has seen the display of your strongest and best qualities, in circumstances that did not call for such non-essentials as mere polish—drawing room culture."

"You mean, for all that counts most with ninety-nine per cent of your class and hers," rejoined Blake. "And there's the craving, too. I'll have to fight that out before I'll be fit to let her do anything. Think I don't know the difference between us? No! I'm going to go the limit, Jimmy. I can't do less, and be square to her. So I give you full leave. You're free to play your hand for all there is in it. I'll stay here—"

"No—no! I'll not hear of it, Tom!"

"Yes, you will. I'll stay here, and you'll see her clear

through to America—to Chicago—right to her papa's house and in through the door. Understand? I don't make a single condition. You're to try your best to win; and if you do, why—don't you see?—it'll show that this which she thinks is the real thing is all a mistake."

"My word, old man! you'd not give her up without a fight? That wouldn't be like you!"

"It all depends. I won't if it's true she loves me— God! no! I'd go through hell-fire for her!"

"If I know you, Tom, you'll suffer that and more, should the event prove she is mistaken as to the nature of her present feeling."

"What of it?" muttered Blake, with a look that told the other the uselessness of persuasion. "Think I'd let her marry me, long as there's a shadow of a chance of her being mistaken?"

"Very well, then," replied his friend. "You've said your say. Now I'll say mine. I can ease the tedium of Miss Leslie's trip up the coast; and I stand ready to do so—on two conditions. In the first place; you're to come aboard and stay aboard. After I find a chaperon for her at Aden, you're to go on home with me, to visit at Ruthby."

"Excuse *me!*" said Blake. "I can see myself parading around your ancestral stone-heap with your ducal dad!"

"You not only can, but will," rejoined the earl. "Come now. You'll be allowed to write that note at Port Mozambique, and keep in covert till Miss Leslie is safe off the ship. But you'll do the rest—you'll not stay here. Another thing—you have my word for it now—I shall endeavor no more than yourself to win her, until after she has returned to her home in the States."

"Lord, Jimmy! that's square—to me, I mean. But how about her?"

"No fear," reassured the Englishman. "She's received everywhere. She's been presented—at Court, y'know. If she stays over on this side a bit, there'll be dozens of 'em dancing attendance on her. Come, now; it's all settled."

"Well, I don't know," hesitated Blake.

"I tell you, you'll sail with us, else I shall leave her at Port Mozambique and come back for you."

"Um-m—if you take it that hard! But are you sure you can keep her satisfied till we put in there?"

"Trust me for that. If she becomes apprehensive, I'll put it that you'd rather be married in port, by the American consul."

"That's no lie. Say, what's the use of waiting till dark? You said there's a stewardess aboard. Jenny will sure be below with her until—until she's ready for the ceremony."

"Quite true, yes. Then it's all settled. At Port Mozambique, your note; you bunk forward, under cover, till Aden; then home with me for a visit; neither of us see her beyond Aden until we follow her to the States."

"Since you insist—yes, it's a go, Jimmy!" agreed Blake. He turned to hasten away along the gorge, past the baobab. "I'll be back soon. Got to pull down that flag."

Lord James followed, and saw him ascend to the cliff crest on the right, up a withered, leafless tree. The trunk had been burned through at the base in such manner that the top had fallen over against the edge of the rocky wall. A pile of stones offered an easy means of reaching the lower branches. The earl climbed up into the top, and watched his friend run forward over the broken ledges of the ridge.

The bamboo flagstaff was wrenched from its supports and lowered amidst a wild commotion of the nesting sea birds. Blake came back at a jog-trot, regardless of the fierce heat of the sun. In his arms were gathered the tattered folds of the signal flag.

"That's one thing I'm going to take away," he said, in response to the other's look of inquiry. "She sewed that leopard-skin dress all by herself, with a thorn for needle, so we could have her skirt for the flag."

"Fancy!" murmured the Englishman. "With a thorn, you say!"

Blake nodded, and followed him down the tree-ladder and back along the cleft to the baobab. There he paused to take down his archery outfit.

"Guess I'll keep these, too, as souvenirs," he remarked. He pointed to the blackened strips of flesh on the curing racks. "May I ask Lord Avondale to stay to dinner?"

"Very kind, I'm sure. But I've a previous engagement," declined his lordship.

"Now, now, Jeems. Needn't turn up your aristocratic nose at first-class jerked antelope. Ought to 've been with us the first three days. Great *menu*—raw fish, cocoanuts, more cocoanuts, and then, just when we were whetting our teeth for a nice fat snake or an *entrée* of caterpillars, I landed that old papa leopard. Managed to haggle some of the india rubber off his bones. Tough!—but it was filling. All the same, we didn't wear out any more teeth on him after we got up the cleft and found the cubs. They were tender as spring lambs."

"And Miss Genevieve went through all that!"

"Yes. Told you she's the grittiest little girl ever—and a

lady! My God, when I think of it all!… Well, she's come through it alive. What's more, she's not going to suffer any bad consequences from it, not if I can help it! Come on. Got your heirloom rag?"

"Safe—inside pocket."

"All right, then. Come on. You don't think I'm aching to hang 'round this cursed hole, do you?—now that she's gone!"

He flung his bow and quiver over his shoulder, thrust the signal flag into the skin pouch, and turned to go.

Lord James stepped before him, with hand outstretched.

"One moment, Tom! Here's for home and America—a fair field, and best man wins!"

"It's a go!" cried Blake, gripping the proffered hand. "May she get the one that'll make her happiest!"

4

THE EARL AND THE OTHERS

MISS DOLORES GANTRY shook the snow from her furs, and with the graceful assurance of a yacht running aslant a craft-swarming harbor, cut into the crowd that surged through the Union Station. She brought up in an empty corner of the iron fence, close beside the exit gate through which passengers were hurrying from the last train that had arrived. Her velvety black eyes flashed an eager glance at the out-pouring stream, perceived a Mackinaw jacket, and turned to make swift comparison of the depot clock and the tiny bracelet watch on her slender wrist.

As she again looked up she met the ardent gaze and ingratiating smile of an elegant young man who was sauntering up the train-platform to the exit gate, fastidiously apart from his fellow passengers. He raised his hat, and at the girl's curt nod of recognition, hastened through the gate for a more intimate greeting.

"My dear Dodie!" he exclaimed, reaching for her hand. "This is a most delightful surprise."

"My dear Laffie!" she mocked, deftly slipping both slender hands into her muff. "I quite agree as to it's being a surprise."

"Then you didn't come down to meet me?"

"You?" she asked, with an irony too fine drawn for his conceit. "Come to meet you?"

"Yes. Didn't you get my note saying that all work on my bridge was stopped by the cold and that I would run down to see you?"

"To see me—plus the world, the flesh, and the devil!"

"Now, Dodie!" he protested, with a smirk on his handsome, richly colored face.

The girl's eyes hardened into black diamonds as she met his assured gaze. "Mr. Brice-Ashton, you will hereafter kindly address me as 'Miss Gantry.' You must be aware that I am now *out*."

"Oh, I've no objections, just so *we're* not out," he punned.

She gave him her shoulder, and peered eagerly through the pickets of the iron fence at a train that was backing into the station. Ashton shrugged, lighted a gilt-tipped cigarette, and asked: "Permit me to inquire, Miss Gantray, if I'm not the happy man for whom you wait, who is?"

She replied without turning: "How can I tell until I see him? I think it will be the hero. If not, it will be the earl."

"Hero?—earl?" repeated Ashton.

"Yes, whichever one Vievie leaves for me."

"What! Genevieve? Miss Leslie? She's not—Is she really coming home so soon?—when she had such a chance for a gay season in London?"

"Don't give yourself away. The London season is in summer."

"You don't say! Well, in England, then. Why didn't you write me?"

"I'm not running a correspondence-school or news agency, Mr. Brice-Ashton."

"Oh, cut it, Dodie! Post me up, that's a good girl! What I've heard has been so muddled. This hero business, for a starter—what about it? I thought it was an English duke that chartered the steamer to rescue Genevieve."

"No, only the son of a duke,—James Scarbridge, the Right Honorable the Earl of Avondale."

"My ante!"

"It's in the jack-pot, and as good as lost. What chance have you now to win Genevieve,—with a real earl and a real hero in the field?"

"Earl *and* hero? I thought he was the hero."

"That's one of the jokes on mamma. Earl Jimmy had nothing to do with the rescue ships that Uncle Herbert cabled to search the Mozambique coast. No; Jeems chartered a tramp steamer on his own account, to look for friend Tommy. He found the heroic Thomas and, incidentally, the fair Genevieve—who wasn't so *very* fair after weeks of broiling in that East African sun."

"It's wonderful—wonderful! To think that she alone of all aboard her steamer should have survived shipwreck on that savage coast!"

"She didn't survive alone—she couldn't have. That's where Tommy came in. There was another man, but he didn't count for much, I guess. Vievie merely wrote that he died during the second cyclone."

"What an experience!—and for a girl like Genevieve!"

"She, of all girls!" chimed in Dolores enviously. "You remember she never went in for sports of any kind, not even riding. And for her to be flung out that way into the tropical jungles, among lions and crocodiles and snakes and things! Why can't I ever have romantic adventures?"

"You wouldn't give the man a chance to prove himself a hero," objected Ashton. "You'd shoot the lions yourself."

"I *am* good at archery. A bow and arrows, you know, were all that Mr. Blake had."

"Blake?" repeated Ashton in rather a peculiar tone.

"Yes, Tommy the hero, otherwise Mr. Thomas Blake."

"Blake—Thomas Blake?" echoed Ashton.

"I—rather odd—I once—seems to me I once knew a man of that name. You don't happen to know if he's a—that is, what his occupation is, do you?"

Ashton was not the kind of man from whom is expected hesitancy of speech. The girl spared him a swift glance from the out-flocking stream of passengers. His fixed gaze and slack lower jaw betrayed even more uneasiness than had his voice.

"Don't be afraid," she mocked. "He's not a minister; so he couldn't marry her without help, and he's not done it since the rescue."

"Not done it?" repeated Ashton vaguely.

"No. According to mamma's letter, Earl Jimmy outgeneraled the low-browed hero. At Aden he put Vievie on a P. and O. steamer, in the charge of Lady Chetwynd. He and the hero followed in the tramp steamer to England, where he kept friend Thomas at his daddy's ducal castle until Vievie made mamma start home with her. You know mamma streaked it for London, at Uncle Herbert's expense, the moment Vievie cabled from Port Mozambique that she was safe. Uncle Herbert would have sent me, too, but mamma wouldn't have it. Just like her! It was her first chance to do England and crowd in on Vievie's noble friends. She said I might spoil the good impression she hoped to make, because I'm too much of a tomboy."

"But if it's your mother and Genevieve you're waiting for—I understood you to say the earl and that man Blake."

"Oh, they followed on the next steamer. Mamma wired that they are all coming on together from New York."

"Where's Mr. Leslie? Did he go to meet them?"

"He? You should know how busy Uncle Herbert always is. I called by his office for him. He sent out word to go on. He would follow."

"What! after all Genevieve went through, all those hardships and dangers? You'd think that even he—"

"Look I oh, look I there she is now!" cried the girl, pressing close against the fence and waving her handkerchief between the pickets.

"Where? Yes, I see! beside your mother!" exclaimed Ashton, and he lifted his hat on his cane.

The signals won them recognition from the approaching ladies, the younger of whom responded with a quietly upraised hand. Beside her walked a rosy-cheeked blonde young Englishman, while in front a big square-built man thrust the crowd forward ahead of them. They were followed by two maids, a valet, and two porters, with hand luggage.

As the party emerged from the gateway the younger lady leaned forward and spoke in a clear soft voice: "Turn to the left, Tom."

The big man in the lead swerved out of the crowd and across the corner past Miss Gantry, who was advancing with outstretched arms, her eyes sparkling with joyous excitement.

"Vievie!" she half shrieked.

Blake glanced over his shoulder and stopped short at sight of the girls locked in each other's arms. After a moment's fervent embrace, Dolores thrust her cousin out at arm's-length and surveyed her from top to toe with radiant eyes.

"Vievie! Vievie! I really can't believe it! To think you're home again—when we never expected to see you—and you've got almost all the tan off already!"

Genevieve looked up into the vivacious face of the younger girl with an affectionate smile on her delicately curved lips and tears of joy in her hazel eyes.

"It is good to be home again, dear!" she murmured. She drew Dolores about to face the big man, who stood looking on with rather a surly expression, in his pale blue eyes. "Tom," she said, "this is my cousin, Miss Gantry. Dolores, Mr. Blake."

"The hee-row!" sighed Dolores, clasping a hand dramatically on her heart.

Blake's strong face lighted with a humorous smile. "Guess I've got to own up to it, Miss Dolores. Anything Jenny—Miss Leslie—says goes."

As he spoke he raised his English steamer cap slightly and extended a square powerful hand. Dolores entrusted her slender fingers to the calloused palm, which closed upon them with utmost gentleness.

"Really, Mr. Blake!" she exclaimed, "I mean it. You *are* a hero."

Blake's smile broadened, and as he released her hand, he glanced at her mother, who had drawn a little apart with the Englishman. "Don't let me shut out your mamma and Jimmy."

"Oh, mamma believes that any display of family affection is immodest," she replied. "But duty, you know—duty!"

She whirled about and impressed a loud salute upon the drooping jowl of the stately Mrs. Gantry.

"Dolores!" admonished the dame. "When *will* you remember you're no longer a hoyden? Such impetuosity—and before his lordship!"

"Goodness! Is he really?" panted her daughter, surveying the Englishman with candid curiosity.

"Is he really!" Mrs. Gantry was profoundly shocked. "If you weren't out, I'd see that you had at least two more years in a finishing school."

"Horrors! that certainly would finish me. But you forget yourself, mamma. You keep his earlship waiting for his introduction."

The Englishman shot a humorous glance at Blake, and drew out his monocle. He screwed it into his eye and stared blandly at the irrepressible Miss Gantry, while her mother, with some effort, regained a degree of composure. She bowed in a most formal manner.

"The Right Honorable the Earl of Avondale: I present my daughter."

The earl dropped his monocle, raised his cap, and bowed with unaffected grace. Dolores nodded and caught his hand in her vigorous clasp.

"Glad to meet you," she said. "It's rare we meet a real live earl in Chicago. Most of 'em are caught in New York, soon as they land."

"It's good of you to say it, Miss Gantry," he replied,

tugging at the tip of his little mustache. "I've been over before, you know. Came in disguise. This time I was able to march through New York with colors flying, thanks to your mother and Miss Leslie."

Dolores sent her glance flashing after his, and saw Genevieve responding coldly to the effusive greeting of Ashton. The young man was edging towards the earl. But Genevieve turned to introduce him first to her companion.

"Mr. Blake, Mr. Brice-Ashton."

"I'm sure I'm—pleased to meet you, Mr. Blake," murmured Ashton, his voice breaking slightly as Blake grasped his gloved hand in the bare calloused palm.

"Any friend of Miss Jenny's!" responded Blake with hearty cordiality.

But as he released the other's hand, he muttered half to himself, "Ashton?—Ashton? Haven't I met you before, somewhere?"

As Ashton hesitated over his reply, Genevieve spoke for him: "No doubt it's the familiarity of the name, Tom. Mr. Brice-Ashton's father is Mr. George Ashton, the financier."

"What! him?" exclaimed Blake. "But no. It's his face. I remember now. Met him in your father's office."

"In father's office?"

"When I was acting as secretary for your father, Miss Genevieve," Ashton hastened to explain. "You remember, I was in your father's office for a year. That was before I succeeded with my—plans for the Michamac cantilever bridge and went to take charge of the construction as resident engineer."

"Your plans?" muttered Blake incredulously.

"To be sure. I remember now," said Genevieve absently,

and she turned to look about, with a perplexed uptilting of her arched brows. "But, Dolores, where is papa?"

"Coming—coming, Viviekins," reassured her cousin, breaking short an animated conversation with the earl. "Don't worry, dear. He'll be along in a few minutes."

Genevieve stepped forward beside Blake to peer at the crowd. Dolores took pity on Ashton, who had edged around, eager for an introduction to the titled stranger.

"Oh, your earlship," she remarked, "this, by the way, is Mr. Laffie Brice-Ashton. I'd like to present him to you, but I'm afraid your Right Honorableness wouldn't take him even as a gift if you knew him as well as I do."

"Oh, now, Do—Miss Gon-tray!" protested Ashton.

The Englishman bowed formally and adjusted his monocle, oblivious of the hand that Ashton had stripped of its glove.

"Your—your grace—I should say, your lordship," stammered Ashton, hastily dropping his hand, "I'm extremely delighted—honored, I mean—at the unexpected pleasure of meeting your lordship."

"Ah, really?" murmured his lordship.

"Mr. Brice-Ashton's father is one of our most eminent financiers," interposed Mrs. Gantry.

"Ah, really? What luck!" politely exclaimed the Englishman. He stepped past the son of the eminent financier, to address Genevieve in an impulsive, boyish tone, "I say, Miss Leslie, hop up on a suitcase between Tom and me. You'll see over their heads."

"Hold on," said Blake, who was staring towards the outer door. "He's coming now."

"Where? Are you sure, Tom?" asked Genevieve, here eyes radiant.

"Sure, I'm sure," said Blake. "Met your father *once*. That was enough for me."

"Tom! You'll not—?"

"Enough for me to remember him," he explained with grim humor. "Don't worry. I don't want a row any more than you do."

"Or than he will! He'll not forget that had it not been for you—"

"And Jimmy!"

"Chuck it, old man," put in Lord James. "Miss Leslie knows as well as you do that one or more of the steamers chartered by her father must certainly have sighted your signal flag within a fortnight. I merely had the luck to be first."

"A lot of things can happen inside two weeks, down on the Mozambique coast. Eh, Miss Jenny?" said Blake.

For the moment, forgetful even of her father, Genevieve clasped her gloved hands and gazed upwards over the heads of the rushing multitude at a vision of swampy lagoons, of palm clumps and tangled jungles, of towering cliffs, and hot sand beaches, all aglare with the fierce downbeat of the tropical sun.

5

A REFRACTORY HERO

A SHORT, STOUT, gray-haired man burst out of the crowd, jerked off his hat to Mrs. Gantry, and hastened forward, his gray-brown eyes fixed hungrily upon Genevieve. A moment later he had her in his arms. She returned his embrace with fervor yet with a well-bred quietness that drew a nod of approval from Mrs. Gantry.

"So! you're home—at last—my dear!" commented Mr. Leslie, patting his daughter's back with a sallow, vein-corded hand.

"At last, papa! I should have hurried to you at once, in spite of your cables, if you hadn't said you were starting for Arizona."

"Couldn't tell how long I'd be on that trip. Wanted you to enjoy the month in England, since Lady Chetwynd had asked you. But come now. I must see you started home. Cut short one Board meeting. Must be at another within half an hour."

He stepped apart from her and jerked out his watch.

"Yes, papa, only—" She paused and looked at him earnestly. "Did you not receive my telegram, that we had met Mr. Blake and Lord James in New York, and that they were to come on with us?"

294

"Hey?" snapped Mr. Leslie, his eyes glinting keen and cold below their shaggy brows. First to be transfixed by their glance was young Ashton, who stood toying with the fringe of Dolores' muff. "What's this, sir? What you doing here?"

Ashton gave back a trifle before the older man's irascibility, but answered with easy assurance: "I thought it would do no harm to run down for a few days. All work at Michamac is stopped—frozen up tight."

"It's not the way your father got his start in life—frivolity! Stick to your work all the time—stick!" rejoined Mr. Leslie. He turned and met the monocled stare of the earl. "H'm. This, I suppose, is the gentleman who—"

"My dear Herbert, permit me," interposed Mrs. Gantry. "Ah—the Right Honorable the Earl of Avondale: I have the honor to present—"

"Glad to meet you, sir!" broke in Mr. Leslie, clutching the Englishman's hand in a nervous grip. "Glad of the chance to thank you in person!"

"But, I say, I'm not the right man, y' know," protested Lord James.

"The small part I had in it is not worth mentioning." He laid a hand on Blake's broad shoulder. "It's my friend Thomas Blake you should thank."

Mr. Leslie stepped back and eyed Blake's impassive face with marked coldness. "Your friend Blake?" he repeated.

"Old friend—camp-mate, chum—all over Western America and South Africa. It's he who's entitled to the credit for the rescue of Miss Leslie."

"We'll talk about your part later. You'll, of course, call on us," said Mr. Leslie. He fixed his narrowing eyes on Blake. "H'm. So you're Tom Blake—the same one."

"That's no lie," replied Blake dryly.

"You heard me say I'm busy. Have no time to-day. I'll give you an appointment for to-morrow, at my office, ten A.M. sharp."

"Thanks. But you're a bit too previous," said Blake. "I haven't asked for any appointment with you that I know of."

"But, Tom!" exclaimed Genevieve, astonished at the hostility in his tone, "of course you'll go. Papa wishes to thank you for—for all you've done. To-day, you see, he's so very busy."

Blake's hard eyes softened before her appealing glance, only to stare back sullenly at her father.

"I'm not asking any thanks from him, Miss Jenny," he replied.

The girl caught the arm of her father, who stood glowering irritably at Blake. "Papa, I—I don't understand why you and Tom—Couldn't you—won't you please be a little more cordial? Wait! I have it!" She flashed an eager glance at Blake. "Tom, you'll dine with us this evening."

He looked at Lord James, and replied steadily: "Sorry, Miss Jenny. You know I'd like to come. But I've got a previous engagement."

"If I ask you to break it, Tom?"

"Can't do it. I've given my word—worse luck!"

"But I do so wish you and papa to come to an understanding."

"Guess I understand him already; so it's no use to—

There now, don't worry. Long as you want me to, I'll accept his polite invitation for to-morrow."

"Ten A.M. sharp!" rasped Mr. Leslie. He drew Genevieve about, and rushed her off, with a curt call to Mrs. Gantry: "Come, Amice. Dolores brought the *coupé*. I'll put you in. The maids and baggage can follow in my car. Hurry up."

Genevieve was whirled away into the thick of the crowd, with scarcely time for a parting glance at Blake and Lord James. Mrs. Gantry lingered an instant to address the young Englishman:

"Pray do not forget, earl, you are to dine with me."

As Lord James bowed in polite agreement, Ashton, who had been scribbling on one of his cards, held it out. "Pardon me, your lordship. Here's a list of my favorite clubs. Look me up. I'll steer you to all the gay spots in little old Chi."

"Mr. Brice-Ashton is one of our hustling young grain speculators," explained Dolores. "Before he went to Michamac he almost cornered the market in wild oats."

"Now, Miss Dodie!" smirked Ashton. "Wait! I'll do your elbowing."

But the girl was already plunging into the crowd, in the wake of her mother, the maids, and the porters. Ashton hastened after, in a vain attempt to overtake her. Crowds part easier before a pretty, smiling, fashionably dressed girl than before a foppish young man who affects the French mode.

The card with the list of clubs fell from the hand that Lord James raised to screw in his monocle.

"Stow it, Jimmy," growled Blake. "I feel just prime for smashing that fool window."

Lord James slipped the monocle into his pocket, and twisted at the end of his short mustache.

"Don't blame you, old man," he remarked. "Her guv'nor *was* a bit crusty. Quite a clever girl that—the cousin—eh?"

"Miss Dolores? She sure is a hummer. Doesn't take after her mother; so she's all right," assented Blake. He added eagerly, "Say, Jimmy, she's just the one for you. You're so blondy blonde you need a real brunette to set off your charms."

"Sorry, Tom. Saw too much of some one else coming up to Aden—and before. Shouldn't have to remind you of that."

"Damn the luck!" swore Blake. "Well, we've come to the show-down. She's home now; agreement's off."

"To-morrow," corrected his friend.

"Lord! If only you weren't you! I'd knock you clean out of the running!"

"Rotten luck!" murmured Lord James sympathetically. "Had it been any other girl, now! But having met her before you did—Deuce take it, old man, how could I help it?"

"'T ain't your fault, Jimmy. You know I don't blame you. I don't forget you began to play fair just as soon as you got next to how matters stood between.—how they stood with me."

"Couldn't play the cad, you know. I say, though, it's time we talked it all over again. Give me your trunk check. I'll have my man send your luggage to my hotel. You're to keep on bunking with me."

"No," replied Blake. "It was all right, long as we were travelling. Now I've got to hunt a hallroom and begin scratching gravel."

"But at least until you find a position."

"No. I'm sure of something first pop, if old Grif is in town. You remember, I once told you all about him—M.F. Griffith, my old engineer—man who boosted me from a bum to a transitman. Whitest man that ever was! Last I heard, he'd located here in Chicago as a consulting engineer. He'll give me work, or find it for me; and Mollie— that's Mrs. Grif—she'll board me, if she has to set up a bed in her parlor to do it."

"Oh, if you're set on chucking me," murmured Lord James. "But I'll stay by you till you've looked around. If you don't find your friend, you're to come with me."

"Must think I need a chaperon," rallied Blake in a fond growl. "Well, signal your Man Friday, and we'll run a line to the nearest directory."

Lord James signed to his valet, who stood near, discreetly observant. On the instant the man stepped forward with his master's hand luggage, and reached down to grasp Blake's suitcase, which had been left by one of the porters. But Blake was too quick for him. Catching up the suitcase himself, he swung away through the crowd and up the broad stairway, to the Bureau of Information.

Two minutes later he was copying an address from the city business directory.

"Got his office O.K.," he informed his friend. "Over on Dearborn Street. Next thing's to see if he's in town. Shunt your collar-buttoner, and come on. We can walk over inside ten minutes."

Lord James instructed his valet to take a taxicab to the hotel. He himself proceeded to button up his overcoat from top to bottom and turn up the collar.

"Your balmy native clime!" he gibed, staring ruefully through the depot windows at the whirling snowstorm without. "If I freeze my Grecian nose, you'll have to buy me a wax one."

Blake chuckled. "Remember that night up in the Kootenay when the blizzard struck us and we lost the road?"

"Pleasant time to recall it!" rejoined Lord James, with a shiver. "But come on. I'm keen to meet your Mr. Griffith."

6

THREE OF A KIND

THEY REACHED THE great office building on Dearborn Street, red-faced and tingling from the whirling drive of the powdery snow. It was so dry with frost that scarcely a flake clung to their coats when they pushed in through the storm doors. The elevator shot them up to the top floor of the building before they could catch their breath in the close, steam-heated atmosphere.

"*Whew!*" said Blake, stepping out and dropping his suitcase, to shed his English raincoat. "Talk about Mozambique! Guess you know now you're in Hammurica, me lud. All the way from the Pole to Panama in one swing of the street door."

"What was your friend's number?" asked Lord James, eying the doors across the corridor.

"Seventeen-fifteen. Must be down this way," answered Blake.

Catching up his suitcase, he led around to the rear corner of the building. At the end of the side hall they came to a door marked "No. 1715." On the frosted glass below the number there was painted in plain black letters a modest sign:

M.F. GRIFFITH, C.E.

CONSULTING ENGINEER

Blake led the way in and across to the plain table-desk where a young clerk was checking up a surveyor's field book.

"Hello," said Blake. "Mr. Griffith in?"

"Why, yes, he's in. But I think he's busy," replied the clerk, starting to rise. "I'll see. What business?"

"Don't bother, sonny," said Blake. "We'll just step in and sit down."

The clerk stared, but resumed his seat, while Blake crossed to the door marked "Private," and motioned Lord James to follow him in. When they entered, a lank, gray-haired man sat facing them at a table-desk as plain as the clerk's. It was covered with drawings, over which the veteran engineer was poring with such intentness that he failed to perceive his callers.

"Hello! What's up now?" asked Blake in a casual tone. "Going to bridge Behring Straits?"

"Hey?" demanded the worker, glancing up with an abstracted look.

His dark eyes narrowed as he took in the trim figure of the earl and Blake's English cap and tweeds. But at sight of Blake's face he shoved back his chair and came hurrying around the end of the desk, his thin dry face lighted by a rare smile of friendship. He warily caught the tip of Blake's thick fingers in his bony clasp.

"Well! I'll be—switched!" he croaked. "What you doing here, Tommy?

Thought we'd got rid of you for good."

"Guess you'll have to lump it," rejoined Blake. "I'm here with both feet, and I want a job—P-D-Q. First, though, I want you to shake hands with my friend, Jimmy Scarbridge— Hold on! Wait a second."

He drew himself up pompously, and bowed to Lord James in burlesque mimicry of Mrs. Gantry. "Aw, beg pawdon, m'lud. Er—the—aw—Right Hon'able the—aw—Earl of Avondale: I present—aw—Mistah Griffith."

"Chuck it! The original's enough and to spare," cut in his lordship. He turned to Griffith with unaffected cordiality. "Glad to meet one of Tom's other friends, Mr. Griffith."

"The only other," added Blake.

"Then I'm still gladder!" said Lord James, gripping the bony hand of Griffith. "Don't let Tom chaff you. My name's just Scarbridge—James Scarbridge."

"Owh, me lud! Himpossible!" gasped Blake. "And your papa a juke!"

At sight of Griffith's upcurving eyebrows, Lord James smiled resignedly and explained: "Quite true—as to His Grace, y'know. But I assure you that even in England I am legally only a commoner. It's only by courtesy—custom, you know—that I'm given my father's second title."

"That's all right, Mr. Scarbridge," assured Griffith, in turn. "Glad to meet you. Have a seat."

While the callers drew up chairs for themselves, he returned to his seat and hauled out a box of good cigars. Blake helped himself and passed the box to Lord James. Griffith took out an old pipe and proceeded to load it with rank Durham.

"Well?" he croaked, as he handed over a match-box. "What's the good word, Tommy?"

"Haven't you heard?" replied Blake. "I'm a hero, the real live article,—T. Blake, C.E., H.E., R.O.— Oh!"

"No joshing, you Injin," admonished Griffith, pausing with a lighted match above the bowl of his pipe.

Lord James gazed reproachfully at the grinning Blake. "He tries to belittle it, Mr. Griffith, but it's quite true. Haven't you seen about it in the press?"

"Too busy over this Arizona dam," said Griffith, jerking his pipe towards the drawings on his desk.

"What dam?" demanded Blake, bending forward, keenly alert.

"Zariba—big Arizona irrigation project. Simple as A, B, C, except the dam itself. That has stumped half a dozen of the best men. Promoters are giving me a try at it now. But I'm beginning to think I've bitten off more 'n I can chew."

"You?" said Blake incredulously.

"Yes, me. When it comes to applying what's in the books, I'm not so worse. You know that, Tommy. But this proposition—Only available dam site is across a stretch of bottomless bog, yet it's got to hold a sixty-five foot head of water."

"Je-ru-salem!" whistled Blake. "Say, you've sure got to give me a shy at that, Grif. It can't be worked out—that's a cinch. Just the same, I'd like to fool with the proposition."

Griffith squinted at the younger engineer through his pipe smoke, and grunted: "Guess I'll *have* to let you try, if you're set on it." He nodded to Lord James. "You know how much use it is bucking against Tommy. The boys used to call him a mule. They were half wrong. That half is bulldog."

"Aw, come off!" put in Blake. "You know it's just because I hate to quit."

"That's straight. You're no quitter. Shouldn't wonder if you held on to this dam problem till you swallowed it."

"Stow the kidding," said Blake, embarrassed.

"I'm giving it to you straight. This dam has made a lot of good ones quit. I'm about ready to quit, myself. But I'll be—switched if I don't think you'll make a go of it, Tommy."

"In your eye!"

"No." Griffith took out his pipe and fixed an earnest gaze on Blake. "I'm not one to slop over. You know that. I can put it all over you in mathematics—in everything that's in the books. So can a hundred or more men in this country. Just the same, there's something—you've got something in you that ain't in the books."

"Whiskey?" suggested Blake, with bitter self-derision.

"Tom!" protested Lord James.

"What's the use of lying about it?" muttered Blake.

"You've no whiskey in you now," rejoined Griffith. "I'm talking about what you are now,—what you've got in your head. It's brains."

"Pickled in alcohol!" added Blake, more bitterly than before.

"That's a lie, and you know it, Tommy. You're not yet on the shelf—not by a long sight."

Blake grinned sardonically at Lord James. "Hear that, Jimmy? Never take the guess of an engineer. They're no good at guessing. It's not in the business."

"Chuck it. You know you've got something worth fighting for now."

"Lots of chance I'll have to win out against you!" Blake's teeth ground together on his unlighted cigar. He jerked it from his mouth and flung it savagely into the wastebasket. But the violent movement discharged the tension of his black humor.

"Lord! what a grouch I am!" he mumbled. "Guess I'm in for a go at the same old thing."

Griffith and Lord James exchanged a quick glance, and the former hastened to reply: "Don't you believe it, Tommy. Don't talk about *my* guessing. You're steady as a rock, and you're going to keep steady. You're on the Zariba Dam now,—understand?"

"It's a go!" cried Blake, his eyes glowing. "That fixes me. You know my old rule: Not a drop of anything when I'm on a job. Only one thing more, and I'm ready to pitch in. I must get Mollie to put me up."

Griffith looked down, his teeth clenching on the pipe stem. There was a moment's pause. Then he replied in a tone more than ever dry and emotionless: "Guess my last letter didn't reach you. I lost her, a year ago—typhoid."

"God!" murmured Blake. He bent forward and gripped his friend's listless hand.

Griffith winced under the sympathetic clasp, turned his face away, coughed, and rasped out: "Work's the one thing in the world, Tommy. Always believed it. I've proved it this year. Work! Beats whiskey any day for making you forget... I've got rooms here. You'll bunk with me. Pretty fair restaurant down around the corner."

"It's a go," said Blake. He nodded to Lord James. "That lets you out, Jimmy."

"Out in the cold," complained his lordship.

"What! With Mamma Gantry waiting to present you to the upper crust?—I mean, present the crust to you."

"Best part of the pie is under the crust."

"Now, now, none of that, Jimmy boy. You're not the sort to take in the town with a made-in-France thing like that young Ashton."

"Ashton?" queried Griffith. "You don't mean Laffie Ashton?"

"He was down at the depot to give our party the glad hand."

"Your party?" repeated Griffith. He saw Blake wink at Lord James, and thought he understood. "I see. He knows Mr. Scarbridge, eh? It's like him, dropping his work and running down here, when he ought to stick by his bridge."

"His bridge?" asked Blake. "Say, he did blow about having landed the Michamac Bridge. But of course that's all hot air. He didn't even take part in the competition. Besides, you needn't tell me he's anything more than a joke as an engineer."

"Isn't he, though? After you pulled out the last time—after the competition,—he put in plans and got the Michamac Bridge."

"You're joking!" cried Blake. "He got it?—that *gent!*"

"You'll remember that all who took part in the competition failed on the long central span," said Griffith.

"No!" contradicted Blake. "*I* didn't. I tell you, it was just as I wrote you I'd do. I worked out a new truss modification. I'd have sworn my cantilever was the only one that could span Michamac Strait."

"And then to have your plans lost!" put in Griffith with keen sympathy beneath his dry croak. "Hell! That bridge would have landed you at the top of the ladder in one jump."

"Losing those plans landed me on a brake-beam, after my worst spree ever," muttered Blake.

"Don't wonder," said Griffith. "What gets me, though, is the way this young Ashton, this lily-white lallapaloozer of a kid-glove C.E., came slipping in with his plans less than a month after the contest. I looked up the records."

"What were you doing, digging into that proposition?" demanded Blake.

"What d' you suppose? Ashton was slick enough to get an ironclad contract as Resident Engineer. His bridge plans are a wonder, but he's proved himself N.G. on construction work. Has to be told how to build his own bridge. I'm on as Consulting Engineer."

"You?" growled Blake. "You, working again for H.V. Leslie!"

"Give the devil his due, Tommy. He's sharp as tacks, but if you've got his name to a straightforward contract—"

"After he threw us down on the Q.T. survey?"

Griffith coughed and hesitated. "Well—now—look here, Tommy, you're not the kind to hold a grudge. Anyway, the bridge was turned over to the Coville Construction Company." He turned quickly to Lord James. "Say, what's that about his being in the papers? If it's anything to his credit, put me next, won't you? I couldn't pry it out of him with a crow-bar."

"So you're going to use a Jimmy instead, eh?" countered Blake.

"Right-o, Tammas," said Lord James. "We're going to open up the incident out of hand."

"Lord!" groaned Blake. He rose, flushing with embarrassment, and swung across, to stare at a blueprint in the far corner of the room.

Lord James flicked the ash from his cigar with his little finger, and smiled at Griffith.

"Tom and I had been knocking around quite a bit, you know," he began.

"Fetched up in South Africa. American engineers in demand on the Rand. Tom was asked to manage a mine."

"He could do it," commented Griffith. "Was two years on a low-grade proposition in Colorado—made it pay dividends. Didn't he suit the Rand people?"

"Better than they suited him, I take it. I left for a run home. Week before I arrived a servant looted the family jewels—heirlooms, all that, you know—chap named Hawkins. Thought I'd play Sherlock Holmes. Learned that my man had booked passage for India. Traced him to Calcutta. Lost two months; found he'd doubled back and gone to the Cape. Cape Town, found he'd booked passage for England under his last alias—Winthrope. Steamer list also showed names of my friend Lady Bayrose, Miss Leslie, and Tom."

"Hey?" ejaculated Griffith, opening his narrowed eyes a line.

"Same time, learned the steamer had been posted as lost, somewhere between Port Natal and Zanzibar."

"Crickey!" gasped Griffith. "Then it was Tom who pulled H.V.'s daughter—Miss Leslie—through that deal! Heard all about it from H.V. himself, when he took me out to Arizona to look over this Zariba Dam proposition. But he didn't name the man. Well, I'll be—switched! Tommy sure did land in High Society that time!"

"They landed in the primitive, so to speak,—he and Miss Leslie and Hawkins,—when the cyclone flung them ashore in the swamps."

"Hawkins? Didn't you just say—"

"Rather a grim joke, was it not? Every soul aboard drowned except those three—Tom and Miss Leslie and Hawkins, of all men!"

"Bet Tommy shook your family jewels out of his pockets mighty sudden."

Lord James lost his smile. "He got them, later on, when the fellow—died."

"Died? How?"

"Fever—another cyclone."

"Eh? Well, God's country is good enough for me. Those tropical holes sure are hell. Tommy once wrote me about one of the Central American ports. You don't ever catch me south of the U.S. This East African proposition, now? Must have been a tough deal even for Tommy."

"They were doing well enough when I found him, both he and Miss Leslie,—skin clothes, poisoned arrows, house in a tree hollow—all that, y'know."

"Well, I'll be—! But that's Tommy, for sure. He's got the kind of brains that get there. If he can't buck through a proposition, he'll triangulate around it. Go on."

"There's not much to tell, I fancy, now that you know he was the man. You're aware that, had it not been for his resourcefulness and courage, Miss Leslie would have perished in that savage land of wild beasts and fever. Yet there is something more than you could have heard from her father, something I'm not free to tell about. Wish I was, 'pon my word, I do! Finest thing he ever did,—something even *we* would not have expected of him."

"Dunno 'bout that," qualified Griffith. "There's mighty little I don't expect of him—if only he can cut out the lushing."

Lord James twisted his mustache. "Ever think of him as wearing a dress suit, Mr. Griffith?"

Griffith looked blank. "Tommy?—in a dress suit!"

"There's one in his box. When we landed in England I took him down to Ruthby. Kept him there a month. You'd have been jolly well pleased to see the way he and the guv'nor hit it off."

"Governor?"

"Yes, my pater—father, y' know."

"So he's a governor? Then Tommy was stringing me about the earl and duke business."

"Oh, no, no, indeed, no. The pater is the Duke of Ruthby, seventh in the line, and twenty-first Earl of Avondale; but he's a crack-up jolly old chap, I assure you. Not all our titled people are of the kind you see most of over here in the States."

"But—hold on—if your father is a real duke, then you're not Mr.—"

"Yes, I must insist upon that. Even in England I am only Mr. Scarbridge—legally, y' know. Hope you'll do me the favor of remembering I prefer it that way."

"I'd do a whole lot for any man *he* calls his friend," said Griffith, gazing across at Blake's broad back. Lord James glanced at his watch, and rose. "Sorry. Must go."

"Well, if you must," said Griffith. "You know the way here now. Drop in any time you feel like it. Rooms are always open. If I'm busy, I've got a pretty good technical library—if you're interested in engineering,—and some photographs of scenery and construction work. Took 'em myself."

"Thanks. I'll come," responded Lord James. He nodded cordially, and turned to call slangily to Blake: "S' long, bo. I'm on my way."

Blake wheeled about from the wall. "What's this? Not going already?"

"Ah, to be sure. Pressing engagement. Must give Wilton time to attire me—those studied effects—last artistic touches, don't y' know," chaffed the Englishman.

But his banter won no responsive smile from his friend. Blake's face darkened.

"You're not going to see her to-day," he muttered.

"How could you think it, Tom?" reproached the younger man, flushing hotly. "I have it! We'll extend the agreement until noon to-morrow. You have that appointment with her father in the morning."

"That's square! Just like you, Jimmy. Course I knew you'd play fair— It's only my grouch. I remember now. Madam G. gave you a bid to dine with her."

Lord James drew out his monocle, replaced it, and smiled. "Er—quite true; but possibly the daughter may be a compensation."

"Sure," assented Blake, a trifle too eagerly, "You're bound to like Miss Dolores. I sized her up for a mighty fine girl. Not at all like her mamma—handsome, lively young lady—just your style, Jimmy."

"Can't see it, old man. Sorry!" replied his lordship. "Good-day. Good-day, Mr. Griffith."

7

THE HERO EXPLAINS

FOR HALF A minute after his titled friend had bowed himself out, Blake stood glowering at the door. The sharp crackle of a blueprint under the thrumming fingers of Griffith caused him to start from his abstraction and cross to the desk, where he dropped heavily into his former seat.

"Well?" demanded Griffith. "Out with it."

"With what?"

"You called him your friend. He's a likely-looking youngster, even if he *is* the son of a duke. Same time, there's something in the wind. Cough it up. Haven't happened to smash any heads or windows, have you, while you were—"

"No!" broke in Blake harshly. "It's worse than that, ten times worse! It's—it's Jenny—Miss Leslie!"

Griffith's thin lips puckered in a soundless whistle. "Well, I'll be—! Don't tell me you've gone and— Why, you never cared a rap for girls."

"No, but this time, Grif— It began when I showed her through that Rand mine. Jimmy has told you what followed."

Griffith blinked, and discreetly said nothing as to what he had heard from Miss Leslie's father. "H'm. I'd like to hear it all, straight from you."

"Can't now. Too long a yarn. I want to tell you about the results. Couldn't do it to any one else," explained Blake, blushing darkly under his thick layer of tropical tan. He sought to beat around the bush. "Well, I proved myself fit to survive in that environment, tough as it was—sort of cave-man's hell. Queer thing, though, Jenny—Miss Leslie—proved fit, too; that is, she did after right at the start. She's got a headpiece, and *grit!*"

"Takes after her dad," suggested Griffith.

"Him!"

"As to the brains and grit."

"Not in anything else, though. They're no more alike than garlic and roses."

"Getting poetic, eh?" cackled Griffith.

"Don't laugh, Grif. It's too serious a matter. I'd do anything in the world for her. She's the truest, grittiest girl alive. She told me straight out, there at the last, that she—she loved me."

"Crickey!" ejaculated Griffith. "She told you that?— she?—Miss—"

"Hush! not so loud!" cautioned Blake. Again the color deepened in his bronzed cheeks. His pale eyes shone very blue and soft. "It was when we heard the siren of Jimmy's steamer. She— You'll forget this, Grif? Never whisper a hint of it?"

"Sure! What you take me for?"

"Well, she wouldn't agree to wait. Wanted to be married as soon as we got aboard ship."

"She—!" Griffith lacked breath even for an expletive.

"I agreed. Couldn't help it, with her looking at me that way. Then we went down around through the cleft to the shore, where the boat was pulling in. Well, there was Jimmy in the sternsheets, in a white yachting suit—Me with my hyena pants, and Jenny in her leopard-skin dress!"

"Say, you *were* doing the Crusoe business!" cackled Griffith.

"It shook me out of my dream all right, soon as I set eyes on Jimmy. I waded out with—Miss Leslie, and put her into the boat. Told him to hurry her aboard. I cut back to the cleft—the place where we'd been staying."

"Off your head, eh?"

"No. Don't you see? I had to save Jenny. I had proved myself a pretty good cave-man, and she had been living so close to that sort of thing that she had lost her perspective. Wasn't fair to her to let her tie herself up to me till she'd first had a chance to size me up with the men of her class."

"You mean to say you passed up your chance?"

"I'd have been a blackguard to 've let her marry me then!" cried Blake, his eyes flashing angrily. He checked himself, and went on in a monotone: "I waited till Jimmy came back to fetch me. Course I had to explain the situation. Asked him to pull out without me, and send down a boat from Port Mozambique. No go. Finally we fixed it up for me to slip aboard into the forecastle."

"Well, I'll be—switched!" croaked Griffith. "You did that, to escape marrying the daughter of a multi-millionaire!"

"It would have been the same if she'd been poor, Grif. She's a lady, through and through, and I—I love her! God! how I love her!"

"Guess that's no lie," commented Griffith in his dryest tone.

Blake relaxed the grip that seemed to be crushing the arms of his chair.

"Well, I went aboard and kept under cover. Jimmy managed to keep her diverted till we put into Port Mozambique. There I sent a note aft to her, letting on that I had already landed, and swearing that I was going to steer clear of her until after she got back to her father. But I kept aboard, in the forecastle, as Jimmy had made me promise to do. At Aden, Jimmy put her on a P. and O. liner in the care of a friend of his, Lady Chetwynd, who was on her way home to England from India."

"He went along, too; leaving you to shift for yourself, eh?"

"Don't you think it! He had been spending half the time forward with me in that stew-hole of a forecastle. Soon as she was safe, I hiked aft and bunked with him. No; Jimmy's as square as they make 'em. To prove it—he had met Jenny before; greatly taken with her. There on the steamer was the very chance he had been after. But he played fair; didn't try to win her. Told me all about it, right at the first, and we came to an agreement. We were both to steer clear of her over on that side. That's why we stuck close to Ruthby Castle till Jenny sailed for home. No; Jimmy is white. He had invitations to more than one house-party where she was visiting around with Lady Chetwynd and Madam Gantry."

"So neither of you have seen her since there at Aden?"

"Yes, we have. Came on from New York with her and her aunt. They had stopped over when they landed, and we blundered into them before we could dodge."

"And Miss Leslie? You look glum. Guess you got what was coming to you, eh?"

Blake's face clouded. "Haven't seen her apart from her aunt yet. She has been kind but—mighty reserved. I'd give a lot to know whether—" He paused, gripping his chair convulsively. "Just the same, I haven't quit. The agreement with Jimmy is off to-morrow afternoon. She's had plenty of time for comparisons. I'll make my try then."

"Don't fash yourself, Tom. If she's the sort you say, and went as far as you say, she's not likely to throw you over now."

"You don't savvy!" exclaimed Blake. "There on that infernal coast I was the real thing—and the only one, at that. Here I'm just T. Blake, ex-bum, periodic drunkard, all around—"

"Stow that drivel!" ordered Griffith. "What if you were a kid hobo? What are you now?—one of the best engineers in the country; one that's going to make the top in short order. I tell you, you're going to succeed. What's more, Mollie said—"

"Mollie!" repeated Blake softly. "Say, but wasn't she a booster! Had even you beat, hands down. Good Lord, to think that she, of all the little women—! Only thing, typhoid isn't so bad as some things. They don't suffer so much."

"Yes," assented Griffith. "That helps—some—when I get to thinking of it. She went out quietly—wasn't thinking of herself."

"She never did!" put in Blake, "Say, but can't a woman make a heap of difference—when she's the right sort!"

"There was a message for you. She said, almost the last

thing: 'Tell Tom not to give up the fight. Tell him,' she said, 'he'll win out, I know he'll win out in the end.'"

"God!" whispered Blake. "She said that?" He bent over and covered his eyes with his hand.

Griffith averted his head and peered at the blueprints on the nearest wall with unseeing eyes. A full minute passed. Keeping his face still averted, he began to tap out the ash and half-smoked tobacco from his pipe.

"H'm—guess you'd better work in a room apart," he remarked in a matter-of-fact tone. "Too much running in and out here. D'you want to start right off?"

"No," muttered Blake. He paused and then straightened to face his friend. His eyes were blood-shot but resolute, his face impassive. "No. I'll wait till after to-morrow. Big order on for to-morrow morning. Appointment to meet H.V."

"Hey?"

"He was down at the depot. You can imagine how effusive he wasn't over my saving his daughter. Curse the luck! If only she had had any one else for a father!"

"Now, now, Tommy, don't fly off the handle. You know there are lots of 'em worse than H.V."

"None I'm in so hard with. First place, there's that Q.T. survey."

"That's all smoothed over. He came around all right. Just ask for your pay-check. He'll shell out."

"I'll ask for interest. Ought to have a hundred per cent. I needed the money then mighty bad."

"We all did. Let it slide. He's her father. You can't afford to buck his game."

"I'd do it quick enough if it wasn't for her," rejoined Blake. "That's where he's got me. Lord! if only he and she weren't—!" Blake's teeth clenched on the end of the sentence.

"Now look here, Tommy," protested Griffith. "This isn't like you to hold a grudge. It's true H.V. did us dirt on the survey pay. But he gave in, soon as I got a chance to talk it over with him."

"'Cause he had to have you on the Michamac Bridge, eh?" demanded Blake, his face darkening.

"Stow it! That may be true, but—didn't I tell you he turned the bridge over to the Coville Company?"

"Afraid he'd be found out, eh?"

"Found out? What do you mean?"

"Mean!" repeated Blake, his voice hoarse with passion. He brought his big fist down upon the desk with the thud of a maul. "Mean? Listen here! I didn't write it to you—I couldn't believe it then, even of him. But answer me this, if you can. I was fool enough not to send my plans for the bridge competition to him by registered mail; I was fool enough to hand them in to his secretary without asking a receipt. After the contest, I called for my plans. Clerk told me he couldn't find them; couldn't find any record that they'd been received. I tell you my plans solved that central span problem. Who was it could use my plans?—who were they worth a mint of money to?"

Griffith stared at his friend, his forehead furrowed with an anxious frown. "See here, Tom—this tropical rough-ing—it must be mighty overtaxing on a man. You didn't happen to have a sunstroke or—"

Blake's scowl relaxed in an ironical grin. "All right, take it that way, if you want to. *He* let on he thought I was trying to blackmail him."

"Crickey! You don't mean to say you—"

"Didn't get a chance to see him that time. Just sent in a polite note asking for my plans. He sent out word by his private-detective office-boy that if I called again he'd have me run in."

"And now you come back with this dotty pipe-dream that he knows what became of your plans! Take my advice. Think it all you want, if that does you any good; but keep your head closed—keep it closed! First thing he'd do would be to look up the phone number of the nearest asylum."

"I'd like to see him do it," replied Blake. He shook his head dubiously. "That's straight, Grif. I'd like to see him do it. I can't forget he's her father. If only I could be sure he hadn't a finger in the disappearance of those plans—Well, you can guess how I feel about it."

"You're dotty to think it a minute. He's a money-grub-ber—as sharp as some others. But he wouldn't do a thing like that. Don't you believe it!"

"Wish I'd never thought of it—he's her father. But it's been growing on me. I handed them in to his secretary, that young dude, Ashton."

"Ashton? There you've hit on a probability," argued Griffith. "Of all the heedless, inefficient papa's boys, he takes the cake! He wasn't H.V.'s secretary except in name. Wine, women, sports, and gambling—nothing else under his hat. Always had a mess on his desk. Ten to one, he got your package mixed in the litter, and shoved all together into his wastebasket."

"I'll put it up to him!" growled Blake.

"What's the use? He couldn't remember a matter of business over night, to save him."

"Lord! I sweat blood over those plans! It was hard enough to enter a competition put up by H. V., but it was the chance of a lifetime for me. Why, if only I'd known in time that they were lost, I'd have put in my scratch drawings and won on *them*. I tell you, Grif, that truss was something new."

"Oh, no, there's no inventiveness, no brains in your head, oh, no!" rallied Griffith. "Wait till you make good on this Zariba Dam."

"You just bet I'll make a stagger at it!" cried Blake. His eyes shone bright with the joy of work,—and as suddenly clouded with renewed moroseness.

"I'll be working for you, though," he qualified. "I don't take any jobs from H. V. Leslie—not until that matter of the bridge plans is cleared up."

8

FLINT AND STEEL

AT THREE MINUTES to ten the following morning Blake entered the doorway of the mammoth International Industrial Company Building. At one minute to ten he was facing the outermost of the guards who fenced in the private office of H.V. Leslie, capitalist.

"Your business, sir? Mr. Leslie is very busy, sir."

"He told me to call this morning," explained Blake.

"Step in, sir, please."

Blake entered, and found himself in a well-remembered waiting-room, in company with a dozen or more visitors. He swung leisurely across to the second uniformed door-keeper.

"Business?" demanded this attendant with a brusqueness due perhaps to his closer proximity to the great man.

Blake answered without the flicker of a smile: "I'm a civil engineer, if you want to know."

"Your business here?"

"None that concerns you," rejoined Blake.

His eyes fixed upon the man with a cold steely glint that visibly disconcerted him. But the fellow had been in training for years. He replied promptly, though in a more civil tone: "If you do not wish to state your business to me, sir, you'll have to wait until—"

"No, I won't have to wait until," put in Blake. "Your boss told me to call at ten sharp."

"In that case, of course—Your name, please."

"Blake."

The man slipped inside, closing the door behind him. He was gone perhaps a quarter of a minute. When he reappeared, he held the door half open for Blake.

"Step in, sir," he said. "Mr. Leslie can spare you fifteen minutes."

Blake looked the man up and down coolly. "See here," he replied, "just you trot back and tell Mr. H. V. Leslie I'm much obliged for his favoring me with an appointment, but long as he's so rushed, I'll make him a present of his blessed quarter-hour."

"My land, sir!" gasped the doorkeeper. "I can't take such a message to *him!*"

"Suit yourself," said Blake, deliberately drawing a cigar from his vest pocket and biting off the tip.

This time the man was gone a full half-minute. He eyed Blake with respectful curiosity as he swung the door wide open and announced: "Mr. Leslie asks you to come in, sir."

As the door closed softly behind him, Blake stared around the bare little room into which he had been shown. He was looking for the third guardian of the sanctum,— the great man's private secretary. But the room was empty. Without pausing, he crossed to the door in the side wall and walked aggressively into the private office of Genevieve's father.

Mr. Leslie sat at a neat little desk, hurriedly mumbling into the trumpet of a small phonograph.

"Moment!" he flung out sideways, and went on with his mumbling.

Blake swung around one of the heavy leather-seated chairs with a twist of his wrist, and drew out a silver match-safe. As he took out a match, Mr. Leslie touched a spring that stopped the whirring mechanism of the phonograph, and wheeled around in his swivel desk-chair.

"Dictate on wax," he explained. "Cuts out stenographer. Any clerk can typewrite. No mislaid stenographer's notes; no mistakes. Well, you're nearly on time."

"Sharp at the door, according to your waiting-room clock," said Blake, striking the match on his heel.

"Good—punctuality. First point you score. Now, what do you expect to get out of me?"

Blake held the match to his cigar with deliberate care, blew it out, and flipped it into the wastebasket, with the terse answer: "Just *that* much."

The other's bushy eyebrows came down over the keen eyes. For a full minute the two stared, the man of business seeking to pierce with his narrowed glance Blake's hard, open gaze. The failure of his attempt perhaps irritated him beyond discretion. At any rate, his silent antagonism burst out in an explosion of irascibility.

"Needn't tell me your game, young man," he rasped. "You think, because you were alone with my daughter, you can force me to pay hush money."

Blake rose to his feet with a look in his eyes before which Mr. Leslie shrank back and cringed.

"Wait! Sit down! sit down! I—I didn't mean that!" he exclaimed.

Blake drew in a deep breath and slowly sat down again. He said nothing, but puffed hard at his cigar.

Mr. Leslie rebounded from panic to renewed irascibility. "H'm! So you're one of that sort. I might have foreseen it."

Blake looked his indifference. "All right. That's the safety-valve. Blow off all the steam you want to through it. Only don't try the other again. You're her father, and that gives you a big vantage. Any one else have said what you did, he wouldn't have had the chance to take it back."

"Do you mean to threaten me?"

"I've smashed men for less."

"You look the part."

"It's not the part of a lickspittle."

"Look here, young man. As the man who happened to save the life of my daughter—"

"Suppose we leave her out of this palaver," suggested Blake.

"Unfortunately, that is impossible. It is solely owing to the obligations under which your service to her have put me that I—"

"That you're willing to let me come in here and listen to your pleasant conversation," broke in Blake ironically. "Well, let me tell you, I'm some busy myself these days. Just now I'm out collecting one of your past-due obligations, I've heard you admit you owe for that first Q.T. Railroad survey."

"There was no legal claim on me. I conceded the point at the request of Mr. Griffith."

"Had to hire him, eh? Best consulting engineer in the city. And he held out for a settlement," rallied Blake.

"You were one of the party?"

"Transitman."

"Then apply to my auditor. He has your pay-check waiting for you."

"How about interest? It's two years over-due."

"I never allow interest on such accounts."

Blake took out his cigar and looked at his antagonist, his jaw out-thrust. "If I had a million, I wouldn't mind spending it to make you pay that interest."

"You could spend twice that, and then not get it," snapped Mr. Leslie. "You'll soon find out I can't be driven, young man. On the other hand—how big a position do you think you could fill?"

"*Quien sabe?*"

"See here. You've put me under obligations. I'd rather it had been any other man than you—"

"Ditto on you!" rejoined Blake.

The blow struck a shower of flinty sparks from Mr. Leslie's narrowed eyes.

"You'll do well to be more conciliatory, young man," he warned.

"Conciliatory? *Bah!*"

"Didn't take you for a fool."

"Well, you won't take me in for one," countered Blake.

"You seem determined to hurt your own interests. Unfortunately you've put me in your debt—an obligation I must pay in full."

"Why not get a receiver appointed, and reorganize?" gibed Blake.

"That's one of the ways you dodge obligations, isn't it?"

Mr. Leslie's wrinkled face quickly turned red, and from red to purple. He thrust a quivering finger against a push-button. Blake grinned exultantly and picked up his hat.

"Don't bother your bouncer," he remarked in a cheerful tone. "I don't need any invitation to leave."

The tall doorkeeper stepped alertly into the room, but turned back on the instant at sight of his master's repellent gesture.

"Mistake," snapped Mr. Leslie, and as the man disappeared, he turned to Blake. "Wait! Don't go yet."

Blake was rising to his feet. He paused, considered, and resumed his seat. Mr. Leslie had regained his normal color and his composure. He put his finger-tips together, and jerked out in his usual incisive tone: "I propose to liquidate this obligation to you without delay. Would you prefer a cash payment?"

"No." Again Blake set his jaw. "You couldn't settle with me for cash, not even if you overdrew your bank account."

"Nonsense!" snapped Mr. Leslie. He studied the young man's resolute face, and asked impatiently, "Well—what?"

"Can't you get it into your head?" rejoined Blake. "I'm not asking for any pay for what I did."

"What, then? If not a money reward—I see. You're perhaps ambitious. You want to make a name in your profession."

"Ever know an engineer that didn't?"

"I see. I'll arrange to give you a position that—"

"Thanks," broke in Blake dryly. "Wait till I ask you for a job."

"What are you going to do?—loaf?"

"That's my business."

Mr. Leslie again studied Blake's face. Though accustomed to read men at a glance, he was baffled by the engineer's inscrutable calm.

"You nearly always win at poker," he stated.

"Used to," confirmed Blake. "Cut it out, though. A gambler is a fool. More fun in a nickel earned than a dollar made at play or speculating."

"So! You're one of these socialist cranks."

Blake laughed outright. "It's the cranks that make the world go 'round! No; I've been too busy boosting for Number One—like you—to let myself think of the other fellow. The trouble with that crazy outfit is they want to set you to working for the people, instead of working the people. No; I've steered clear of them. 'Fraid I might get infected with altruism. Like you, I'm a born anarchist— excuse me!—individualist. What would become of those who have the big interests of the country at heart if they didn't have the big interests in hand?"

Mr. Leslie ignored the sarcasm. "Either you're a fool, or you're playing a deep game. It occurs to me you may have heard that my daughter has money in her own right."

"Three million, she said," assented Blake.

"She told you!"

"Guess she told me more than she seems to have told you."

"About what?"

"Ask her."

Mr. Leslie's eyes narrowed to thin slits. "Her aunt wrote

me that she suspected you had the effrontery to—aspire to my daughter's hand. I couldn't believe it possible."

"That so?" said Blake with calm indifference.

Mr. Leslie started as though stung. "It's true, then! You—you!—" He choked with rage.

"I thought that would reach you," commented Blake.

"You rascal! you blackguard!" spluttered Mr. Leslie. "So that's your game? You know she's an heiress! Think you have the whip-handle—bleed me or force her to marry you!— Alone with her after the other man—! You—you scoundrel! you blackguard! I'll—"

"Shut up!" commanded Blake, his voice low-pitched and hoarse, his face white to the lips. For the second time during the interview Mr. Leslie cringed before his look. His pale eyes were like balls of white-hot steel.

Slowly the glare faded from Blake's eyes, and the color returned to his bronzed face. He relaxed his fists.

"God!" he whispered huskily. "God!... But you're her father!"

Something in his tone compelled conviction, despite Mr. Leslie's bitter prejudice. He jerked out reluctantly: "I'm not so sure—perhaps I spoke too—too hastily. But—the indications—"

"Needn't try to apologize," growled Blake.

"I'll not—in words. How about a twenty-five-thou-sand-dollar position?"

"What?" demanded Blake, astonished.

"That, as a beginning. If you prove yourself the kind of man I think you are,—the kind that can learn to run a railroad system,—I'll push you up the line to a hundred thousand, besides chances to come in on stock deals with George Ashton and myself."

"But if you think I'm a—"

"You're the only man that ever outfaced me in my own office. I'll chance the rest,—though I had your record looked up as soon as your name was cabled to me. I know not only who you are but *what* you are."

Blake bent forward, frowning. "I've stood about enough of this."

"Wait," said Mr. Leslie. "I'm not going to drag that in. I mention it only that you will understand without argument why my offer is based on the condition that you at once and for all time give over your ridiculous idea of becoming my son-in-law."

"You—mean—that—?"

"That I'd rather see my daughter in her grave than married to you. Is that plain enough? You're a good engineer—when you're not a *drunkard.*"

For a moment Blake sat tense and silent. Then he replied steadily: "I haven't touched a drop of drink since that steamer piled up on that coral reef."

"Three months, at the outside," rejoined Mr. Leslie. "You've been known to go half a year. But always—"

"Yes, always before this try," said Blake. "It's different, though, now, with the backing of two such—ladies!"

"Two?" queried Mr. Leslie sharply.

"One's dead," replied Blake with simple gravity.

"H'm. I—it's possible I've misjudged you in some things. But this question of drink—I'll risk backing you in a business way, if it costs me a million. I owe you that much. But I won't risk my daughter's happiness—supposing you had so much as a shadow of a chance of winning her. No! You saved her life. You shall have no chance whatever to make her miserable. But I'll give you opportunities—I'll put you on the road to making your own millions."

Blake raised his cigar and flecked off the ash. "*That* for your damned millions!" he swore.

Mr. Leslie stared and muttered to himself: "Might have known it! Man of that kind. Crazy fool!"

"Fool?" repeated Blake contemptuously. "Just because money is *your* god, you needn't think it's everybody else's. You—money—hog! You think I'd sell out my chance of winning *her!*"

"You have no chance, sir! The thought of such a thing is absurd—ridiculous!"

"Well, then, why don't you laugh? No; you hear me. If I knew I didn't have one chance in a million, I'd tell you to take your offer and—"

"Now, now! make no rash statements. I'm offering you, to begin with, a twenty-five-thousand-dollar position, and your chance to acquire a fortune, if you—"

Blake's smouldering anger flared out in white heat. "Think you can bribe me, do you? Well, you can just take your positions and your dollars, and go clean, plumb to hell!"

"That will do, sir!—that will do!" gasped Mr. Leslie, shocked almost beyond speech.

"No, it won't do, Mr. H.V. Leslie!" retorted Blake. "I'm not one of your employees, to throw a fit when you put on the heavy pedal, and I'm not one of the lickspittles that are always *baa-ing* around the Golden Calf. You've had your say. Now I'll have mine. To begin with, let me tell you, I don't need your positions or your money. Griffith has given me work. I'm working for him, not you. Understand?"

"You are? He's my consulting engineer."

"That cuts no ice. I'm doing some work for him—for *him;* understand? It's not for you. He gave me the job—not you. After what you've said to me here, I wouldn't take a *hundred*-thousand-dollar job from you, not if I was walking around on my uppers. Understand?"

"But—but—"

Blake's anger burst out in volcanic rage. "That's it, straight! I don't want your jobs or your money. They're dirty! You've looked up my record, have you? How about your own? How about the Michamac Bridge? Griffith says the Coville Company has taken it over; but you started it—you called for plans—you advertised a competition. Where are my plans?—you!"

Mr. Leslie shrank back before the enraged engineer.

"Calm yourself, Mr. Blake!" he soothed in a quavering voice. "Calm yourself! This illusion of yours about lost plans—"

"Illusion?" cried Blake. "When I handed them in myself to your secretary—that dude, Ashton."

Mr. Leslie sat up, keenly alert. "To him? You say you handed in a set of bridge plans to my former secretary?"

"He wasn't a *former* secretary then."

"To young Ashton, at that time my secretary. Where was it?"

"In there," muttered Blake, jerking his thumb towards the empty anteroom. "I had to butt in to get even that far."

"Why didn't you show your receipt when you applied for your plans?"

"Hadn't a receipt."

"You didn't take a receipt?"

"And after that Q.T. survey, too!" thrust Blake. "I sure did play the fool, didn't I? But I was all up in the air over the way I had worked out that central span, and didn't think of anything but the committee you'd appointed to pass on the competing plans. Those judges were all right. I knew they'd be square."

"Sure you had any plans? Where's your proof?" demanded Mr. Leslie with a shrewdness that won a sarcastic grin from Blake.

"Don't fash yourself," he jeered. "You're safe—legally. Of course my scratch copy of them went down in the steamer. The fact I wrote Griffith about them before the contest wouldn't cut any ice—with your lawyers across the table from any I could afford to hire."

"Griffith knows about your plans?"

"Didn't get a chance to show them to him. All he knows is I wrote him I was drawing them to compete for the bridge—which of course was part of my plan to blackmail you," gibed Blake. He rose, with a look that was almost good-humored. "Well, guess we're through swapping compliments. I won't take up any of your valuable time discussing the weather."

With shrewd eyes blinking uneasily under their shaggy brows, Mr. Leslie watched his visitor cross towards the door. The engineer walked firmly and resolutely, with his head well up, yet without any trace of swagger or bravado.

As he reached for the doorknob, Mr. Leslie bent forward and called in an irritable tone: "Wait! I want to tell you—"

"Excuse *me!* My time's too valuable," rejoined Blake, and he swung out of the room.

Mr. Leslie sat for a few moments with his forehead creased in intent thought. He roused, to touch a button with an incisive thrust of his finger. To the clerk who came hastening in he ordered tersely: "Phone Griffith—appointment nine-fifteen to-morrow. Important."

9

PLAYS FOR POSITION

ABOUT THREE O'CLOCK of the same day a smart electric *coupé* whirled up Lake Shore Drive under a rattling fusillade of sleet from over the lake. At the entrance of the grounds of the Leslie mansion it curved around and shot in under the porte-cochère.

A footman in the quiet dark green and black of the Leslie livery sprang out to open the *coupé* door, while the footman with the *coupé*, whose livery was not so quiet, swung down to hand out the occupants. Before the servant could offer his services, Dolores Gantry darted out past him and in through the welcome doorway of the side entrance. Her mother followed with stately leisure, regardless of a wind-flung dash of sleet on her sealskins.

Having been relieved of their furs, the callers were shown to the drawing-room. As the footman glided away to inform his mistress of their arrival, Dolores danced across to the door of the rear drawing-room and called in a clear, full-throated, contralto voice: "Ho, Vievie! Vievie! You in here? Hurry up! There's something I do so want to tell you."

Mrs. Gantry paused in the act of seating herself.

"Dolores! Why must you shriek out like a magpie? Will you never forget you're a tomboy?"

"I'm not, mamma. I'm simply acting as if I were one. You forget I'm a full-blown *débutante*. Vievie has already promised me a ball."

"Behave yourself, if you wish to attend it."

Dolores jumped to a chair and sank into it with an air of elegant languor. "Yes, mamma. This—ah—driving in moist weather is so fatiguing, don't you find it?"

Mrs. Gantry disposed herself upon the comfortable seat that she had selected, and raised her gold lorgnette. "Do not forget that the ball Genevieve has so generously promised you is to be honored by the presence—"

"Of a real live earl and a real hero, with Laffie Ashton thrown in for good—I mean, bad—measure!" cut in Dolores with enthusiasm. "You know, I asked Vievie to 'put him on her list, else he never may be kissed!'"

Again Mrs. Gantry raised her lorgnette to transfix her daughter with her cold stare. "*You* asked her to invite Lafayette Ashton? And you know his reputation!"

"Of course. But you mustn't ask for the details, mamma," reproved the girl. "It's best that you should not become aware of such things, my dear. Only, you know, 'boys will be boys,' and we must not lose sight of the fact that poor dear Laffie will be worth twenty millions some day—if his papa doesn't make a will. Besides, he dances divinely. Of course Earl Jimmy's mustache is simply too cute for anything, but, alas! unless Vievie clings to her heroic Tommy—"

"Tommyrot!" sniffed Mrs. Gantry. "The presumption of that low fellow! To think of his following her to America!"

"You should have forewarned the authorities at Ellis Island, and had him excluded as dangerous—to your plans."

"No more of this frivolity! I've confided to you that that man is dangerous to Genevieve's happiness. I'll not permit it. What a fortunate chance that the earl came with him! I shall see to it that Genevieve becomes a countess."

Dolores pulled a mock-tragic face. "Oh, mamma," she implored, "why don't you root for me, instead? I'm sure a coronet would fit me to perfection, and his mustache is *so* cute!"

To judge by Mrs. Gantry's expression, it was fortunate for her daughter that Genevieve came in upon them. Dolores divined this last from the sudden mellowing of her mother's face. She whirled up out of her chair and around, with a cry of joyous escape: "Oh, Vievie! You're just in time to save me!"

"From what, dear?" asked Genevieve, smilingly permitting herself to be crumpled in an impetuous embrace.

"Mamma was just going to run the steam-roller over me, simply because I said Jimmy's mustache is cute. It *is* cute, isn't it?"

"'Jimmy'?" inquired Genevieve, moving to a chair beside Mrs. Gantry.

"His honorable earlship, then—since mamma is with us."

"You may leave the room," said her mother.

"I may," repeated the girl. She pirouetted up the room and stopped to look at a painting of a desolate tropical coast.

"It's such a dreadful day out, Aunt Amice," said Genevieve. "And you can't be rested from the trip."

"Quite true, my dear," agreed Mrs. Gantry. "But I had to see you—to talk matters over with you. I did not wish to break in on your enjoyment of those delightful English house parties; and crossing over, you know, I was too wretchedly ill to think of anything. Can I never get accustomed to the sea!"

"It's so unfortunate," condoled Genevieve. "I believe I'm a born sailor."

"You proved it, starting off with that globe-trotting Lady Bayrose."

"Poor Lady Bayrose! To think that she—" The girl pressed her hands to her eyes. "The way that frightful breaker whirled the boat loose and over and over!—and the water swarming with sharks!"

"Do not think of it, my dear! Really, you must not think of it!" urged Mrs. Gantry. "Be thankful it happened before the sailors had time to put you in the same boat. Better still, my dear, do not permit yourself to think of it at all. Put all that dreadful experience out of your mind."

"But you do not understand, Aunt Amice. I fear you never will. Except for that—for poor Lady Bayrose—I've told you, I do not wish to forget it."

"My dear!" protested Mrs. Gantry, "cannot you realize how very improper—? That man! What if he should talk?"

"Is there anything to be concealed?" asked Genevieve, with quiet dignity.

"You know how people misconstrue things," insisted her aunt. "That newspaper notoriety was quite sufficiently— It's most fortunate that Lord Avondale is not affected. I must admit, his attitude towards that man puzzles me."

"I can understand it very well," replied Genevieve, firmly.

"You both insist that the fellow is—is not absolutely unspeakable! I should never have thought it of you, Genevieve, nor of such a thorough gentleman as Lord Avondale—gentleman in *our* sense of the term,—refined, cultured, and *clean*. Were he one of the gentry who have reasons for leaving England,—who go West and consort with ruffians—remittance men—But no. Lady Chetwynd assured me he has been presented at Court, and you know the strictness of Queen Mary."

"You admit that Lord Avondale is, shall I say—perfect. Yet—"

"He is irreproachable, my dear, except as regards his extraordinary insistence upon an intimate friendship with that man."

"That is what confirms my good opinion of him, Aunt Amice."

"That!"

"It proves he is himself manly and sincere."

Mrs. Gantry raised a plump hand, palm outward. "Between the two of you—"

"We know Mr. Blake—the real man. You do not."

"I never shall. I will not receive him—never. He is impossible!"

"What! never?—the man who saved me from starvation, fever, wild beasts, from all the horrors of that savage coast?—the intimate friend of the Earl of Avondale?"

"Does he paint, Vievie?" called Dolores. "Is this a picture of your Crusoe coast?"

"No, dear. I bought that in New York. But it is very like the place where Tom—"

"'Tom'!" reproached Mrs. Gantry. She looked around at her daughter.

"Dolores, I presumed you left us when I ordered you."

"Oh, no, not 'ordered,' mamma. You said 'may,' not 'must.'"

"Leave the room!"

The girl sauntered down towards the arched opening into the rear drawing-room. As she passed the others, she paused to pat her cousin's soft brown hair.

"I do believe the sun has burnt it a shade lighter, Vievie," she remarked. "What fun it must have been! When *are* you going to show me that leopard-skin gown?"

"Leave the room this instant!" commanded Mrs. Gantry.

Dolores crossed her hands on her bosom and crept out with an air of martyred innocence. Her mother turned to Genevieve for sympathy. "That girl! I don't know what ever I shall do with her—absolutely irrepressible! These titled Englishmen are so particular—she is your cousin."

Genevieve colored slightly. "You should know Lord Avondale better. If he is at all interested—"

"He is, most decidedly. He dined with us last evening. Laffie Ashton called; so I succeeded in getting the earl away from Dolores. We had a most satisfying little *tête-à-tête*. I led him into explaining everything."

"Everything?" queried Genevieve.

"Yes, everything, my dear. His aloofness since you reached Aden has been due merely to his high sense of honor,—to an absurd but chivalrous agreement with that fellow to not press his suit until after your arrival home. At Aden he had given the man his word—"

"At Aden?" interrupted Genevieve. "How could that be, when Tom left the ship at Port Mozambique?"

"He didn't. It seems that the fellow was aboard all the time, hiding in the steerage or stoke-hole, or somewhere—no doubt to spy on you and Lord Avondale."

Genevieve averted her head and murmured in a half whisper: "He was aboard all that time, and never came up for a breath of air all those smothering days! I remember Lord James speaking of how hot and vile it was down in the forecastle. This explains why he went forward so much!"

"It explains why he did not book passage with you from Aden—why he did not hasten to you at Lady Chetwynd's—all because of his chivalrous but mistaken sense of loyalty to that low fellow."

"If you please, Aunt Amice," said Genevieve, in a tone as incisive as it was quiet, "you will remember that I esteem Mr. Blake."

Mrs. Gantry stared over her half-raised lorgnette. She had never before known her niece to be other than the very pattern of docility.

"Well!" she remarked, and, after a little pause; "Fortunately, that absurd agreement is now at an end. The earl intimated that he would call on you this afternoon. I am sure, my dear—"

Of what the lady was sure was left to conjecture. The footman appeared in the hall entrance and announced: "Mr. Brice-Ashton."

Ashton came in, effusive and eager. "My dear Miss Genevieve! I—ah, Mrs. Gantry! Didn't expect to meet you here, such a day as this. Most unexpected—ah—pleasure! *N'est-ce pas?*— No, no! my dear Miss Leslie; keep your seat!"

Genevieve had seemed about to rise, but he quite deftly drew a chair around and sat down close before her. "I simply couldn't wait any longer. I felt I must call to congratulate you over that marvellous escape. It must have been terrible—terrible!"

Genevieve replied with perceptible coldness: "Thank you, Mr. Ashton. I had not expected a call from you."

"'Mr.' Ashton!" he echoed. "Has it come to that?—when we used to make mudpies together! Dolores said that you—"

"Not so fast, Laffie!" called the girl, as she came dancing into the room in her most animated manner. "Don't forget I'm Miss Gantry now."

Ashton continued to address Genevieve, without turning: "I came all the way down from Michamac just to congratulate you—left my bridge!"

"You're too sudden with your congratulations, Laffie," mocked Dolores.

"Genevieve hasn't yet decided whether it's to be the hero or the earl."

"Dolores," admonished her mother. "I told you to leave the room."

"Yes, and forgot to tell me to stay out. It's no use now, is it? Unless you wish me to drag out Laffie for a little *tête-à-tête* in the conservatory."

"Sit down, dear," said Genevieve.

Mrs. Gantry turned to Ashton with a sudden unbending from hauteur. "My dear Lafayette, I observed your manner yesterday towards that—towards Mr. Blake. Am

I right in surmising that you know something with regard to his past?"

"About Blake?" replied Ashton, his usually wide and ardent eyes shifting their glance uneasily from his questioner to Genevieve and towards the outer door.

"About my friend Mr. Blake," said Genevieve.

"You call him a friend?—a fellow like that!" Ashton rashly exclaimed.

"He has proved himself a disinterested friend,—which I cannot say of all with whom I am acquainted."

"Oh, of course, if you feel that way."

"My other friends will remember that he saved my life."

"If only he had been a gentleman!" sighed Mrs. Gantry.

"Yes, Vievie," added Dolores. "Next time any one goes to save you, shoo him off unless he first offers his card."

"Mr. Blake is what many a seeming gentleman is not," said Genevieve, her levelled glance fixed upon Ashton. "Tom Blake is a man, a strong, courageous man!"

"We quite agree with you," ventured Ashton. "He is a man of the type one so frequently sees among firemen and the police."

Mrs. Gantry intervened with quick tact: "Mr. Blake is quite an eminent civil engineer, we understand. As a fellow engineer, you have met him, I dare say—have had dealings with him."

"I?—with him? No—that is—" Ashton stammered and shifted about uneasily under Genevieve's level gaze. "It was only when I was acting as Mr. Leslie's secretary. Blake handed me the bridge plans that he afterwards claimed were lost. I tell you, I had nothing to do with them—nothing! I merely received them from him. That was all. I went

away the very next day—resigned my position. I don't
know what became of his plans,—nothing whatever! I tell
you, the Michamac Bridge—"

"Why, Lame!" giggled Dolores. "What makes you
squirm so? You're twitching all over. I thought you'd had
enough of the simple life at Michamac to recover from the
effects of that corner in oats. You haven't started another
corner already, have you?"

"No, I have—I mean, yes—just a few cocktails at the
club—yes, that's it. So bitter cold, this sleet! You'll understand, Mrs. Gantry—perhaps one too much. Haven't had
any since I went back to the bridge last time."

"Then up at Michamac you take it straight?" asked
Dolores.

Ashton forced a nervous laugh. "Keep it up, Dodie!
You'll make a wit yet." He bent towards Genevieve. "You'll
pardon me, won't you, Genevieve?"

The girl raised her fine brows ever so slightly. "'Miss
Leslie,' if you please."

"Of course—of course! Just another slip—that last cock-
tail and the sleet. Wet cold always sends it to my head. That
about Blake, too—I oughtn't to 've spoken of it after you
said he was your friend. It's, of course, your father's affair."

"Then you need say no more about it," said Genevieve
with ironical graciousness. He shifted about in his chair,
and she caught him deftly. "Must you be going?—really!
Good-day."

He rose uncertainly to his feet, his handsome face
flushed, and his full red lower lip twitching.

"I—I had not intended—" he began.

"Good-day!" said Mrs. Gantry with significant emphasis.

"So sorry you must rush off so soon, Laffie," mocked Dolores.

Social training has its value. Ashton pulled himself together, bowed gracefully, and started up the room with easy assurance.

As he neared the doorway, the footman appeared and announced with unction: "The Right Honorable, the Earl of Avondale."

Ashton stopped short, and when the Englishman entered, met him with an effusive greeting: *"Mon Dieu!* Such a fortunate chance, your lordship! So glad to meet you again,—and here, of all places! Don't forget to look me up at my clubs."

"Hearts are trumps, Laffie—not clubs," called Dolores, as Lord James passed him by with a vague nod.

10

THE SHADOW OF DOUBT

BEFORE THE EARL had reached them Mrs. Gantry was rising.

Genevieve rose to protest. "You're not going so soon, Aunt Amice? You'll stay for a cup of tea?"

"Not to-day, my dear. Ah, earl! you're just in time to relieve Genevieve from the ennui of a solitary afternoon. I regret so much that we cannot stay with you. Come, Dolores."

Dolores settled back comfortably on her chair. "Go right on, mamma. Don't wait for me. I'll stay and help Vievie entertain Lord Avondale."

"Come—at once."

"Oh, fudge! Well, start on. I'll catch you."

Mrs. Gantry stepped past Lord James. Genevieve met his eager glance, and hastened to overtake her aunt. "Really, won't you stay, Aunt Amice? I'll have tea brought in at once."

"So sorry, my dear," replied Mrs. Gantry, placidly sailing on towards the reception hall.

Dolores simulated a yawn. "O-o-ho! I'm so tired. Will nobody help me get up?"

With a boyish twinkle in his gray eyes but profound

gravity In his manner, Lord James offered her his hand. She placed her fingers in his palm and sprang up beside him. The others were still moving up the room. She surprised him by meeting his amused gaze with an angry flash of her big black eyes.

"Shame!" she flung at him. "You, his friend, and would take her from him!"

He stared blankly. The girl whirled away from him with a swish of silken skirts and fled past her mother, all her anger lost in wild panic.

"Dolores! Whatever can—" cried Mrs. Gantry. But Dolores had vanished.

"Really, Genevieve, that madcap girl—! About yourself, my dear. Promise me now, if you cannot say 'yes,' at least you'll not make it a final 'no.'"

"But, Aunt Amice, unless I feel—"

"Promise me! You must give yourself time to make sure. He will wait. I am certain he will wait until you have found out—"

"I cannot promise anything now," replied Genevieve.

Mrs. Gantry did not press the point. It was the second time during the call that her niece had proved herself less docile than she had expected. As she left the room, Genevieve returned to Lord James without any outward sign of hesitancy. She seated herself and smiled composedly at her caller, who still stood in the daze into which Dolores's outburst had thrown him.

"Won't you sit down?" she invited. "How is Mr. Blake?"

With rather an abstracted air, Lord James sank down on the chair opposite her and began fiddling with the cord of his monocle.

"Haven't seen him since yesterday," he replied, "Left him at the office of a Mr. Griffith—engineer—old friend. Gave him work immediately—something big, I take it. Asked Tom to bunk with him."

"It's so good to hear he has work already—and to stay with a friend! You mean, live with him?"

"Yes."

"He—the friend—seems desirable?"

"Decidedly so, I should say. Engineer who first started him on his career, if I remember aright what Tom once told me of his early life."

"Oh, that is such good news! But have you seen him since—since this morning? He had that appointment with papa, you know."

"No, I regret to say I haven't; and I fear I cannot reassure you as to the outcome. You know Tom's way; and your father, I take it, is rather—It would seem that they had a disagreement before Tom went West the last time."

"Yes. He once referred to it. Some misunderstanding with regard to the payment of a railway survey. I asked papa about it last evening, and he told me that it had been made all right—that Tom would get his pay for his share in the survey."

"Little enough, in the circumstances," remarked Lord James.

"That was not all. Papa promised to give him a very good position. He had intended to offer money. But I explained to him that, of course, Tom would not accept money."

"Very true. I doubt if he would have accepted it even had it not been for his hope that—" Lord James paused and stared glumly at his finger-tips. "Bally mess, deuce take it! He and your father at outs, and he and I—"

"You have not quarrelled? You're still friends?" exclaimed Genevieve.

"Quarrelled? No, I assure you, no! Yet am I his friend? Permit me to be candid, Miss Leslie. I'm in a deuce of a quandary. On the trip up to Aden, you'll remember, I told you something of the way he and I had knocked about together."

"Yes. Frankly, it added not a little to my esteem for you that you had learned to value his sterling worth."

"I did not tell you how it started. It was in the Kootenay country—British Columbia, you know. Bunch of sharpers set about to rook me on a frame-up—a bunco game. Tom tipped me off, though I had snubbed him, like the egregious ass I was. I paid no heed; blundered into the trap. Wouldn't have minded losing the thousand pounds they wanted, but they brought a woman into the affair—made it appear as if I were a cad—or worse."

"Surely not that, Lord James. No one could believe that of you."

"You don't know the beastly cleverness of those bunco chaps. They had me in a nasty hole, when Tom stepped in and showed them up. Seems he knew more about the woman and two of the men than they cared to have published. They decamped."

"That was so like Tom!" murmured Genevieve.

"Claimed he did it because of an old grudge against the parties. Had to force my thanks on him. Told you how we'd chummed together since. Deuce take it! why should it have been you on that steamer—with him?"

"Why?" echoed Genevieve, gazing down at her clasped hands, which still showed a trace of tropical tan.

"You know it—it puts me in rather a nasty box," went on Lord James. "Had I not met you before he did, it is possible that I could have avoided—You see my predicament. He and I've been together so much, I can foresee the effect on him of—er—of a great disappointment."

Genevieve gazed up at him with startled eyes. "Lord James, you must explain that; you must be explicit."

"I—I did not intend to so much as mention it," stammered the young Englishman, bitterly chagrined at himself. "It was only—pray, do not ask me, Miss Leslie!"

"You referred, of course, to his drinking," said Genevieve, in a tone as tense as it was quiet. "Do not reproach yourself. When we were cast ashore together, he was—not himself. But when I remember all those weeks that followed—! You cannot imagine how brave and resolute, how truly courageous he was!—and under that outward roughness, how kind and gentle!"

"I too know him. That's what makes it so hard. The thought that I may possibly cause him a disappointment that may result in—" Lord James came to a stop, tugging at his mustache.

Genevieve was again staring at the slender little hands, from which the most expert manicuring had not yet entirely removed all traces of rough usage.

"He told me something of—of what he had to fight," she murmured in a troubled voice. "But I feel that—that if something came into his life—" She blushed, but went on bravely—"something to take him out of what he calls the grind—"

"Shame!" she flung at him. "You, his friend,
and would take her from him!"

Lord James had instantly averted his gaze from her crimsoning face.

"That's the worst of it!" he burst out. "If only I could feel sure that he—I've seen him fight— Gad! how he has fought—time and again. Yet sooner or later, always the inevitable defeat!"

"I cannot believe it! I cannot!" insisted Genevieve. "With his strength, his courage! It's only been the circumstances; that he has had nobody to—I—I beg your pardon! Of course you—What I mean is somebody who—" She buried her face in her hands, blushing more vividly than before.

The Englishman's face lightened. "Then you've not let my deplorable blunder alter your attitude towards him?"

"Not in the slightest."

He leaned forward. "Then— I can wait no longer! You must know how greatly I— All those days coming up to Aden I could say nothing. Before coming aboard, he had told me why he could not permit you to—to commit yourself irrevocably."

He paused. Genevieve bent over lower. She did not speak.

He went on steadily: "It was then I realized fully his innate fineness. I own it astonished me, well as I thought I knew him. With his brains, his 'grit,' and *that*, I'd say he could become anything he wished—were it not for his— for the one weakness."

Genevieve flung up her head, to gaze at him in indignant protest.

"Weakness! How can you say that? He is so strong—so strong!"

"In all else than that," insisted Lord James. "You must

face the hard fact. Gad! this is far worse than I thought it would be. But I knew you before he did, and I've played fair with him. It was not easy to say nothing those days before we reached Aden, or to stay away from you after I reached home. Even he could not have found it so hard. He has all that stubborn power of endurance; while I—"

"You have no cause to reproach yourself. I cannot say how greatly it pleased me that you took him to Ruthby Castle."

"Could you but have been there, too! He and the pater hit it off out of hand. Jolly sensible chap, the pater—quiet, bookish—long head."

"He must be!"

"Not strange about Tom, though. It's odd how his bigness makes itself felt—to those who've any sense of judgment. And yet it's not so odd, when you come to think. My word! if only it were not for his— Forgive me, Miss Genevieve! I've the right to consider what it might mean to you. It gives me the right to speak for myself. He himself insisted that, in justice to you, I should not withdraw."

"Lord James!"

"Pray, do not misunderstand, Miss Genevieve. He knew what it meant to me. But our first thought was for you. He wished you to have the full contrast of your own proper environment, that you might regain your perspective—the point of view natural to one of your position."

"He could think I'd go back to the shams and conventions, after those weeks of *real* life!"

"Sometimes life is a bit too real in the most conventional of surroundings," said his lordship, with a rueful smile. "No. He saw that you had no right to commit yourself then; that you should reconsider matters in the environment in which you belong and for which he is not now fitted—whatever may be the outcome of his efforts to make himself fit."

"He will succeed!"

"He may succeed. I should not have the slightest hesitancy in saying that success would be certain, were it not for that one flaw. It's not to be held against him—an inherited weakness."

"Do you not believe we can overcome heredity?"

"In some cases, I daresay. But with him— You must bear in mind I've seen the futility of his struggle. All his resolution and courage and endurance seem to count for nothing. But it's too painful! Can't we leave him out of this? You are aware that I missed my opportunity when Lady Bayrose changed her plans and rushed you off on the other ship. After that you may imagine how difficult I found it to say nothing, do nothing, coming up to Aden."

"Please, please say no more!" begged Genevieve, her eyes bright with tears of distress. "I regard you too highly. You have my utmost esteem, my respect and friendship, my— you see he has taught me to be sincere—you have my affection. Dear friend, I shall be perfectly candid. I was a silly girl. I had never sensed the realities of life. I had a young girl's covetousness of a coronet—of a title. Yet that was not all. I felt a warm regard for you. Had you spoken before I met him, before I learned to know him—"

"Before you knew him? Then you still—? The contrast of civilization—of your own environment—has made no difference?"

"I do not say that. Yet it is not in the manner you suppose." She looked away, with a piteous attempt to smile.

"It's strange how much pain can be caused by the slightest shadow of a doubt."

"Miss Genevieve! I—I shall never be able to forgive myself! For me to have said a word—it was despicable!"

"No, do not say it. Can you think me capable of misunderstanding? Dear friend, I esteem you all the more for what I know it must have cost you. But no; what I spoke of was something that was already in my own mind."

"Ah—then you, too—Miss Genevieve, it's been so good of you. Let me beg that you do not consider this as final."

"But I can promise you nothing. It would not be right to you."

"I ask only that you do not consider this final. You have admitted a shadow of a doubt. With your permission, I propose to wait until you have solved that doubt. You have given me cause to hope that, were it not for him—"

"It is not right for me to give you the slightest hope."

"But I take it. Meantime, no more annoyance to you. We'll be jolly good friends, no more. You take me?"

"I'll ring for tea. You deserve it."

"No objections, I assure you. I'll serve as stopgap till Tom turns up."

Genevieve rose quickly, her color deepening. "He is coming?—this afternoon!"

"I should not have been surprised had I found him here. And now—" He glanced at his watch. "It's already half after four."

"Oh, and papa said he'd be home early to-day!—though his custom is to come barely in time to dress for dinner."

"Hope Tom hit it off with him this morning—but—" Lord James shook his head dubiously—"I fear he was not in a conciliatory mood."

11

REBELLION

GENEVIEVE RANG FOR tea, and changed the conversation to impersonal topics. A footman brought in a Russian samovar and a service of eggshell china. They sipped their tea and chatted lightly about English acquaintances, but with frequent glances towards the hall entrance. Each was wondering which one would be first to come, Blake or Mr. Leslie.

The conversation had languished to a mere pretext when Blake was announced. The engineer entered slowly, his face red and moist from the fierce drive of the sleet off the lake. He had come afoot.

Genevieve placed a trembling hand on the cover of her samovar, and called to him gayly: "Hurry here at once and have a good hot cup of tea. You must be frozen."

Blake came to them across the waxed floor with an ease and assurance of step in part due to his visit to Ruthby Castle and in part to his walk over the sleet-coated pavements.

"No tea for me, Miss Jenny," he replied with cheerful heartiness.

"Thanks, just the same. But I'm warm as toast—look it, too, eh?"

"Then take it to cool you off," suggested Lord James. "That's the Russian plan. When you're cold, hot tea to warm you; when you're hot, hot tea to cool you."

"Not when water tastes good to me," replied Blake with a significance that did not escape his friend. "Well, Jimmy, so you beat me to it."

"Waited till after three," said Lord James.

"Thought you'd hang back to give me the start? Went you one better, eh?" replied Blake. He stared fixedly into the handsome high-bred face of his friend and then at Genevieve's down-bent head. "Well? What's the good word? Is it—congratulations?"

"Not this time, old man," answered the Englishman lightly. He rose.

"Take my seat. Must be going."

Blake's eyes glowed. "You're the gamest ever, Jimmy boy."

"Don't crow till you're out of the woods," laughed his friend. "Can't wish you success, y'know. But it's to continue the same between us as it has been, if you're willing."

"That's like you, Jimmy!"

"To be sure. But I really must be going. Good-day, Miss Genevieve."

The girl looked up without attempting to conceal her affection and sympathy for him.

"Dear friend," she said, "before you go, I wish to tell you how highly I value and appreciate—"

"No more, no more, I beg of you," he protested, with genial insistence.

"Tom, I'll be dropping in on you at your office."

He bowed to Genevieve, and still cloaking his hurt with a cheerful smile, started to leave them. At the same moment Mr. Leslie came hurrying into the room. The sight of Lord James brought him to a stand.

"H'm!" he coughed. "So it's you, Lord Avondale? Hodges said—" His keen eyes glanced past the Englishman to the big form across the corner of the table from Genevieve. "What! Right, was he?—Genevieve."

"Yes, papa?" replied the girl, looking at Blake with a startled gaze. She was very pale, but her delicately curved lips straightened with quiet determination. She did not rise.

"Er—glad to meet you again so soon, Mr. Leslie," said Lord James, deftly placing himself so that the other could not avoid his proffered hand without marked discourtesy. Mr. Leslie held out his flaccid fingers. They were caught fast and retained during a cordial and prolonged hand-shake.

"When we first met," went on his lordship suavely, "time was lacking for me to congratulate you on the fact that your daughter came through her terrible experience so well. She has assured me that she feels all the better for it. Only one, like myself, accustomed to knocking about the tropics, can fully realize the extraordinary resourcefulness and courage of the man who had the good fortune to bring her through it all safely and, as she says, bettered."

"Yes, yes, we all know that, and admit it," replied the captive, attempting to free his hand.

Lord James gave it a final wring. "To be sure! You, of all men, will bear in mind what he accomplished. Yet I must insist that my own appreciation is no less keen. It is the greatest satisfaction to me that I am privileged to call Thomas Blake my friend."

"Your friend has put me under obligations," answered

Mr. Leslie. "I have acknowledged to him that I owe him a heavy debt for what he has done. I stand ready to pay him for his services, whenever he is ready to accept payment."

"Ah, indeed," murmured Lord James. "'Pon my word, now, that's what I call deuced generous."

"No; that's not the question at all. It's merely a matter of a business settlement for services rendered," replied Mr. Leslie.

"Yet one does not—er—value gratitude in pounds and dollars, y'know."

"No, no, of course you do not, papa!" exclaimed Genevieve. "Please remember—please try to consider—"

She would better have remained silent. Her evident concern alarmed her father to the point of exasperation.

"I am considering how this friend of Lord Avondale's bore himself towards me, in my office, this morning," he interrupted her. He turned again to Lord James. "I should not need to tell you, sir, that the manner of expressing gratitude depends altogether on the circumstances. We are now, however, considering another matter. You were about to leave— You will always be welcome to my house, Lord Avondale, and so will be your friends, *when they come and go with you.*"

"Father!" protested Genevieve, rising to face him.

"My mistake, Miss Jenny," said Blake, coolly drawing himself up beside her. "I thought it was *your* house."

He swung about to Mr. Leslie, and said, with unexpected mildness: "Don't worry; I'm going. We don't want to fuss here, do we?—to make it any harder for her. But first, there's one thing. You're her father—I want to say I'm sorry I cut loose this morning."

"What! you apologize?"

"As to what I said about my bridge plans—yes. If you had left out about—If you hadn't rubbed it in so hard about me and—You know what I mean. It made me red-hot. I couldn't help cutting loose. But, just the same, I oughtn't to've said that about the plans, because—well, because, you see, I don't believe it."

"You don't? Then why—?"

"I did believe it before. I believed it this morning, when I was mad. But I've had time to cool off and think it over. Queer thing—all the evidence and probabilities are there, just the same; but somehow I can't believe it of you any longer—simply can't. You're her father."

"H'm—this puts a different face on the matter," admitted Mr. Leslie. "I begin to think that I may have been rather too hasty. Had you been more conciliatory, less—h'm—positive, I'm inclined to believe that we—"

"I don't care what *you* believe," was Blake's brusque rejoinder. "I'm not trying to curry favor with you. Understand? Come on, Jimmy."

But Genevieve was at his elbow, between him and the door.

"You are not going now, Tom," she said.

"Genevieve," reproved her father. "This is most unlike you."

"Unlike my former frivolous, pampered self!" cried the girl. "I'm no longer a silly *débutante,* papa. I've lived the grim hard realities of life—there on that dreadful coast—with him. I'm a woman."

"You child! You're not even twenty-one."

"I am old—older than the centuries, papa—old enough

to know my own mind." She turned to Blake. "You were right, Tom. This is my home—legally mine. You are welcome to stay."

"Mr. Leslie!" interposed Lord James, before her father could reply. "One moment, if you please. I have told you that Mr. Blake and I are friends. More than that, we are intimate friends—chums. I wish to impress on you the very high esteem in which I hold him, the more than admiration—"

"Chuck it, Jimmy," put in Blake.

Lord James concluded in a tone of polite frigidity. "And since you place conditions on his welcome to your house, permit me to remark that I prefer his acquaintance to yours." He bowed with utmost formality.

"H'm!" rasped Mr. Leslie. "You should understand, sir. Had you not interrupted me—" He abruptly faced Blake. "You, at least, will understand my position—that I have some reason—It is not that I wish to appear discourteous, even after this morning. You've apologized; I cannot ask you to go—I do not ask you to go. Yet—"

"If you please, papa," said Genevieve with entrancing sweetness.

"Well?"

"Isn't it time for you to dress?"

"No—came home early," replied Mr. Leslie, jerking out his watch. He searched his daughter's face with an apprehensive glance, and again addressed Blake. "Too early. There's time for a run out to George Ashton's. Want to see him on a matter of business. Valuable acquaintance for you to make. Jump into the runabout with me, and I'll introduce you to him."

"Thanks," said Blake dryly. "Not to-day."

"Mr. Blake has just come, papa," said Genevieve. "You would not deprive us of the pleasure of a little visit."

"H'm. By cutting it close, I can wait a few minutes."

"You need not trouble to wait, papa. You can introduce him to Mr. Ashton some other time."

"May I offer myself as a substitute?" put in Lord James. "Mrs. Gantry has told me so much about the elder Mr. Ashton. Quite curious to meet him."

Blandly taking Mr. Leslie's assent as a matter of course, he started toward the door. "Good-day, Miss Leslie. Ah— do we go out this way? Can't tell you how I value the opportunity. Very good of you, very!"

"Wait," said Mr. Leslie. "Genevieve, haven't you an engagement out, this afternoon?"

"If I had a dozen, papa, I should not deprive Mr. Blake of his call."

"Mr. Blake is welcome to his call. But—since you force me to say it—I must expressly tell you, it is my wish that you should not see him alone."

"I'm very sorry, papa, that you should forbid me," said Genevieve with a quiet tensity that should have fore-warned him.

"Sorry?"

"Yes, papa, because, if you insist, I shall have to disobey you."

"You will?"

He stared at her, astounded, and she sustained his gaze with a steadiness that he perceived could not be shaken.

Lord James again interposed. "I beg your pardon, Mr.

Leslie, if I may seem to interfere. But as he is my friend, I, too, request you—"

"You?" exclaimed Mr. Leslie, with fresh astonishment. "You also side with him?—when my sister-in-law tells me—"

"That is all by-the-bye, I assure you, sir. The least I can do for the man who saved her life is to play fair. Permit me to say that you can do no less."

Mr. Leslie looked at Genevieve with a troubled frown.

"At least, my dear, I hope you'll remember who you are," he said.

She made no reply, but stood white-faced and resolute until he went from the room. Lord James followed close after him.

Blake and Genevieve were left alone.

12

THE DEEPENING OF DOUBT

BLAKE STOOD AS motionless as a carved figure, his eyes glowing upon the girl, blue and radiant with tenderness and compassion and profound love.

The clang of a heavy door told her that her father had left the house. On the instant all her firmness left her. She hid her face in her hands and sank into the nearest chair, quivering and weeping, in silent anguish.

Blake came near and stood over her. He spoke to her in a voice that was deep and low and very soft: "There, there, little girl, don't you mind! Just cry it out. It'll do you good. You know I understand. Have a good cry!"

The sympathetic urging to give way freely to her weeping almost immediately soothed her grief and checked the flow of tears. She rose uncertainly, dabbing at her eyes.

"I—I couldn't help it, Tom. It's the fi-first time papa's ever been so cross with me!"

"My fault, I guess. Rubbed his fur the wrong way this morning pretty hard. But don't you fret, girlie. It'll be all right. Only we mustn't blame him. Think of what it means to him. You're all he has, and if he thinks you're—if he thinks he's going to lose you—"

"But it was so cruel!—so unjust!—the way he treated you!"

"Oh, that's all right, little woman. I don't mind that. We'll all forget it by to-morrow. He didn't mean half he said. It was just the thought that I—that somebody might take you away from him. Jenny!" His eyes glowed upon her blue as sapphires. "You're home now."

He held his arms open for her to come to him. She swayed forward as if to give herself into the clasp of those strong arms, but instantly checked the movement and shrank back a little way.

"Wait, Tom," she murmured hesitatingly. "We must first—"

"Wait longer, Jenny?" he exclaimed, his deep voice vibrant with the intensity of his feeling. "No, I must say it! I've waited all these weeks—good Lord!—when maybe you've thought it was because I didn't want to—to do as you asked!"

"It's not that, Tom, truly it's not that. I was hurt and—shamed. But even then I divined why you had done it and realized the nobility of your motive."

"Nobility? That's a good joke! You know I was only trying to do the square thing. Any man would have done the same."

"Any *man* would. I'm not so certain as to some who call themselves gentlemen."

"There're some who're real gentlemen—worse luck to me—Jimmy, for one. I can never catch up with him in that line, girlie, but I can make a stagger at it."

"You can become anything you will, Tom," she said with calm conviction.

"Maybe," he replied. "But, Jenny, I can't wait for that. Wish I could. I'm still only—what you know. Same time, you're back home now, and you've been visiting with your titled friends. Also you've seen how your father looks at it, and how—"

"What does all that amount to—even papa's anger? If only that were all!"

"Jenny! then you still—?" His voice quivered with passion. "My little girl!—how I love you! God I how I love you! I never thought much of girls, but I loved you the first time I ever set eyes on you, there in the Transvaal. That's why I threw up the management of the mine. I knew who your father was; I knew I hadn't a ghost of a show. But I followed you to Cape Town—couldn't help it!"

"You—you old silly!" she murmured, half frightened by the greatness of his passion. "You should have known I was only a shallow society girl!"

"Shallow?—you? You're deep as blue water!"

"The ocean is fickle."

"You're not; you're true! You've *lived!* I've seen you face with a smile what many a man would have run from."

"Because with me was one who would have died sooner than that harm should come to me! Those weeks, those wonderful weeks that we lived, so close to primitive, savage Nature—bloody fanged Nature!—those weeks that I stood by your side and saw her paint for us her beautiful, terrible pictures of Life, pictures whose blue was the storm-wave and the sky veiled with fever-haze, whose white was the roaring surf and the glare of thunderbolts, whose red was fire and blood! And you saved me from all—all! I had never even dreamt that a man could be so courageous, so enduring, so strong!"

His face clouded, and he gave back before her radiant look.

"Strong?" he muttered. "That's the question. Am I?"

"Of course you are! I'm sure you are. You *must* be. It was that which compelled my—which made me—" She paused, and a swift blush swept over her face from forehead to throat—"made me propose to you, there on the cliff, when the steamer came."

"That a lady should have loved me like that!" he murmured. "I still can't believe it was true! My little girl, it's not possible—not possible!"

"You say 'loved,'" she whispered. Her eyelids fluttered and drooped before his ardent gaze; her scarlet face bent downward; she held out her hands to him in timid surrender.

He caught them between his big palms, but not to draw her to him. A jagged mark on her round wrist caught his eye. It was the scar of a vicious thorn. The last time he had seen it was on the cliff top,—that other time when she put out her arms to him. He bent over and kissed the red scar.

"Jenny," he replied in bitter self-reproach, "here's another time I've proved I'm not in your class—not a gentleman. You've raised a point—the real point. Am I what you think me? You think I'm at least a man. Am I?"

She looked up at him, her face suddenly gone white again. "Tom! You don't mean—?"

"About my being strong. All that you've seen so far are my leading suits. There's that other to be reckoned with yet.

I told your father I hadn't touched a drop since the wreck. But you know how it was before."

"Yes, dear, but that *was* before!"

"I know. Things are different now. I've something at stake that'll help me fight. You can't guess, though, how that craving—Lucky I'll have Jimmy, as well, to back me up. He's great when it comes to jollying a fellow over the bumps. He'll help."

"It's little enough, after all you've done for him! He told me."

"Just like him. But let's not get sidetracked. What I wanted to make clear is that I'm not so everlastingly strong as you seem to think."

"Tom, you'll not give way! You'll fight!"

"Yes, I'll fight," he responded soberly.

"And you'll win!"

"I hope so, girlie. I've fought it before, and it has downed me, time and again. But now it's different—unless you've found you were mistaken. But if you still feel as when you—as you did there on the cliff that morning— Good God! how *could* I lose out, with you backing me up?"

She looked at him with a quick recurrence of doubt. "You ask help of me?"

"If you care enough, Jenny. It's not going to be a joke. I've tried before, and gone under so many times that some people would say I've no show left. But let me tell you, girlie, I'm going to fight this time for all I'm worth. I'm going to break this curse if I can. It is a curse, you'll remember. I told you about my mother."

"You should not think of that. What does heredity count as against environment!"

"Environment?—heredity? By all accounts, my father was the man you've thought me, and a lot more—railroad engineer; nerviest man ever ran an engine out of Chicago on the Pennsylvania Line; American stock from way back—Scotch-Irish; sober as a church, steady, strong as a bull. Never an accident all the years he pulled the fast express till the one that smashed him. Could have jumped and saved himself—stayed by his throttle, and saved the train. They brought him home—what was left of him. Papers headlined him; you know how they do it. That was my father."

"Oh, Tom! and with such a father!"

"Wait a minute. You spoke of heredity and environment. I'm giving you all sides, except anything more about my mother. Her father was a cranky inventor... Well, inside six months we were living in a tenement. I was a little shaver of six. The younger of my sisters was a baby. Talk about environment! Wasn't many years before I was known as the toughest kid in Rat Alley."

"Don't dwell on that, Tom. Don't even speak of it," begged Genevieve.

He shook his head. "I want you to know just what I've been. It's your right to know. I wasn't one of the nasty kind and I wasn't a sneak. But I was the leader of my gang. Maybe you know what that means. Of course the police got it in for me. Finally they made it so hot I had to get out of Chicago. I took to the road—became a bum."

"Not that!—surely not that!"

"Well, no, only a kid hobo. But I'd have slid on down if I hadn't dropped into a camp of surveyors who were heading off into the mountains and had need of another man.

Griffith, the engineer in charge, talked me into joining the party as axman. I took a fancy to him. He proved himself the first real friend I'd ever had—or was to have till I met Jimmy Scarbridge."

"A man's worth is measured by the friends he makes," she observed.

"Not always. Well, Griffith got me interested. I joined the party. *Whew!*—seven months in the mountains, and not a saloon within fifty miles any of the time. But I stuck it out. Nobody ever called me a quitter."

"And now, Tom, you'll not quit! You'll win!"

"I'll try—for you, girlie! You can't guess how that braces me—the thought that it's for you! You see, I'm beginning to count on things now. I'm not even afraid of your money now. Good old Grif—Griffith, you know—has given me a shy at a peach of a proposition—toughest problem I was ever up against. It's a big irrigation dam that has feazed half a dozen good engineers."

"But you'll solve the problem! You can do anything!"

"I'm not so sure, Jenny. I've only begun to dig into the field books. Even if I do make a go of it in the end, chances are I'll have to work like—like blazes to get there. But that'll help me on this other fight—help choke down the craving when it comes. A whole lot turns on that dam. If I make good on it, I'm made myself. Tack up my ad as consulting engineer, and I'll have all the work I want. Won't be ashamed to look your three millions in the face."

"My money! Can you still believe that counts with me? Money! It is what we are ourselves that counts. If you acquired all the money in the world, yes, and all the fame, but failed to master yourself, you'd not be the man I thought you—the man whom I—whom I said I loved."

"Jenny! Then it's gone—you no longer care?"

"You have no right to ask anything of me until you've—"

"I'm not, Jenny! Don't think it for a moment. I'm not asking anything now. I wanted to wait. It's only that I want you to know how I love you. I wouldn't dream of asking you to—to marry me now—no, not till I've won out, made good. Understand? All I want is for you to wait for me till I've made my name as an A-1 engineer and until I've downed that cursed craving for drink."

"You will, Tom—you *must!*"

"With you to back me, little woman! Yes, I guess I can make it this time, with you waiting for me!"

Genevieve met his smile and enthused gaze with a look of firm decision.

Her doubt and hesitancy had at last crystallized into a set purpose.

She replied in a tone that rang with a hardness new to him: "No. It must be more than that."

"More?" he asked, surprised.

"More, much more. That morning, after I so shamelessly forced you to listen to me, nothing could have altered my purpose had you come aboard the steamer with me."

"But I couldn't then. 'T wouldn't have been fair to you."

"Yet it might have been wise. Who knows? At the least, the question would have been settled 'for better or for worse.' It is easier to face the trouble which one cannot escape than deliberately to make choice of entering into the state that may or may not bring about the dreaded misfortune. Had you married me then, Tom, I would surely have been happy for a time. But now—you have made me believe that you were right."

Blake drew back from her, his head downbent in sudden despondency. "So you've found out you don't feel the same?"

Her eyes dimmed with tears of compassion for him, but her voice was as firm as before. "I loved Tom Blake because he was so manly, so strong! I still love that Tom Blake. You are not sure that you are strong."

"But if I knew I had your love back of me, Jenny!"

"That's it—you wish to lean on me! It's weak; it's not like you. You won my love by your courage, your resolution, your strength! All my love for you is based on your strength. If that fails—if you prove weak—how am I to tell whether my love will endure?"

"I'll win out. I know I can win out if I have you to fight for."

"If you have me to *lean* on! No; you must prove yourself stronger than that. I had no doubts then. I urged you to marry me—flung myself at you. But now, after what I've been forced to realize since then—"

She stopped short, leaving him to infer the rest. He took it at the worst. He replied despairingly yet without a trace of bitterness: "Yes, you'd better take Jimmy. He's your kind."

"Tom! How can you? I've a great esteem for Lord James, I like him very much, but—"

"He's the right sort. You could count on being happy with him," stated Blake, in seeming resignation. She looked at him, puzzled and hurt by his calmness. The look fired him to a passionate outburst. "Don't you think it, though! He's not going to have you! I can't give you up! I'm going to win you. My God! I love you so much I'd try to win you—I'd have to win you, even if I thought you'd be unhappy!"

Her voice softened with responsive tenderness. "Oh, Tom, if only I knew we would have—would have and keep that great love that covers all things! I'd rather be miserable with you than happy without you!"

"Jenny! you do love me!" he cried, advancing with outstretched arms.

She drew back from him. "Not now—not now, Tom!"

He smiled, only slightly dashed. "Not now, but when I've made good. You'll wait for me! I can count on that!"

"No," she answered with utmost firmness.

"Jenny!"

"I'll make no promise—not even a conditional one. You must make this fight without leaning on any one. I must know whether you are strong, whether you are the real Tom Blake I love."

"But I'm not asking anything—only in case I make good."

"No; I'll not bind myself in any way. I'll not promise to marry you even if you should win. It was you who made me wait, and now I shall make sure. Unless I feel certain that we would be bound together for all time by the deepest, truest love, I know it would be a mistake. If I were certain, right now, that you lack the strength to conquer yourself for the sake of your own manhood, I would accept Lord James."

Whether or not the girl was capable of such an act, there could be no doubt that she meant what she said, and her tone carried conviction to Blake. He was silent for a long moment. When he replied, it was in a voice dull and heavy with despondency. "You don't realize what you're putting me up against."

"I realize that you must clear away all my doubt of your strength," she rejoined, with no lessening of her firmness. "You were strong there on that savage coast, in the primitive. But you must prove yourself strong enough to rise *out* of the primitive—to rise to your true, your higher self."

He bent as if he were being crushed under a ponderous weight. His voice dulled to a half articulate murmur. "You—won't—help—me?"

"I cannot—I dare not!" she insisted almost fiercely. "If I did I should doubt. This dreadful fear! You must prove you're strong! You *must* master yourself for the sake of your own manhood!"

At last he was forced to realize that it was necessity, not desire, that impelled her to thrust him from her. He must fight his hard battle alone—he must fight without even the thought that he had her sympathy.

He should have divined that she would be secretly hoping, perhaps praying for him, striving for him in spirit with all the might of her true love. But by her insistence she had at last compelled him to doubt her love.

He thought of the many times that he had gone down in disgraceful defeat, and black despair fell upon him. His broad shoulders stooped yet more.

"What's the use?" he muttered thickly.

But the question itself served as the goad to quicken all his immense reserve of endurance. He looked up at Genevieve, heavy-eyed but grim with determination.

"You don't know what you've put me up against," he said. "But I'll not lay down yet. Nobody ever called me a quitter.

You've a right to ask me to make good. I'll make a stagger at it. Good-bye!"

He turned from her and walked up the room with the steady deliberation of one who bears a heavy burden.

It was almost more than she could endure. She started to dart after him, and her lips parted to utter an entreaty for him to come back to her. But her spirit had been tempered in that fierce struggle for life on the savage coast of Mozambique.

She checked herself, and waited until, without a backward glance, he had passed out through the curtained doorway. Then, and not until then, she sank down in her chair and gave way to the anguish of her love and doubt and dread.

13

PLANS AND OTHER PLANS

A QUARTER AFTER nine the next morning found Griffith at the door of Mr. Leslie's sanctum. He stuffed his gauntlet gloves into a pocket of his old fur coat, and entered the office, his worn, dark eyes vague with habitual abstraction.

Mr. Leslie was in the midst of his phonographic dictation. He abruptly stopped the machine and whirled about in his swivel-chair to face the engineer.

"Sit down," he said. "How's the Zariba Dam?"

"No progress," answered Griffith with terse precision. He sat down with an air of complete absorption in the act, drew out an old knife and his pipe, and observed: "You didn't send for me for that."

"How's the bridge?"

"Same," croaked the engineer, beginning to scrape out the bowl of his pipe with the one unbroken blade of his knife.

"That young fool still running around town?"

"Can't say. It'd be a good thing to have him do it all the time if work was going on. Had a letter from McGraw, that man I put in as general foreman. He says everything is frozen up tight; may keep so for two weeks or more."

"You've laid off most the force?"

"No, not even the Slovaks."

Mr. Leslie frowned. "Two or three weeks at full pay, and no work?

That's an item."

"Hard enough to hold together a competent force on such winter work as that," rejoined Griffith. "Almost impossible with your kid-glove Resident Engineer. I've said nothing all this time; but he's made some of my best men quit—bridge workers that've stayed by me for years. Said they couldn't stand for his damned swell-headedness, not even to oblige me."

"Well, well, I leave it to you. Do the best you can. It's a bad bargain, but we've got to go through with it. Only time the young fool ever showed a glimmer of sense was when he had his father's lawyers drew his contract with me. My lawyers can't find a flaw in it."

"Not even diamond cut diamond, eh?" cackled Griffith. He ceased scraping at his pipe to peer inquisitively into the bowl. "What I've never been able to figure out is how he happened to solve the problem of that central span. Don't think you've ever realized what a wonderful piece of work that was. It's something new. Must have been a happy accident—must have come to him in what I'd call a flash of intuition or genius. He sure hadn't it in him to work such a thing out in cold blood."

"Genius?—*pah!*" scoffed Mr. Leslie.

"Hey?" queried Griffith, glancing up sharply. "What else, then?"

"I've recently been given reason to suspect—"began Mr. Leslie. He paused, hesitated, and refrained. "But we'll talk of that later. First, my reason for sending for you. I understand that you know this man Blake, who, unfortunately, was the person that saved my daughter."

Griffith replied with rather more than his usual dryness. "If I've got a correct estimate of what Miss Leslie had to be pulled through, it's lucky that Tom Blake was the man."

"You've a higher opinion of him than I have."

"We've worked together."

"He's in your office now," snapped Mr. Leslie.

"Yes, and he stays there long as he wants," rejoined Griffith in a quiet matter-of-fact tone. "It's your privilege to hire another consulting engineer."

Mr. Leslie brought his shaggy eyebrows together in a perplexed frown. "Must say, I can't understand how the fellow makes such friends. Your case is hardly less puzzling than that of the Earl of Avondale."

"Hey? Oh, you mean young Scarbridge. He seems to be one of the right sort—even if he *is* the son of a duke. But if Tommy hadn't introduced him as a friend—"

"We're talking about Blake," interrupted Mr. Leslie. "I want your help."

"Well?" asked Griffith warily.

"He has put me under obligations, and refuses to accept any reward from me. It's intolerable!"

"Won't accept anything, eh? Well, if he says he won't, he won't. No use butting your head against a concrete wall."

"He's a fool!"

"I'd hardly agree as to that. He doesn't always do as people expect him to. Same time, he usually has a reason."

"But for him to refuse to take either cash or a position!"

"I notice, though, he drew his pay-check for the Q.T. survey. No; Tommy isn't altogether a fool—not altogether."

"Twenty-five-thousand-dollar position!" rasped Mr. Leslie.

"Hey?"

"Offered him that, and—"

"You offered him—?" echoed Griffith, his lean, creased face almost grotesque with astonishment.

"Think I don't value my daughter's life?" snapped Mr. Leslie. "I was ready to do that and far more for him. He refused—not only refused but insulted me."

Griffith peered intently into the angry face of his employer. "Insulted you, eh? Guess you prodded him up first."

"I admit I had rather misjudged him in some respects."

"So you gave him the gaff, eh?—and got it back harder!" cackled Griffith.

"He shall be compelled to accept what I owe him, indirectly, if not directly. You have given him work?"

"Yes."

"You've, of course, told him that I'm the Coville Construction Company."

"Not yet."

"What! You're certain of that?"

Griffith nodded. "He sailed into me, first thing, for taking work from you. To ease him off, I said the Coville Company had taken over the bridge from you. The matter hasn't happened to come up again since."

"You're certain he doesn't know I'm interested in the company?"

"Not unless somebody else has told him."

"Then—let's see— We'll appoint him Assistant Resident Engineer on the bridge."

"He'll not take it under young Ashton."

"Not if his salary is put at twenty-five thousand?"

"As Assistant Engineer?" said Griffith, incredulous.

"You'll be too busy with my other projects to keep up these visits to Michamac. Besides, you said the bridge is coming to the crucial point of construction."

"That central span," confirmed Griffith.

"If you consider Blake sufficiently reliable, you can give him detailed instructions and send him up to take charge."

"How about Ashton's contract?"

"He'll be satisfied with the glory. Reports will continue to name him as Resident Engineer. If he won't listen to reason, I'll ask his father to drop him a line. The young fool has had his allowance cut twice already. He'd consider his pay as engineer a bare pittance."

"Heir to the Ashton millions, eh?" croaked Griffith.

"If I know George Ashton, he has a good safe will drawn, providing that his fortune is to be held in trust. That fool boy won't have any chance to squander more than his allowance,—and he won't keep me now from paying off this obligation to Blake."

"Perhaps not. I'm not so sure, though, that Tom will— One thing's certain. He won't go up to Michamac right away."

"He won't? Why not? It's just the time for him to get the run of things, now while there's no work going on."

"He'd catch on quick enough. It's not that. Fact is, he's got hold of something a lot bigger, and I know he'll not quit till he has either won out or it has downed him. Never knew of but one thing that ever downed him."

Mr. Leslie glared at the engineer, his face reddening with rage.

"Something bigger!" he repeated. "So the fellow has bragged about it!"

Griffith stared back, perplexed by the other's sudden heat. "Guess we've got our wires crossed," he said. "I told him, of course. He didn't know anything about it."

"What you talking about?" demanded Mr. Leslie, puzzled in turn.

"The Zariba Dam."

"That!" exclaimed Mr. Leslie, and his face cleared. "H'm,—what about the dam?"

"I had about thrown it up. I'm giving Tom a go at it."

Mr. Leslie's eyebrows bristled in high curves. "What! wasting time with a man like that? If *you've* given it up, we'll try England or Europe."

"No use. Plenty of good men over there. They can give us pointers on some things. But if they've ever done anything just like this Zariba Dam, they've kept it out of print."

"But an unknown second-rate engineer!"

"That's what's said of every first-rater till he gets his chance."

"You're serious?"

"I don't guarantee he can do it. I do say, I won't be any too surprised if he pulls it off. It's a thing that calls for invention. He'll swear he hasn't an ounce of it in him—says he just happens to blunder on things, or applies what he has picked up. All gas! He once showed me some musty old drawings that made it look like one of his grandfathers ought to be credited with the basic inventions of a dozen machines that to-day are making the owners of the patent-rights rich. Guess some of that grandfather's bump can be located on Tom's head."

"Inventor—h'm—inventor!" muttered Mr. Leslie half to himself. "That puts rather a different face on that bridge matter."

"As how?" casually asked Griffith, beginning to scrape afresh at his pipe-bowl.

Mr. Leslie considered, and replied with another question: "At the time of the competition in plans for the bridge, did you know that Blake was to be a contestant?"

"He writes letters about as often as a hen gets a tooth pulled. But I got a letter the time you mention,—a dozen lines or so, with another added, saying that he was in for a whirl at the Michamac cantilever."

"You've shown him Ashton's bridge plans?"

"Not yet. He's been too busy on the Zariba field books."

"You've seen his own plans for the bridge?"

"No. They were lost."

"The originals, I mean—his preliminary copy. He must have kept something."

"Yes. But I guess they're pretty wet by now," replied Griffith, his face crackling with dry humor. "They're aboard that steamer, down on the African coast. If you want to see them, you might finance a wrecking expedition. But Tom says she went down mast-under, and there are plenty of sharks nosing along the coral reef."

Mr. Leslie winced at the word *sharks,* and reluctantly admitted: "I've had a long talk with my daughter. He played the part of a man. I acknowledge that I've held a strong prejudice against him. It seems, however, that in part I've been mistaken."

"Now you're talking, Mr. Leslie!"

"Only in part, I say—about his lost bridge plans. I had thought he was trying to blackmail me."

"More apt to be a black eye, if you let him know you thought that," was Griffith's dry comment.

"He came near to resorting to violence. As I look at it now, I can't say I blame him. Those bridge plans, though— Knowing this about his inventiveness, has it not occurred to you that his plans may not have been lost, after all?"

"Look here, Mr. Leslie," said Griffith, rising with the angularity of a jumping-jack, "we've rubbed along pretty smooth since we got together last year; but Tom Blake is my friend."

"Sit down! *sit* down!" insisted Mr. Leslie. "You ought to see by this time that I'm trying to prove myself anything but an enemy to him."

Griffith sat down and began mechanically to load his pipe with the formidable Durham. Mr. Leslie put the tips of his fingers together, coughed, and went on in a lowered tone. "Those plans disappeared. His charge was preposterous, ridiculous—*as against me*. Yet if the plans were not lost, what became of them? He told me yesterday that he himself handed them to the person who was at that time acting as my secretary. You catch the point?"

"Um-m," grunted Griffith, his face as emotionless as a piece of crackled wood.

"Young Ashton was my secretary. He resigned the next day. Said he had been secretly working on plans for the Michamac cantilever; thought he had solved the problem of the central span; might go ahead and put in his plans if none of the competitors were awarded the bridge. Within a month he did put in plans."

"Well?" queried Griffith.

"Don't you make the connection?" demanded Mr. Leslie. "Blake handed his plans to Ashton, and took no receipt. The plans disappeared. Ashton leaves; comes back in a month with plans that he hasn't the skill to apply in the construction of the bridge—plans include an entirely new modification of bridge trusses—stroke of inventive genius, you called it."

Griffith's lean jaw dropped. "You—you don't mean to say he—the son of George Ashton—that he could—God A'mighty, he's heir to twenty millions!"

"You don't believe it? Suppose you knew he was about to be cut off without a cent? George had stood about all he could from the young fool. Those bridge plans came in just in time to prevent the drawing of a new will."

The hand in which Griffith held his pipe shook as if he had been seized with a fever chill, but his voice was dry and emotionless. "That accounts for those queer slips and errors in the plans. He couldn't even make an accurate copy, and was too much afraid of being found out to take time to check Tom's drawings. Jammed them into his fireplace soon's he'd finished. The thief!—the infernal thief!—the—!" Griffith spat out a curse that made even Mr. Leslie start.

"Good Lord, Griffith," he remonstrated. "That's the first time I ever heard you swear."

"I keep it for *dirt!*... Well, what you going to do about it?"

"I am going to have you show Ashton's plans to Blake. If he recognizes them as a copy of his own—"

"Better get ready to ship Laffie out of the country. Once saw Tom manhandle a brute who was beating his wife—one of those husky saloon bouncers. The wife had a month's nursing to do. Tom will pound that—that sneak to pulp."

"Show him the plans. If he recognizes them, I'll let the thief know he has been found out. He'll run, and we'll be rid of him without any scandal. We'll arrange for Blake to get the credit for the bridge, after a time. George Ashton and I are rather close together. I don't want him to be hit harder than's necessary."

"Say, Mr. Leslie, I don't mind admitting you *are* square!" exclaimed Griffith. "You don't like Tom, and you know he hasn't a line of proof. It would be only his word against Laffie's. Unknown engineer trying to blackmail the son of George Ashton. You know what would be said."

"I told you, I owe him a debt. I intend to pay it in full."

"One thing though," cautioned Griffith. "Even a cornered rat will fight. There's the chance that Laffie may not run. He'd be a drivelling idiot if he did, with his father's millions at stake. Don't forget we've no proof. It won't look even possible to outsiders. Suppose I hold off showing Tom those plans till we see if he can make it on the Zariba Dam? If he pulls that off, no engineer in the U.S. will doubt his claims to the bridge."

"That means a delay," said Mr. Leslie irritably. "My first plan was to send Blake to Michamac at once."

"Lord! With one cantilever finished and the other out to the central span—if it's Tom's bridge, he'd recognize it as quick as his plans. And if he did—well, I'd not answer for what would happen to that damn thief."

"H'm—perhaps you're right," considered Mr. Leslie. He thought a moment, and added with quick decision, "Very well. Keep him on at the dam. What are you paying him?"

"Two hundred."

"Double it."

"No go. He'd suspect something."

"Suspect, would he? H'm—several expert engineers have failed on that dam. If it can be put through, the project will net me a half-million. Ten per cent of my profits might stimulate you engineers. I offer fifty thousand dollars as reward to the man who solves the problem of the Zariba Dam."

"Say, that's going some!" commented Griffith.

"Plain business proposition. If I can't get it done for wages, it is cheaper to pay a bonus than to have the project fail."

"Good way to put it," admitted Griffith. "Don't just know, though, what I'll do with all that money."

"You? Thought you said that Blake—"

"D'you suppose he'd take a cent of it? He's working for me."

"But if he does the work?"

"He might accept the credit. The cash would come to me, if he had to cram it down my throat. He won't touch your money."

"Crazy fool!" rasped Mr. Leslie. Again he paused to consider, and again he spoke with quick decision. "The Coville Company takes over the project. I don't believe the dam can be built; I'm tired of the whole thing. So I unload on the Coville Company. You see? The company offers the fifty thousand bonus as a last hope. It hires Blake direct on some of its routine work. You insist that he try for the dam, between times."

"That's the ticket!" said Griffith. "We'll try it on him."

"Then call by the Coville office. I'll phone over for them to have the transfer made and a letter waiting for you," said Mr. Leslie, and he jerked out his watch.

Griffith rose at the signal. He fumbled for a moment with his hat and gloves, and spoke with a queer catch in his voice. "I'd like to—let you know how I—appreciate—"

"No call for it! no call for it!" broke in Mr. Leslie. "Good-day!"

He whirled about to his desk and caught up the receiver of one of his private-line telephones.

14

BETWEEN FRIENDS

LORD JAMES SAUNTERED into the office of Griffiths, C.E., and inquired for Mr. Blake. The cleric stared in vague recognition, and answered that Mr. Blake was busy. Nothing daunted, the visitor crossed to the door toward which the clerk had glanced.

When he entered, he found Blake in his shirtsleeves, humped over a small desk. He was intently absorbed in comparing the figures of two field books and in making little pencil diagrams.

"Hello, old man. What's the good word?" sang out his lordship.

Blake nodded absently, and went on with his last diagram. When he had finished it, he looked up and perceived his friend standing graceful and debonair in the centre of the room.

"Why, hello, Jimmy," he said, as if only just aware of the other's presence. "Can't you find a chair?"

"How's the dam?"

"Dam 'fi 'no," punned Blake. He slapped his pencil down on the desk, and flung up his arms to stretch his cramped body.

"You need a breather," advised Lord James.

"Young Ashton came 'round to my hotel last evening. Wanted me to go to some bally musical comedy—little supper afterward with two of the show-girls—all that. I had another engagement. He then asked me to drop around this morning and take my pick of his stable. Wants me to ride one of his mounts while I'm here, you know. Suppose you come up-town with me and help me pick out a beast."

"No," said Blake. "Less I see of that papa's boy the better I'll like him."

"Oh, but as a fellow-engineer, y'know," minced Lord James.

"You love him 'bout as much as I do."

Lord James adjusted the pink carnation in his lapel, and casually remarked: "You'll be calling at the Leslies' this afternoon, I daresay."

"No," said Blake.

"Indeed?" exclaimed the younger man. He flushed and gazed confusedly at Blake, pleased on his own account, yet none the less distressed for his friend.

Blake explained the situation with sober friendliness. "It's all up in the air, Jimmy. I've got to make good, and she won't promise anything even if I succeed."

"Not even if you succeed?" Lord James was bewildered.

"Can't say I blame her, since I've had time to think it over," said Blake. "If it was you, for instance, she might have a show to get some happiness out of life, even with the whiskey. But think of her tied up to me, whiskey or no whiskey!"

"You'll down the habit this time, old man."

Blake smiled ironically. "That's what you've said every

time. It's what I've said myself, every time since I woke up to what the cursed sprees meant. No; don't be afraid. You'll have your chance soon enough. She has cut me clean off from outside help. She wouldn't even give me so much as a 'good luck to you'!"

"She wouldn't? But of course you know that she wishes it."

"Does she? But that's not the point. She's made me believe she isn't sure of her—of her feelings toward me. Don't think I blame her. I don't. She's right. If I can't stand up and fight it out and win, without being propped up by my friends, I ought to lose out. I'm not fit to marry any woman—much less her."

Lord James tugged and twisted at his mustache, and at last brought out his reply: "Now, I—I say, you look here, old chap, you've got to win this time. It means her, y'know. You must win."

"Jimmy," stated Blake, his eyes softening, "you're the limit!"

"You're not!" flashed back his friend. "There's no limit to you—to what you can do."

"Heap of good it does—your saying it," grumbled Blake.

"This—er—situation won't prevent your calling at the Leslies', I hope."

"I'm not so sure," considered Blake. "Leastways you won't see me there till I begin to think I see a way to figure out this dam."

Lord James swung a leg over the corner of the desk and proceeded to light a cigarette. Through the haze of the first two puffs he squinted across at the glum face of his friend, and said: "Don't be an ass. She hasn't told you not to call."

"No," admitted Blake. "Just the same, she said she wouldn't give me any help."

"That doesn't bar you from calling. The sight of her will keep you keen."

"I tell you, I'm not going near her house till I think I've a show to make good on this dam."

"Then you'll lunch with me and make an early call at the Gantrys'. Miss Dolores requested me to give you an urgent invitation."

"Excuse *me!*" said Blake. "No High Society in mine."

"You'll come," confidently rejoined his friend. "You owe it to Miss Genevieve."

Blake frowned and sat for some moments studying the point. Lord James had him fast.

"Guess you've nailed me for once," he at last admitted. "Rather have a tooth pulled, though."

"I say, now, you got along swimmingly at Ruthby."

"With your father. He wasn't a Chicago society dame."

"Oh, well, you must make allowances for the madam. Miss Dolores explained to me that 'Vievie has only to meet people in order to be received, but mamma has to keep butting in to arrive—that's why she cultivates her grand air.'"

"No sham about Miss Dolores!" approved Blake.

"Right-o! You'll come, I take it. What if the dragon does have rather a frosty stare for you? She said I might bring you to call. Seriously, Tom, you must learn to meet her without showing that her manner flecks you. Best kind of training for society. As I said just now, you owe it to Miss Genevieve."

"Well—long as you put it that way," muttered Blake.

"You'll get along famously with Miss Dolores, I'm sure," said Lord James. "She's quite a charming girl,—vivacious and all that, you know. She's taken quite a fancy to you. The mother is one of those silly climbers who never look below the surface. You have twice my moral stamina, but just because I happen to have a title and some polish—"

"Don't try to gloze it over," cut in Blake. "Let's have it straight. You're a thoroughbred. I'm a broncho."

"Mistaken metaphor," rejoined his friend. "I'm a well-bred nonentity. You're a diamond in the rough. When once you've been cut and polished—"

"Then the flaws will show up in great shape," gibed Blake.

"Never think it, old man! There is only one flaw, and that will disappear with the one cutting required to bring the stone to the best possible shape."

"Stow it!" ordered Blake. The rattling of the doorknob drew his gaze about. "Here's Grif, back at last. He's been to chin with Papa Leslie." He squinted aggressively at the older engineer, who entered with his usual air of seeming absorption in the performance of his most trivial actions. "Hello, you Injin! Gone into partnership with H.V.? You've been there all morning."

"Other way 'round, if anything," answered Griffith. He nodded cordially in response to the greeting of Lord James, and began rummaging in his pockets as he came over to the desk. "Now, where's that letter? Hey?—Oh, here it is." He drew out a long envelope, and started to open it in a precise, deliberate manner.

"So he fired you, eh?" rallied Blake.

"In a way," said Griffith, peering at the paper in his hand.

"It seems he's unloaded the Zariba project onto the Coville Company."

"Thought it couldn't be put through, eh?" said Blake. "Bet he didn't let it go for nothing, though."

"It's not often he comes out at the little end of the horn," replied Griffith. "Didn't take the Coville people long to wake up to the situation. Look here."

Blake took the opened letter, which was headed with the name and officers of the Coville Construction Company. He read it through with care, whistled, and read it through the second time.

"Well, what you think of it?" impatiently demanded Griffith.

"*Whee!* They sure must think H. V. has left them to hold the bag. Fifty thousand bonus to the engineer that shows 'em how the dam can be built!"

"Strict business," croaked Griffith. "The company is stuck if they quit. Fifty thousand is only ten per cent of their net profits if the project goes through. Wish I had a show at it."

"Well, haven't you? It says any engineer."

"I had quit before you came, only I didn't like to own up to H. V."

"You needn't yet a while. I'll keep digging away at it. If I put it through, we divvy up. I'm working for you. See?"

"Not on your life, Tommy! I don't smouge on another man's work."

"Well, then, we'll say I'm to split it because you put me next to the chance."

"No go. I've no use for three-fourths of what I'm making nowadays. It's just piling up on me. Look here. I happened to speak about you to the Coville people—looking ahead, you know. They want me to try you out on some work I'm too busy to do myself. It's not much, and they offer only one-fifty a month as a starter, but it may lead to something better than I can do for you."

"Yes, that's so," considered Blake.

"It is checking field work reports that come in slowly this time of year. That's the only trouble. You'll be sitting around doing nothing half the time—that is, unless you're fool enough to waste any more time on this dam' dam."

"Waste time?" cried Blake, his eyes flashing. "Watch me! Wait till you get your next bill for electric lights! You've given me my cue, Grif. I'm going to buck through this little proposition in one-two-three style, grab my fifty thousand, and plunge into the New York Four Hundred as Tommy Van Damdam. Clear out, you hobos. I'm going to work!"

"Don't forget I've got you on for lunch and Mrs. Gantry's," reminded Lord James.

Blake paused, pencil in hand. "Aw, say, Jimmy, you'll have to let me off now."

"Can't do it, old man, really."

"At least that infernal call."

"No, you've got to get used to it. Tell you what, I'll let you off on the lunch if you'll be at my hotel at four sharp. Don't squirm. That gives you as many hours to grind as are good for you at one stretch. If you try to funk it, I'll hold you for both lunch and call. Your social progress is on my conscience."

"Huh!" rejoined Blake. "Don't wish you any hard luck, but if you and your conscience were in—"

"Four sharp, remember!" put in Lord James, dodging from the room.

Griffith followed him closely and shut the door.

"I'm not so busy, Mr. Scarbridge. Step into my private office and have a cigar," he invited, and as Lord James hesitated, he added in a lower tone, "Want your idea about him."

Lord James at once went with the engineer into his office.

"You wish to speak about Tom?" he said.

"Yes. Did you notice that look about his eyes? It's the first sign."

"Oh, no! let us hope not, Mr. Griffith. I happen to know he has suffered a severe disappointment. It may be that."

"Well, maybe. I hope so," said Griffith dubiously. With innate delicacy, he refrained from any inquiry as to the nature of Blake's disappointment. As he handed out his box of cigars, he went on, "I don't quite like it, though. He's a glutton for field work, but this indoors figuring soon sets him on edge. He can't stand being cooped up."

"Count on me to do all I can to get him out."

"Yes, I'm figuring on you, Mr. Scarbridge. He's told me all about you. Between the two of us, we might stave it off and keep him going for months. Wish I knew more about the girl—Miss Leslie. If she's the right sort, there's just a chance of something being done that I gave up as being impossible, last time he was with me—he might be straightened out for good."

"It's possible, quite possible! Others have been cured,— why not he?" exclaimed Lord James, his face aglow with boyish enthusiasm. But as suddenly it clouded. "Ah, though, most unfortunate—this stand of Miss Leslie's!"

"What about her?" queried Griffith, as the other hesitated.

"She has told him that he must win out absolutely on his own strength, without her aid or sympathy."

"Well, I'll be—switched! Thought she loved him."

Lord James flushed, yet answered without hesitancy. "It is to be presumed she does, otherwise she would not have forced this test upon him."

"How d'you make that out?"

"Mere grateful interest in his welfare would have been satisfied by the assurance of his material success. On the other hand, her—ah—feeling toward him is at present held in restraint by her acute judgment. She had reason to esteem him in that savage environment. She now realizes that he must win her esteem in her own proper environment. She is not merely a young lady—she is a lady. Her rare good sense tells her that she must not accept him unless he proves himself fit."

"He's a lot fitter than all these lallapaloozer papa's boys and some of their fathers,—all those empty-headed swells that are called eligibles," rejoined Griffith.

"It's not a question of polish or culture, believe me. She is far too clever to doubt that he would acquire that quickly enough. My reference was to this one flaw, which may yet shatter him. The question is whether it penetrates too deep into his nature. If not—if he can rid himself of it—then even I admit that he would make her happy."

"Yet she won't lift a finger to help him fight it out?"

"Courage is the fundamental virtue in a man. It includes

moral strength. If she cannot be sure of his strength, she will always doubt him and her love for him."

"Can't see it that way. If she helped him, and he won out, he'd be cured, wouldn't he?"

"I've been trying to guess at a woman's reason, but I'm not so rash as to attempt to argue the matter," said Lord James. He picked up his hat and held out a cordial hand to the engineer. "She may or may not be right. I'm not altogether certain as to the intuitive wisdom of women. However that may be, we at least shall do our best to pull him through."

"That's talking, Mr. Scarbridge!" exclaimed Griffith.

15

BY-PLAY

PROMPTLY AT FOUR that afternoon Blake was shown to the rooms of his friend at the hotel. He entered with a glum look not altogether assumed.

"Well, here I am," he grumbled. "Hope you're satisfied. You're robbing me of the best part of the day."

"I daresay," cheerfully assented Lord James. "Now look pleasant till I see if you're dressed."

"No, I haven't a thing on. Just clothed in sunshine and a sweet smile," growled Blake, throwing open his raincoat to show his suit of rough gray homespun. "You don't ever get me into that skirty coat again. I can stand full dress, but not that afternoon horror-gown. I'm no minister."

"Don't fash yourself, old man. At least you've been tailored in London, and that's something. You'll do—in Chicago."

"I'll do O.K. right here," said Blake. "What say? You've spoiled my afternoon. We'll call it quits if you settle down with me and put in the time chinning about things."

"Tammas, I'm shocked at you," reproved Lord James. "You cannot wish to disappoint Mrs. Gantry, really!"

"Mrs. Gantry be—"

"No, no! Do not say it, my deah Tammas! When one is

in Society, y'know, one is privileged to think it, but it's bad form to express it so—ah—broadly—ah—I assure you."

He adjusted his monocle and stared with a vacuous blandness well calculated to madden his friend. Blake hurled a magazine, which his lordship deftly sidestepped. He reached for his hat, and faced Blake with boyish eagerness.

"Come on, Tom. Chuck the rotting. We're wasting time."

"Must have a taxicab waiting for you," bantered Blake.

"No, a young lady. Miss Dolores is really eager to become acquainted with you, and—er—she may have a friend or two—"

"Excuse *me!*"

"Tammas the quitter!"

Lord James started for the door, and Blake followed him, striving hard to maintain his surly look. At the street entrance he sought to postpone the coming ordeal by urging his need for exercise.

"Don't worry. I'll pay," said Lord James, pretending to misunderstand, and he raised his finger to the chauffeur of the nearest cab. "You can walk home, if you wish to save pennies. Now, you know, we desire to reach Mrs. Gantry's as soon as possible."

"Yes, we do!" growled Blake.

He seemed more than ever determined to remain in his glum mood, and the pleasant badinage of his friend during their run out to Lincoln Park Boulevard rather increased than lessened his surliness. When they entered through the old Colonial portal of the Gantry home, he jerked off his English topcoat unaided, contemptuously spurning the assistance of the buff-and-yellow liveried footman. But as they were announced, he assumed what Lord James termed his "poker face," and entered beside his friend, with head well up and shoulders squared.

"Good boy! Keep it up," murmured Lord James. "She'll take you for a distinguished personage."

Blake spoiled the effect by a grin, which, an instant later, was transformed into a radiant smile at sight of Genevieve beside Mrs. Gantry.

Dolores came darting to meet them, her black eyes sparkling and her lithe young body aquiver with animation.

"Oh, Lord Avondale!" she cried. "So you did make him come. Mr. Blake, why didn't you call at once?"

"Wasn't asked," answered Blake, his eyes twinkling.

"You are now. So please remember to come often. Never fear mamma. I'll protect you. Oh, I'm just on tiptoe to see you in those skin things you wore in Africa. I made Vievie put on her leopard-skin gown, and I think it's the most terrible romantic thing! And now I'm just dying to see your hyena-skin trousers and those awful poisoned arrows and—"

"Dolores!" admonished Mrs. Gantry.

"Oh, piffle!" complained the girl, drawing aside for the men to pass her.

Even Mrs. Gantry was not equal to the rudeness of snubbing a caller in her own house—when she had given an earl permission to bring him. But the contrast between her greetings of the two men was, to say the least, noticeable.

Blake met her supercilious bearing toward him with an impassiveness that was intended to mask his contemptuous resentment. But Genevieve saw and understood. She rose and quietly remarked: "You'll excuse us, Aunt Amice. I wish Mr. Blake to see the palm room. I fancy it will carry him back to Mozambique."

Mrs. Gantry's look said that she wished Mr. Blake could be carried back to Mozambique and kept there. Her tongue said: "As you please, my dear. Yet I should have thought you'd had quite enough of Africa for a lifetime."

"One never can tell," replied Genevieve with a coldness that chilled the glow in Blake's eyes.

They went out side by side yet perceptibly constrained in their bearing toward one another.

Dolores flung herself across the room and into a chair facing her mother and Lord James.

"Did you see that?" she demanded. "I do believe Vievie is the coldest blooded creature! When she knows he's just dying for love of her! Why, I never—"

"That will do!" interrupted Mrs. Gantry.

"I'll leave it to Lord Avondale. Isn't it the exact truth?"

"Er—he still looks rather robust," parried Lord James.

"You know what I mean. But I didn't think she'd behave in this dog-in-the-manger fashion. She might have at least given me a chance for a *tête-à-tête* with him, even if he is her hero."

"I am only too well aware what Lord Avondale will think of *you*, going on in this silly way," observed Mrs. Gantry.

"If Lord Avondale doesn't like me and my manners, he needn't. Need you, Mr. Scarbridge?"

"But how can I help liking you?" asked the young Englishman with such evident sincerity that the girl was disconcerted. She flashed a bewildered glance into his earnest face, and turned quickly away, her cheeks scarlet with confusion.

"Ah, Earl," purred her mother, "I fully appreciate your kindness. She is Genevieve's cousin. You are therefore pleased to disregard her gaucheries."

"Ho! so that's it?" retorted Dolores. "Lord Avondale needn't trouble to disregard anything about me."

"Believe me, I do not, Miss Gantry," replied Lord James. "I find you most charming."

"Because I'm Vievie's cousin! Well, if you wish to know what I think, I think all Englishmen are simply detestable!" cried the girl, and she sprang up and flounced away, her face crimson with anger.

"You had better go straight to your room," reproved her mother.

The girl promptly dodged the doorway for which she was headed, and veered around to a window, where she turned her back on them and perched herself on the arm of a chair.

Mrs. Gantry sighed profoundly. "*A-a-ah!* Was ever a mother so tried! Such temper, such perversity! Her father, all over again!"

"If you'll permit me to offer a suggestion," ventured Lord James, "may it not be that you drive with rather too taut a rein?"

"Too taut! Can you not see? The slightest relaxation, and I should have a runaway."

"But a little freedom to canter? It's this chafing against the bit. So high spirited, you know. I must confess, it's that which I find most charming about her."

"Impossible! You cannot realize."

"Then, too, her candor—one of the rarest and most admirable traits in a woman."

"Simply terrible! That she should fling her—opinion of you in your face!"

"Better that than the usual insincerity in such cases of dislike. It gives me reason to hope that eventually I can win her friendship."

"Your kindness is more than I can ever repay!"

"You can by granting me a single favor."

"Indeed?" Mrs. Gantry raised her eyebrows in high arches.

"By receiving my friend as my friend."

"Ah! Had you not asked permission to bring him, he would not have been received at all."

"Not even as the man who saved your niece?"

"That is an obligation to be discharged by her father."

"I see. Very well, then. Regarding him simply as my friend, I ask you to consider that he is undergoing a most difficult, I may say, cruel test. He must overcome something that he has vainly fought for years—something that has crushed many of the greatest intellects the world has known."

"The more reason for me to save Genevieve from ruin. From what you say, I imply that it is a hopeless case of degeneracy."

"Not hopeless; and degenerate in that respect alone—if you must insist on the term."

"I do insist."

"What if he should succeed in overcoming it?"

"He cannot. Even should he seem to, there will always be a weakness to be feared."

"Is that just?"

"It is just to Genevieve."

"Everything for Vievie, coronet included!" called Dolores over her shoulder.

Mrs. Gantry's English complexion deepened to the purple of mortification. The frank smile that told of his lordship's enjoyment of her discomfiture was the last straw. She rose in her stateliest manner.

"I shall leave you a few moments to be entertained by the dear child, since you find her so amusing," she said. "Genevieve must not be permitted to remain too long in the close hot air of the palm room."

"There's some hot air outside the conservatory, mamma," remarked Dolores.

But Mrs. Gantry sailed majestically from the room, without deigning to heed the pleasantry.

Lord James sauntered across to the window and perched himself on a chair arm close before the girl.

"When do you begin?" he asked. "Your mamma said you were to entertain me."

"Best possible reason why I shouldn't," she snapped, staring hard out of the window.

"What if I should try to entertain you?"

"You wouldn't succeed. I wanted to talk to a man. It's too bad! Simply because you asked me to, I was silly enough to tease Vievie into coming over this afternoon—and the minute he comes, she rushes him off to the conservatory."

"Believe me, I regret quite as keenly that she did not take me instead."

"That's complimentary—to me!"

"Can you blame me for agreeing, when you express a preference for the man instead of the mere son of a duke?"

"Perhaps you're a man yourself. Who knows?"

"*Quien sabe*, Señorita Dolores?" he rallied her. "Tell me how to prove it."

She flashed him a glance of naive coquetry. "You ask how? If I were my great grandmother, you might try to kiss me, and chance a stiletto thrust in return."

"Your great grandmother was an Italian?"

The girl's red lips curled disdainfully. "No, she was Spanish. Though she lived in Mexico, her family were Castilian and related to the royal Valois family of France. So you see how far back it goes. We have the journal of her husband. She married Dr. Robinson, who accompanied Lieutenant Pike on his famous expedition."

"Pike? Leftenant Pike?"

"No, he wasn't 'left.' He came back and became the General Pike who died at the moment of his glorious victory over the English, in the War of 1812."

"Ah, come to think—Pike of Pike's Peak. Never heard of the battle you mention; but as an explorer— So one of his companions married your ancestress?"

"Yes. He must have been another such man as Mr. Blake."

"The kind to risk stiletto thrusts for kisses?"

"Yes. I know I must be exactly like her—that haughty Señorita Alisanda."

"Indeed, yes. I can almost see her dagger up your sleeve."

The girl's black eyes flashed fire. "If it *was* there, you'd get a good scratch!"

"Believe me," he apologized, "you quite failed to take me."

"It's no question of taking you. I prefer heroes."

"Can't say I blame you. You've all the fire and charm of a Spanish girl, and, permit me to add, the far greater charm of an American girl."

She looked to see if he was mocking her. Finding him unaffectedly sincere, she promptly melted into a most amiable and vivacious though unconventional *débutante*.

16

THE AMARYLLIS

THE CONSTRAINT BETWEEN Blake and Genevieve had rather increased than lessened when they left the others. Neither spoke until they had passed through the outer conservatory into the tropical heat of the palm room. But there the first whiff of the odor from the moist warm mould brought with it a flood of pungent memories.

"The river jungle," muttered Blake, sniffing. "Air was drier out under the cocoanut palms."

"That first night, in the tree!" murmured Genevieve. "How easily you hauled us up with the vine rope! Ah, then—and now!"

Blake drew away from her, his face darkening. "Hope you don't think I expected to see you here? If Jimmy knew, he didn't tell me."

"How could he know? Dolores did not phone to me until mid-afternoon. But even had you been told, I see no reason why you shouldn't have come."

"You don't?" he asked, his face brightening. "I was afraid you might think I was trying to dodge your conditions. Besides, I had promised myself not to call on you till I thought I saw a way to work out a big piece of engineering that I'm on."

"Then you have a good position? I'm so glad!"

"Not a regular position. But I've been given work and a chance at one of the biggest things in hydraulics—the Zariba Dam, out in Arizona."

"You're not going away?" Calmly as she tried to speak, she could not entirely repress an under-note of apprehension. Slight as was the betrayal of feeling, it enheartened him immensely. He beamed up at the palm crests that brushed the glazed dome.

"Looks like they're going to raise the roof, doesn't it?" he said. "Feel that way myself. Your father unloaded the Zariba project onto the Coville Construction Company, and they've offered a cool fifty thousand dollars to the man that figures out a feasible way to construct the dam. I spoke about it before, you may remember; but this bonus wasn't up then. If I put it through, I'll be recognized as a first-class engineer."

"You will succeed, of course," said Genevieve with perfect confidence in his ability to overcome such a relatively easy difficulty.

"Hope so," responded Blake. "I'm still tunnelling in the dark, though. Not a glimmer of a hole out."

"That is of small concern."

"Isn't it, though? I'm counting on that to boost me along on the other thing. Nothing like a little good luck to keep a fellow braced up."

"But I'm sure you have some Dutch blood,—and you know the Dutch never fight harder than when the odds are against them."

"Then it's too bad I'm not Hans Van Amsterdam. He'd have the scrap of his life."

"Do you mean that the odds are so greatly against you?" asked Genevieve, with sudden gravity.

"What's the use of talking about it?" said Blake, almost brusquely. "If I win, I win; and I'm supposed to believe that is all it means. If I lose, you're rid of me for good."

Genevieve bit her lip and turned her head to hide her starting tears.

"I did not think you would be so bitter over it!" she half sobbed.

"Can't you take a joke?" he demanded. "Great joke!—me thinking I've a ghost of a show of winning you! No; the laugh's on me, all right. Idea of me dreaming I can down that damnable thirst!"

"Tom, you'll not give up—you'll not!" she cried with a fierceness that shook him out of his bitter despondency.

"Give up?" he rejoined. "What d' you take me for? I'll fight—course I'll fight, till I'm down and out. People don't much believe in hell nowadays, Jenny. I do. I've been there. I'm bound to go there again, I don't know how soon. Don't think I'm begging for help or whining. Nobody goes to hell that hasn't got hell in him. He always gets just what's coming to him."

"No, no! It's not fair. I can't bear to hear you blame yourself. There's no justice in it. Both heredity and environment have been against you."

"Justice?" he repeated. He shook his head, with rather a grim smile. "Told you once I worked in a pottery. Supposing the clay of a piece wasn't mixed right, it wasn't the dish's fault if it cracked in the firing. Just the same, it got heaved on the scrap-heap."

Genevieve looked down at her clasped hands and whispered: "May not even a flawed piece prove so unique, so valuable in other respects, that it is cemented and kept?"

Blake laughed harshly. "Ever know a cracked dish to cement itself?"

"This is all wrong! The metaphor doesn't apply," protested the girl. "You're not a lifeless piece of clay; you're a man— you have a free, powerful will."

"That's the question. Have I? Has anybody? Some scientists argue that we're nothing but automatons—the creatures of heredity and environment."

"It's not true. We're morally responsible for all we do— that is, unless we're insane."

"And I'm only dippy, eh?" said Blake.

He moved ahead around the screening fronds of a young areca palm, and came to an abrupt halt, his eyes fixed on an object in the midst of the tropical undergrowth.

"Look here!" he called in a hushed tone.

Genevieve hesitated, and came to him with reluctant slowness. But when she reached his side and saw what it was he was looking at so intently, her cold face warmed with a tender glow, and, unable to restrain her emotion, she pressed her cheek against his arm. He quivered, yet made no attempt to take advantage of her weakness.

"Tom! oh, Tom!" she whispered. "It's exactly the color of the other one!"

"Wish *this* snake was as easy to smash!" he muttered.

"It will be!" she reassured him. He made no response. After a short silence, she said, "In memory of that, Tom, I wish you would kiss me."

He bent over and touched his lips to her forehead with reverent tenderness. That was all.

When Mrs. Gantry came in on them, they were still standing side by side, but apart, contemplating the great crimson amaryllis blossom. Their attitude and their silence were, however, sufficient to quicken her apprehensions.

"My dear child," she reproached Genevieve, "you should know that this damp mouldy air is not wholesome for you."

"She's right, Miss Jenny," agreed Blake. "It's too much like Mozambique—gets your thoughts muddled. You've failed to do as you said you would. I ought to've gone sooner. Good-day, Mrs. Gantry. Good-day, Miss Jenny."

He turned away with decisive quickness.

"Must you go?" asked Genevieve, with a trace of entreaty that did not escape her aunt.

"Yes," said Blake.

"You'll come to see me soon!"

"Not till I see daylight ahead on the dam. Don't know when that will be. Best I can say is *Adios!*"

"I trust it will be soon."

"Same here," he responded, and he left the palm room with head down-bent, as if he were already pondering the problem, the solving of which was to free him from the self-imposed taboo of her house.

"My dear Genevieve!" Mrs. Gantry hastened to exclaim. "Why must you encourage the man?"

The girl pointed to the gorgeous blossom of the amaryllis. "That is one reason, Aunt Amice."

"That? What do you mean?"

"Your amaryllis—not the flower itself, but what it stands for to me."

"Still, I do not—"

"Not when you recall what I told you about that frightful

puff adder—that I was stooping to pick an amaryllis when the hideous creature struck at me?"

"You mentioned something about a snake, but there was so much else—"

"Yes, it was only once of the many, many times when he proved himself a man. Though the adder only struck the fold of my skirt, I stood paralyzed with horror. Winthrope, as usual, was ineffectual. Tom came running with his club—and then—" The girl paused until the vivid blush that had leaped into her cheeks had ebbed away. "It was not alone his courage but his resourcefulness. Most men would have turned away from the writhing monster, full of loathing. He saw the opportunity to convert what had been a most deadly peril into a source of safety. He sent me away, and extracted the poison for his arrow tips."

"My dear child, I freely admit that he is an admirable savage," conceded Mrs. Gantry.

"Say rather that he was fit to survive in a savage environment. We shall now see him adapt himself to the other extreme."

"Young girls always tend to idealize those whom they chance to fancy."

"Chance? Fancy? Dear Aunt Amice, you and papa do not, perhaps cannot, realize that for those many weeks I lived with storm and starvation, sun and fever, serpents and ferocious beasts all striving to destroy me. I saw the hard realities of life, and learned to think. Mentally I am no longer a young girl, but a woman, qualified to judge what her future should be."

The glowing face of her usually composed niece warned Mrs. Gantry to be discreet. She patted the coils of soft hair.

"There, there, my dear. Pray do not misunderstand me. All I ask is that you make sure before you commit yourself,—a few months of delay, that you may compare him with the men of our own class."

Genevieve smiled. "I have gone quite beyond that already, Aunt Amice."

"Indeed?" murmured the elder woman. Too tactful to venture further, she placed a ring-crowded hand upon her ample bosom. "It is too close in here. I feel oppressed."

Genevieve readily accompanied her from the conservatory.

Blake had gone, alone, for they found Lord James in the midst of a lively *tête-à-tête* with Dolores.

At sight of the merry couple, Genevieve paused in the doorway to recall to her companion some previous conversation. "You see, Aunty. Confess now. They would make a perfect couple."

"Nonsense. He would never dream of such a thing, even were you out of his thoughts. What is more, though he seems to have caught her in one of her gay moods, I know that she simply abominates him. She told him as much, within a minute after you left us."

"I'm so sorry!" sighed Genevieve. "At least let us slip out without interrupting them. I must be going, anyway."

"My dear, I have you to consider before Dolores," replied Mrs. Gantry, and she advanced upon the unconscious couple. "Genevieve is going."

Lord James looked about, for the slightest fraction of a moment discomposed. Genevieve perceived the fleeting expression, and hastened to interpose. "Do not trouble. It is so short a distance."

But the Englishman was already bowing to Dolores. The girl turned her back upon him with deliberate rudeness.

"You see!" murmured Mrs. Gantry to Genevieve.

When Lord James and her niece had gone, the outraged dame wheeled upon her daughter. But at the first word, Dolores faced her with such an outblazing of rebellious anger that the mother thought best to defer her lecture.

17

ENTRAPPED

ON A FROSTY Sunday morning, some ten days later, Blake came swinging out Lake Shore Drive at a space-devouring stride that soon brought him to the Leslie mansion. He turned in, and the footman, who had received orders regarding him, promptly bowed him in.

After a moment's hesitancy, Blake handed over a calling card. All his previous cards had been printed, with a "C.E." after his name and nothing before it. These social insignia had been ordered for him by Lord James. Blake wondered how the innovation would impress Genevieve.

She presently came down to him, dressed for church but without her hat. He was quick to note the fact. "You're going out. Didn't mean to call at the wrong time."

"No," she replied. "I am going to church, but not until Aunt Amice and Dolores call by for us. That may not be for half an hour. I am very glad to see you. I remember what you said about your next call. This means, does it not, that you believe you can solve the problem of the Zariba Dam?"

"Yes. I sidetracked the proposition four days ago. Had all the facts and factors in my head, but couldn't seem to get anywhere. Well, I hadn't tried to think about the dam since then, but this morning, all of a sudden, the idea came to me."

"You had set your subconscious mind to working," remarked Genevieve. "The ideas of many of the great inventions and discoveries have come that way."

"Don't know about any subconscious mind," said Blake. "But that idea flashed into my head when I wasn't thinking of the dam at all—just like I'd dreamed it."

"You mean 'as if' you'd dreamed it, not 'like,'" said Genevieve, with a look of playful reproof.

"How's that?" he queried. "Never thought that was wrong. But I like your telling me. Is that right?"

"Quite,—grammatically as well as otherwise," she answered, smiling at his soberness. But her tone was as earnest as his. "The speech of a great engineer should be as correct as his figures."

"That's a go!" agreed Blake. "I'll hire a grammar expert just as soon as I work out this dam idea—um—you know what I mean—this idea about the dam. Don't know how long that will take. But I'm pretty sure I've got the thing cinched—else I wouldn't have had the nerve to come here this morning. You'll believe that, Jenny?"

"Of course. Yet there was no reason why you should have remained away even had you not succeeded. I did not mean you to—to take it that way, Tom."

"All right, then. I'll drop around often if it's not against rules."

"You'll come to church with me this morning?"

"Church!" echoed Blake, in mock-tragic fright. "Haven't been inside a church since I don't know when."

"All the more reason why you should go with us now," she argued.

"Us?"

"Aunt Amice always calls by for papa. He is one of the vestrymen of the Cathedral, you know, but he'd never go if aunty did not come for him. We share the same pew. But it's a large one. There'll be room for you."

"Not in the same pew with your aunt and father," rejoined Blake. "It'd take a larger pew than was ever made, to hold them and me."

"Oh, but you must come, Tom. You'll enjoy the music. Here they are now."

"O-ho, Vievie, you in here?" called Dolores, and she darted in upon them. "Goodness! who's the man? Why, it's Mr. Blake. Hail to the hero!"

She pirouetted down to them and shook Blake's hand vigorously, chattering her fastest. "You can't imagine how glad I am to see you. I've had less than half of Jeems, with mamma butting in all the way over. Of course he'll sit between her and Vievie. If you'll come along as my own particular, I'll feed you on chocolates and keep you nudged during the sermon."

"Oh, but I say, Miss Gantry, those were to be my chocolates," protested Lord James from the doorway.

"Hello," said Blake. "So you're the man, are you? Better look out.

First thing you know, you'll get roped."

"Roped? What's that?" demanded Dolores.

"Ask Jeems," laughed Blake.

"Er—seems to me I've heard the expression in relation to the term 'steer,'" observed Lord James.

"Oh, something to do with a ship," said the girl.

"Yes, with what the sailormen would call a trim craft. Eh, Jeems?" chuckled Blake.

"You're laughing at me!" accused the girl. "To make up for it, you'll have to come and hold my prayer-book for me. Just think!—a real hero to hold my prayer-book!"

"Excuse *me!*" objected Blake. "I don't know the places."

"Never mind. We can study the styles quite as well. Vievie, let's hurry on. Mamma has gone up to rout out Uncle Herbert. They'll be late—as usual."

"Well, then, I'll clear the track," said Blake. "Take good care of Jeems for me. Good-bye, Miss Jenny."

"Don't leave, Tom," replied Genevieve. "If you do not wish to go to the Cathedral—"

"We'll all stay home," cut in Dolores.

"What's this about staying home?" came the voice of Mrs. Gantry from the hall.

"Quick, Mr. Blake!" exclaimed Dolores in a stage whisper. "Hide behind me. I'm taller than Vievie."

Her mother came in upon them in time to catch Blake's broadest grin.

"Stay at home, indeed! Such a delightful day as—Ah!"

"It is Mr. Blake, Aunt Amice," said Genevieve in a tone that compelled the stiffening matron to bow.

"Well, good-bye," repeated Blake.

"Please wait," said Genevieve. "If you do not wish to go to church, you must stay to— Here's papa."

"Not late this time, am I?" demanded Mr. Leslie, bustling into the room. "All ready, my dear? No, you've not got on your hat. Hello!" He stopped short, staring at Blake. "Didn't know you were to be with us."

"I'm not," said Blake.

"You're not? H'm,—why not? Not afraid of church, are you? Better join us."

Blake stared in open astonishment. "Thanks, I—Not this time, I guess," he replied.

Mr. Leslie seemed about to press the point, but paused and glanced at his watch.

"Please do not wait for me," said Genevieve. "I have decided not to go."

If Blake expected an outburst over this, he had another surprise in store for him. Mrs. Gantry turned away, tight-lipped and high of chin, either too full for utterance or else aware that it was an instant when silence was the better part of diplomacy.

Mr. Leslie followed her, after a half-irritable, half-cordial word to Blake. "Very well, very well. Some other time, then."

As Lord James took his leave of Genevieve with apparent nonchalance, Blake noted an exultant sparkle in the black eyes of Dolores. Yet the look was flatly contradicted by her words as she flounced about toward the door: "You needn't say good-bye, Mr. Scarbridge. You may as well stay right here, since she's not going."

"You see how she rags me," complained Lord James, hastening out after her.

Blake watched them go, his eyes keen with eager observation. He was still staring at the doorway when Genevieve offered banteringly, "A penny for your thoughts, Mr. Blake."

"You'll have to bid higher. Make it a coronet—I mean, half a crown."

"Only half a crown? Why not a crown—the oak crown of the conqueror? You know the Bible verse: 'He that over-cometh himself is greater than he that taketh a city.'"

"Can't say as to that; but I've taken in the town, after having failed to overcome," said Blake with bitter humor.

"Tom! You must not speak of your defeats. They are past and of the Past. You must not even think of them. Have you ever been baptized?"

"Baptized? Let's see... Yes, I remember the question was brought up when I came back from my first hoboing and my sisters got me going to the Episcopal Mission. They even persuaded me to join what's called a confirmation class. That's when it had to be proved I'd been baptized."

"Oh, Tom! then you've been confirmed—you're an Episcopalian!"

"I was confirmed. That's not saying I'm an Episcopalian now."

"Have you joined another denomination?"

"No. It was just that my religious streak pinched out, and some years after that I read Darwin and Spencer and Haeckel."

"But that's no reason. If only you had read Drummond first, you'd have seen that true science and true religion are not opposed but are complementary to each other."

"Drummond?" queried Blake. "Never heard of him, that I remember. Anyway, I guess I'm not one of the religious kind. It was only to please my sisters I started in that time."

"But you'll go to church with me now, Tom?"

Blake hesitated. "Thought you told them you'd decided not to go?"

"Not to the Cathedral. There's the little chapel down

the street, in which I was confirmed. It's nearer. We could walk. The bishop officiates at the communion this morning, but he is ill; so Mr. Vincent, the vicar, will preach. He's a young clergyman and is said to be as popular with the men of his congregation as with the women. His text to-day for morning service is—No, I'll not tell it to you, but I'm sure you'll find the sermon helpful."

"If you're so anxious to have me go, Jenny, I'll go. But it's to be with you, not because I'm interested in that kind of religion. I don't believe in going to a church every week and whining about being full of sin and iniquity and all that. The people that do it are either hypocrites and don't believe what they are saying, or else it's true, and they ought to go to jail."

Genevieve smiled regretfully. "You and I live in such different worlds.

Will you not try to at least look into mine?"

"Well, I'll not sleep during the sermon," promised Blake.

She shook her head at his levity, and left him, to fetch her hat and furs.

When they went out, Blake had no need to stop in the hall. He had brought no overcoat. The first breath of the clear frosty air outside caused her to draw her furs about her graceful throat. She glanced at Blake, and asked with almost maternal concern. "Where's your topcoat? You'll take cold."

"What, a day like this?" he replied. "On a good hustling job I'd call this shirtsleeve weather."

"You're so hardy! That is part of your strength."

"Um-m," muttered Blake. "That cousin of yours is a hummer, isn't she?"

"If you but knew how she envies me my Crusoe adventures!"

"I'm not surprised to hear it. What gets me is seeing her go to the same church as her mother."

"She doesn't usually. But how could she miss such a chance to tease aunty and Lord James? She's a dear contrary girl."

"Then she's not an Episcopalian?"

"Oh, yes. Isn't it nice that we all are?"

"We all?" queried Blake.

"If you've been confirmed, you are, too. That's why I'm so glad you're coming with me. We'll take the communion together."

Blake's face darkened, and he replied hesitatingly: "Why, you see, Jenny, I—I don't think I want to."

"But, Tom, when it will please me so much!"

"You know I'd like to please you—only, you see, I'm not—I don't believe in it."

"Do you positively disbelieve in it?"

"Well, I can't say just that."

"Then I'm sure it will be all right. You'll not be irreverent, and maybe it will reawaken your own true spiritual self."

"Sorry," said Blake uneasily. "I'm afraid I can't do it, even to please you."

"But why not? Surely, Tom, you'll not allow your hard cold science to stand in the way of a sacrament!"

"I don't know whether it is a sacrament or isn't."

"Is that your reason for refusing what I so greatly desire?"

He looked away from her, and asked in a tone that was meant to be casual, "Do they use regular wine, or the unfermented kind?"

"So that's your reason!" she exclaimed. "I did not think you'd be afraid."

"Anything that has alcohol in it—" he sought to explain. "It's the very devil to rouse that craving! There have been times when I've taken a drink and fought it down—but not when—No, I can't risk it, Jenny."

"Not the communion wine? Surely no harm could come from that! You need take only the slightest sip."

"One taste might prove to be as bad as a glassful. You can't guess what it's like. I'm apt to go wild. Just the smell is bad enough."

"But it's the *communion*, Tom. You have been confirmed in the Church. You know what the consecrated bread and wine symbolize. You can recall to mind all the sacred associations."

"I'm mighty sorry," replied Blake. "If only that meant to me what it does to you, I might risk it. I'm no blatant atheist or anti-religionist. I'm simply agnostic; I don't believe. That's all. You have faith. I haven't. I didn't wish to get rid of my faith. It just went."

"It may come to you again, if you seek to partake of the spiritual communion," urged Genevieve.

"I'm willing enough to try that. But I'll not risk any wine."

"You'll not?" she cried. "Afraid to taste the consecrated wine? Then you *are* weak!—you *are* a coward! And I thought you strong, despite your own confession!"

The outburst of reproach forced Blake to flinch. He muttered in protest, "Good Lord, Jenny! you don't mean to say you make this a part of the test?"

"Does it mean nothing to you that I long to have you

share the communion with me?" she rejoined. "What must I think of you if you dare not venture to partake of that holy symbol, in the communion of all that is highest within you with the Father?"

Blake quivered as though the frosty air had at last sent a chill through his powerful frame.

"You insist?" he asked huskily.

"You are strong. You will do it," she replied.

"You don't know what it means. But, since you insist—" he reluctantly acquiesced. He added almost inaudibly, "Up against it for sure! Still—there have been times—"

18

HOLY COMMUNION

THEY REACHED THE chapel and entered during the last verse of the Processional Hymn. As Genevieve was known to the usher in charge of the centre aisle, they were shown to a pew farther forward than Blake would have chosen.

Genevieve produced a dainty hymnal and prayer-book, and gave her companion the pleasurable employment of helping her hold first one and then the other, throughout the service. If his spirit was quickened by a re-hearing of the prayers in which he had once believed, he did not show it. But he seemed pleased at the fact that Genevieve was too intent upon worship to gaze around at the hats and dresses of the other ladies.

The chapel choir could not boast of any exceptional voices. It was, however, very well trained. Throughout the anthem Blake sat tense, almost quivering, so keen was his delight. At the close he sank back into the corner of the pew, his gaze shifting uneasily from the infirm and aged bishop in the episcopal chair to the thin, eager-faced young vicar who had hastened around to mount up into the pulpit.

With a quick movement, the vicar opened the thick

Bible to his text, the announcement of which caused Blake to start and fix his attention upon him:

"'He that is slow to anger is better than the mighty, and he that ruleth his spirit than he that taketh a city.' Proverbs 16:32."

Genevieve glanced at Blake, who recalled how she had expressed her certainty that he would find the sermon helpful. The text was apt, to say the least. His hard-set face momentarily softened with a smile that caused her to settle back, in serene contentment. He assumed what Lord James would have termed his "poker face" and leaned up in the corner of the pew, to gaze at the preacher, as impassive as a wooden image.

The manner in which the Reverend Mr. Vincent elucidated his text soon won a stare of pleased surprise from Blake. He began by describing, no less vividly than briefly, the walled cities of the ancients and the enormous difficulty of capturing them, either by siege or assault. This was followed by a graphic summary of the life of Alexander the Great.

Blake listened with such intentness to this novel sermon that he did not perceive that Genevieve was no less intently studying him. It was evident he was deeply impressed by the obvious inference to be drawn from the life of the mighty young Macedonian,—the youth who conquered worlds, only to be himself conquered by his own vices.

But when, warming to his theme, the young vicar entered upon a eulogy of asceticism, Blake bent over and stared moodily at the printed "Suggestions to Worshippers" pasted on the back of the next pew. His big body, to all appearances, was absolutely still and rigid, but the fingers of his right hand moved about restlessly, tapping his knee or clenching upon the broad palm.

In the midst of Mr. Vincent's explanations of what he considered the fundamental differences between the self-torture of the Hindu yogis and the mortifications of spirit and body practised by the mediaeval monks, Blake shook his head in an uneasy, annoyed gesture. Yet if he meant this as an indication of dissent, he gave no other sign that he was following the thread of the sermon.

Even the close of the eloquent peroration, in which Mr. Vincent besought his hearers to prepare for the fasting and prayer of the Lenten season, failed to rouse Blake from his moody abstraction. But at the end of the regular service, when the white-gowned choir-boys flocked out and the majority of the congregation began to crowd into the aisles with decorous murmurings and the soft rustling of silken skirts, Blake raised his head and followed their departure with a shifting, disquieted gaze.

At last all others than those who had remained for the communion had passed out into the vestibule, and the closing of the doors muffled the loud clear voices of those on the outer steps. Genevieve touched Blake's arm. He started, and glanced up into the chancel. As he caught sight of the bishop and Mr. Vincent behind the rail, his uneasiness became so pronounced that Genevieve was alarmed.

"What is it? Are you ill?" she whispered.

"No," he replied. He thrust his shaking hands into his coat pockets, forced himself to take a deep breath, and added in a thick, half-inarticulate mutter, "no—won't give in—not a quitter."

She could not catch the words, but the resolute tone reassured her.

"It's the air in here. It's stifling. But we shall not be long now," she murmured, and she lapsed into devotional concentration.

Blake, however, followed the service with increasing restlessness. His fingers twitched within the sheltering pockets, and the lines of his face drew tense. He glanced about two or three times as though half inclined to bolt.

A little more, and he might have broken under the strain and run away. But then the communicants began to leave their pews and drift forward into the chancel. At the touch of Genevieve's hand upon his arm he started more sharply than before.

"Tom, you really are ill!" she insisted.

"No," he mumbled, "I guess I— Wait, though. I've forgotten. Does he mean we're supposed to take it as real flesh and blood?"

"Only the Romanists hold to that. We take it symbolically."

"Then why doesn't he say so?"

"He did. Besides, every one understands. You are coming?"

"Wine—alcohol—and she still insists!" he muttered in a thick, almost inarticulate voice.

Intent upon the sacrament, she failed to heed either his tone or the despair in his tense face.

"Come. We are the last," she urged. "We'll soon be out in the open air."

With a heaviness that she mistook for solemnity, he

stepped out into the aisle for her to leave the pew, and walked beside her up into the chancel.

She knelt near the extreme end of the altar rail, and bent over with her face in the little hand that she had bared to receive the communion bread. For a moment Blake stood beside her, staring dubiously at the venerable figure of the bishop. Mr. Vincent passed between. Blake took a step to the left and knelt down beside Genevieve.

The only sounds in the chancel were the intoned murmurings of the bishop and Mr. Vincent and the labored breathing of an asthmatic woman next to Genevieve. The less indistinct of the murmuring voices drew near. Genevieve thrust out her palm a little way. Blake, without looking up, did the same.

Mr. Vincent reiterated his intoned statement above them, as though in invocation, and placed tiny squares of bread in their palms. They were the last in the line of kneeling communicants. Blake waited until Genevieve raised her hand to her mouth. Mechanically he followed her example. He swallowed the little morsel of bread with perceptible effort. Again he pressed his forehead down upon the hand that gripped the brass rail.

The bishop's voice now murmured near them, feeble and broken, yet very solemn: "'The Blood of our Lord Jesus Christ, which was shed for thee, preserve thy body and soul unto everlasting life. Drink this in remembrance that Christ's Blood was shed for thee, and be thankful.'"

Both of Blake's hands now clutched the rail in a grip that whitened the knuckles. Persons from the other end and the centre of the line were rising and softly retiring to their pews. The asthmatic woman gasped and fell silent as the bishop held the communion cup to her lips.

The bishop shuffled quietly along another step and stood bowed over the last two communicants. He was a very old man and he was ill. His voice sank to an inaudible murmur: "The Blood... shed for thee, preserve... life. Drink this...."

Blake waited, tense and rigid, as one about to meet the shock of a deadly attack. The bishop drew the chalice back from Genevieve's lips in his trembling hands, and paused for Blake to reach out and take it.

Blake did not move. The bishop bent farther over. The fumes of the wine rose in the face of the kneeling man. He quivered and shrank back—then, almost violently, he flung up his head and caught the cup to his lips.

Genevieve was rising. Blake stood up abruptly and followed her down to their pew. She knelt at once; but he caught up his soft hat, and holding it before his face, bent down close to her ear. He spoke in a strained whisper: "Excuse me. I've got to go."

She half rose. "You're ill! I'll go with you and—"

"No. Sit still. I've a—a most important engagement with, a friend—Mr. Griffith. Got to hurry!"

"Not so loud!" she cautioned him. "If you must go, Tom!"

"Yes, must! Sorry, but—" His hand sought and closed upon hers in a sudden caressing clasp, and his voice became husky. "Good-bye, girlie! May not see you for a—for a time!"

"Why, are you going out of town?" she asked.

But he was already turning away. Without pausing to answer her question, he started rapidly down the aisle, his head and shoulders bent forward in a peculiar crouch.

A slight frown of perplexity and displeasure marred the serenity of Genevieve's face. But the benign voice of the bishop immediately soothed her back into her beatific abstraction.

When the service was ended, she walked home in a most devotional frame of mind, and after luncheon, spent the afternoon searching out scriptural verses that she thought would aid in the spiritual re-awakening of Blake. Later in the afternoon she accompanied her father to the Gantrys', her face aglow with reverent joy. It was as if she felt that she had already guided Blake into the straight and narrow way that leads up out of the primitive.

They found Dolores industriously shocking her mother by a persistent heckling of Lord James, who was smiling at her quips and sallies and twirling his little blond mustache as if he enjoyed the raillery.

"Oh, here's Vievie, at last!" cried the girl. "Vievie darling, your eyes positively shine! Have you and the heroic Thomas been talking about the sharks and crocodiles of your late paradise? That was so cute of you, waiting this morning till we had gone, and then slipping off with him alone."

"We went to my little chapel. I knew the dear old bishop would be there. And the new vicar, Mr. Vincent, preached a splendid sermon."

"Which you talked about all the way home—I don't think," mocked Dolores.

"No, you never think," agreed Mrs. Gantry.

"Mr. Blake had to hasten away, just before the close of the communion service," explained Genevieve. "He remembered an important engagement with Mr. Griffith."

"About the Zariba Dam?" queried her father with alert eagerness.

"He did not say. I am not altogether sure that he—"

"Pardon me," interrupted Lord James. "Do you really believe that, in the circumstances, he would leave you for a business appointment?"

"Why shouldn't he?" said Mr. Leslie. "If he solves the problem of that dam, his fortune is as good as made. He'll have big positions thrust upon him. Did he seem excited, my dear—abstracted?"

"Oh, do you think it was that?" replied Genevieve. "I feared he was ill. The ventilation of the chapel is so wretched. He did look odd; yet he would not admit that he felt ill. I was half doubtful whether it was right to insist that he stay to communion."

"Communion!" gasped Mrs. Gantry. "You don't mean to say, my dear, that you've made a convert of him? Impossible!"

"I'm afraid not," sighed Genevieve. "I believe he took the communion merely to oblige me."

"Took the communion?" echoed Lord James, no less astonished than Mrs. Gantry. "Surely you do not—er—It seems quite impossible, you know."

"Is it so very amazing, when I asked him—urged him?" said Genevieve, flushing ever so slightly under his incredulous look.

"My word!" he murmured. "Tom did that!"

"I regret that he was not in a condition to receive the utmost good from it. But he was either ill or else rendered uneasy over his business with Mr. Griffith," remarked Genevieve.

"Of course, of course!" assented Lord James, bending over to brush a speck from his knee. "Quite a pity, indeed!" He straightened and turned to Mrs. Gantry, with a forced smile. "Er—it's deuced stupid of me—agreeing to dine, y'know—deuced stupid. Must beg pardon for cutting it! I'd quite forgotten I was to meet Tom—er—and Griffith, at their offices. They may be waiting for me now."

"Why, of all things!" protested Dolores. "You don't mean to say you are going to run off, just when dinner is ready?"

"Lord Avondale has made his excuses," said her mother. "No doubt another time—"

"Very soon, I trust—very soon," assented Lord James, with a propitiatory glance at Dolores. "It's a keen disappointment, I assure you." He looked about at Genevieve. "If you ladies will be so kind—It's a most pressing matter. Er—Griffith is not in the best of health. He may have to take a trip to Florida."

"No, he won't," broke in Mr. Leslie. "Not unless he leaves some one to manage Lafayette Ashton. The young cub isn't fit to be left alone with that bridge. Isn't that what this appointment is about? Griffith may have it in mind to put Blake in charge of the bridge."

"Er—must say it wouldn't surprise me if he takes a run up there with Griffith," said Lord James. "May go along myself."

"But you'll be back for the ball!" exclaimed Dolores.

"Right-o! Count on me for the ball. That's a fortnight off. Ample time."

"Then I promise you two waltzes. Bring back Laffie with you. He dances divinely."

Lord James smiled in rather an absent manner, and

turned to Genevieve. "You take me? I expect to be away with Tom for a few days. He will probably lack opportunity to call on you before he leaves town. You may have a message for me to take to him."

"Give him my best wishes for the success—of his work."

"That is all?"

For a few moments Genevieve stood hesitating, too intent upon her own thoughts to heed the covert stare of Dolores and the open scrutiny of her aunt and father. Lord James waited, with his averted gaze fixed upon the anxious face of Mrs. Gantry.

"That is all," quietly answered the girl, at last.

Mrs. Gantry sighed with relief, but Dolores frowned, and Mr. Leslie stared in irritable perplexity. Lord James bowed and hastened out before any of the others had observed his expression.

19

THE FALL OF MAN

GRIFFITH, C.E., SAT in the inner room of the bare living apartments adjoining his office. His feet, clad in white socks and an ancient pair of carpet slippers, were perched upon the top of a clicking steam radiator. His lank body balanced itself perilously in a rickety cane-seated chair, which was tilted far back on the rear legs. His pipe, long since burnt out and cold, hung from his slack jaw, while his eyes, bright and excited, galloped through the last pages of a sensational society novel.

He reached the final climax of the series of climaxes, and sat for a moment tense; then, flirting the cheap thing into a corner, he drew down his feet and stood up, stretching and yawning. Having relieved his cramped muscles, he drew out a tobacco pouch. But while in the act of opening it, he glanced at the alarm-clock on the book-shelves, and ended by replacing the pouch, without loading his pipe.

"Nine," he croaked, and again he stretched and yawned.

A sharp knock sounded at the hall-door of the outer room. Before he could start in response, a second and far louder knock followed.

"H'm—must be a wire," he muttered, and he shuffled quickly over the faded carpet into the front room.

The door shook with a third knocking that sounded like fist blows. Griffith's eyes sharpened with the look of a man who has lived in rough places and scents danger. He turned the night-catch and stepped to one side as he flung the door open. Before him stood a tall young man in an English topcoat. The visitor's curly yellow hair was bare and his handsome face scarlet with embarrassment.

"I—er—I beg your pardon, Mr. Griffith. I—" he stammered.

A big hand swung up on his shoulder, and a deep voice, thick and jocular, cut short his apology. "Thash all ri', Cheems. Wash ri' in. Ish on'y ol' Grishsh. Wash ri' in, I shay."

Propelled by the hand on his shoulder, Lord James entered with a precipitancy that carried him half across the room. Blake followed with solemn deliberation, keeping a hand upon the door casing. Griffith stepped around and shut and bolted the door. Without a second glance at Blake, he shuffled close up to Lord James and demanded in a rasping, metallic voice, "What's the meaning of this, Mr. Scarbridge?"

"Thash all ri', Grish," interposed Blake, "thash all ri'. M'frensh Chimmy Ear' Albondash. Hish fa'er's Dush Rubby—y' shee?"

Without raising his voice, Griffith gave utterance to a volley of blasphemous expletives that crackled on the air like an electric discharge.

"If you will kindly permit me, sir—"

"Hell!" cut in the engineer. "You call yourself his friend. Good friend you are, to let him touch a drop!"

"This is no time for misunderstandings between his

friends, Mr. Griffith," said Lord James, with a quiet insistence that checked the other's anger. "He was hard at it when, I found him—had been for hours."

"Ri' she are, Chi-Chimmy boy! Ching o' it, Grishsh!—thish ish a relish—relishush lushingsh—church shaloo—loon."

Griffith went over to the swaying figure, and stared close into the pallid face and glittering, bloodshot eyes.

"You damned fool!" he jerked out.

"Whash—whash 'at? Whash you shay, Grishsh?"

"You damned idiot!"

"Thash all ri'. Goo' frensh, Grishsh, youm me. Lesh hash a dro-drop."

"Come on in," said the engineer. "I'll give you several drops." He shot a glance at the Englishman. "Lend a hand, will you?"

Lord James stepped quickly to the other side of Blake, who clasped each about the neck in a maudlin but vice-like embrace. As they moved toward the bedroom, Griffith exclaimed with strategic enthusiasm: "That's it, boys, come right on in. It's so confounded dusty here, let's have a bath."

"All ri', Grishsh, en'ching you shay. Bu' you wanna wash ou' y' don' gi' wa'er insish. Wa'er insish a man'sh wor' ching—"

"That's all right, old man," cut in Lord James, "I'll see to that. Leave it to me."

By this time they had come in beside Blake's own cot, which extended out of the corner of the room, at the foot of Griffith's equally simple bed. Griffith opened the door of a tiny bathroom and turned on the hot water in the tub.

Lord James fell to stripping Blake, regardless of his protests that he could undress himself.

"Chuck it!" ordered his lordship, as Blake sought to interfere. "You don't want to keep us waiting our turn, do you?"

Blake launched upon an elaborate and envolved disclaimer that he had harbored the remotest idea of causing his friends the slightest trouble. In the midst Griffith came out of the bathroom. With his help, Blake was soon got ready, and the two led him in between them. In the corner of the bathroom was a small cabinet shower-bath with a wooden door. Blake turned toward it, but Griffith drew him about to the steaming tub.

"Hot room first, Tommy," he said. "Haven't forgotten how to take a Turkish, have you?"

Blake entered upon another profuse apology, meantime docily permitting the others to immerse him in the tub of hot water. Griffith promptly added still hotter water to the bath, while Lord James held the vapor curtains tight about the patient's neck. Before many minutes Blake began to grow restless, then to curse. But between them, Griffith and Lord James managed to keep him in the tub for more than a quarter of an hour.

"All right, Tommy. Now for the shower," said Griffith, at last.

Blake came out of the tub red and still wobbly. They rushed him over and shoved him into the cabinet. Lord James stepped clear, and Griffith slammed shut the door, latched it with an outside hook, and jerked open the lever of the shower-faucet, which was outside the cabinet.

"*Oof!*" grunted Blake, as the cold deluge poured down upon his bare head and body.

"Fine, hey?" called Griffith.

"*Wow!* Lemme ou'! *Oo-ou!*"

The cabinet shook with a bump that would have upset it had it not been screwed fast to the wall.

"Aw, now, don't do the baby-act, Tommy!" jeered Griffith. "Yowling like a bum, over a bath!"

"Be game, old man!" chimed in Lord James. "Take your medicine."

"Bu-but 'sh cole! *W-whew!*"

"Stay with it, old man—stay with it!" urged Lord James. "Don't lay down. Be a sport!"

"G-gosh! 'M free-freezin'! Lemme out!"

Griffith rubbed his hands together and cackled: "Stay with it, Tommy. It's doing the work. Stay with it."

"Damnation!" swore Blake. "O-open that door!"

"Time we were moving, Mr. Scarbridge," said Griffith.

He followed Lord James out of the bathroom, and closed the door. He led the way through into the front room, and closed that door. They stood waiting, silent and expectant.

The walls shook with a muffled crash.

"Repairs, five dollars," said Griffith. "Better stand farther over this way."

The bathroom door slammed open violently. The two men glanced into each other's eyes.

"You've played football?" croaked the engineer.

Lord James nodded.

"Tackle him low—fouler the better," advised Griffith.

There was a pause.... One of the cots in the bedroom creaked complainingly.

"Huh," muttered Griffith. "Sulking, eh? Good thing for us." He gazed full into the Englishman's face, and offered his hand. "I hope you'll overlook what I said, Mr. Scarbridge—Lord Scarbridge. Under the circumstances—"

"Don't mention it, Mr. Griffith! It's—it's the most positive proof of your friendship for him—that you should have been so angered. Deuce take it, I'd give anything if this hadn't happened!"

"How did it happen?" asked Griffith. "Sit down— No; no chance of his coming out now."

Lord James slipped off his heavy topcoat, and seated himself, his dress clothes and immaculate linen offering an odd contrast to the shabby room. But the engineer looked only at the face of his visitor.

"It's a beastly shame—when he was holding his own so well!" exclaimed the Englishman.

"That's what gets me," said Griffith. "He seemed to have staved it off indefinitely. I didn't notice a single one of the usual signs. And he has let out that the dam was almost a certainty. If he had fizzled on it, I could understand how that and the way he's been grinding indoors night and day—"

"No; he's stood that better than I had feared. What a shame! what a beastly shame! When Miss Leslie learns—"

"Miss Leslie?" cut in Griffith. "If she shakes him for this, she's not much account—after all he did for her. If she's worth anything, now's the time for her to set to and help pull him up again. But you haven't said yet how it happened."

"That's the worst of it! To be sure, she was perfectly

innocent. She must have thought it simply impossible that the communion wine—"

"Hey!—communion wine? That's what he meant by church saloons and religious lushing, then. She steered him up against that—knowing his one weakness?"

"My dear sir, how could she realize?"

"He told me she knew."

"But the communion wine!"

"Communion alcohol! Alcohol is alcohol, I don't care whether it's in a saloon or a church or pickling snakes in a museum. I tell you, Tommy's case has made a prohibition crank of me. Talk about it's being a man's lack of will and moral strength—*bah!* I never knew a man who had more will power than he, or who was more on the square. You know it."

"I—to be sure—except, you know, when he gives way to these attacks."

"Gives way!—and you've seen him fight! It's a disease, I tell you—a monomania like any other monomania. Why don't they say to a crazy man in his lucid intervals, 'Trouble with you is your lack of will power and moral strength. Brace up. Go to church'?"

"But you'd surely not say that Tom's insane? He himself lays it to his own weakness."

"What else is insanity but a kind of weakness—a broken cog in the machine which slips and throws everything out of gear, no matter how big the dynamo? I tell you, a dipsomaniac is no more to be blamed for lack of will power or moral strength than is a kleptomaniac, or than an epileptic is to be blamed for having fits. It's a disease. I'm giving it to you straight what the doctors say."

All the hopefulness went out of the Englishman's boyish face.

"Gad!" he murmured. "Gad! Then he can't overcome it."

"I don't know. The doctors don't seem to know. They say that a few seem to outgrow it—they don't know how, though. But all agree that the thing to do is to keep the patient braced—keep him boosted up."

"Count on me for that!" exclaimed Lord James.

"It's where this girl—Miss Leslie—ought to come in, if she's worth anything," thrust Griffith.

"But—but, my dear sir, you quite fail to understand. It will never do to so much as hint to her that he has failed."

"Failed!" retorted Griffith. "When she herself forced him to take the first drink—Don't cut in! If you know Tommy as well as you ought, you know he would never have taken that drink in the condition he was in—not a single drop of anything containing alcohol! No! the girl forced him—she must have. He's dead in love with her. He'd butt his head against a stone wall, if she told him to. Hell!—just when he had his chance at last!"

"His chance?"

"I've been figuring it as a chance. Supposing he had pulled off this big Zariba Dam, he'd have felt that he had made good. It might have brought around that change the doctors tell about. Don't you see? It might have fixed that broken cog—straightened him up somehow for good. But now—hell!"

Griffith bent over, with a groan.

"Gad!" murmured Lord James. After a long pause, he added slowly, "But, I assure you, regarding Miss Leslie, it will never do to tell her. If she hears of this, he will have no chance—none! That occurred to me immediately I inferred the deplorable truth. I told her we were thinking of going with you to the bridge—Michamac."

"You did? Say, I thought Britishers were slow, but you got your finger on the right button first shove. It's the very thing for him—change, open air, the bridge— Wait a minute, though! With the chances more than even that it's Tommy's own— Until he makes good on the dam, nobody would take his word against that lallapaloozer's."

"I—er—beg pardon. I fail to take you," said Lord James.

"Just the question of his finding out something that's apt to make him manhandle young Ashton."

"Ah—all the better, I say. Anything to divert his mind."

Griffith looked at the Englishman with an approving smile. "You sure are the goods, Mr. Scarbridge! It'll take two or three days for him to fight down the craving, even with all the help we can give him. Wait a minute till I phone to a drug-store."

He shuffled out through a side doorway that led into his private office. While he was telephoning, Lord James heard low moans from the bedroom. He clenched his hands, but he did not go in to his friend until Griffith returned and crossed to the inner door.

"Come in, Mr. Scarbridge," he said. "Next thing is to see if we can talk him into going to Michamac."

20

DE PROFUNDIS

HE OPENED THE door and, seemingly heedless of all else, hastened through to the bathroom, to shut off the flow of the shower. Lord James followed him as far as the corner cot, where Blake, wet-haired and half dressed, sat bowed far over, his elbows on his knees and his face between his hands.

"Head ache, old man?"

Blake raised his head barely enough for his friend to catch a glimpse of his haggard face and miserable eyes.

"Come now, Tommy," snapped Griffith, shuffling back from the bathroom, "we all admit you've made a damned fool of yourself; but what's the use of grouching? Sit up now—look pleasant!" He swung around a chair for Lord James, and seated himself in an old rocker. "Come, sit up, Tommy. We're going to hold an inquest on the remains."

"They need it—that's no lie," mumbled Blake.

"*Bah!* Cherk up, you rooster! It isn't the first time you've lost your feet. Maybe your feelings are jolted, but—the instrument is safe. Remember that time you fell down the fifty-foot bank and never even knocked your transit out of adjustment? You never let go of your grip on it! Come; you'll soon be streaking out again, same as ever."

"No, you're clean off this time, Grif." Instead of raising his head, Blake hunched over still lower. He went on in a dreary monotone, "No, I'm done for this trip—down for the count. I'm all in."

"Rot!" protested Lord James.

"All in, for keeps, this time. I'm not too big a fool to see that. Everything coming my way,—and to go and chuck it all like this. Needn't tell me she'll overlook it. Wouldn't ask her to. I'm not worth it."

"She's got to!" cried Griffith, with sudden heat. "She steered you up against this."

"What if she did? Only makes it all the worse. Didn't have sand enough to refuse. I'm no good, that's all—not fit to look at her—she's a lady. You needn't cut in with any hot air. I'm no more 'n a blackguard that got my chance to impose on her—and took it. That's the only name for it— young girl all alone!"

"No, no, old man, just the contrary, believe me!" exclaimed Lord James.

"I doubt if I myself could have done what you did when she—er—"

"'Cause there'd have been no need. You're in her class, while I—" He groaned, and burst out morosely: "You know I'm not, both of you. What's the use of lying?"

The two friends glanced across at each other and were silent. Blake went on again, in his hopeless, dreary monotone. "Down and out—down and out. Only son of his mother, and she a drunkard. Nothing like Scripture, Jimmy, for consoling texts."

He began to quote, with an added bitterness in his despair: "'Woe unto them that are mighty to drink, and men of strength to mingle strong drink… their root shall be as rottenness, and their blossom shall go up as dust—' 'Awake, ye drunkards, and weep and howl, all ye drinkers of wine.' 'For while they are drunken as drunkards, they shall be devoured as stubble fully dry.'—Dry? Good Lord! Ring up a can of suds, Grif. I've got ten miles of alkali desert down my throat!"

"All right, Tommy," said Griffith. "We'll soon fix that. I've sent in an order already."

"You have not!" rejoined Blake, in an incredulous growl. "Well, suppose you ring 'em up again. If that can doesn't get here mighty sudden, I'll save the fellow the trouble of bringing it."

"Hold on, young man," ordered Griffith, as Blake started to heave himself to his feet. "I'm running this *soirée.*"

He stood up and shuffled out into the front room. Blake shifted around restlessly, and was again about to rise, when there came a sharp rapping at the outer door.

"That's the man now," said Lord James. "Hold tight. It will now be only a moment."

Blake restrained himself. But it was a very long moment before Griffith came in with a pitcher and three glasses upon a battered tray. At the tinkle of the glasses Blake looked up, his face aflame. He made a clutch at the pitcher.

Griffith gave him his shoulder, and cackled: "Don't play the hog, Tommy. I've been up in Canada enough to know that the nobility always get first helping. Eh, Lord Scarbridge?"

"You—you—" gasped Blake.

"But this time," went on Griffith, hastily pouring out a

brimming glassful of liquid from the pitcher, "we'll make an exception."

He turned about quickly, and with his hand clasped over the top of the glass, reached it out to Blake. Half maddened by his thirst, the latter clutched the glass, and, without pausing to look at its contents, drained it at a gulp. An instant later the glass shattered to fragments on the floor, and Blake's fist flung out toward Griffith.

"Quassia!" he growled. "You dotty old idiot! Needn't think you're going to head me off this soon!"

Griffith set the tray on his bed, and crossing to the door, locked it and put the key in his pocket.

"Now, Tommy," he croaked, "you've got just two friends that I know of. They're here. Maybe you can take the key from us; but you know what you'll have to do to us first."

Blake stared at him with morose, bloodshot eyes.

"You're dotty!" he growled. "You know you can't stop me, once I'm under way. I don't want to roughhouse it, but I want something for this thirst, and I'm going to have it. Understand?"

"H'm. If that's all," said Griffith.

"That's all, if you're reasonable," replied Blake less morosely. "They gave me all I wanted when I took the gold cure."

"Cured you, too," jeered Griffith.

"That's all right. The point now is, do I get something? If I do, I agree to stay here. If I don't, I'm going out."

"Try another glass of this while you're waiting," suggested Lord James, and he poured out a second glassful of the bitter decoction.

"No," answered Blake.

"You tossed down the other too fast. Sip it. You'll find that it will ease the dryness while you are waiting," insisted Lord James. "Try it, to oblige me."

"*Ugh!*" growled Blake. He hesitated, then reluctantly took the glass and began to sip the quassia. After the last swallow, he turned sullenly to Griffith. "Well, what you waiting for? Get a move on you."

"It does help, doesn't it?" interposed Lord James.

Blake muttered something behind his lips that the others chose to take for assent.

"Yes, it's the real thing," said Griffith. "Try another, Tommy, same way."

"Another? *Bah!* You can't fool me. I'm on to your game."

"Sure you are," assented Griffith. "What's more, you're sober enough now to know that our game is your game. Own up. Don't lie."

Blake looked down morosely, and for a long quarter of a minute his friends waited in anxious suspense. At last, without looking up, he held out his empty glass for Lord James to refill it. The second battle was won.

As Lord James took the glass, Griffith interposed. "Hold on. We'll keep that for later. I've something else now."

"More dope!" growled Blake.

"No, good stuff to offset the effects of the poison you've been swilling since morning. Next course is bromide of potassium."

"Take your medicine, bo!" chimed in Lord James.

"*Ugh!*" groaned Blake. "Dish it out, then. Only don't forget. You know, well as I do, that if the craving comes on that bad again, I'm bound to have a drink. I tell you, I can't help myself. I've told you about it time and again. It's

He went on in a dreary monotone, "No, I'm done for
this trip—down for the count. I'm all in."

hell till I get enough aboard to make me forget. You know I don't like the stuff. I've hated the very smell of it since before my first real spree."

Griffith shot a significant glance at Lord James. "That's all right, Tommy,—we understand how it is. But we've got hold of it this time. You'll never quit if you can help it, and we know now you can help it, with this quassia to keep your throat from sizzling. Here's your bromide."

Blake gulped down the dose, but muttered despondently: "What's the use? You know you can't head me off for keeps, once I'm as far under way as I've got to-day. Think you're going to stop me now, do you?"

"That's what," rejoined Griffith. "You'll think the same in about ten minutes. I'm going to talk to you like a Dutch uncle."

"And I've got to sit here while you unwind your jaw! Cut it short. Don't see why you want to chin, anyway. All that's left is to haul me to the scrapheap…. You don't think I'd go near her after this, do you? I've got a little decency left. Only thing I can do is to open wide and cut loose. D.T. finish is the one for me. Won't take long for her to forget me. Any fool can see that."

"We're going up to Michamac, first thing tomorrow," remarked Griffith in a casual tone.

"You may be. I'm not."

"It's all arranged, Tammas," drawled Lord James. "I told Miss Leslie—"

"You told her! Mighty friendly of you! Good thing, though. Sooner she knows just what I am, the better. How soon do you figure on the wedding?"

"Chuck it, you duffer!" exclaimed the Englishman, flushing scarlet. "I didn't tell her *this*. She doesn't know."

Blake's haggard face lighted with a flash of hope, only to settle back into black despair.

"She'll learn soon enough. I'm done for, for good, this trip!" he groaned. He clenched his fist and bent forward to glare at them in sullen fury. "Damn you! Call yourselves my friends, and sit here yawping, you damned Job's comforters! Think I'm a mummy?—when I've lost her! God!—to sit here with my brains going—to know I've lost all—all! Give me some whiskey—anything!... My girl—my girl!"

He bent over, writhing and panting, in an agony of remorse.

Griffith fetched a tablet and a glass of water, to which he added some of the quassia.

"Here's your dose of sulphonal," he said, in his driest, most matter-of-fact tone. "You've got to get to sleep. It's an early train."

"What's the use? Leave me alone!" groaned Blake.

"Gad, old man," put in Lord James. "Any one who didn't know you would think you were a quitter."

"What's the use? I've lost out. I'm smashed."

"All right. Let's call it a smashup," croaked Griffith. "Just the same, you don't go out of commission till you've squared accounts. You're not going to leave the Zariba Dam in the air."

"Guess I've got enough on paper for you to work out the solution, if it's workable."

"And if not?"

"I'm all in, I tell you. I'm smashed for good."

"No, you're not. Anyway, there's one thing you've got to

do. You've got to settle about that bridge. You've been too busy over the dam to think of asking for a look at Ashton's plans, and I've said nothing. I've been waiting for you to make good on the dam. With that behind you, no engineer in the U.S. would doubt your word if you claimed the bridge."

"What of that? What do I care?" muttered Blake. "The game's up. What's the use?"

"This!" snapped Griffith. "Either Laffie Ashton is a dirty sneak thief, or he's a man that deserves my apologies. It's a question of fair play to me as well as to him. You're square, Tom. You'll come up to Michamac with me and settle this matter."

"Lord! Why can't you let me alone?" groaned Blake. But he took the sulphonal and washed it down with the quassia-flavored water.

Lord James went out into the office to phone his man at the hotel to fetch over clothes for a short trip. When he reentered the bedroom Blake was stretched out in bed, and Griffith was spreading a blanket for himself on the floor.

"Should I not run over to my hotel for the night?" remarked the Englishman. "Don't want to put you out of your bed, y' know."

"No. I sleep as well, or better, on the floor. We want to be sure of an early start," said Griffith.

Blake rose on his elbow and blinked at them. His eyes were still bloodshot and his face haggard, but the change in his voice was unmistakably for the better. "Say, bos, it does pay to have friends—sometimes!"

"Forget it!" rejoined Griffith. "You go to snoozing. It's an early train, remember."

Blake sighed drowsily, and stretched out again on the flat of his back.

Within a minute he was fast asleep.

21

THE BRIDGE

AT DAWN THEY roused him out of his drugged sleep and gave him a showerbath and rubdown that brought a healthy glow to his cold skin. He turned pale at the mere mention of food, but after a drink of quassia, Griffith induced him to take a cup of clear coffee and some thickly buttered toast. After that the three hastened in a cab to the station, stopping on the way to buy half a case each of grapefruit and oranges. Aboard the train Blake was at once set to eating grapefruit and chewing the bitter pith to allay the burning of his terrible thirst.

Throughout the trip, which lasted until mid-afternoon, one or the other of the two friends was ever at his side, ready to urge more of the acid fruit upon him and continually seeking to divert and entertain him by cheerful talk. Until after the noon hour they were on the main line and had the benefit of the dining-car. Griffith ordered a hearty meal, more dinner than luncheon, and Blake was able to eat the greater part of a spring chicken.

The most trying and critical time during the trip was the short wait at the junction, where they transferred to the old daycoach that was attached to the train of structural steel for the Michamac Bridge. Blake caught sight of a saloon, and the associations roused by it quickened his craving to an almost irresistible fury. When, none too soon, the train pulled out of the little town, he sank back in his seat morose and almost exhausted by his struggle.

Though Lord James made every effort to rouse him to a more cheerful mood, his face was still sullen and heavy when the train clanked in over the switches of the material yards at the bridge. Before they left the car Griffith made certain that Blake was wrapped about in overcoat and muffler and had on the arctics that he had bought for him.

Having directed one of the trainmen to bring the boxes of fruit to the office, Griffith led the way up the path formed by the bridge-service track. The rails had been kept shovelled clear from the February snowdrifts and ran straight out through the midst of the bleak unlovely buildings grouped near the edge of Michamac Strait, at the southern terminus of the bridge.

Hardly had the three passengers stepped from the train, when Blake lifted his head for a clear view of the big electric derricks, the vast orderly piles of structural steel, floor beams, and planking, the sheds containing paint, machinery, and other stores, the gorged coal-bins, and all the other evidences of a vast work of engineering.

His gaze followed the bridge-service track past the cookhouse and bunkhouse and the storehouses, out across the completed shore span to the gigantic structure of the south cantilever. Far beyond, between its lofty skeleton towers and upsweeping side webs, appeared, in seemingly reduced proportions, the towers and webs of the north cantilever, across on the north edge of the channel of the strait.

Blake drew in a deep breath, and stared at the titanic structure, eager-eyed. There was no need for Lord James to nudge Griffith. The engineer had not missed a single shade of the great change in Blake's expression. He asked casually, "Well, how does the first sight strike you, Tommy?"

"You didn't say she was so far along," replied Blake.

"Didn't I? H.V., you know, has a pull with the Steel Trust. We've had our material delivered in short order, no matter who else waited. North cantilever is completed; ditto the south, except for part of the timbering and flooring. The central span is built out a third of the way from the north 'lever. But several miles of the feed track on that side the strait have been put into such bad shape by the weather that we'll have the central span completed from this side before the road over there is open again."

"That so?" said Blake. "I want to see about that span."

"We'll go out for a look at once, soon as we dump our baggage in on Laffie," said Griffith.

"Is that thing here?" growled Blake.

"Now, just you keep on your shirt, Tommy," warned Griffith. "He may be here, or he mayn't. You are here to look at the Michamac Bridge and hold on to yourself. Understand?"

Blake scowled and stared menacingly toward a snow-embanked, snow-covered building, the verandahs of which distinguished it as the office and quarters of the Resident Engineer.

"I want your promise you'll do nothing or say nothing to him till after you've made good on the Zariba Dam," went on Griffith. "You don't want your blast to go off before you've tamped the hole."

Blake's scowl deepened, and he clenched his fist in its thick fur glove. But after a long moment he answered morosely, "Guess you're right. He holds the cards on me now and has the drop. But if I find he slipped the aces out of my hand, it won't be long before I get the drop on him."

"And then something will drop!" added Lord James.

"I'll smash him—the dirty sneak!" growled Blake.

"Now, now, Tommy; you're not sure yet," cautioned Griffith.

"That so?" replied Blake in a tone that brought a glint of excitement into the worn eyes of the older engineer.

But before he could speak, a silk-robed figure stepped out onto the verandah of the Resident Engineer's office, and called delightedly, "Ah, Lord Avondale!—welcome to Michamac! You escaped my hospitality in town, but you can't here!"

"Thanks. Very good of you, I'm sure," replied Lord James dryly.

"I see you've come with old Grif," Ashton gayly rattled on. "Hello, Griffith! Hurry in, all of you. It's cold as the South Pole. I'll have a punch brewed in two shakes. Who's the other gentleman?"

At the question, Blake, who had been staring fixedly at the bridge, turned his muffled face full to the effusive welcomer. Before his hard, impassive look Ashton shivered as if suddenly struck through to the marrow by the cold.

"Blake!" he gasped. "Here?"

"No objections, have you?" asked Blake in a noncommittal tone. "Just thought I'd run up with Mr. Griffith and take a look at your bridge. He says it's worth seeing. But of course, if you don't allow visitors—"

"Just the opposite, Tommy," put in Griffith, quick to catch his cue. "Mr. Ashton is always glad to have his bridge examined by those who know what's what. Isn't that so, Mr. Ashton?"

"Why, of—of course—I—" stammered Ashton, his teeth chattering.

"Sure," went on Griffith. "Any man who's invented such a modification of the truss as this bridge shows, ought to have all the fame he can get out of it. In England he'd be made a lord, I suppose. Eh, Mr. Scarbridge?"

"Er—we've knighted brewers and soap-boilers. But then, y'know, with us beer and soap are two of the necessities," drawled Lord James.

"W-won't you come in?" urged Ashton. "It's chi-illy out here! I'll have that punch brewed in half a s-second."

"My God!" gasped Blake, his jaws clenched and face black with the agony of his temptation.

All unintentionally Ashton had turned the tables on his tormentors.

Griffith scowled at him and demanded: "Where's McGraw?"

"B-bunkhouse," answered Ashton.

Griffith spoke to Lord James in a low tone. "Go in and keep him there, will you? Might stay with him all night. We'll stop at the bunkhouse."

"I'm on," said Lord James.

Griffith raised his voice. "Well, then, if you prefer it that way, Mr. Scarbridge. It's true Ashton can make you more comfortable, and I'll be busy half the night checking over reports and so forth with McGraw. Ashton, if you'll send over your report, it'll leave you free to entertain Mr.

Scarbridge. And say, send over the boxes that'll be coming along in a little while. I'm trying a diet of grapefruit." He turned to Blake. "Come on. We don't want to keep Mr. Ashton out here, to shiver a screw loose."

Blake uttered an inarticulate growl, but turned away with Griffith as Lord James sprang up the verandah steps and blandly led the vacillating Resident Engineer into his quarters. The visiting engineers crossed over to the big ungainly bunkhouse, and entered the section divided off for the bosses and steel workers and the other skilled men.

Within was babel. Kept indoors by the cold that enforced idleness on all the bridge force, the men were crowded thickly about their reading and card tables or outstretched in their bunks, talking, laughing, grumbling, singing, brooding—each according to his mood and disposition, but almost all smoking.

At sight of Griffith a half-hundred voices roared out a rough but hearty welcome that caused Blake's face to lighten with a flush of pleasure. The greeting ended in a cheer, started by one of the Irish foremen.

Griffith sniffed at the foul, smoke-reeking air, and looked doubtfully at Blake. He held up his hand. Across the hush that fell upon the room quavered a doleful wail from the Irish foreman: "Leave av hivin, Misther Griffith, can't ye broibe th' weather bur-r-reau? Me Schlovaks an' th' Eyetalians'll be afther a-knifin' wan another, give 'em wan wake more av this."

"There are indications that the cold snap will break within a week," replied Griffith. "You'll be at it, full blast, in two or three days. Where's McGraw?"

A big, fat, stolid-faced man ploughed forward between

the crowded tables. As he came up, he held out a pudgy hand, and grunted: "Huh! Glad t' see you."

Griffith shook hands, and motioned toward Blake. "My friend Mr. Blake.

Trying to get him to take charge here—nominally as Assistant Engineer—in case I have to go to Florida."

McGraw's deep-set little eyes lingered for a moment on the stranger's mouth and jaw. "Good thing," he grunted.

"The company is offering him double what Mr. Ashton gets; but he's not anxious to take it as Assistant."

The big general foreman was moved out of his phlegmatic stolidity.

"Huh? He's not?"

"Not under that thing," put in Blake grimly.

"Must know him."

"He may change his mind," said Griffith. "The company has authorized me to make it a standing offer. So if he turns up any time—"

McGraw nodded, and offered his hand to Blake. "Hope you'll come. C'n do m' own work. Bridge needs an engineer, though—resident one."

"H'm,—Mr. Ashton might call that a slap on the wrist," remarked Griffith. "Get on your coat. We're going out to the bridge."

McGraw headed across for his separate room. While waiting for him, Griffith introduced Blake to the engine-driver of the bridge-service train, two or three foremen, and several of the bridge workers. But the moment McGraw reappeared in arctics and Mackinaw coat, Griffith hurriedly led the way out of the smother of smoke and foul air.

As the three started bridgeward along the clean-shovelled service-track Blake fell in behind his companions. Seeing that he did not wish to talk, Griffith walked on in the lead with McGraw.

They were soon swinging out across the shore, or approach, span of the bridge. This extended from the high ground on the south side of the strait to an inner pier at the edge of the water, where it joined on to the anchor arm of the south cantilever. Almost all the area of the bridge flooring, which had been completed to beyond the centre of the cantilever, was covered with stacked lumber and piles of structural steel and rails, and kegs of nails, rivets, and bolts.

Here every chink and crevice was packed with snow and ice. But all the titanic steel structure above and the unfloored bottom-chords and girders of the outer, or extension, arm of the cantilever had been swept bare of snow by the winter gales and left glistening with the glaze of the last shower of sleet.

Blake swung steadily along after the others, his face impassive. But his eyes scrutinized with fierce eagerness the immense webs of steel posts and diagonals that ran up on either side, under the grand vertical curves of the top-chords, almost to the peaks of the cantilever towers. He had to tilt back his head to see the tops of those huge steel columns, which reared their peaks two hundred and fifty feet above the bridge-floor level and a round four hundred feet above the water of the strait.

Presently the three were passing the centre of the cantilever, between the gigantic towers, whose iron heels were socketed far below in the top-plates of the massive concrete piers, built on the very edge of deep water. From this point the outer arm of the cantilever extended far out over the broad chasm of the strait, where, a hundred and fifty feet beneath its unfloored level, the broken ice from the upper lake crashed and thundered on its wild passage of the strait.

Blake looked down carelessly into the abyss of grinding, hurtling ice cakes. The drop from that dizzy height would of itself have meant certain death. Yet without a second glance at the ice-covered waters, he followed his companions along the narrow walk of sleeted planks that ran out alongside the service-track. Though his gaze frequently shifted downward as well as upward, it went no farther than the ponderous chords and girders and posts of the bridge's framework.

Striding along the narrow runway of ice-glazed planks with the assurance of goats, the three at last passed under the main traveller, a huge structure of eleven hundred tons' weight that straddled the bridge's sides and rose higher than the towers. Its electromagnetic cranes were folded together and cemented in place by the ice.

A few yards beyond they came to the end of the extension arm of the cantilever and out upon the uncompleted first section of the central, or suspension, span. It was poised high in space, far out over the dizzy abyss. Many yards away, across a yawning gap, the completed north third of the suspension span reached out, above the gulf, from the tip of the north cantilever, like the arm of a Titan straining to clasp hands with his brother of the south shore.

Yet the mid-air companionship of this outreaching skeleton-arm served only to heighten the giddiness and seeming instability of the south-side overhang. From across the broad gap, the eye followed the curve of the bottom-chords of the north cantilever away down into the abyss toward the far shore of the strait, where the lofty towers upreared upon their massive piers.

From this viewpoint there was no relieving glimpse of the shoreward curving anchor-arm that balanced the outer half of the north cantilever alike in line and weight. There was only the vast upcurve of the top-chords and the stupendous down-curve of the bottom-chords and the line between that stood for the foreshortened sixteen hundred feet of bridge-floor level extending from the north shore to the swaying tip of that unanchored north third of the central span.

Few even among men accustomed to great heights could have stood anywhere upon the outer reach of the over-hang without a feeling of nausea and vertigo. Not only did the gigantic structure on the far side of the gap seem continually on the verge of toppling forward into the abyss, but the end of the south cantilever likewise quivered and swayed, and the mad flow of the roaring, ice-covered waters beneath added to the giddiness of height the terrifying illusion that the immense steel skeleton had torn loose from its anchorage to earth and was hurtling up the strait through mid-air, ready to crash down to destruction the instant its winged driving-force failed.

Yet Griffith and Blake followed McGraw out to the extreme end of the icy walk and poised themselves, shoulder to wind, on narrow sleet-glazed steel beams, as uncon-cerned as sailors on a yardarm. Griffith and McGraw were absorbed in a minute inspection of the bridge's condition and in estimating the time it would take to throw forward the remaining sections of the central, or suspension, span, upon the termination of the irksome spell of extreme frosty weather.

Blake looked, as they looked, at post and diagonal, eyebolt and bottom-chord, and across the gap at the swaying tip of the north cantilever. But his face showed clearly that his thoughts were not the same as their thoughts. His eyes shone like polished steel, and there was a glow in his haggard face that told of an exultance beyond his power of repression.

At last Griffith roused from his absorption. He immediately noticed Blake's expression, and dryly demanded: "Well?"

"Well your own self!" rejoined Blake, striving to speak in an indifferent tone.

"Something of a bridge, eh?"

"It's not so bad," admitted Blake. He glanced at McGraw, who had paused in his ox-like ruminating.

Griffith addressed the general foreman. "Mr. Blake is a bit off his feed. A friend that came with us will occupy my room in Mr. Ashton's quarters. I'd like a room in the bunkhouse for Mr. Blake and myself, with a good stove and a window that'll let in lots of fresh air."

"C'n have mine," grunted McGraw. "Extra bunk in yardmaster's room,"

"It'll be a favor," said Griffith. "You might get it ready, if you will. Mr. Blake must have clean air when he goes inside. He and I will take our time going back. There are two or three things I want another look at."

McGraw at once started shoreward, without making any verbal response, yet betraying under his dull manner his eagerness to oblige the Consulting Engineer. When he had gone well beyond earshot, Griffith turned upon Blake with a quizzical look.

"So!" he croaked. "It's a certainty."

"Knew that soon's I got the first look," said Blake.

Griffith's forehead creased with an anxious frown. "You promise not to mix it with him."

"Don't fash yourself," reassured Blake. "I've waited too long for this, to go off at half-cock now."

"That's talking! You'll wait till you're sure you can settle him—the skunk! Come on, now. We'll start inshore before you get chilled."

"How about yourself?" chuckled Blake, as he led back along the runway. "Won't take the frost two shakes to reach the centre of your circumference, once it gets through that old wolfskin coat."

"Huh! I can still go you one better, young man. I'll soon be thawing out in Florida, while you'll be trotting back here to boss the completion of T. Blake's cantilever—largest suspension span cantilever in the world."

"God!" whispered Blake, staring incredulously at the titanic structure born of his brain. "But it's mine—it *is* mine!... I sweat blood over those plans!"

"Doggone you, Tommy, you're no engineer—you're an inventor, Class A-1!" exulted Griffith. "First this; then the Zariba Dam. After that, the Lord only knows what! Trouble with you, you're a genius."

"And a whiskey soak!" added Blake, with a sudden upwelling of bitterness.

"Hey! what!—after this?" demanded Griffith, his voice sharp with apprehension. He could not see the face of his companion, but the manner in which Blake's head bent forward between his hunching shoulders was more than enough to confirm his alarm.

"Come, now, Tommy!" he reproached. "Don't be a fool— just when things are coming your way."

"Think so?" muttered Blake. "What d'you suppose I care for what I'd get out of this or the dam? Good God! You can't see it—yet you had Mollie!"

For a moment the older man was forced to a worried silence. It ended in an outflashing of hope. "I told you what she said about you—almost her last words. You'll win out—she said it!"

Blake halted and turned about to his friend, his face convulsed with doubt and a despondency that verged on despair. They were still halfway out on the overhang of the extension arm. He pointed down to the crashing, tumbling ice far beneath his feet.

"Do you know what I'd do if I had any nerve?" he cried. "I'd step over... end it!... You could tell her I slipped. There wouldn't be any need to tell her about—yesterday. She would remember me as she knew me there in Mozambique. After a time she'd make Jimmy happy—and be happy herself. Trouble is, I'm what she suspected. I haven't the nerve, when it comes to the real showdown."

"Damnation!" swore Griffith. "Have you gone clean dotty? You're not the kind to quit, Tom!—to slide out from under because you haven't the grit to hang on!"

"That's it. I'm booked for the D.T. route," muttered Blake. "Wasn't born for a watery end. Whiskey for mine!"

"Rats! You're over the worst of this bump already. You're going back to-morrow and dig in to make good on the dam."

"The dam! What's it to me now?"

"Fifty thousand dollars, the credit for your bridge, and a place among the top-notchers."

"Much that amounts to—when I've lost her!" retorted Blake.

He turned about again and plodded heavily shoreward, his chin on his breast and his big shoulders bowed forward.

22

CONDEMNED

THOUGH HE SANK into a taciturn and morose mood from which no efforts of his friends could rouse him, Blake sullenly accepted the continued treatment that Griffith thrust upon him. In the morning he muttered a confirmation of the statement of Lord James that he was looking better and that the attack must be well over.

Ashton, forced probably by an irresistible impulse to learn the worst, followed Lord James to the room occupied by the engineers. Blake cut short his vacillating in the doorway with a curt invitation to come in and sit down. Having satisfied what he considered the requirements of hospitality, Blake paid no further attention to the Resident Engineer. As nothing was said about the bridge, Ashton soon regained all his usual assurance, and even went so far as to comment upon Blake's attack of biliousness.

When, beside the car step, an hour later, Ashton held out his hand, Blake seemingly failed to perceive it. Ashton's look of relief indicated that he mistook the other's profound contempt for stupid carelessness. To one of his nature, the fact that Blake had not at once denounced him as a thief seemed proof positive that the sick man had failed to recognize in the bridge structure the embodiment of his stolen plans.

He turned from Blake to Lord James. "Ah, my dear earl, this has been such a pleasure—such a delight! You cannot imagine how intolerable it is to be cut off from the world in this dreary hole—deprived of all society and compelled to associate, if at all, with, these common brutes!"

"Really," murmured Lord James. "For my part, y' know, I rather enjoy the company of intelligent men who have their part in the world's work. Though one of the drones myself, I value the 'Sons of Martha' at their full worth."

"Oh, they have their place. The trouble is to make them keep it."

"'Pon my word, I scarcely thought you'd say that—so clever an engineer as yourself!"

Ashton glanced up to be certain that both Griffith and Blake had passed on into the car.

"Your lordship hasn't quite caught the point," he said. "One may have the brains—the intellect—necessary to create such a bridge as this, without having to lower himself into the herd of common workers."

"Ah, really," drawled the Englishman, swinging up the car steps.

Ashton raised his hat and bowed. "*Au revoir,* Earl. Your visit has been both a delight and an honor. I shall hope soon to have the pleasure of seeing you in town."

"Yes?" murmured Lord James with a rising inflection. "Good-day."

He nodded in response to Ashton's final bow, and hastened in to where Blake and Griffith were making themselves comfortable in the middle of the car. The three were the only passengers for the down trip.

"So he didn't get you to stay over for the winter?" remarked Griffith as the Englishman began to shed his topcoat.

"Gad, no! He couldn't afford it. Tried to show me how to play poker last night. I've his check for two thousand. He insisted upon teaching me the fine points of the game."

"Crickey!—when you've travelled with T. Blake!" cackled Griffith. "Hey, Tommy? Any one who's watched you play even once ought to be able to clean out a dub like Lallapaloozer Laf. Say, though, I didn't think even you could keep on your poker face as you have this morning. It's dollars to doughnuts, he sized it up that you had failed to get next."

"Told you I wasn't going to show him my cards," muttered Blake.

Lord James looked at him inquiringly, but he lapsed into his morose silence, while Griffith commenced to write his report on the bridge, without volunteering an explanation. Lord James repressed his curiosity, and instead of asking questions, quietly prepared for his friend one of the last of the grapefruit.

An hour or so later Blake growled out a monosyllabic assurance that he was now safely over his attack. Yet all the efforts of Lord James to jolly him into a cheerful mood utterly failed. Throughout the trip he continued to brood, and did not rouse out of his sullen taciturnity until the train was backing into the depot.

"Here we are," remarked Lord James. "Get ready to make your break for cover, old man. What d' you say, Mr.

Griffith? Will it be all right for him to keep close to his work for a while—to lie low?"

"What's that?" growled Blake.

"Young Ashton's a bally ass," explained Lord James. "He bolted down whole what I said about your attack of bile. Others, however, may not be so credulous or blind. You'd better keep close till you look a bit less knocked-up. There's no need that what's happened should come to Miss Leslie."

"Think so, do you?" said Blake. "Well, I don't."

"What's that?" put in Griffith.

"There's not going to be any frame-up over this, that's what," rejoined Blake, reaching for his hat and suitcase. "Soon 's I get a shave I'm going out to tell her."

"Gad, old man!" protested Lord James. "But you can't do that—it's impossible! You surely do not realize—"

"I don't, eh?" broke in Blake bitterly. "I'm up against it. I know it, and you know it. You don't think I'm going to do the baby act, do you? I've failed to make good. Think I'm going to lie to her about it? No!—nor you neither!"

His friends exchanged a look of helplessness. They knew that tone only too well. Yet Lord James sought to avert the worst.

"Might have known you'd be an ass over it," he commented. "Best I can do, I presume, is to go along and explain to her my view of what started you off."

"Best nothing. You'll keep out of this. It's none of your funeral."

"There's more than one opinion as to that."

"I tell you, this is between her and me. You'll keep out of it," said Blake, with a forcefulness that the other could not withstand. "Don't worry. You'll have your turn later on."

"Deuce take it!" cried the Englishman. "You can't fancy I'm dwelling on that! You can't think me such a cad as to be waiting for an opportunity derived from an injustice to you!"

"Injustice, *bah!*" gibed Blake. "I'll get what's coming to me. It's of her I'm thinking, not you. She was right. I'm going to tell her so. That's all."

"But, in view of what she herself did——"

"I'll tell her the facts. That's enough," said Blake, and he led the way from the car.

He hastened out of the depot and would have started off afoot, had not Lord James hailed a taxicab and taken him and Griffith home. He went in with them, and when Blake had shaved and dressed, proposed that they should go on together as far as the hotel. To this Blake gave a sullen acquiescence, and they whirred away to the North Side. But instead of stopping at the hotel, their cab sped on out to the Lake Shore Drive.

Lord James coolly explained that he intended to take his friend to the door of the Leslies. Blake would have objected, but acquiesced as soon as he understood that Lord James intended to remain in the cab.

During the day the cold had moderated, and when Blake swung out of the cab he was wrapped about in the chilly embrace of a dripping wet fog from off the lake. He shivered as he hurried across and up the steps and into the stately portico of the Leslie house.

At the touch of his finger on the electric button, the heavy door swung open. He was bowed in and divested of hat and raincoat by an overzealous footman before he could protest. Silent and frowning, he was ushered to a door that he had not before entered. The footman announced him and drew the curtains together behind him.

Still frowning, Blake stepped forward and stopped short to stare about him at the resplendent room of gold and ivory enamel that he had entered. Only at the second glance did he perceive the graceful figure that had risen from the window-seat at the far end of the room and stood in a startled attitude, gazing fixedly at him.

Before he could speak, Genevieve came toward him with impetuous swiftness, her hands outstretched in more than cordial welcome.

"Tom! Is it really you?" she exclaimed. "I had not looked for you back so soon."

"It's somewhat sooner than I expected myself," he replied, with a bitter humor that should have forewarned her.

But she was too relieved and delighted to heed either his tone or his failure to clasp her hands, "Yes. You know, I've been so worried. You really looked ill Sunday, and I thought Lord James' manner that evening was rather odd—I mean when I spoke to him about you."

"Shouldn't wonder," said Blake in a harsh voice. "Jimmy had been there before. He knew."

"Knew? You mean—?" The girl stepped back a little way and gazed up into his face, startled and anxious. "Tom, you *have* been sick—very sick! How could I have been so blind as not to have seen it at once? You've been suffering terribly!"

Again she held out her hands to him, and again he failed to take them.

"Don't touch me," he replied. "I'm not fit. It's true I've

suffered. Do you wonder? I've been in hell again—where I belong."

"Tom! oh, Tom!—no, no!" she whispered, and she averted her face, unable to endure the black despair that she saw in his unflinching eyes.

"Jimmy and old Grif, between them, managed to catch me when I was under full headway," he explained. "They stopped me and took me up to the Michamac Bridge. I'm on my feet again now. Just the same, I went under, and if it hadn't been for them, I'd be beastly, roaring drunk this minute."

"No, Tom! It's impossible—impossible! I can't believe it!"

"Think I'd lie about a little thing like that?" he asked with the terrible levity of utter despair.

"But it's—it's so awful!"

"I've known funnier jokes. God! D'you think I've done much laughing over being smashed for good? It's rid you of a drunken degenerate. It's you who ought to laugh. How about me? I've lost *you!* God!"

He bent over, with his chin on his breast and his big fists clenched down at his sides.

She stared at him, dazed, almost stunned by the shock. Only after what seemed an age of waiting could she find words for the stress of bitter disappointment and mortified love that drove the blood to her heart and left her white and dizzy.

"Then—you have—failed. You *are*—weak!" she at last managed to say.

Simple as were the words, the tone in which they were spoken was enough for Blake.

"Yes," he answered, and he swung about toward the door.

"Have you no excuses—no defence?" she demanded.

"I might lay it to that wine at the church—and prove myself still weaker," said Blake.

"The holy communion!" she reproached.

"I never made fun even of a Chinaman's religion," he said. "Just the same, if I don't believe a thing, I don't lie and let on I do. I told you that wine meant nothing to me in a religious way. But even if it had, I don't think it would have made any difference. Drop nitric acid on the altar rail, and it will eat the brass just the same as if it was in a brass foundry. Put alcohol inside me, and the craving starts up full blast."

"Then you believe I should excuse—"

"No," he interrupted with grim firmness. "I might have thought it then—but not now. I've had two days to think it over. It all comes down to this: If, knowing how you felt about it, I could not kneel there beside you and take that taste of wine without going under, I'm just what you suspected—weak, unfit."

She clasped her hands on her bosom. "You—admit it?"

"What's the use of lying about it?" he said. "If it hadn't come about that way, you can see now it was bound to happen some other way."

"I—suppose—yes. Oh! but it's horrible!—horrible! I thought you so strong!"

"I won't bother you any more," he muttered. "Good-bye."

He went out without venturing a glance at her white face. She waited, motionless, looking toward the spot where he had stood. Several moments passed before she seemed to realize that he had gone.

23

A REPRIEVE

LORD JAMES DID not call upon Genevieve until late
afternoon of the next day, and then he did not come alone.
He had called first upon Mrs. Gantry and Dolores, who
brought him on in their *coupé*.

Genevieve came down to them noticeably pale and with
dark shadows under her fine eyes, but her manner was, if
anything, rather more composed than usual. She even had
a smile to exchange for the gay greeting of Dolores. Mrs.
Gantry met her with a kiss a full degree more fervent than
was consistent with strict decorum.

"My dear child!" she exclaimed. "I have hastened over to
see you. Lord Avondale has told me all about that fellow."

"Yes?" asked Genevieve, looking at Lord James calmly
but with a slight lift of her eyebrows that betrayed her
astonishment.

"Hasn't your father told you?" replied Mrs. Gantry,
reposing herself in the most comfortable seat. "It seems
that he has arranged—"

"Beg pardon," said Lord James. "It was the Coville
Construction Company that made the offer."

"Very true. An arrangement has been made, my dear,
that will take that person to the bridge and keep him there."

"Provided he accepts the offer," added Lord James.

"How can it be otherwise? The salary is simply stupendous for a man of his class and standing."

"Laffie gets only twelve thousand a year, yet he designed the bridge," remarked Dolores. "He told me it wasn't even enough for pin-money."

"I fancy he must contrive to make it go farther since his last trip to town," said Mrs. Gantry. "The little visit proved rather expensive. His father made another reduction in his allowance."

"Goodness!" exclaimed Dolores. "Poor dear Laffie boy! If I conclude to marry him, I shall insist that Papa Ashton is to give me a separate allowance."

"My word, Miss Dolores!" expostulated Lord James. "You're not encouraging that fellow?"

"Oh, it's as well to have more than one hook on the line. Ask mamma if it isn't. Besides, Laffie would be a gilt-edged investment—provided his papa made the right kind of a will. Anyway, I could get Uncle Herbert's lawyers to fix up an agreement as to that—a kind of pre-nuptial alimony contract between me and Laffie's papa's millions."

Mrs. Gantry held up her hands. "Could you have believed it, Genevieve! She was frivolous enough before I went over for you. But now!"

Dolores coolly disregarded her mother, to turn a meaning look on Lord James. "If I have frivolled enough, it's about time you said something."

The young Englishman put an uneasy hand to his mustache. "Er—I should have preferred a—a rather more favorable time, Miss Dolores."

"Yes, and have mamma slam him before you put in the

buffer," rejoined the girl. "See here, Vievie. It's too bad, but you must have tattled something to Uncle Herbert, and he—"

"Tattled!" repeated Genevieve. "I have always been candid with papa, if that is what you mean, Dolores."

"All right, then, Miss Candid. Though we called it tattling ten years ago. Anyway, Uncle Herbert wrote about it to mamma. He sent the letter out this noon. Next thing, it'll be all over Chicago—and England."

"Dolores! I must insist!" admonished Mrs. Gantry.

"So must I, mamma! If it's wrong to destroy the property of others, it's no less wrong to destroy their reputations."

Her mother expanded with self-righteous indignation. "Well, I never!—indeed! When the fellow has neither character nor reputation!"

"Dear auntie," soothed Genevieve, "I know you too well to believe you could intentionally harm any one."

"I would do *anything* to save you from ruining your life!" exclaimed Mrs. Gantry, moved almost to tears.

"I shall not ruin my life," replied Genevieve, with a quiet firmness that brought a profound sigh of relief from her aunt.

"*A-a-h!*—My dear child! Then you at last realize what sort of a man he is."

"Vievie knows he *is* a man—which is more than can be said of some of them," thrust Dolores, with a mocking glance at Lord James.

"My dear," urged Mrs. Gantry, "give no heed to that silly chit. I wish to commend your stand against the fatal attraction of mere brute efficiency."

"Oh, I say!" put in Lord James. "It's this I must protest

against, Miss Leslie—this talk of his brute qualities—when it's only the lack of polish. You should know that. He's a thistle, prickly without, but within soft as silk."

"Do I not know?" exclaimed Genevieve, for the moment unable to maintain her perfect composure.

"The metaphor was very touching and most loyal, my dear earl," said Mrs. Gantry. "Yet you must pardon me if I suggest that your opinion of him may be somewhat biased by friendship."

"But of course mamma's opinion isn't biased," remarked Dolores. She shot an angry glance at her mother, and added—"by friendship."

"It would relieve me very much if no more were said about Mr. Blake," said Genevieve.

"We can't—now," snapped Dolores, frowning at the footman who had appeared in the doorway. "Some one must have sighted the right honorable earl in our *coupé*."

Her irony was justified by the actions of the three young matrons who fluttered in on the breeze of the footman's announcement. They immediately fell into raptures over his lordship, who was forced in self-defence to tug and twist at his mustache and toy with his monocle. At this last Dolores flung herself out of the room in ill-concealed disdain.

She was not to be found when, all too soon, her mother tore the "charming Earl Avondale" away from his chattering adorers. After the worshipful one had been borne off, the dejected trio did not linger long. Their departure was followed by the prompt reappearance of Dolores.

She came at her cousin with eyes flashing. "Now you're all alone, Vievie! I've been waiting for this. Do you know what I'm going to do? I'm going to give you a piece of my mind."

"Please, dear!" begged Genevieve.

"No. I'll not please! You deserve a good beating, and I'm going to give it to you. That poor Mr. Blake! Aren't you 'shamed of yourself? Breaking his big noble heart!"

"Dolores! I must ask you—"

"No, you mustn't! You've got to listen to me, you know you have. To think that you, who've always pretended to be so kind and considerate, should be a regular cat!"

"You foolish dear!" murmured Genevieve. "Do you imagine that anything that you can say can hurt me, after— after—" She turned away to hide her starting tears.

"That's it!" jeered her cousin. "Be a snivelly little hypocrite.

Pretend to be so sorry—when you're not sorry at all. *Pah!*"

Genevieve recovered her dignity with her composure. "That is quite enough, my dear. I can overlook what you have already said. You know absolutely nothing about love and the bitter grief it brings."

"You don't say!" retorted Dolores, her nostrils quivering. "Much you know about me. But you!—the idea of pretending you love him—that you ever so much as dreamed of loving him!"

Genevieve shrank back as if she had been struck. "Oh! for any one to say that to me!"

"It's true—it must be true!" insisted Dolores, half frightened yet still too surcharged with anger to contain herself. "If it isn't true, how could you break his heart?—the man who saved you from that terrible savage wilderness!"

"I—I cannot explain to you. It's something that—"

"I know! You needn't tell me. It's mamma. She's been knocking him. I'll bet she started knocking him when she first cabled to you—at least she would have, had she known anything about him. Think I don't know mamma and her methods? If only he'd been his lordship—Owh, deah! what a difference, don't y' know! She'd never have let you get out of England unmarried!"

"Dolores! this is quite enough!"

"The Countess of Avondale, future Duchess of Ruthby! Think I don't see through mamma's little game? And you'd shillyshally around, and throw over the true, noble hero to whom you owe everything—whom you've pretended you loved—to run after a title, an Englishman, when you could have that big-hearted American!"

Genevieve's lips straightened. "What a patriot!" she rejoined with quiet irony. "You, of course, would never dream of marrying an Englishman."

"That's none of your business," snapped Dolores, not a little taken aback by the counter attack.

"You spoke about pretence and hypocrisy," went on Genevieve. "How about the way you tease and make sport of Lord Avondale?"

For a moment the younger girl stood quivering, transfixed by the dart. Suddenly she put her hands before her eyes and rushed from the room in a storm of tears.

Genevieve started up as if to hasten after her, but checked herself and sank back into her chair. For a long time she sat motionless, in the blank dreary silence of profound grief, her eyes fixed upon vacancy, dry and lustreless.

When, a few minutes before their dinner hour, her father

hurried into the room, expectant of his usual affectionate welcome, she did not spring up to greet him. The sound of his brisk step failed to penetrate to her consciousness. He came over to her and put a fond hand on her shoulder.

"H'm—how's this, my dear?" he asked. "Not asleep? Brown study, eh?"

She looked up at him dully; but at sight of the loving concern in his eyes, the unendurable hardness of her grief suddenly melted to tears. She flung herself into his arms, to weep and sob with a violence of which he had never imagined his quiet high-bred daughter capable. Bewildered and alarmed by the storm of emotion, he knew not what to do, and so instinctively did what was right. He patted her on the back and murmured inarticulate sounds of love and pity.

His sympathy and the blessed relief of tears soon restored her quiet self-control. She ceased sobbing and drew away from him, mortified at her outburst.

"There now," he ventured. "You feel better, don't you?"

"I've been very silly!" she exclaimed, drying her tear-wet cheeks.

"You're never silly—that is, since you came home this time," he qualified.

"Because—because—" She stopped with an odd catch in her voice, and seemed again about to burst into tears.

"Because *he* taught you to be sensible,—you'd say."

"Ye—yes," she sobbed. "Oh, papa, I can't bear it—I can't! To think that after he'd shown himself so brave and strong—! But for that, I should never have—have come to this!"

"H'm,—from the way you talked last night, I took it

that the matter was settled. You said then that you could no longer—h'm—love him."

"I can't!—I mustn't! Don't you see? He's proved himself weak. How, then, can I keep on loving him? But they—they infer that it is my fault. I believe they think I tempted him."

"How's that?"

"Because I urged him to take the communion with me. I told you what he himself said about alcohol. But he did not blame me. He pointed out that if he was too weak to resist then, he would have yielded to the next temptation."

"H'm,—no doubt. Yet I've been considering that point—the fact that you did force him against his will."

"Surely, papa, you cannot say it was my fault, when he himself admits that his own weakness—"

"Wait," broke in her father. "What do you know about the curse of drink? It's possible that he might be able to resist the craving if not roused by the taste."

"Yet if he is so weak that a few drops of the holy communion wine could cause him to give way so shamelessly—"

"Holy?—h'm!" commented Mr. Leslie. "Alcohol is a poison. Suppose the Church used a decoction containing arsenic. Would that make arsenic holy?"

"Oh, papa! But it's so very different!"

"Yes. Alcohol and arsenic are different poisons. But they're similar in at least one respect. The effects of each are cumulative. To one who has been over-drugged with arsenic a slight amount more may prove a fatal dose. So of a person whose will has been undermined and almost paralyzed with alcohol—"

"That's it, papa. Don't you see? If he lacks the will, the strength, the self-control to resist!"

"No, that isn't the point. It's your part in this most unfortunate occurrence that I'm now considering."

"My part?"

"You told him that he must not look to you for help or even sympathy. I can understand your position as to that. At the same time, should you not have been as neutral on the other side? Was it quite fair for you to add to his temptations?"

"Yet the fact of his weakness—"

"I'm not talking about him, my dear. It's what you've done—the question whether you do not owe him reparation for your part in his—misfortune."

"My part?"

"Had you not forced him into what I cannot but consider an unfair test of his strength, he would not have fallen. Griffith tells me that he was well along toward a solution of the Zariba Dam. Had you not caused this unfortunate interruption in his work, he might soon have proved himself a master engineer. That would have strengthened him in his fight against this hereditary curse."

"He was to fight it on his own strength."

"What else would this engineering triumph have been but a proof to himself of his strength? You have deprived him of that. Griffith tells me that, hard as he is striving to work out the idea which he was certain would meet the difficulties of the dam, he now seems unable to make any progress."

"So Mr. Griffith and you blame all upon me?"

"You mistake me, my dear. What I wish to make clear to

you is that, however hopeless Blake's condition may be, you are responsible for his failure upon this occasion."

"And if so?"

"Premising that in one respect my attitude toward him is unalterable, I wish to say that he has risen very much in my esteem. I have had confidential talks with Griffith and Lord Avondale regarding him. I have been forced to the conclusion that you were justified in considering him, aside from this one great fault, a man essentially sound and reliable. He has brains, integrity, courage, and endurance. Given sufficient inducement, those qualities would soon enable him to acquire all that he lacks,—manners and culture."

"Oh, papa, do not speak of it! It was because I saw all that in him that I felt so certain. If only it were not for the one thing!"

"H'm," considered Mr. Leslie, scrutinizing her tense face. "Then I gather it's not true what yesterday you said and no doubt believed. You still regard him with the same feelings as before this occurrence."

"No! no! He has destroyed all my faith in him. I—I can pity him. But anything more than that is—it must be— dead."

"Can't say I regret it. But—this is another question. You've lost him one chance. I believe you should give him another."

"Another chance?—you say that?" she asked incredulously.

"You should cancel this record—this occurrence. Blot it out. Start anew."

"How can I? It is impossible to forget that he has failed so utterly."

"Thanks to the poison you put into his mouth."

"Father! I did not think that you—"

"I was unjust to him. You also have done him a wrong. I am seeking to make reparation. In part payment, I wish to make clear to you what you should do to offset your fault. In view of the development of your character (which, by the way, you claim was brought about by your African experience), I feel that I should have no need to urge this matter. You are not a thoughtless child. Think it over. Here's Hodges."

She went in with him to dinner, perfectly composed in the presence of the grave-faced old butler. But after the meal, when her father left for his customary cigar in the conservatory, she sought the seclusion of the library, and attempted to fight down the growing doubt of her justice toward Blake that had been roused by her father's suggestions.

It was easy for her to maintain the resolute stand she had taken so long as she kept her thoughts fixed on his fall from manhood. But presently she began to recall incidents that had occurred during those terrible weeks on the savage coast of Mozambique.

She remembered, most vividly of all, a day on the southern headland—the eventful day before the arrival of the steamer—when he had spoken freely of the faults of his past life.... He had never lied to her or sought to gloze over his weakness.

And he could have concealed this present failure. She divined that both Griffith and Lord James would never have betrayed him. Yet he had come direct to her and confessed, knowing that she would condemn him.

The thought was more than she could withstand. She crossed over to her desk, and wrote swiftly:—

DEAR FRIEND:

You are to consider that all which has taken place since Sunday is as if it had never happened.

Come to me to-morrow, at ten.

JENNY.

Enclosing the note in an envelope addressed to Blake, she gave it to a servant for immediate delivery. As soon as the man left the room, she went to the telephone and arranged for a private consultation with one of the most eminent physicians in the city.

24

THE WAY OF A WOMAN

BLAKE WAS HUMPED over his desk, his fingers deep in his hair, and his forehead furrowed with the knotted wrinkles of utter weariness and perplexity, as his eyes pored over the complex diagrams and figures jotted down on the plan before him.

Griffith came shuffling into the room in his old carpet slippers. He looked anxiously at the bent form across the desk from him, and said: "See here, Tommy, what's the use of wasting electricity?"

Blake stared up at him, blear-eyed with overstudy and loss of sleep.

"Told you 'm going to keep going long as the wheels go 'round," he mumbled.

"They'd keep going a heap longer if you laid off Sundays," advised Griffith. "I'm no fanatic; but no man can keep at it day and night, this way, without breaking."

"Sooner the better!" growled Blake. "You go tuck yourself into your cradle."

Griffith shook his head dubiously and was shuffling out when he heard a knock at the hall door of the living-room. He hastened to respond, and soon returned with a dainty envelope. Blake was again poring over his plans and figures. The older man tossed the missive upon the desk.

"Hey, wake up," he cackled. "Letter from one of your High Society lady friends. Flunkey in livery for messenger."

"Livery?" echoed Blake. "Brown and yellow, eh?—as if his clothes had malaria."

"No. Dark green and black."

Blake started to his feet, his face contorted with the conflict of his emotions. "Don't joke!—for God's sake! That's hers!"

Griffith ripped the note from its envelope and held it out. Blake clutched it from him, and opened up the sheet with trembling fingers, to find the signature. For a moment he stood staring at it as if unable to believe his own eyes. Then he turned to the heading of the note and began to read.

"Well?" queried Griffith, as the other reached the end and again stood staring at the signature.

Instead of replying, Blake dropped into his chair and buried his face in his arms. Griffith hovered over him, gazing worriedly at the big heaving shoulders.

"Must say you're mighty talkative," he at last remarked, and he started toward the door. "Good-night."

"Wait!" panted Blake. "Read it!"

Griffith took the note, which was thrust out to him, and read it through twice.

"Huh," he commented. "She wasn't so awfully sudden over it. 'Bout time, I'd say."

"Shut up!" cried Blake, flinging himself erect in the chair, to beam upon his friend. "You've no license to kick, you old grouch. I'm coming to bed. But wait till to-morrow after-noon. Maybe the fur won't fly on old Zariba!"

"Come on, then. I'll get your sulphonal."

"You will—not! No more dope in mine, Grif. I've got something a thousand per cent better."

"She ought to've come through with it at the start-off," grumbled Griffith. But he gladly accompanied his friend to the bedroom.

In the morning Blake awoke from a profound natural sleep, clear-eyed and clear-brained. His first act was to tele-phone to a florist's to send their largest crimson amaryllis to Miss Genevieve Leslie.

Though he forced himself to walk, he reached the Leslie mansion a full half-hour before ten. To kill time, he swung on out the Drive into Lincoln Park. He went a good mile, yet was back again five minutes before the hour. Unable to wait a moment longer, he hastened up into the stately portico and rang.

As on the previous day, he was at once bowed in and ushered to the beautiful room of gold and ivory enamel. He entered eagerly, and was not a little dashed to find himself alone. His spirits rebounded at the remembrance that he was early. He stopped in the centre of the room and stood waiting, tense with expectancy.

Very soon Genevieve came in at one of the side door-ways. He started toward her the instant he heard her light step. But her look and bearing checked his eager advance. She was very pale, and her eyelids were swollen from hours of weeping.

"Jenny!" he stammered. "What is it? Your note—I thought that—that—"

"You poor boy! you poor boy!" she murmured, her eyes brimming over with tears of compassion.

"What is it?" he muttered, and he drew nearer to her.

She put out her hands and grasped his coat, and looked up at him, her forehead creased with deep lines of grief, and the corners of her sweet mouth drooping piteously.

"Oh, Tom! Tom!" she sobbed, "I know the worst now! I know how greatly I wronged you by forcing you into temptation. I have been to one who knows—one of the great physicians."

"About me?" asked Blake, greatly surprised.

"I used no names. He does not know who I am. But I told him the facts, as you have told them to me, dear. He said—Oh, I cannot—I cannot repeat it!"

She bent forward and pressed her face against his breast, sobbing with an uncontrollable outburst of grief. He raised his arms to draw her to him, but dropped them heavily.

"Well?" he asked in a harsh voice. "What of it?"

She drew herself away from him, still quivering, but striving hard to control her emotion.

"I—I must tell you!" she forced herself to answer. "I have no right to keep it from you. He said that it is a—a disease; that it is a matter of pathology, not of moral courage."

"Disease?" repeated Blake. "Well, what if it is? I don't see what difference that makes. If I fight it down—all well and good. If I lose out, I lose out—that's all."

"But don't you see the difference it makes to me?" she insisted. "I blamed you—when it wasn't your fault at all. But I did not realize, dear. I've been under a frightful strain ever since we reached home. Just because I do not weep and cry out, every one imagines I'm cold and unfeeling.

I've been reproached for treating you cruelly. But you see now—"

"Of course!" he declared. "Don't you suppose I know? It's your grit. Needn't tell me how you've felt. You're the truest, kindest little woman that ever was!"

"Oh, Tom! that's so like you!—and after I *have* treated you so cruelly!"

"You? What on earth put that into your head? Maybe you mean, because you didn't give me the second chance at once when I owned up to failing. But it was no more than right for you to send me off. Didn't I deserve it? I had given you cause enough to despise me—to send me off for good."

"No, no, not despise you, Tom! You know that never could be, when there in that terrible wilderness you proved yourself so true and kind—such a man! And not that alone! I know all now—how you, to save me—" She paused and looked away, her face scarlet. Yet she went on bravely: "how, in order that I might be compelled to make certain, you endured the frightful heat and smother of that foul forecastle, all those days to Aden!"

"That wasn't anything," disclaimed Blake. "I slept on deck every night. Just a picnic. I knew you were safe—no more danger of that damnable fever—and with Jimmy to entertain you."

"While you had to hide from me all day! James said that it was frightful in the forecastle."

"Much he knows about such places! It wasn't anything to a glass-factory or steelworks. If it had been the stokehole, instead—I did try stoking, one day, just to pass the time. Stood it two hours. Those Lascars are born under the equator. I don't see how any white man can stoke in the tropics."

"You did that?—to pass the time! While we were aft, under double awnings, up where we could catch every breath of air! Had I known that you did not land at Port Mozambique, I should have—should have—"

"Course you would have!" he replied. "But now you see how well it was you didn't know."

"Perhaps—Yet I'm not so sure—I—I—"

She clasped her hands over her eyes, as all her grief and anguish came back upon her in full flood.

"Oh, Tom! what shall we do? My dear, my poor dear! That doctor, with his cold, hard science! I have learned the meaning of that fearful verse of the Bible: 'Unto the third and fourth generation.' You may succeed; you may win your great fight for self-mastery. But your children—the curse would hang over them. One and all, they too might suffer. Though you should hold to your self-mastery, there would still be a chance,—epilepsy, insanity, your own form of the curse! And should you again fall back into the pit—"

She stopped, overcome.

He drew back a little way, and stood regarding her with a look of utter despair.

"So that is why you sent for me," he said. "I came here thinking you might be going to give me another chance. Now you tell me it's a lot worse than even I thought."

"No, no!" she protested. "I learned what I've told you afterward—after I had sent you the note. You must not think—"

He broke in upon her explanation with a laugh as mirthless as were his hard-set face and despairing eyes. She shrank back from him.

"Stop it!—stop it!" she cried. "I can't bear it!"

He fell silent, and began aimlessly fumbling through his pockets. His gaze was fixed on the wall above and beyond her in a vacant stare.

"Tom!" she whispered, alarmed at his abstraction.

He looked down at her as if mildly surprised that she was still in the room.

"Excuse me," he muttered. "I was just wondering what it all amounts to, anyway. A fellow squirms and flounders, or else drifts with the current. Maybe he helps others to keep afloat, and maybe he doesn't. Maybe some one else helps him hold up. But, sooner or later, he goes down for good. It will all be the same a hundred years from now."

"No!" she denied. "You know that's not true. You don't believe it."

He straightened, and raised his half-clenched fist.

"You're right, Jenny. It's the facts, but not the truth. It's up to a man to pound away for all he's worth; not whine around about what's going to happen to him to-morrow or next year or when he dies. Only time I ever was a floater was when I was a kid and didn't know the real meaning of work. Since then I've lived. I can at least say I haven't been a parasite. And I've had the fun of the fight."

He flung out his hand, and his dulled eyes flashed with the fire of battle.

"Lord!—what if I *have* lost you! That's no reason for me to quit. You did love me there—and I'll love you always, little woman! You've given me a thousand times more than I deserve. I've got that to remember, to keep me up to the fighting pitch. I'm going to keep on fighting this curse, anyway. Idea of a man lying down, long as he can stagger! Even if the curse downs me in the end, there're lots of things I can do before I go under. There're lots of things to be done in the world—big things! Pound away! What if a man is to be laid on the shelf to-morrow? Pound away! Keep doing—that's life! Do your best—that's living!"

"I know of *one* who has lived!" whispered Genevieve. "Jenny! Then it's not true? You'll give me another chance? You still love me?"

"Wait! No, you must not!" she replied, shrinking back again. "I cannot—I will not give way! I must think of the future—not mine, but *theirs!* I must do what is right. I tell you, there is one supreme duty in a woman's lot—she should choose rightly the man who is to be the father of her children! It is a crime to bring into the world children who are cursed!"

A flame of color leaped into her face, but she stood with upraised head, regarding him with clear and candid eyes that glowed with the ecstasy of self-sacrifice.

Before her look, his gaze softened to deepest tenderness and reverence.

When he spoke, his voice was hushed, almost awed.

"Now I understand, Jenny. It's—it's a holy thing you've done—telling me! I'll never forget it, night or day, so long as I live. Good-bye!"

He turned to go; but in an instant she was before him with hands outflung to stop him.

"Wait! You do not understand. Listen! I did not mean what you think—only—only if you fail! Can you imagine I could be so unjust? If you do not fail—if you win— Oh, can't you see?"

He stared at her, dazed by the sudden glimmering of hope through the blackness of his despair.

"But you said that, even if I should win—" he muttered.

"Yes, yes; he told me there would still be a risk. But I cannot believe it. At least it would not be so grave a risk. Oh, if you can but win, Tom!"

"I'll try," he answered soberly.

"You will win—you shall win! I will help you."

"You?"

"Yes. Don't you understand? That is why I sent for you—to tell you that."

"But you said—"

"I don't care what I said. It's all different now. I see what I should do. I have failed far worse than you. There on that savage coast you required me to do my share; but always you stood ready to advise and help me. Yet after all that—How ungrateful you must think me!"

"No, never!" he cried. "You sha'n't say that. I can't stand it. You're the truest, kindest—"

"It's like you to say it!" she broke in. "But look at the facts. Did you ever set me a task that called for the very utmost of my strength—perhaps more; and then turn coldly away, with the cruel word that I must win alone or perish?"

"It's not the same case at all," he remonstrated. "You're not fair to yourself. I'm a man."

"And I've called myself a woman," she replied. "After those weeks with you I thought myself no longer a shallow, unthinking girl. A woman! Now I see, Tom—I know! I have failed in the woman's part. But now I shall stand by you in your fight. I shall do my part, and you will win!"

Blake's eyes shone soft and blue, and he again held out his arms to her. But in the same moment the glow faded and his arms fell to his side.

"I almost forgot," he murmured. "You said that I must win by my own strength—that you must be sure of my strength."

"That was before I learned the truth," she replied. "I no longer ask so much. I shall—I must help you, as you helped me. I owe you life and more than life. You know that. You cannot think me so ungrateful as not to do all I can."

"No," he replied, with sudden resolve. "You are to do as you first said—as we agreed."

"You mean, not help you? But I must, Tom, now that I realize."

"All I want is another chance," he said. "It's more than I deserve. I can't accept still more."

"You'll not let me help you? Yet what the doctor said makes it all so different."

"Not to me," replied Blake, setting his jaw. "I've started in on this fight, and I'm going through with it the way I began. It'll be a big help to know how you feel now; but, just the same, I'm going to fight it out alone. The doctors may say what they please,—if I haven't will power enough to win, without being propped up, I'm not fit to marry any woman, much less you!"

"Tom!" she cried. "You *are* the man I thought you. You *will* win!"

She held out her hands to him. He took them in his big palms, and bent over to kiss her on the forehead.

"There!" he said, stepping away. "That's a lot more than I'm entitled to now, Jenny. It's time I left, to go and try to earn it."

"You won't allow me to help?" she begged.

"No," he answered, with a quiet firmness that she knew could not be shaken.

"At least you cannot keep me from praying for you," she said.

"That's true; and it will be a help to know how you feel about it now," he admitted.

"You will come again—soon?"

"No, not until I begin to see my way out on the Zariba Dam."

"Oh, that will be soon, I'm sure."

"I hope so. Good-bye!"

He turned and hurried from the room with an abruptness that in other circumstances she might have thought rude. But she understood. He was so determined in his purpose that he would not take the slightest risk that might be incurred by lingering.

She went to a front window, and watched him down the Drive. His step was quick but firm, and his head and shoulders were bent slightly forward, as if to meet and push through all obstacles.

25

HEAVY ODDS

FOR A FEW days Lord James was able to bring Genevieve encouraging reports of a vast improvement in Blake's spirits. But still the engineer-inventor failed to make the headway he had expected toward the solution of the complex and intricate problem of the dam. In consequence, he re-doubled his efforts and worked overtime, permitting himself less than four hours of sleep a night. His meals he either went without or took at his desk.

All the urgings of Griffith and Lord James could not induce him to cease driving himself to the very limit of endurance. Day by day he fell off, growing steadily thinner and more haggard and more feverish; yet still he toiled on, figuring and planning, planning and figuring.

But on the morning of the day set for Genevieve's ball, the weary, haggard worker tossed his pencil into the air, and uttered a shout that brought his two friends on a run from Griffith's office.

"I've got it! I've got it!" he flung at them, as they rushed in. He thrust a tablet across the table. "There's the proof. Check those totals, Grif."

Lord James leaned over the table to grasp Blake's hand.

"Gad, old man!" he said. "Just in time for you to go to the ball."

Griffith paused in his swift checking of Blake's final computations.

"Ball? Not on your sweet life! He's going to bed."

"You promised to go, Tom," said Lord James.

"Did I?" replied Blake. "Well, then, of course I'm going."

"Of course!" jeered Griffith. "It's no use arguing against a mule.

Can't help but wish you hadn't reminded him, Mr. Scarbridge."

"The change will do him good," argued Lord James.

"I'm in for it, anyway," said Blake. "Only thing, I wish I could get some sleep, in between. Well, here's for a good hot bath and a square meal. That'll set me up."

Griffith shook his head. "I'm not so sure. What you need is twelve hours on your back."

That he was right the Englishman had to admit himself with no little contrition before the ball was half over.

Blake presented a good figure, and though he talked little and danced less, yet on the whole he produced a very good impression. As Lord James had once observed, with regard to his visit at Ruthby Castle, Blake's bigness of mind seemed to be instinctively sensed by nearly all those with whom he came in contact on favorable terms.

But, from the first, he avoided Genevieve with a persistence so marked as almost to disarm Mrs. Gantry.

Most of his few dances were with Dolores, who discovered that, notwithstanding his evident weariness, he was astonishingly light on his feet and by no means a poor waltzer. But after midnight she found it increasingly difficult to lure him out on the floor whenever she was seized with the whim to favor him by scratching the name—and feelings—of some other partner.

More than once Lord James urged him to go home and turn in. Blake's reply was that he knew he ought not to have come to the ball, but since he had come, he proposed to stick it out,—he would not be a quitter. So he stayed on, hour after hour, weary-eyed and taciturn, but by no means ill-humored. Many of the wall-flowers and elderly guests poured their chatter into his unhearing ear, and thought him a most sympathetic listener.

Genevieve, however, with each glimpse that she caught of him, perceived how his fatigue was constantly verging toward exhaustion. At last, between three and four in the morning, she cut short a dance with young Ashton and asked Lord James to take her into the library for a few minutes' rest. He was with Dolores, but immediately relinquished her to Ashton, and went off with Genevieve.

They soon passed out of the chatter and whirl of the crowd into the seclusion of the library. Genevieve led the way to her father's favorite table, but avoided the big high-backed armchair. Lord James placed a smaller chair for her at the other side of the table, facing the door of the card-room, and as she sank into it he took the chair at the corner.

"Ah!" sighed Genevieve. "It's so restful to get away from them all for a few moments."

"I wonder you're not still more fatigued. Awful crush," replied Lord James. "I daresay you haven't had any chance all evening for a nibble of anything. Directed that something be brought to us here."

"That was very thoughtful of you. I do need something.

I'm depressed—It's about Tom. I brought you in here to ask your opinion. He has looked so haggard and worn to-night."

"Overwork," explained Lord James. "He's been hard at it, day and night, in that stuffy office. He could stand any amount of work out in the open. But this being cooped up indoors and grinding all the time at those bally figures!"

"If only it's nothing worse! I'm so afraid!"

"No. It hasn't come on again; though that may happen any time when he's so nearly pegged. Must confess, I blame myself for urging him to come to-night. But he said he had solved the big problem, and I thought the change would do him good—relax his mind, you know. Egregious mistake, I fear. I've urged him to go; but he insists upon sticking it out."

"But you're certain that he—has—done nothing as yet?"

"No, indeed, I assure you! This over-fatigue—I'm not even certain whether the craving is on him or not.... You'll pardon me, Miss Genevieve—but do you realize how hard you have made it for him, cutting him off from all help in his desperate struggle?"

"Then he *is* fighting all alone?" she exclaimed.

"Yes. He won't allow even me to jolly him up now. He's given me the cold shoulder. Said the inference to be drawn from your conditions was that he should have no help whatever."

"Isn't that brave!—isn't that just like him!" cried the girl, her eyes sparkling and cheeks aglow. "He *will* win! I feel sure he'll win!"

Lord James looked down at the table, and asked in rather

an odd and hesitating tone: "We must hope it. But—if he does win—what then?"

Blake came slowly into the room through the doorway behind them, his head downbent as if he were pondering a problem.

Unaware of the newcomer, Genevieve looked regretfully into the troubled face of her companion, and answered him with absolute candor. "Dear friend, need I repeat? I am very fond of you, and I esteem you very highly. Yet if he succeeds, I must say 'no' to you."

As the young Englishman bent over, without replying, Blake roused from his abstraction and perceived that he was not alone in the room.

"Hello—'scuse me!" he mumbled. Half startled, they turned to look at him. He met them with a rare smile. "So it's you, Jeems—and Miss Jenny. Didn't mean to cut in on your 'tates-an'-tay, as the Irishman put it."

He started to turn back. Genevieve sought to stop him. "Won't you join us, Tom?"

"Thanks, no. It's Jimmy's sit-out. I just stepped in here to see if I could find a book on the differential calculus. Been figuring a problem in my head all evening, and there's a formula I need to get my final solution. I know that formula well as I know you, but somehow my memory seems to've stopped working."

"Those bally figures! Can't you ever chop off?" remonstrated Lord James. "You're pegged. Come and join us. Miss Genevieve will be interested to hear about the dam."

"I'm interested, indeed I am, Tom. Papa says you are working out a piece of wonderful engineering."

Blake stared. "What does *he* know about it?"

"I suppose his consulting engineer told him—your friend Mr. Griffith."

"Grif's not working for him now."

"Indeed? Then I misunderstood. Anyway, you must come and explain all about the dam."

"Well, if you insist," said Blake. He went around to the big armchair, across from Genevieve, and sat down wearily while explaining: "But the dam is a long way from being built. It's all on paper yet, and I've had to rely on the reports sent in by the field engineers."

A footman came in and set food and wine before Genevieve and Lord James. Blake went on, with quick-mounting enthusiasm, heedless of the coming and going of the soft-footed, unobtrusive servant.

"That's the only thing I'm afraid of. Would have liked to've gone over the ground myself first. But they had two surveys, and the field notes check fairly well. Barring mistakes in them, I've got the proposition worked out to a T. It's all done except some figuring of details that any good engineer could do. Just as well, for I'm about all in. Stiffest proposition I ever went up against."

He sank back into the depths of the big chair, with a sudden giving way of enthusiasm to fatigue. Lord James reached out his plate to him.

"You *are* pegged, old man," he said. "Have a sandwich."

"No," replied Blake. "I'm too played out to eat. Just want to rest."

Genevieve had been scrutinizing his face, and her deepening concern lent a note of sharpness to her reproach: "You're exhausted! You should not have come to-night!"

"Couldn't pass up a dance at your house, could I?" he

smilingly rejoined. "Don't you worry about me. It's all right, long's I've got that whole damn irrigation system worked out."

"Ha! ha! old man!" chuckled Lord James. "That expresses it to a T, as you put it. But wouldn't it be better form to say, 'the whole irrigation dam system'?"

Blake smiled shamefacedly. "Did I make a break like— such as that? 'Scuse me, Miss Jenny. I'm sort of—I'm rather muddled to-night."

"No wonder, after all you've done," said Genevieve. She added, with a radiant smile, "But isn't it glorious that you've finished such a great work! Papa says that you've actually invented a new kind of dam."

The silent footman had reappeared with another plate and glass of wine. He glided around behind Blake, who had leaned forward again with the right arm upon the edge of the table. Unconscious of the servant, who placed the plate and wine glass near him on his left and quietly glided from the room, the engineer responded to Genevieve's remark with an animation that might have been likened to the last flare of a dying candle.

"No," he said, "it's not exactly a new kind of dam—not an invention. I did work out once a modification of bridge trusses which some might call an invention,—new principle in the application of trusses to bridge structure. Allows for a longer suspension span on cantilever bridges."

"But this Zariba Dam," remarked Lord James; "I've yet to learn, myself, just how you worked it out."

"Well, it wasn't any invention; just a sort of discovery how to combine a lot of well-known principles of construction to fit the particular case. You see, it's this way. There was only one available site for the dam, and the mid-section of that was bottomless bog; yet provision had to be made for a sixty-five foot head of water."

"You take him, Miss Genevieve," said Lord James. "They have no solid ground to build on, and the water above the dam is to be sixty-five feet deep."

"I should think the dam would sink into the bog," remarked Genevieve.

"That was one factor in the problem," said Blake. "Solved it by putting the steel reinforcement of the concrete in the form of my bridge-truss span. The whole central section could hang in midair and not buckle or drop. That was simple enough, long's I had my truss already invented. The main difficulty was that deep bog. If you studied hydrostatics, you'd soon learn that a sixty-five foot head of water puts an enormous pressure on the bed of a reservoir."

Absorbed in his explanation, Blake unconsciously grasped the wine glass in his left hand, as he went on:

"That pressure would be enough to make the water boil down through the bog and clear out under the deepest foundation any of the other engineers had been able to figure out. Well, I figured and figured, but somehow I couldn't make anything in the books go. At last, when I had almost given up—"

"No! you couldn't do that," put in Lord James.

Blake smiled at him, and paused to grasp again his broken thread of thought. In the fatal moment when his wakeful consciousness was diverted, and before Lord James could interpose to avert the act, his subconsciousness automatically caused his left hand to raise the glass which it held to his lips.

Before he was aware of what he was doing, he had taken a sip of the wine. An instant afterward the glass shattered on the floor beside his chair, and he clutched at the edge of the table, his face convulsed and his eyes glaring with the horror of what he had done.

"Hell!" he gasped.

Genevieve rose and started back from the table, shocked and frightened by what she mistook for an outburst of rage or madness. Lord James rose almost as quickly, no less shocked and quite as uncertain as to what his friend would do.

"Tom!" he called warningly, and he laid his hand on Blake's shoulder.

Almost beside himself in the paroxysm of fear and craving that had stricken his face white and half choked him with seeming rage, Blake shook off the restraining hand, and gasped hoarsely at Genevieve: "Wine!—here—in your house! God! Shoved into my hand! Smell wasn't enough—must taste it! God! Tough deal!"

"Lord Avondale!" cried Genevieve, and she turned to leave the room, furiously indignant.

"Gad! old man!" murmured Lord James, staring uncertainly from Blake to the angry girl, for once in his life utterly disconcerted and bewildered. He was unable to think, and the impulse of his breeding urged him to accompany Genevieve. After a moment's vacillation, he sprang about and hastened with her from the room.

Blake sat writhing in dumb anguish, his distended eyes fixed upon the doorway for many moments after they had gone. Then slowly yet as though drawn by an irresistible force, his gaze sank until it rested upon the half-filled wine glass left by Lord James. He glared at it in fearful fascination. Suddenly his hand shot out to clutch at it,—and as suddenly was drawn back.

There followed a grim and silent struggle, which ended in a second clutch at the glass. This time the shaking fingers closed on the slender stem. The wine was almost wetting his lips when, with a convulsive jerk, he flung it out upon the rug beside his chair.

Shuddering and quivering, Blake sank back in the chair, with his left arm upraised across his face as if he were expectant of a crushing blow or sought to shut out some horrible sight. His right arm slipped limply down outside the chair-arm, and the empty glass dropped to the floor out of his relaxing fingers.

Yet the lull in the contest was only momentary. As his protecting arm sank down again, his bloodshot eyes caught sight of the wine in Genevieve's glass. Instantly he started up rigid in his chair and clutched the edge of the table, as if to spring up and escape. But he could not tear his gaze away from the crimson wine.

Again there came the grim and silent struggle, and again the fierce craving for drink compelled his hand to go out to grasp the glass. But his will was not yet totally benumbed. As his fingers crooked to clutch the glass-stem, he made a last desperate effort to withstand the all but irresistible impulse that was forcing him over the brink of the pit. Beads of cold sweat started out on his forehead. His face creased with furrows of unbearable agony. His mouth gaped. The serpent had him by the throat.

The struggling man realized that he was on the verge of defeat. He was almost overcome. In a flash he perceived

*His jaw closed fast,—and in the same instant his
outstretched hand smashed down upon the wine glass.*

the one way to escape. For a single instant his slack jaw closed fast,—and in the same instant his outstretched hand clenched together and upraised and smashed down upon the wine glass.

Utterly exhausted, the victor collapsed forward, with head and arms upon the table, in a half swoon that quickly passed into the sleep-stupor of outspent strength.

26

TURNING THE ODD TRICK

THUS IT WAS Lord James found his friend when he came hurrying back into the library. He did not rouse Blake to ask questions. One glance at the shattered glass and Blake's bleeding hand was enough to tell him what had happened. There could be no doubt that Blake had won. It was no less certain, however, that the struggle had cost him the last ounce of his strength. What he now needed was absolute rest.

With utmost gentleness, Lord James examined the cut hand for fragments of glass and bound it up with his own handkerchief. As quietly, he gathered up the broken glass and the dishes, and wiped the blood and wine from the table. Another hour would see the end of the ball. Many of the guests already had gone, and it was not probable that any of those who remained would leave the ballroom or the cardroom to wander into the secluded library. Yet he thought it as well to remove the traces of Blake's struggle. He placed the bandaged hand of his unconscious friend down on the chair-arm, in the shadow of the edge of the table, and went out with the plates and glass, closing the door behind him.

He had been gone only a few minutes when the door of

the cardroom swung open before a sharp thrust, and Mr. Leslie stepped into the library, followed by Mrs. Gantry. Mr. Leslie closed the door, and each took advantage of the seclusion to blink and yawn and stretch luxuriously. They had just risen from the card table, and were both cramped and sleepy. Also neither perceived Blake, who was hidden from them by the back of the big chair.

"Ho-ho-hum!" yawned Mr. Leslie, in a last relaxing stretch. "That ends it for this time." He wagged his head at his sister-in-law, and rubbed his hands together exultantly. "For once you'll have to admit I *can* play bridge."

"For once," she conceded, as she moved toward the table. "You're still nothing more than a whist-player, yet had it not been for the honor score, you'd have beaten us disgracefully. One is fortunate when one has the honor score in one's favor."

"H'm! h'm!" he rallied. "I'll admit you women can *score* honor, but the question is, do you know what honor is?"

"Most certainly—when the score is in our favor. One would fancy you'd been reading Ibsen. Of all the bad taste—" Mrs. Gantry stopped short, to raise her lorgnette and stare at the flaccid form of Blake. "Hoity-toity! What have we here?"

"Hey?" queried Mr. Leslie, peering around her shoulder. "Asleep? Who is he?"

Mrs. Gantry turned to him and answered in a lowered voice: "It's that fellow, Blake. I do believe he's intoxicated."

"Intoxicated?" exclaimed Mr. Leslie. He went quickly around and bent over Blake. He came back to her on tiptoe and led her away from the table.

"You're mistaken," he whispered. "I'm certain he hasn't touched a drop."

"Certain?"

"Yes. Some one has spilled wine on the table; but his breath proves that he hasn't had any. It's merely that he's worn out—fallen asleep. Poor boy!"

"'Poor boy'?" repeated Mrs. Gantry, quizzing her brother-in-law through her lorgnette.

"H'm. Why not?" he demanded. "I was most unjust to him. I've been compelled to reverse my judgment of him on every point that was against him. As you know, he refused everything I offered in the way of money or position. He has proved that his intentions are absolutely honorable,— and now he has proved himself a great engineer. By his solution of the Zariba Dam problem, he has virtually put half a million, dollars into my pocket."

"I understood that you turned that project over to some company."

"The Coville Company—of which I own over ninety-five per cent of the stock. He would quit if he knew it, and I can't afford to lose him. The solution of the dam is a wonderful feat of engineering. That's what's the matter with him now. He worked at it to the point of exhaustion—and then for him to come here, already worn out!"

"I'm sure he was quite welcome to stay away," put in the lady.

Mr. Leslie frowned, and went on: "Griffith tells me that he can stand any amount of outdoor work, but that office work runs him down fast. But I'll soon fix that. We arranged to put him in charge of the Michamac Bridge."

"In charge? How will you get rid of Lafayette? You've

grumbled so often about his having a contract to remain there as chief builder, because he drew the bridge plans."

"Copied them, you should say."

"Ah, is that the term?"

"For what he did, yes—unless one uses the stronger term."

"I quite fail to take you."

"You'll understand—later on. Griffith and I are figuring that Tom will take the bridge and keep it."

"He has my heartfelt wish that he will take it soon, and remain in personal possession for all time!"

"H'm. I presume Genevieve could come down to visit us occasionally."

"Herbert! You surely cannot mean—?"

"Griffith has told me something in connection with this bridge that proves Thomas Blake to be one of the greatest engineers, if not the greatest, in America. I'd be proud to have him for a son-in-law."

"Impossible! *impossible!* It can't be you'll withdraw your opposition!"

"Not only that; I'll back him to win. I like your earl. He's a fine young fellow. But, after all, Blake is an *American.*"

"He's a brute! Herbert, it is impossible!"

"They said that dam was impossible. He has mastered it. He's big; he's got brains. He'll be a gentleman within six months. He's a genius!"

"*Poof!* He's a degenerate!"

"You'll see," rejoined Mr. Leslie. He went back to the table and tapped the sleeper sharply on the shoulder.

Blake stirred, and mumbled drowsily: "Huh! what—whatcha want?"

"Wake up," answered Mr. Leslie. "I wish to congratulate you."

Blake slowly heaved himself up and blinked at his disturber with haggard, bloodshot eyes. He was still very weary and only half roused from his stupor.

"Huh!" he muttered. "Must 'uv dropped 'sleep— Dog tired." His bleared gaze swung around and took in Mrs. Gantry. He started and tried to sit more erect. "Excuse me! Didn't know there was a lady here."

"Don't apologize. That's for me to do," interposed Mr. Leslie, offering his hand. "My—that is, the Coville Company officers tell me you've worked out a wonderful piece of engineering for them."

Blake stared hard at the bookcase behind Mrs. Gantry and answered curtly, oblivious of the older man's hand. "That remains to be seen. It's only on paper, so far."

"But I—h'm—it seems they are sufficiently satisfied to wish to put you in charge of the Michamac Bridge."

"In charge?"

"Yes."

"How about Ashton—their contract with him?"

"That's to be settled later. I wish—h'm—I understand that you are to be sent nominally as Assistant Engineer."

"I am, eh? Excuse *me!*"

"At double the salary of Ashton, and—"

"Not at ten times the salary as *his* assistant!"

"But you must know that Griffith's doctor has ordered him to Florida, and with the work rushing on the bridge— He tells me it has reached the most critical stage of construction—that suspension span—"

"You seem mighty interested in a project you got rid of,"

remarked Blake, vaguely conscious of the other's repressed eagerness.

"Yes. I was the first to consider the possibility of bridging the strait."

"Your idea, was it?" said Blake, with reluctant admiration. "It was a big one, all right."

"Nothing as compared to the invention of that bridge," returned Mr. Leslie.

"Your young friend Ashton sure is a great one," countered Blake.

"The man who planned that bridge is a genius," stated Mr. Leslie with enthusiasm. "That's one fact. Another is that Laffie Ashton is unfit to supervise the construction of the suspension span. I'll see to it myself that the matter is so arranged that you—"

"Thanks, no. You'll do nothing of the kind," broke in Blake. He spoke without brusqueness yet with stubborn determination. "I don't want any favors from you, and you know why. I can appreciate your congratulations, long as you seem to want to be friendly. But you needn't say anything to the company."

"Very well, very well, sir!" snapped Mr. Leslie, irritated at the rebuff. He jerked himself about to Mrs. Gantry. "There's time yet. What do you say to another rubber?"

"You should have spoken before we rose," replied the lady. "There'll be others who wish to go. You'll be able to take over some one's hand. I prefer to remain in here for a *tête-à-tête* with Mr. Blake."

Blake and Mr. Leslie stared at her, alike surprised. The younger man muttered in far other than a cordial tone:

"Thanks. But I'm not fit company. Ought to've been abed and asleep hours ago."

"Yet if you'll pardon me for insisting, I wish to have a little chat with you," replied Mrs. Gantry.

At her expectant glance, Mr. Leslie started for the door of the cardroom. As he went out and closed the door, Mrs. Gantry took the chair on the other side of the table from Blake, and explained in a confidential tone: "It is about this unfortunate situation."

Blake stared at her, with a puzzled frown. "Unfortunate what?"

"Unfortunate situation," she replied, making an effort to moderate her superciliousness to mere condescension. "I assure you, I too have learned that first impressions may err. I cannot now believe that you are torturing my niece purposely."

Blake roused up on the instant, for the first time wide awake.

"What!" he demanded. "I—torturing—her?"

"Most unfortunately, that is, at least, the effect of the situation."

"But I—I don't understand! What is it, anyhow? I'd do anything to save her the slightest suffering!"

"Ah!" said Mrs. Gantry, and she averted her gaze.

"Don't you believe me?" he demanded.

"To be sure—to be sure!" she hastened to respond. "Had I not thought you capable of that, I should not have troubled to speak to you."

"But what is it? What do you mean?" he asked, with swift-growing uneasiness.

"I do not say that I blame you for failing to see and understand," she evaded. "No doubt you, too, have suffered."

"Yes, I've— But that's nothing. It's Jenny!" he exclaimed, fast on the barbed hook. "Good God! if it's true I've made her suffer— But how? Why? I don't understand."

Mrs. Gantry studied him with a gravity that seemed to include a trace of sympathy. There was an almost imperceptible tremor in her voice.

"Need I tell you, Mr. Blake, how a girl of her high ideals, her high conception of *noblesse oblige,* of duty (you saved her life as heroically as—er—as a fireman)—need I point out how grateful she must always feel toward you, and how easily she might mistake her gratitude for something else?"

"You mean that she—that she—" He could not complete the sentence.

Mrs. Gantry went on almost blandly. "A girl of her fine and generous nature is apt to mistake so strong a feeling of gratitude for what you no doubt thought it was."

"Yet that morning—on the cliffs—when the steamer came—"

"Even then. Can you believe that if she really loved you then, she could doubt it now?"

"You say she—does—doubt it? I thought that—maybe—" The heavy words dragged until they failed to pass Blake's tense lips.

"Doubt it!" repeated Mrs. Gantry. "Has she accepted you?"

"No. I—"

"Has she promised you anything?"

"No. She said that, unless she was sure—"

"What more do you need to realize that she is not sure?

Can you fancy for a moment that she would hesitate if she really loved you—if she did not intuitively realize that her feeling is no more than gratitude? That is why she is suffering so. She realizes the truth, yet will not admit it even to herself."

Blake forced himself to face the worst. "Then what—what do you—?"

"Ah! so you really are generous!" exclaimed Mrs. Gantry, beaming upon him, with unfeigned suavity. "Need I tell you that she is extremely fond of Lord Avondale? With him there could be no doubts, no uncertainties."

"Jimmy is all right," loyally assented Blake. "Yes, he's all right.

Just the same, unless she—" He stopped, unable to speak the word.

"In accepting him she would attain to—" The tactful dame paused, considered, and altered her remark. "With him she would be happy."

"I'm not saying 'no' to that," admitted Blake. "That is, provided—"

"Ah! And you say you love her!" broke in Mrs. Gantry. "What love is it that would stand between her and happiness—that would compel her to sacrifice her life, out of gratitude to you?"

Blake bent over and asked in a dull murmur: "You are sure it's that?"

"Indeed, yes! How can it be otherwise?—a girl of her breeding; and you—what you are!"

Blake bent over still lower, and all his fortitude could not repress the groan that rose to his lips. Mrs. Gantry watched him closely, her face set in its suave smile, but her eyes hard and cold. She went on, without a sign of compunction: "But I now believe you are possessed of sterling qualities, else I should not have troubled to speak the truth to you."

She paused to emphasize what was to follow. "There is only one way for you to save her. She is too generous to save herself. I believe that you really love her. You can prove it by—" again she paused—"going away."

Blake bent over on the table and buried his face in his arms. His smothered groan would have won him the compassion of a savage. It was the cry of a strong man crushed under an unbearable burden. Mrs. Gantry was not a savage. Her eyes sparkled coldly.

"You will go away. You will prove your love for her," she said.

Certain that she had accomplished what she had set out to do, she returned to the cardroom, and left her victim to his misery and despair.

27

A PACKING CASE

ALREADY EXHAUSTED BY the stress of the fierce fight that he had so hardly won, Blake could no longer sustain such acute grief. Nature mercifully dulled his consciousness. He sank into a stupor that outwardly was not unlike heavy slumber.

Mrs. Gantry had been gone several minutes when the other door swung open. Dolores skipped in, closely followed by Lafayette Ashton. The young man's face was flushed, and there was a slight uncertainty in his step; but as he closed the door and followed the girl across the room, he spoke with rather more distinctness than usual.

"Here we are, *ma cher.* I knew we'd find a place where you could show me how kind you feel toward your fond Fayette."

"So that's the way you cross the line?" criticised Dolores. "What a get-away for a fast pacer who has gone the pace!"

"Now, Dodie, don't hang back. You know as well as I do—"

"Hush! Don't whisper it aloud!" cautioned the girl, pointing dramatically to Blake. "Betray no secrets. We are not alone!"

Ashton muttered a French curse, and went over to the table.

"It's that fellow, Blake," he whispered, over his shoulder.

"Mr. Blake?" exclaimed Dolores, tiptoeing to the table. "He's gone to sleep. Poor man! I know he must be awfully tired, else he would have waltzed with me again the last time I scratched your name."

"What you and Genevieve can see in him gets me!" muttered Ashton, with a shrug. "Look at him now. Needn't tell me he's asleep. He's intoxicated. That's what's the matter with him."

Dolores leaned far over the table toward Blake, sniffed, and drew back, with a judicial shake of her head. "Can't detect it. But, then, I couldn't expect to, with you in the room."

"Now, Dodie!"

She again leaned over the table. "See," she whispered. "His hand is tied up. It's hurt."

"Told you he's intoxicated," insisted Ashton.

The girl moved toward a davenport in the corner farthest from Blake.

"Come over here," she ordered. "It's a nuisance to sit it out with you, when it's one of the last waltzes. At least I won't let you disturb Mr. Blake."

"Mr. T. Blake, our heroic cave-man!" replied Ashton, as he followed her across the room.

"How you love him!" she rallied. "What's the cause of your jealousy?"

"Who says I'm jealous?"

"Of course there's no reason for you to be. He's not interested in me, and you're not in Genevieve—just now."

"My dear Dodie! You know you've always been the only one."

"Since the last!" she added. "But if it's not jealousy, what is it?—professional envy? You've been knocking him all the evening. You began it the day he came. What have you against him, anyway? He has never wronged you."

Ashton's eyes narrowed, and one corner of his mouth drew up.

"Hasn't he, though!" he retorted. "The big brute! I can't imagine how your mother can allow you and Genevieve to speak to him, when she knows what he is. And your uncle—the low fellow tried to blackmail him—accused him of stealing his bridge plans. First thing I know, he'll be saying *I* did it!"

"Did you?" teased the girl, as she seated herself on the heap of pillows at the head of the davenport.

Ashton's flushed face turned a sickly yellow. He fell, rather than seated himself, in the centre of the davenport.

"What—what—" he babbled; "you don't mean—No! I didn't!—I tell you, I didn't! They're my plans; I drew them all myself!"

"Why, Laffie! what is the matter with you?" she demanded, half startled out of her mockery. "Can it be you've mixed them too freely? Or is it the lobster? You've a regular heavy-seas-the-first-day-out look."

He managed to pull himself together and mutter in assent: "Yes, it must be the lobster. But the sight of that brute is enough to—to—"

"Then perhaps you had better leave the room," sweetly advised Dolores.

"Mr. Blake happens to be one of my friends."

"No, he isn't," corrected Ashton.

"Really!"

"No. I won't have it. You needn't expect me to have anything to do with you unless you cut him."

"Oh, Laffie! how could you be so cruel?" she mocked.

He was so far intoxicated that he mistook her sarcasm for entreaty. He responded with maudlin fervor. "Don't weep, Dodiekins! I'll be as easy on you as I can. You see, I must inform you on such things, if you're to be my *fiancée*."

She was quick to note his mistake, and sobbed realistically: *"Fi-fiancée!* Oh! Oh, Laffie! Bu-but you haven't asked me yet!"

He moved along the davenport nearer to her, and attempted to clasp her hand.

"You're a coy one, Dodiekins!" he replied. "Of course I'm asking you, you know that. You can't think I don't mean it. You know I mean it."

"Really?"

"Of course! Haven't I been trying to get a chance to tell you, all the evening? Of course I mean it! You're the fair maiden of my choice, Dodiekins, even if you aren't so rich as some."

"Fair?—but I'm a brunette," she corrected. "It's Genevieve you're thinking of. Confess now, it is, isn't it?"

"No, indeed, no!" he protested. "I prefer brunettes— always have! You're a perfect brunette, Dodiekins. I've always liked you more than Genevieve. You're the perfect brunette type, and you have all that *verve*—you're so *spirituelle.* Just say 'yes' now, and let's have it over with. To-morrow I'll buy you the biggest solitaire in town."

"Oh, Laffie!—the biggest? You're too kind! I couldn't think of it!" she mocked.

"But I mean it, Dodie, every word, indeed I do!" he insisted, ardently thrusting out an arm to embrace her.

She slipped clear, and sprang up, to stand just beyond his reach.

"So great an honor!" she murmured. "How can I deprive all the other girls of the greatest catch in town?"

"They've tried hard enough to catch me," he replied. "But I'd rather have you than all the blondes put together. I mean it, every word. I don't mind at all that you're not so rich as Genevieve. I'll have enough for two, as soon as the old man shuffles off this mortal coil. You'll bring him dead to rights on the will question. He likes you almost as well as he likes Genevieve. You're second choice with him."

"Second!—not the third?—nor the fourth? You're sure?"

"No, second; and you can count on it, he'll do the handsome thing by Mrs. Lafayette, even if he keeps me on an allowance. So now, say the word, and come and cuddle up."

"Oh, Laffie!—in here? We might disturb Mr. Blake."

"Blake!" he muttered, and he looked angrily at the big inert form half prostrate on the table. "He's intoxicated, I tell you—or if he's not, he ought to be. The insolence of him, hanging around Genevieve! I hope he is drunk! That would settle it all. We'd be rid of him then."

"'We'?" queried Dolores.

He caught her curious glance, and hastened to disclaim: "No, not we—Genevieve—I meant Genevieve, of course!"

Dolores affected a coquettish air. "Oh, Mr. Brice-Ashton! I do believe you want to get him out of the way."

"I? No, no!" he protested, with an uneasy, furtive glance at Blake.

"Don't try to fool me," she insisted. "I know your scheme. But it's of no use. If she doesn't take the hero, she'll accept the earl. Ah, me! To think you're still scheming to get Vievie, when all the evening you've pretended it was I!"

In the reaction from his fright, he sprang up and advanced on her ardently. "It *is* you, Dodie! you know it is. Own up, now—we're just suited to each other. It's a case of soul-mates!"

"Oh, is it, really?" she gushed. He sought to kiss her, but she eluded him coquettishly. "Wait, please. We must first settle the question. If it's a case of soul-mates, who's to be the captain?"

"See here, Dodie," he admonished; "we've fooled long enough. I'm in earnest. You don't seem to realize this is a serious proposal."

"Really?" she mocked. "A formal declaration of your most honorable intentions to make me Mrs. L. Brice-Ashton?"

"Of course! You don't take it for a joke, do you?"

She smiled upon him with tantalizing sweetness. "Isn't it? Well, it may not be. But how about yourself?"

"Dolores," he warned, "unless you wish me to withdraw my—"

"Your solemn suit!" she cut in. "With that and the case you mentioned, the matter is complete. A suit and a case make a suitcase. You have my permission to pack."

"Dodie! You can't mean it!"

"Can't I? You may pack yourself off and get a tailor to press your suit. He can do it better. Run along now. I'm going to make up to Mr. Blake for that waltz of yours that he wouldn't let me give to him."

"You flirt!" cried Ashton, flushing crimson. "I believe your heart is made of petrified wood."

"Then don't ask me to throw it at you. It might hurt your soft head."

"Dolores!" he warned her.

"Yes," she went on, pretending to misunderstand him. "Wouldn't it be awful?—a chunk of petrified wood plunking into a can of woodpulp!"

"I wish you to remember, Miss Gantry—" he began,

"Don't fret," she impatiently interrupted. "I'll not forget 'Miss Gantry,' and I wish you wouldn't so often. 'Dodie,' 'Dodie,' 'Dodie,' all the evening. It's monotonous."

"Indeed. Am I to infer, Miss Gantry, that you are foolish enough to play fast and loose with me?"

"You're so fast, how could I loose you?" she punned.

He muttered a French oath.

"Naughty! Naughty!" she mocked. "Swearing in French, when you know I don't speak it! Why not say, 'damn it' right out? That would sound better."

"See here, Dodie," he warned. "I've stood enough of this. You know you're just dying to say 'yes.' But let me tell you, if you permit this chance to slip by—"

"Oh, run along, do!" she exclaimed. "I want to think, and it's impossible with you around."

"Think?" he retorted. "I know better. What you want is a chance to coquet with him."

He looked about at Blake, with a wry twist in his lower lip.

"One enjoys conversing with a man once in a while," she replied, and she turned from him a glance of supreme contempt and loathing that pierced the thickness of his conceit. Disconcerted and confused, he beat a flurried retreat, jerking shut the door with a violent slam.

28

THE SHORTEST WAY

THE NOISE OF the door jarred Blake from his lethargy. He groaned and sluggishly raised his head. His face was bloodless and haggard, his bloodshot eyes were dull and bleared. He had the look of a man at the close of a drunken debauch.

Dolores hastened to him, exclaiming, "Mr. Blake, you are ill! I shall phone for a doctor!"

"No," he mumbled apologetically. "Don't bother yourself, Miss Dolores. It's not a doctor I need. I'm only—"

"You *are* ill! I'll call Genevieve." She started toward the door.

"Don't!" he cried. "Not her—for God's sake, not her!" He rose to his feet heavily but steadily. "I'm going—away."

"Going away? Where?" asked Dolores, puzzled and concerned.

"Alaska—Panama—anywhere! You're the right sort, Miss Dolores. You'll explain to her why I had to go without stopping to say good-bye."

"Of course, Mr. Blake—anything I can do. But why are you leaving?"

"Your mother—she told me."

"Told you what? I do believe you're dreaming."

Blake quivered. "Wish it *was* a nightmare!" he groaned. He steadied himself with an effort. "No use, though. She told me the truth about—your cousin. Said her feeling for me is only gratitude."

"What! Vievie's?—only gratitude? Don't you believe it! Mamma is rooting for Jeems. She may believe it; she probably does. She wants to believe it. She *wants* a countess in the family."

"She couldn't do better in that line, nor in any other," replied Blake with loyal friendship. "Jimmy is all right; he's the real thing."

"Yes, twenty-four carats fine!"

"Don't joke, Miss Dolores. I know you don't like him, but it's true, just the same. I knocked around a whole lot with Jimmy, in all sorts of places. I give it to you straight,—he's square, he's white, and he's what all kinds of people would call a gentleman."

"But as for being a man?" she scoffed.

Blake's dull eyes brightened with a fond glow.

"Man?" he repeated. "D'you think I'd fool around with one of these swell dudes? No; Jimmy is the real thing, and he's a thoroughbred."

"Such a cute little mustache!" mocked the girl.

"It's one of the few things I couldn't cure him of—-that and his monocle." Forgetful of self, Blake smiled at her regretfully and shook his head. "It's too bad, Miss Dolores. No use talking when it's too late; but couldn't you have liked him enough to forget the English part? You and he would sure have made a team."

"Yes, isn't it too bad? A coronet would fit my head just as

well as Vievie's. But mamma is so silly. She never thought of that."

Blake stared in surprise. "You don't mean—?"

"Mamma has been so busy saving Vievie from you, she's not had time to consider me."

"Say," exclaimed Blake, "I've half a notion you do like him. That would account for the way you keep at him with your nagging and teasing."

"You don't say!"

"Yes. That's the way one of my sisters used to treat me."

"How smart you are!" cried the girl, and she faced away from him petulantly, that he might not see her flaming cheeks. "Oh, yes, of course I like him! I'm head over heels in love with him! How could I help but be?"

"Some day you'll know such things aren't joking matters," he gravely reproved her.

She turned to him, unable longer to sustain her pretence. Her voice quavered and broke: "But it's—it's true! I do!"

She bent over with her face in her hands, and her slender form shook with silent sobs. He came quickly around to her, his eyes soft with commiseration. "You poor little girl! So you lose out, too!"

She looked up at him with her tearful dark eyes, and clutched eagerly at the lapel of his coat.

"Mr. Blake! He has told me how resolute you are. You must not give up! I'm certain Vievie likes you. If only mamma hadn't meddled! She's always messing things. It's just because she can't realize I'm in long frocks. If—if only she had seen how much grander it would be to make herself the mother-in-law of an earl, instead of a mere aunt-in-law!"

Blake's face darkened morosely. "That's the way things are—misdeal all around. Your mother is right. You've lost out; I've lost out. What's the use?"

"Surely you're not going to give up?" she demanded.

"I've never before been called a quitter; but—sooner I get out from between her and Jimmy, the better," he rejoined, and turning on his heel, he started toward the door by which Ashton had left.

"But, Mr. Blake," she urged, "wait. I wish to tell you—"

"No use," he broke in, without turning or stopping.

She was about to dart after him, when the door opened, and Ashton entered, carrying a bottle of champagne and a glass. He nodded familiarly to Blake and approached him with an air of easy good-fellowship.

Blake saw only the glass and the bottle. He glared at them, his face convulsed with fierce craving. Then he forced himself to avert his gaze. But as he started to turn aside, his jaw clenched and his eyes burned with a sudden desperate resolve. He stopped and waited, his face as hard as a granite mask. Dolores did not see his expression. She was eying Ashton, whom she sought to crush with her scorn.

"Ho!" she jeered. "So you're going to drown your sorrows in the flowing bowl. You ought to've remembered that absence makes the heart grow fonder."

To better show her contempt, she turned her back on him.

He instantly stepped forward beside Blake and began pouring out a glass of the champagne. He smiled suavely, but his eyes narrowed, and his full lower lip twisted askew.

"Look here, Blake," he began, "I know you're on the water-wagon; but you have it in for me for some reason, and I want to make it up with you. Take a glass of fizz with me."

Dolores whirled about and saw him with the glass of sparkling wine outreached to Blake, who was eying it with a peculiar oblique gaze.

"Lafayette Ashton!" she cried. "Aren't you ashamed of yourself?—aren't you ashamed?"

Ashton shrugged cynically, and urged the wine on Blake. "Come on! One glass wouldn't hurt a fly. I've heard of your wonderful success with the Zariba Dam. I want to congratulate you."

"Congratulate—that's it!" replied Blake, in a harsh, strained voice. "Best man wins. Loser gets out of the way. All right. I'll take the short-cut."

He reached out his bandaged right hand to take the glass. Dolores darted toward him, crying out shrilly in horrified protest: "Stop! stop! Mr. Blake! Think what you're doing!"

"I know what I'm doing," he said taking the glass and facing her with a smile that brought tears of pity to her eyes. "Your mother is right. I'm in your cousin's way. I'm going to get out of her way, and I'm going to do it in a fashion that'll rid her of me for keeps. Hell is nearer than Alaska."

"Wait! wait!" she cried, as he raised the glass to his lips. "For her sake, don't. Wait!"

"For her sake!" he rejoined, still with that heart-rending smile.

"Here's to her and to him—congratulations!"

He tossed down the wine at a swallow before she could clutch his upraised arm.

She turned upon Ashton, in a fury of scorn and anger. "You—you beast!"

"Why, what's the matter?" he protested, feigning innocence. "What's the harm in a glass of fizz?"

"You knew!" she cried, pressing upon him so fiercely that he gave back. "You knew what it means for him to drink anything—a single drop! You scoundrel!"

"There, now, Miss Dolores!" soothed Blake, patting her on the shoulder. "What's the use of telling him what he is? He knows it as well as we do. Anyhow, I didn't have to take the drink. I'm the only one to blame."

"Oh, Mr. Blake! how could you? How could you?" she cried.

"It was easy enough—doing it for her," he answered.

"For her! How can you say it?"

"Well, it's done now. Good-bye. I'm not likely to see you again soon.

It's a long trip from hell to heaven," he explained with grim humor.

Great as was his fortitude, she caught a glimpse of the anguish behind his mask. But his tone, as he swung Ashton around, repulsed her. "Come on, Mephistopheles. You've turned the trick. We've less than three hours before daylight. It's whiskey straight we're after."

29

LIGHT AND DARKNESS

NOT UNNATURALLY DOLORES failed to realize at once the utter ruin that Blake had brought upon himself by overthrowing the pillars of his temple. She was too intent upon her own tragedy. With Blake out of the way, Lord James would of course have no difficulty in winning Genevieve. There was now no hope for her.

She flung herself down in a chair, with a childlike wail. "Why did he do it? Oh! why did he do it? Oh, Jimmy! you'll never look at me now! If only I could *hurt* mamma!"

She bent over, weeping with bitter grief and anger.

She was still sobbing and crying when, sometime later, Lord James slipped hastily in from the cardroom. He closed the door swiftly and hurried toward the table, his eyes widening with his attempt to see clearly in the half light of the library.

"Tom, old man!" he called eagerly. "I'm now free to see you home. We'll slip out the side entrance—" He stopped short, perceiving that the big chair was empty, and that the figure in the chair across was not a man's.

"Er—beg pardon!" he stammered. "I—er—expected to find my friend here. Believe me, I would not have intruded—"

"So you d—don't consider me a friend!" retorted Dolores, vainly striving to hide her grief under a scornful tone.

"Miss Gantry!" he exclaimed. "Is it you?"

"It's not Vievie, that's certain. The sooner you run along and mind your business, the better."

"Miss Dolores, I—I really can't see why you hold such a dislike to me. I'll go immediately. I hadn't the remotest idea of intruding. You'll believe that? Only, y'know, I left Tom—Mr. Blake—in here. I came to go home with him. He was quite knocked-up. He should not have come to-night."

"You knew it!—you knew it, and left him in here alone!"

"Why, what do you mean, Miss Dolores? You alarm me! I left him asleep—fancied he'd not be disturbed in here—that an hour or so of sleep would freshen him up for the drive home."

"So you left him—alone—for mamma and that despicable creature to do their worst!"

"Miss Dolores, I—I beg your pardon, but I quite fail to take you. If anything has happened to Tom—"

"Regrets! What's the good of them, when it's too late?"

"Too late? Surely you cannot mean that he—?"

"Yes, the worst, the very worst,—and that miserable, detestable creature knew it when he offered him the wine. I believe he brought it in deliberately to tempt him."

"Wine? He drank! How long ago? Where is he now? I must try to check him."

"If only you could! But it's too late. He went off with Laffie."

"Not too late! The craving has been checked once—I've seen it done."

"But this time it's not the craving."

"How's that?"

"It's because he was driven desperate. He took it deliberately—intentionally."

"Impossible! Tom would never—"

"He would! He did! I saw him. But don't you blame him. She's the one. How could he know better, in his condition?—utterly tired out! She drove him to it, I tell you."

"She—Genevieve? I assure you—"

"No, no! mamma, of course! She told him a pack of lies—took away all his hope. She made him think that Vievie had never really loved him."

"Impossible!—unless your mother herself believes it."

"Oh, she believes it—or thinks she does. She's so anxious—so anxious!" The girl sprang up and stamped her foot. "Oh! I wish she and her meddling were in Hades!"

"My dear Miss Dolores!" protested Lord James, tugging nervously at his mustache.

She whirled upon him in hysterical fury. "Don't you call me that! Don't you dare call me that! I won't have it! I won't! I'm not your dear! I tell you—"

His look of blank astonishment checked her in the midst.

"I—I—I didn't mean—" she gasped. "Oh! what must you think of me!"

She turned from him, her face scarlet with shame. But in the same instant she remembered Blake, and forgot herself in the disaster to him.

"How selfish of me, when he— Poor Mr. Blake! What can be done? We must do something—at once!"

"If anything can be done!" said Lord James in a hopeless tone. "You say he took it deliberately?"

"Yes. Can't you see? Mamma had stuffed him with a lot of rot about gratitude—about Vievie sacrificing herself to him on account of gratitude. It's easy enough to guess mamma's little game. Oh! it's simply terrible! Of course he believed it, and of course he planned at once to go away— that's the kind of man he is! He planned to go away—run off—so that Vievie couldn't sacrifice herself."

"My word!"

"And just then Laffie Ashton came back with the wine. I believe he did it a-purpose—that he *wanted* to get Mr. Blake intoxicated!"

"The unmitigated cad! Yet why should he? It seems impossible that any man—"

"How should I know? He's vicious enough to do *anything*. But what does that matter? It's Mr. Blake. Can't you see why he took it? He was getting himself out of the way. I didn't understand then what he said—about the bad place being nearer than Alaska—but now I do. What he was determined to do was to get himself out of Vievie's way for good. The quickest that he could do it was to start drinking—go on a spree."

"Gad!"

"And now you stand here like a dummy, when there's a way to save him."

"Yes, yes! I'll go after him!" He started alertly toward the door.

She sprang before him, "No! What good would that do? You know he's set on saving Vievie. He'll not listen to you."

"Gad! That's true. He's hard enough to handle, at best. With this added—Yet I cannot but make the effort. I'll phone Mr. Griffith."

"Griffith? What's the use of wasting time? There's just one person who can save him, and you know it."

"No, unless Griffith—"

"Are you absolutely stupid? Can't you see? It's Vievie alone who—"

"Genevieve!"

"Now's the time for her to do something. She must prove her love. That alone can stop him."

"If she does love him."

"Can you doubt it?"

"She has doubted it."

"She may think she does. But it's all due to mamma's knocking and suggesting. Vievie loves him as much as he loves her. Needn't tell me! I know all about it. She made him fail—the time you took him up to Michamac. This time it's all mamma's fault. Vievie has got to save him!"

"Most assuredly it is hopeless unless she—"

"That's no reason for you to stand here gawking! You've got to go and tell her. She wouldn't listen to me; but you're a man and his friend. You can make her see the injustice of it all. She's to blame as much as mamma. This never would have happened if it hadn't been for her shillyshallying."

Lord James paused before replying, his clear gray eyes dark with doubt and indecision.

"My word!" he murmured. "Could I but feel certain— This second failure, in so short a time! There is her future to be considered, as well."

"Her future as Countess of Avondale!" scoffed the girl.

"No, I assure you, no!" he insisted. "Can you believe I could be so low?—and at such a time as this! It was of the consequences to her as well as to him—He has failed again. Can he ever win out, even should he have her aid?"

"You claim to be his friend!"

"For his sake, no less than hers—Consider what it would mean to a man of his nature, unable to check himself in his downward course, yet conscious that it was wrecking her happiness, possibly her life."

"It won't happen, not if she really loves him. You don't half know him. He could do anything—anything!—if she went to him and asked him to do it for her sake."

"Could I but be sure of that!"

"*Pah!* You pretend to be his friend. How long would you stand here fiddling and fussing, if you didn't want her yourself?"

"That—it is too much!" he said, his face pale and very quiet. "I had ventured to hope that I might overcome your dislike. Now I see that it is as well that you have refused to regard me other than as you have."

"Why, what do you mean? I—I don't understand."

"You have always been candid. Permit me to be the same. The truth is that I had begun to wish Tom success—not alone because of my friendship for him. But now I realize that his fight is hopeless. I shall do my utmost to make your cousin happy."

Dolores stared at him with dilating eyes. "Jimmy!" she whispered. "It can't be you mean that you—that you—?"

"Yes," he answered. "Pardon me for saying anything about it. I shall not bother you again."

"Oh, thank you!" she scoffed. "So now you're going to stay quiet and wait for Vievie to fling herself into your arms when she hears about your rival."

The young Englishman flushed and as suddenly became white, yet his voice was as steady as it was low. "I shall do whatever she wishes, if she finds that she does not love him."

"And that's all?" she jeered. "You'll calmly keep out of it while he commits *hara-kiri,* and then you'll step into his shoes."

"No. I shall go to her at once and ask her to save my friend—if she loves him."

"You will?"

"Yes."

"You will!" cried the girl, her cheeks flushing and her black eyes sparkling with delight— "You will! Oh, Jimmy!"

Even as the words left her lips, she became conscious of what she had done, and her flush brightened into a vivid scarlet blush. She turned and fled from him, panic-stricken.

He stood dazed, unable at first to believe what her tone and look had betrayed to him. When, after some moments, his doubt gave way to certainty, his face lighted with what might be termed joyous exasperation.

"My word!" he murmured. "The little witch! I'll pay her out jolly well for it all!"

But his blissfully exultant vexation was no more than a flash that deepened the gloom with which he recalled the disaster to his friend.

"Gad!" he reproached himself. "What am I thinking of—with her and Tom—"

He turned quickly to the door of the cardroom.

30

THE END OF DOUBT

WHEN THE ENGLISHMAN entered the card-room, the last of the players to linger at their table had risen and were taking their leave of Genevieve. Her father and aunt were disputing over their last game. But at sight of the newcomer, Mrs. Gantry bowed and beckoned to him, instantly forgetful of her argument.

"You are always in time, Earl," she remarked. "We are just about to leave. May I ask if you have seen Dolores?"

"Not a moment ago. I daresay she has gone for her wraps."

"Huh! Ran off from you, eh?" bantered Mr. Leslie. "She's a coltish kitten. Didn't scratch, did she?"

"She misses no opportunity for that, the hoyden!" put in Mrs. Gantry. "Ah, Earl, we are the last." She rose and went to meet Genevieve, who was coming to them from the farther door. "My dear girl, I congratulate you! It has been a grand success!"

"Thank you, Aunt Amice," replied Genevieve in rather a listless tone.

"Must you be going?"

"Lord Avondale has just come in to let me know that it is time."

"Er—beg pardon," said Lord James. "I wish to speak with Miss Leslie before going."

"Ah, in that case," murmured Mrs. Gantry, with a gratified smile, "you are excused, of course! Herbert, you may see me out."

Mr. Leslie looked from Lord James to his daughter doubtfully. But the Englishman was fingering a pack of cards with seeming nonchalance, and Genevieve met her father's glance with a quiet smile. He shook his head, and went out with Mrs. Gantry.

As they left the room, Lord James faced Genevieve with a sudden tensity that compelled her attention.

"What is it?" she asked, half startled by his manner. "You said you wished to speak with me?"

"If you'll be so kind as to come into the library. It's a most serious matter. There'll be less chance of interruptions."

She permitted him to lead her in to her former seat at the library table. He took the big chair across from her.

"You look so grave," she said. "Please tell me what it is."

"Directly. Yet first I ask you to prepare yourself. Something has happened—most unfortunate!"

She bent toward him, startled out of her fatigue and lassitude. "You alarm me!"

"I cannot help it," he replied. "Genevieve, matters have come to an unexpected crisis. There can be no more delay. I must ask you to make your decision now. Do you love Tom?"

"You have no right to ask that. I did not give you the right. You said you would wait."

"I am not asking for myself," he insisted. "It is for him. He has the right to know."

"The right? How?" she asked, with growing agitation. "I do not understand. You spoke of some misfortune. Has papa—?"

"Quite the contrary. Yet Tom is in a very bad way, and unless you—"

"Tom ill—ill?" she cried. "And I did not realize it! That I should have been angered—should have left him—because I thought he was in a rage—and all the time it was because of his suffering, his illness! It was despicable of me—selfish! Oh, Tom, Tom!"

She covered her face with her hands, and bent over, quivering with silent grief and penitence.

"You have answered me," said Lord James, regarding her with grave sympathy. "You love him."

She looked up at him, dry-eyed, her face drawn with anxiety. "Where is he? Why aren't you with him? He has a doctor? He must have the best!"

"That rests with you, Genevieve," he replied. "There is one person alone who can save him—if she loves him enough to try."

The truth flashed upon her. She stared at him, her eyes dilating with horror. "It is *that* you mean! He has failed—again!"

He sought to ease her despair. "Believe me, it is not yet too late— Permit me to explain."

"Explain?" she asked. "What is there to explain? He has failed!" Her voice broke in a sob of uncontrollable grief. "I tried to forget, still hoping he was strong—that he would prove himself strong. How I have hoped and prayed—and now!"

She bent over, with her face on the table, in a vain effort to conceal and repress her grief.

Lord James leaned forward, eagerly insistent. "You must listen to me. He has not had fair play. Such a gallant fight as he was making! I believe he would have won, I really believe he would have won, had it not been for that woman."

"What woman?" asked Genevieve, half lifting her head.

"Pardon me," he replied. "But your aunt— It was most uncalled for, most unfair. It seems she sought him out— to-night, of all times!—when he was pegged—completely knocked-up. You have seen that yourself. This was after we deserted him."

"Deserted? Yes, that is the word—deserted!"

"At the moment when he tasted the wine, quite unaware of what he was doing. We deserted him at the time when he had utmost need of us. What clearer proof of his great strength than that he fought off the temptation?"

"Yet now you say—?"

"He fought it off then. He proved himself as strong as even you could desire. When I hastened in I found him still where I am sitting, but doubled over, utterly spent— asleep, poor chap. His hand was bleeding. He had shattered your—he had crushed one of the glasses with his fist."

"Crushed a glass! But why?"

"To prevent himself from drinking what was in it. Can't you see? The struggle must have been frightful; yet he won. Had I but foreseen! I fancied he would be undisturbed in here—would get a bit of refreshing sleep to pull him up. But your aunt came in. She took her opportunity—convinced him that you did not love him; that your feeling was only gratitude."

Genevieve bent over, with renewed despair. "And for that he gave up the fight!"

"He fought and won when we left him, when we deserted him in his need. It was only after your aunt had convinced him that you did not—"

"He foresaw that he would lose!" she cried. "He foresaw! But I—I could not believe it possible!"

"But you do not understand. It was not that he really lost. He did not give way because of weakness. He did it deliberately—"

"Deliberately?" she gasped. Surprise gave place to an outflashing of scorn. "Deliberately! Oh, that he could do such a thing—deliberately!"

"No, no! I must insist. To cut himself off from you, that was his purpose. He thought to save you from sacrificing yourself. However mistaken he was, you must see how high a motive—how magnanimous was his intention."

But the girl was on the verge of hysteria, and quite beyond reason.

"You may believe it—I don't! I can't! He's weak—utterly weak!"

"Genevieve, no! There's still time to save him. A word from you, if you love him."

"Love him!" she cried, almost beside herself. "How can I love him? He did it deliberately! I despise him!"

"You are vexed—angry. Pray calm yourself. I remember what you had to say about him, there on the steamer, coming up from Aden. You loved him then."

"But now— Oh, how could he? How could he?"

The Englishman failed to understand the real cause of her half-frenzied anger and despair—the thought that Blake had ruined himself deliberately. "But don't you see it was not weakness? He proved it when he shattered the glass. His hand was cut and bleeding. He has proved that he can master that craving. I've sought to explain how it was. It is not yet too late. A word from you would save him, a single word!"

"No. It is too late. I can't see it as you do. It was weakness—weakness! I cannot believe otherwise."

"Yet—if you love him?"

"James, it is generous of you—noble!—when you yourself—"

"That's quite out of it now. It's of him I am thinking, and of you."

"Never of yourself!" she murmured. She looked down for a short moment. When she again raised her eyes, she had regained her usual quiet composure. She spoke seriously and with a degree of formality: "Lord Avondale, when you honored me with your offer, you asked me to wait before giving you a final answer."

He was completely taken unawares. "I—I— To be sure. But I cannot permit you—Your happiness is my first consideration."

"It is that disregard of self, that generosity, which enables me to speak. As I told you, I can now give you no more than the utmost of my esteem and affection. But if you are willing to take that as a beginning, perhaps, later on, I may be able to return your love as you deserve."

"But you— I do not know how to say it— In justice to yourself, no less than to him, you should make sure."

"I have never been more sure," she replied. "You have been most generous and patient. It is not right or considerate for me to longer delay my decision."

"Er—very good of you, very!" he murmured, gazing down at his interlocked fingers. "Yet—if you would care to wait—to make sure, y' know."

"But why should I wait? No, James, I am clear in what I am doing. I know that I can trust you absolutely."

Lord James slowly raised his head and met her gaze, too intent upon repressing the stress of his emotions to perceive the big fur-clad form that stood rigid in the doorway beyond Genevieve.

"Miss Leslie," he said, speaking in the same formal and serious tone that she had used in giving her decision, "I am then to understand that you accept my proposal—you will marry me?"

"Within the year, if you desire," she responded, without any sign of hesitancy.

"It's very good of you!" he replied. "I shall devote myself to your happiness."

If his voice lacked the joyful ring and his look the ardent delight of a successful lover, she failed to heed it. He rose and bent over the table with grave gallantry to kiss the hand that she held out to him.

"Gratulations!" said a harsh voice, seemingly almost in their ears.

They looked up, startled. Blake stood close to them, at the end of the table, with his soft hat in his half-raised left hand, and his shaggy fur coat hanging limp from his bowed shoulders. He stood with perfect steadiness. Only in the fixed stare of his bloodshot eyes and the twitching of the muscles in his gray-white face could they perceive the mental stress and excitement under which he was laboring.

"Tom!" stammered the Englishman. "You here!"

"Couldn't get Ashton started," replied Blake. His voice was hoarse and rasping but not thick. Though he spoke slowly, his enunciation was distinct. "His man just carried him out. I've been waiting to slip out, unseen, this way. I ask you to excuse me. Long's I'm here, I'll make the best of it I can. Congratulations to you! Best man wins!"

While he was speaking, Genevieve had drawn her hand out of the unconscious clasp of Lord James and slowly risen from her chair. Her face was as white as Blake's; her eyes were wide with fear and pity and horror.

"You!—how could you do it?" she gasped. "When I had given you the second chance—to fail again!" The sight of his powerful jaw, clenched and resolute, stung her into an outburst of angry scorn. "Fail, fail! always fail! yet with that look of strength! To come here with that look, after failing again so utterly, miserably—in my house! You coward!"

"That's it," assented Blake in a dead monotone. "Only pity is you couldn't see it sooner. But you know me now. Ought to 've known me from the first. I didn't get drunk there in Mozambique 'cause I hadn't the stuff. You might have known that. But now it's settled. I've proved myself a brute and a fizzle—been proving it ever since Ashton got a bottle and showed me into a little room. We've been guzzling whiskey in there ever since. His man took him out dead drunk. So far I'm only—"

"Tom!" broke in Lord James. "No more of that! Tell the truth—tell her why you did it!"

"Tell her—when she's guessed already. But if you say so, Jimmy—It's the first time I ever owned up I'm a quitter. Great joke that, when all my life I haven't been anything else,—hobo, fizzle, quitter, bum—"

"Gad! Not that drivel! If you can't explain to her, then keep silent."

"No, I don't keep silent till I've had my say," rejoined Blake morosely. "Needn't think I don't know just what I'm saying and what I'm doing." His voice harshened and broke with a despair that was all the more terrible for the deadness of his tone. "God! That's why the whiskey won't work. I've poured it down like water, but it's no use—it won't work! I can't forget I've lost out!"

Genevieve leaned toward him, half frenzied, her face crimson and her gentle eyes ablaze with scorn. "And you— you!—claiming to be sober—come in here and say that to me!—that you've deliberately sought to intoxicate yourself in my house—in my house! You haven't even the decency to go away to do it! You must flaunt your shame in my face!"

"I told you I meant to slip out unseen," he mumbled, for the moment weakening in his determination to vilify himself. "Didn't think you'd give me the gaff—when it was all for you."

"For me!" she cried, in a storm of hysteria—"for me! Oh! To destroy all my love for you—my trust in the courage, the strength, the heroism I thought was yours! Oh! And to prove yourself a brute, a mere brute!—here in my own house!—my guest! Oh! oh! I hate you! I hate you!"

*Lord James dropped without a groan. "You
coward!—you murderer!" she gasped.*

She flung herself, gasping and quivering, into her chair, in a desperate effort to regain self-control.

Blake bent over her and murmured with profound tenderness: "There, there, little girl! Don't take on so! I ought to 've cleared out right at first—that's a fact. But I didn't mean to bother you. Just blundered in. But I'm glad to know you've found out the truth. Long's you know for sure that you hate me, 't won't take you long to feel right toward him. He's all I'm not. Mighty glad you're going to be happy. Good-bye!"

Genevieve had become very still. But she neither looked up at him nor spoke when he stopped. He turned steadily about and started toward the door of the cardroom. Lord James thrust back the heavy chair and sprang to place himself before his friend.

"Wait, Tom!" he demanded. "Can't you see? She's overcome. Good God! You can't go off this way! You must wait and tell her the truth—how it happened—why you did it!"

Blake looked at him quietly and spoke in a tone of gentle warning, as one speaks to a young child: "Now, now, Jimmy boy, get out of my way. Don't pester me. Just think how easily I could smash you—and I'm not so far from it. Stand clear, now."

"No! In justice to yourself—to her!"

"That's all settled. Let me by."

He stepped to one side, but Lord James again interfered. "No, Tom, not till you've told her! You shall not go!"

The Englishman stood resolute. Blake shook his head slowly, and spoke in a tone of keen regret: "Sorry, Jimmy; but if you *will* have it!"

His bandaged right fist drove out and struck squarely on

the point of his friend's jaw. His nerves of sensation were so blunted by the liquor he had drunk that he struck far harder than he intended. Lord James dropped without a groan, and lay stunned. Blake stared down at him, and then slowly swung around to look at Genevieve.

She had risen and stood with her hands clutching the edge of the table.

Her face was distorted with horror and loathing.

"You coward!—you murderer!" she gasped.

"Yes, that's it," he assented—"brute, drunkard, coward, murderer—all go together. You're right to hate me! But you can't hate me half as much as I hate myself. That's hell all right—to hate yourself."

Suddenly he flung out his arms toward her and his voice softened to passionate tenderness. "God! but it's worth the price!—to save you, Jenny! I'd do it all over again, a thousand times, to make you happy, little girl!"

She shrank back and flung up her arm in a gesture of bewilderment, which he mistook for fear.

"Don't be afraid," he reassured. "I'm going."

He turned hastily, stooped to feel the heart of the unconscious man, and rose to swing across to the cardroom door. He passed out swiftly and closed the door behind him, without pausing for a backward glance.

Genevieve stared after him, dazed and bewildered by her half realization of the truth. The door had closed between them—what seemed to her an age had passed—when the full realization of what he had done flashed in upon her clouded brain like a ray of glaring white light.

She flung out her arms and cried entreatingly: "Tom! Tom—dearest!"

She tried to dart around the table, but swayed and tottered, barely saving herself from the fall by sinking into a chair. The heavy, muffled clang of the street door came to her as from a vast distance. The merciful darkness closed over her.

31

A BRIDGE GAME

THE COLD SNAP at Michamac had been broken for nearly a month, and work on the bridge was progressing with unprecedented rapidity.

Two days after the ball, Ashton had returned to the bridge sobered and chastened. The change in him may have been due to another cut in his allowance, or to a peppery interview during which Mr. Leslie had sought to browbeat him into resigning his position.

Whatever the cause of his change of heart, Ashton had so far proved himself almost feverishly eager to establish a record. Griffith, badly shaken by the failure and disappearance of Blake, had been peremptorily ordered South by his physician. Seizing the opportunity, Ashton, instead of interfering with the work, as McGraw expected, had astonished the phlegmatic general foreman by pushing operations with utmost zeal and energy.

More mechanics and laborers had been hired, and the augmented force divided into three eight-hour shifts. All day, in sun or fog or snow, and all night, under the bluish glare of the arc-lights, the expert bridgemen toiled away upon the gaunt skeleton of the gigantic bridge, far out and above the abyss of the strait. Not a moment of the twenty-four hours was lost.

But the Resident Engineer's brief spurt of energy had already notably relaxed, when, one sunny day near the end of March, a man not a member of the train crew nor a regular passenger came in on the afternoon train. As he emerged from under a coal car, one of the switchmen stared at him blankly, swore a few lurid oaths, and laughed.

The brake-rider had paid for his ride, though not in money. He limped as he walked off, and the gray pallor of his unshaven face was grotesquely shaded and blotched with coal dust. His shoddy clothes were torn and mud-stained, his soft hat begrimed and shapeless, his cheap shoes too far gone for repair. Yet for all his shiftless footwear and his limp, his stride was long and quick.

A watchman caught sight of him, and hurried after, to warn him off the grounds. The hobo disappeared behind a pile of girders. When the watchman turned the corner, his quarry had disappeared. He shook his head doubtfully at the bridge-service train, which was backing out along the track before him with a load of eyebars and girders. There was reason to believe that the hobo had boarded it; but if so, it was under too speedy headway for the rheumatic watchman to follow.

His suspicions were well founded. As the train clattered past the unlovely buildings of rough lumber and sheet iron clustered about the bridge terminus, the stranger clambered up between two of the swaying cars and perched himself upon the wheel-like top of the handbrake. Seated thus, with feet dangling and hands thrust carelessly into the pockets of his disreputable coat, he gazed intently about at the bridge, regardless of the bitter sting of the lake wind.

The train rattled out across the shore span and along the anchor arm of the south cantilever. The brake-rider scrutinized the immense webs and lofty towers with the look of a father greeting his first-born. The train rolled on out between the towers and beyond, where swarms of carpenters and laborers were laying beams and stringers and floor planking and piling up immense stacks of material to be used farther out. The finishing gangs were following up the steel workers as fast as they could be pushed.

Beyond them, out near the end of the extension-arm, the electro-magnetic cranes of the huge main traveller were sorting and shifting forward a great heap of structural steel. The material thus handled came within the reach of the smaller traveller, which crouched upon the top-chords like a skeleton spider, swinging out the steel as wanted to the end of the unfinished suspension span.

At sight of the great heaps of structural steel and flooring material and of the ponderous main traveller so far out toward the end of the overhang, the glow in the sunken eyes of the brake-rider died out, and his grimy brows gathered in a troubled frown.

The airbrakes hissed, the cars bumped and clanked, and the train came to a laborious stop with the outermost cars beneath the lofty latticed framework of the main traveller. At once the electro-magnetic cranes began to descend, ready to swing off whole carloads of steel in their magic monstrous clutch.

The brake-rider had slipped down and was walking rapidly outward along the narrow plank footway. As he advanced he looked about him with an anxious gaze, but it was at the unfloored substructure of the bridge, not at the awesome spectacle of the swift-flowing, ice-covered stream a hundred and fifty feet beneath. Once he paused and stooped over to look closer at a rivet head.

He hurried on to where, under the smaller traveller, the uncompleted south part of the central, or suspension, span poised dizzily in space, over-arching the abyss. Many yards of gap still yawned between its tip and the tip of the sections that strained out to meet it from the end of the north cantilever.

The sections built on to the southern part of the central span had brought the overhang still more dizzily out over the broad strait. The wonder was that men could be found who were willing to work day after day in a position of such real peril. Yet since Ashton's change of attitude, McGraw had experienced no difficulty in securing and holding enough and to spare of expert bridge-workers, who toiled and sweat at their task with seemingly never a thought of the abyss that yawned beneath them.

When the brake-rider left the train, the men of the evening shift, just come on, were swarming about the end of the overhang like ants upon the tip of a broken twig,— alert-eyed, quick-handed, cool-brained "Sons of Martha," who, balanced unconcernedly in mid-air on narrow stringers, clenched fast the rivets in Death's steel harness. During the lulls between the furiously rattling volley-blows of the electric riveting-machines they grumbled about the deterioration of smoking tobacco or speculated on next season's baseball scores.

With his beefy shoulders braced against the last

top-chord post, McGraw stood chewing the end of a fat black cigar while he watched the placing of a bottom-chord of a new sub-panel. From the ox-like unconcern of his stolid face and deepset eyes, his interest in the proceedings seemed to be of the most casual nature. But at the slightest gesture of his pudgy hand, cranes swung up and down, men hauled upon guy ropes, riveters moved alertly forward with their machines.

One of the men caught McGraw's eye, and jerked a thumb over his shoulder. The general foreman looked about and saw the grimy stranger standing on the plank walk a few yards back. McGraw stared, ruminated, signed to a sub-foreman, and walked stolidly back along a string of single planks to where the stranger stood waiting for him.

The soft hat of the brake-rider was now pulled down over his eyes, and his chin was hidden in the upturned collar of his tattered coat. As McGraw approached him, he drew back out of the deafening clatter of the riveting-machines. McGraw followed, his heavy face of a sudden grown truculent. He came up close to the stranger.

"You dirty bum!" he threatened. "What you doin' here? Get t' hell outer here, or I'll trow you over!"

The stranger pushed back his hat, and met the other's menacing stare with a grin. His pale blue eyes were twinkling. McGraw's heavy jowl fell slack.

"Well, McGraw—thought you wouldn't forget me this soon. What's the latest from Mr. Griffith?"

"Jacksonville—Holy saints! you've sure been lushin' some, Mr. Blake."

"Looks like it; but as it happens I haven't. Tried to turn

loose, but got switched. Instead of a spree, I've been on a bum—tour of the Sunny South."

"Bum?" repeated McGraw.

"Yes. Needed a change. Too much indoors work; so I got out."

"*Uh?*" mumbled McGraw in slow astonishment. "No booze?"

"No. That's the funny part of it. Didn't touch a drop of anything. I used to be afraid of it when I wasn't on a tear, but now I don't even think of it. Seems as if I couldn't get up a thirst if I tried. Can't make it out."

"Sick," commented McGraw.

"No. I'm eating like a horse, and getting my strength back, hand over fist."

"In your head," qualified McGraw, touching his forehead.

"Guess that's it. Must be. Never before opened the throttle and cut loose, to come to a dead stop this way. It's as if you got up a full head of steam, and then drew the fire. Mighty queer, though,—my head is as clear as crystal."

"Huh," grunted McGraw ambiguously. "Come to take your job—assistant?"

Blake's face darkened. "No, just dropped by on my way to Canada. Thought I'd have a look at my—" he paused, and altered his statement—"that I'd see how your old scrap-heap is getting along."

"Huh."

"But, long as I'm here, guess I'll take hold for a turn or two, just to keep my hand in."

"Good! Need an engineer."

"I might as well earn enough for railroad fare. This

brake-beaming and riding the rods isn't as soft a snap as it used to seem when I was a kid."

"Soft? Y'look like a second-hand garbage-can!"

"Thanks. Where's your resident swell?"

"Quarters. Hit up the pace—work—been goin' some." McGraw swept his fat arm around in an explanatory gesture. "Laid down a'ready."

"All right. I'm on the job. But I've got to get some sleep soon. And say, just pick out a spry kid to steer me up against the wash-house, will you?"

McGraw signed to the nearest man. "Pete—Mr. Blake, our 'Sistant Engineer—t' my room." He turned to Blake. "Help y'self. Safety razor 'n' tub handy. Clothes in locker. You c'n wear 'em over to commissary. Guess you c'n git into 'em."

He nodded, unaware that he had said anything humorous, and pivoted around to return to his work. Blake limped briskly away after the puzzled but silent Pete. At the bunkhouse Pete showed his charge into McGraw's room, and went to order hot water for a bath.

When he returned, Blake, with half the stubble already shorn from his lathered face, handed over a telegraph message addressed to Griffith.

Eager to be of service to the Consulting Engineer, the man hurried the message to the telegraph operator. The latter, no less friendly to Griffith, corrected the address to the sick engineer's hotel in Tampa, and wired the despatch "rush."

The message could hardly have been more laconic:

On the job.   Tom.

When Pete returned for further orders, he met the Assistant Engineer at the door of the commissary, baggily draped in a suit of McGraw's clothes, which fitted nowhere except across the shoulders.

Blake dismissed him, and went in to outfit himself with a costume in keeping with his position. Almost asleep, he then went back to the bunkhouse, stumbling and yawning, and stretched out in McGraw's bed, utterly fagged.

32

LAFFIE PLAYS—BLAKE TRUMPS

AFTER AN EVENING at poker with one of the new bridge-workers, Ashton had retired at midnight. He had not heard of Blake's coming, for McGraw had presumed that the Assistant Engineer had reported to the office before turning in to sleep.

When he awoke, the sun was half way up the eastern sky. He yawned, glanced at the sun, and rang for his breakfast. It was presently brought in to him by his English valet, who, like the chef, was not unused to the city social hours of his employer. Ashton did not trouble to go into his elegant little dining-room, but ordered the meal served at his bedside.

Sometime later, Blake, over in the bunkhouse, opened his eyes, yawned, and sprang out into the middle of McGraw's unaesthetic room. He had slept eighteen hours without a break. He awoke still stiff and sore, but brimming over with energy, and hungry as a shark. He gave himself a cold rubdown, jumped into his new clothes, and ran to the cookhouse for a hearty meal.

When he came out again, he headed straight across the tracks for the office of the Resident Engineer. He smiled ironically as he noted the green and white paint and the trimmings of the verandahs with which Ashton had endeavored to give a bungalow effect to the shack-like structure. But as he swung up the steps into the front verandah, the grimness of his look increased and the humor vanished. His heavy tread through the weather vestibule announced his entrance into the office. He took no pains to walk softly.

Ashton, attired in a lounging-robe of scarlet silk, was half reclining in an easy chair. The big desk beside him was littered with engineering journals, reports, and blue-prints of bridge plans, topped with detail drawings in ink of the long central span. The Resident Engineer was not studying the plans. He was reading a French novel of the variety seldom translated.

At Blake's entrance, he looked up, his delicate high-arched eyebrows gathered in a frown of annoyance. Almost in the same moment he recognized the intruder, and started to his feet in open alarm.

"How!—why!" he stammered. "You here? I thought you—that after—"

"Too bad, eh?" bantered Blake. "But you mustn't blame yourself. You did your best. But accidents will happen."

"Then you're—you're not—Yet you look—"

"Appearances often deceive," quoted Blake lightly. "You gave me a great start-off—had me going South. So I went."

"Going South?"

"Yes. But that's all by-the-bye, as my friend, the Right Honorable the Earl of Avondale, would say. I'm here now for you to enter my acceptance of the standing offer of the Assistant Engineership."

"You—you agree to take it—under me?" cried Ashton in astonishment.

"Why not?" asked Blake with well-feigned surprise.

"Why, of course if—You see, it's—it's rather unexpected," Ashton sought to explain as he regained assurance. "Old Griffith wrote me about the way you had put through the Zariba Dam. After that I never dreamed you'd accept any position as Assistant."

"Well, I like to please Grif," was Blake's easy reply. "He's been worrying because office work uses me up. Nothing suits me better than an outdoor job, and I happened to take a fancy to your bridge the other time I came. It's a good deal like those plans of mine that got mislaid. Of course you can't know that."

"No, of course not!" assented Ashton, moistening his lower lip.

"Course not," repeated Blake. "So I can't blame you if you find it hard to believe that my plans would have been accepted before you drew yours if they hadn't been mislaid."

"Then you—no longer accuse Mr. Leslie of—having taken them?" Ashton ventured to ask.

"Couldn't prove it on him, could I? No use *baa-ing* over spilt milk. Well, you understand I'm on the job now; I've accepted the offer."

"Ye-es," reluctantly admitted Ashton. "Not that I see the use. There's no need for another engineer."

"That's no lie. One *engineer* is enough," said Blake dryly. "You sure proved yourself one when you planned this little old cantilever. However, I'm short of cash. I'll hang around and do what I can. May be able to save you bother by carrying orders out to McGraw or checking over reports for you."

He picked up the vellum-cloth drawings of the central span and some of the blueprints, and began in a matter-of-fact manner to roll them up.

"Hold on!" sharply interposed Ashton. "What are you about?"

"I'm going to bunk with McGraw. Thought I'd take these over and try to get in touch with the work."

"No, you sha'n't! I can't allow you to take those. They're the original drawings. They must not be taken out of my office."

"Original drawings?" repeated Blake in a tone of perfect innocence.

"Excuse me. I took them for copies."

"C-copies!" stuttered Ashton, turning white even to his lips.

"Yes. Hasn't Grif the originals?" asked Blake in a careless tone that was barely touched with surprise.

Ashton rallied from his fright. "No, you're mistaken, completely mistaken! These are the originals. I drew them myself. I couldn't trust to a draughtsman."

"Sure not, such important work as this span of yours. Grif tells me there's never before been anything built like this suspension span," agreed Blake, bending over to study the drawings. "But you'll admit some of these figures are rather slipshod for work on original drawings put in to win a competition."

"But I—I didn't compete. The idea came to me too late for that. I tried my utmost to be in time for the contest. I was working fast to get my plans drawn. That's why I made some errors—which you may have noticed."

Blake looked up with an ironical smile.

Ashton moistened his lips, hesitated, and asked in an uneasy tone: "About—about how long do you expect to stay? I suppose you will stay, won't you?"

"Well, three or four days, maybe. As you probably know, Grif screwed the company up to offer me a stiff salary— on the strength of that Zariba work, I suppose. I didn't intend to take the offer at all, but my clothes were—they got rather out of repair on my Southern tour, and I came on up here without stopping at my tailor's. Happened to leave my checkbook, too, and it's a long walk to town."

"Oh, if it's only that you're strapped," Ashton hastened to reply; "I'll be pleased to draw you a check—little loan, you know—anything from a hundred to a thousand. No hurry about paying it back. I'm flush."

"You're too kind!" said Blake dryly.

"It's nothing—nothing—a mere trifle!" assured Ashton, with a touch of condescension. "You know I'll have scads of money to burn some day." He opened a drawer of his desk and took out a checkbook. "I know you can't be anxious to hang around a dreary hole like this. Suppose I make it five thousand? You can keep the money as long as you wish. There's just time for you to catch the extra train we're sending down to the junction for more steel."

"Thanks. But I need a good rest," said Blake.

"I'll think it over, and let you know. Maybe I'll decide to loaf around with you a few days and save borrowing."

"Oh, well, if you can stand this jumping-off place," replied Ashton, visibly disappointed.

He glanced down into the open drawer, and his eyes narrowed with a look of furtive eagerness that did not escape Blake. In a corner of the drawer was a squat black bottle and a tumbler. Ashton lifted them out and poured a half-glassful of whiskey that was thick and oily with age.

"The real stuff!" he said, holding out the tumbler to Blake. "Older than your grandmother. Let's wet your welcome to Michamac!"

"Here's how!" replied Blake, with a geniality of tone and manner that diverted the other's attention from the glint in his eyes. He took the glass and deliberately twisted his hand backward so that the whiskey poured out on the bare floor in front of the desk.

"Look out! You're spilling it!" exclaimed Ashton.

"No, just pouring it," explained Blake. "German custom. Next time you're in a beer-garden do it, and they'll let you know what it means."

"Means?" echoed Ashton.

"In this case, it means I never drink when I'm on a job. One of my rules. Told you I had accepted that standing offer, didn't I?"

"Yes. But I didn't know that you—"

"Well, you know now. I'm on this job."

Ashton shot a covert glance at his square-jawed opponent.

"Then it's a mistake—the report that you refused to accept any position from Mr. Leslie," he murmured.

"Mistake? No," curtly answered Blake. "Needn't try to fool me. Mr. Leslie turned the bridge over to the Coville Company months ago."

"Fool you?" sneered Ashton. "You're too easy! The Coville Company is only another name for Papa Leslie."

"Look here," warned Blake. "You're apt to learn soon that some lies aren't healthy."

"It's the truth," replied Ashton, giving back a little, but insistent on the facts. "It's a way he avoids responsibility. But he owns ninety-nine per cent of the stock. Griffith must have told you that. He knows all about it."

This obstinate insistence, despite the young fellow's evident fear, convinced Blake. He half raised his clenched fist.

"And I fell to it!" he muttered. "Let him bunco me into putting through that dam for him! Scheme to make me take his money!"

"You as good as put half a million into his pocket," jeered Ashton.

"What do I care about that?" rejoined Blake.

"It's that fifty thousand bonus. He'll be trying to force it on me."

Ashton thought he had misunderstood. "Don't fear he'll not pay up. He's good pay when you have it in black and white. There's still time to catch the train. You'll find your check waiting you at the offices of the company."

Blake did not reply. One of the dimensional figures on a blueprint of the south cantilever had caught his glance, and he had bent over to peer at it. A sudden stillness seemed to have fallen upon him.

After a perceptible pause, he asked in a tone that was very low and quiet and deliberate: "Would you mind telling me if this blueprint was made direct from your originals—from the original drawings used in ordering the structural steel?"

"Yes, of course," answered Ashton. "Why?"

"You are sure?"

"I'm certain. You don't think I'd let any one with a pen fool around my drawings, do you?"

"Lord, no! Might correct your damn errors!" cried Blake, all his stony calm fluxing to lava before an outflare of volcanic excitement. "You fool!—Lord! Wasting time! Sit down—scratch off an order. That cantilever must be relieved P.D.Q.—every ounce skinned off it!"

"What—what's that?" asked Ashton, staring blankly. He had never before seen Blake agitated.

"You fool!" shouted Blake. "You've got that outer arm loaded down with material 'way beyond the margin of safety. You damned fool, you made an error here in the figures—over the bottom-chords and posts. They'll hold anything, once the suspension span is completed, but now! Lord! McGraw is a mule—he'll insist on a written order. Weather report says wind. And another train loading to run out on the overhang, when we ought to be hauling steel off!"

"Oh, we ought, ought we?" blustered Ashton, venturing bravado in view of Blake's agitation. "Who d'you think is running this bridge, you barrel-house bum? I'll give you to understand I'm the engineer in charge here. You're my Assistant—my Assistant! D'you hear?"

"Yes, yes!" urged Blake. "Only scratch off an order! There's no time to lose! I'll do the work. For God's sake, hurry! You've a hundred men out there on that deadfall—a million dollars' worth of steel-work! Those bottom-chords may buckle any second!"

From eager pleading, Blake burst out in an angry roar: "Damn you! Get busy! Write that order!"

Seized with desperate fear of the big form that leaned menacingly toward him over the desk, Ashton snatched an automatic pistol from the top drawer, and thrust it out toward Blake.

"Stand back! Stand back! Keep away!" he cried shrilly.

Blake hastily stepped back. It was not the first time he had seen a panic-stricken fool with a pistol. The quick retreat instantly restored Ashton's assurance. He rebounded from fear to contempt.

"You big bluff!" he jeered. "Good thing you hopped lively. I'll show you! Thought I wasn't armed, did you?"

"You doughhead!" rejoined Blake. "Can't you understand? I tell you that bridge—"

"*Bah!* You knocker! I see your game. You know now that it's Papa Leslie's job; you want to get in charge—knock out my work—spoil the record I'm making. That's it! You think you'll get my place, and try to smooth things up with Genevieve."

"Shut up!" commanded Blake, raising his fist.

Ashton hastily sighted the pistol, which he had half lowered. "You—you—don't you threaten me! I'll shoot!" As Blake made no attempt to attack, he went on viciously: "You'd better not! I'll show you! I'm the boss here—get out of here! You're fired! Get out; keep off my bridge; leave the grounds, or I'll have you kicked off!"

"You fool!" said Blake. He swung around and started off with stern determination. But within three strides he faced about again. "You dotty fool! I had intended to let you down easy."

He came back toward the desk, grim-faced and very quiet. Ashton was puzzled and disconcerted by this sudden change of front. The pistol wavered in his trembling hand.

"Keep away! Don't you touch me! Don't you come near me!" he half whimpered.

Blake advanced to the opposite side of the desk, and spoke in a tone of cool raillery: "You're rattled. Better put up that gun. It might go off."

"It will in half a second!" snapped Ashton.

Blake leaned forward and transfixed him with a stare of cold contempt.

"You thief!" he said. "Your game is up. You sneak thief!"

Ashton lowered his pistol and cowered as though Blake had struck him.

"No, no! I'm not—I'm not! You haven't any proof—you can't prove it!"

"Proof?" growled Blake. "When I've known it ever since I came up before—knew it the first look. My bridge from shoe to peak—every girder, every rivet—and my truss! Not another bridge in the world has that truss. You dirty sneak thief!—*Huh!* you would, would you?"

Ashton had sought to raise and aim the pistol. This time Blake did not step back. Instead, he flung himself forward, and his hand closed in an iron grip on the wrist of the hand that held the pistol. The weapon fell from the paralyzed fingers.

Ashton made a frantic clutch with his left hand to regain the pistol, but he was jerked violently forward, up and over the desk. As he floundered across in a flurry of rustling, tearing maps and papers, he swore in shrill anger. Blake's left hand gripped his throat, His anger gave place to terror. He sought to scream, but the fingers tightened and throttled him. He was dragged across and down upon the floor, choking and gurgling. Blake bent lower.

"Lie still!" he ordered. "I'm going to let go your throat. If you squawk, I'll break your neck!"

He removed his grip alike of wrist and throat, and Ashton, gasping and panting, felt gingerly of his throat with his soft fingers. He could not see the dark marks left by Blake's terrible clutch, but he could feel the bruises. He glared up, terror-stricken, into the pale hard eyes that blazed down into his own with a light like that of molten steel.

"You—you'll not—not murder me!" he panted.

"I'll break your neck if you don't keep quiet and mind," menaced Blake.

He sprang erect. "Get up to your desk—quick!"

Ashton needed no urging. As he scrambled around to the chair, Blake picked up the automatic pistol and tested its mechanism with expert swiftness.

"Don't! Don't!" implored Ashton, dodging down.

"*Bah!* Take that pen—write!" commanded Blake. Ashton clutched at his pen and an order pad. "Steady, you fool! Now write, *'Bridge in danger. Strip bare. Blake in charge.'* " Ashton scribbled with frantic swiftness. "Got that? Sign your name in full as Resident Engineer."

The moment Ashton obeyed, Blake reached over and snatched up the order pad and an indelible pencil. In his other hand he thrust out the pistol to press its muzzle against Ashton's temple.

"Oh!—oh!—don't!" whimpered the coward.

"You skunk!" growled Blake. "Keep your mouth shut, or I'll smash you like a rattlesnake. I'm going to save my bridge. Don't get in my way!" He pointed with the pistol toward the rear door of the room. "What's in there?"

"My—my quarters."

"Get in there! Stay in! No yawping!" The terse orders ended in a flash of grim humor. "You're sick. Mind you don't get worse."

Ashton was already slinking into his apartment.

There was a rumble of freight cars outside. Blake spun about on his heel and rushed out through the vestibule.

33

ABOVE THE ABYSS

A TRAIN LOADED with steel was backing out to the bridge. Blake ran down the track to the engine and swung up into the cab.

"Stop her!" he shouted.

The engine-driver was among the men who had been introduced to Blake on his visit with Griffith. He recognized the engineer at the first glance.

"Hello, Mr. Blake!" he sang out. "You here?"

"Brakes!" cut in Blake so incisively that the driver closed his throttle and applied the airbrakes with emergency swiftness.

Anticipating his questions, Blake tersely explained: "Bridge in danger. I'm in charge. Have you a lot of empties handy?"

"How?—bridge?" queried the fireman, peering around at the stranger.

"Dozen empties—" began the driver.

"Good!" said Blake. "Clear these cars and—"

"What's this?" demanded the yardmaster, who had run up at the sudden stoppage of the train. "Back on out, Jones. There's the coal to switch."

"Damn your coal!" swore Blake. "Get a big string of empties out the bridge, quick as you can!"

"Who the hell are you?" blustered the yardmaster.

"Engineer in charge," answered Blake, holding out Ashton's order. "Bridge in danger—error in plans—overloaded—and weather report says wind! Jones, toot up your whistle—fire-call—anything! I want every man of every shift out here in two shakes."

Without waiting for orders from the yardmaster, Jones signed to his fireman, reversed, and threw open his throttle. The fireman clutched the whistle-cord and began jerking out a succession of wild shrieks and toots. As the train started away from the bridge, Blake swung to the ground to meet the excited men who came running from all directions.

He held Ashton's order close under the nose of the yardmaster, and shouted above the din of the engine whistle: "See that? She'll go when the wind rises. Hustle out those empties, with every man you have."

Impelled by the engineer's look, the yardmaster sprang about and sprinted alongside the train, waving signals to his switch crew. Blake no less swiftly sprang into the midst of the mob of off-shift men streaming from the bunkhouse.

"I'm Blake—engineer in charge—from Griffith!" he shouted. "Bridge overloaded—will go down when wind rises. We've got to clear her. She may go down when the empties back out. Any yellow cur that wants to quit can call for his pay-check. I'm going out. Come on, boys!"

He started along the service-track at a quick jog-trot. The men, without a single exception, followed him in a mass, jostling each other for the lead. Near the outer end of

the approach span they met the morning shift of carpenters and laborers, who were hurrying shoreward in response
to the wild alarm of the engine whistle. Blake waved them
about.

"Bridge in danger!" he shouted. "Volunteers to clear
material."

Few of the carpenters and none of the chattering Slovaks
and Italians caught anything except the word "danger." But
zeal and fearlessness are sometimes as contagious as fear. A
half-dozen or so drew aside to slink on shoreward. All the
others joined the silent eager crowd behind Blake. Before
they had gone a hundred feet every man in the crowd knew
that at any moment the huge cantilever might crash down
with them to certain destruction in the chasm, yet not one
turned back.

A short distance beyond the cantilever towers they
came to the foremost of the on-shift steel workers, who
had halted in their shoreward run when they saw that the
outcoming party showed no sign of halting. But those in
their rear and McGraw, who had been left behind farthest
of all in the race, were still moving forward.

Blake waved his pad to McGraw and called out to
him over the heads of the others: "Here's my order! I'm
in charge. Take every man you can handle, and work the
main traveller to the towers. Hustle!"

"Your order!" wheezed McGraw stubbornly.

Blake was already close upon him. He had dealt before
with men of McGraw's character. He tore off Ashton's
order, thrust it into the other's pudgy hand, and paused to
scribble an order to hold the train on the shore span.

On occasion McGraw could be nimble both in mind

and body. The moment he had read Ashton's order, he wheeled about to rush back the way he had come, and let out a bull-like bellow: "Hi, youse! clear f'r trav'ller! Out-shift, follow me!"

The steel workers who had been on shift raced after and past him to the main traveller. He followed at a surprisingly rapid pace, bellowing his instructions. Blake, holding back in the lead of his far larger party from the shore, began to issue terse orders to the gangs of carpenters and laborers. They strung along the extension arm, outward from the point where the floor-system was completed. Before Blake could pass on ahead, tons of beams and stringers, iron fittings and kegs of bolts and nails began to rain down into the abyss.

Having detailed half of the two shore shifts of steel workers to clear the way for the inrolling of the huge traveller, Blake took the other half out with him to the extreme end of the overhang. As soon as the main traveller began its slow movement shoreward, he ordered the smaller traveller run back several yards, in readiness to load the heavier pieces of structural steel.

All his own men being now engaged in the most effectual manner, he turned about to quiet McGraw, who, for once shaken out of his phlegmatic calm, had been reduced to a state of apoplectic rage by the inability of his men to perform miracles. Blake's cool manner and terse directions almost redoubled the efficiency of the workers. The main traveller began to creep toward the towers with relative rapidity.

Blake walked ahead of it, to steady and encourage the gangs that toiled and sweat in the frosty sweep of the rising wind. He came back again to the overhang and stood for a few moments gazing across at the outstretched tip of the north cantilever.

Suddenly his face lightened. He glanced over his shoulder at the lofty towers behind him, nodded decisively, and hastened back to where McGraw, once more his usual stolid taciturn self, was extracting every ounce of working energy out of the men who swarmed about the main traveller.

"Goin' some!" he grunted, as Blake tapped his arm.

"Stop her fifty feet this side towers," ordered Blake. "How many central-span sections have you stacked up out here?"

"All 'cept four north-side 'uns. Last come this mornin'. In yards yet."

"How long'll it take us to rig a cable tram from the traveller across to the north 'lever?"

"Huh?" demanded McGraw blankly.

"We'll run the north-side steel across by tram, and push the work from both ends. Once the central span's connected, this bridge'll stand up under any load that can be piled on her."

"Wind risin'—an' you figurin' on construction work!" commented McGraw.

"If she doesn't go to smash in the next half-hour, we'll be O.K.," answered Blake coolly. "That train has waited long enough. You look to the steel. Load the first sections for this end on the outermost car. We can cut it off the train at the towers."

At McGraw's nod, he scratched off an order and sent a man running with it to the waiting train. Very shortly the three outermost cars came rolling toward him, pushed by the switch crew and a gang of laborers. Their weight was several times offset by the weight of flooring material that had already been hurled from the bridge.

Blake tested the force of the wind, noted the distance that the main traveller had moved shoreward, and promptly ordered the work of destruction to cease. Some forty or fifty thousand dollars' worth of material had already gone over into the strait, and he was too much of an engineer to permit unnecessary waste.

The electro-magnetic crane of the smaller traveller was already swinging up a number of pieces of structural steel to load on the cars as they rolled out to the extreme end of the service-track. McGraw came hurrying to take charge of the eager loading gang. Blake went out past them to the end of the overhang, and perching himself on a pile of steel, began to jot down figures and small diagrams on the back of his pad.

He was still figuring when a cheer from the carloaders caused him to look up. The cars, which had been stacked with steel to their utmost capacity, were being connected with the rear of the train by means of a wire rope. In response to the signals of McGraw, the engine started slowly shoreward.

Before the train had moved many yards the slack of the steel rope was taken up. It tautened and drew up almost to a straight line, so tense that it sang like a violin string in the sharp wind gusts. Then the steel-laden cars creaked, started, and rolled shoreward after the train, groaning under their burden. The men all along the bridge raised a wild cheer.

Blake stepped back beside McGraw.

"Well, Mac, guess we've turned the trick," he said.

"Close,—huh?" replied the general foreman, holding up his hand to the wind.

"Close enough," agreed Blake. "She might have gone any minute since we came out. *Whee!*—if I hadn't headed off that train of steel! Well, a miss is as good as a mile. She'll stand now. Next thing is to connect the span."

"Huh?" ejaculated McGraw. "Ain't goin' t' tackle that, Mr. Blake, 'fore reinforcin' bottom-chords?"

"What! Wait for auxiliary bracing to come on from the mills? Not on your life! Once connected, she'll be unbreakable—all strains and stresses will be so altered as to give a wide margin of safety, spite of that damned skunk!"

"Huh?" queried McGraw.

Blake's lips tightened grimly, but he ignored the question.

"We'll drive the work on twelve-hour shifts,—double pay and best food that can be bought. Divide up the force now, and turn in with your shift—those who most need sleep."

34

"THE GUILTY FLEE"

IN THE MIDST of the wild flurry of work on the bridge, an engine from the junction had puffed into the switching yards with a single coach, the private car of H. V. Leslie.

Despite the shrill whistle that signalled its approach, no one ran out to meet the special,—no workman appeared in the midst of the sheds and material piles to stare at the unexpected arrival. Irritated at this inattention, Mr. Leslie swung down from his car, closely followed by Lord James.

"What can this mean?" he demanded. "Not a man in sight. Entire place seems deserted."

"Quite true," agreed Lord James. "Ah, but out on the bridge—great crowd of men working out there. Seems to be fairly swarming with men."

"So there are—so there are. Yet why so many out there, and none in the yards?"

"Can't say, I'm sure. I daresay we'll learn at the office."

"Learn what, Mr. Scarbridge?" asked Dolores, who had popped out into the car vestibule. Without waiting for an answer or for his assistance, she sprang down the steps, waving her muff. "Come on, Vievie. Don't wait for mamma."

"What are you going to do?" demanded Mr. Leslie.

"Hunt for our heroic hero, of course," answered the girl.

"You shall do no such thing," said her mother, appearing majestically in the vestibule.

Genevieve, pale and calm and resolute, came out past her aunt.

"We shall go to Mr. Ashton's office, papa," she said, as Lord James handed her down the steps. "If Mr. Blake is not there, Mr. Ashton will know where to send for him."

"Tom's out on the bridge," stated Lord James.

"He is? How do you know?" queried Mr. Leslie.

"It's a hundred to one odds. That wire to Griffith—'On the job,' y' know. He'll be where the most work is going on. I'll go fetch him."

"If you will, James," said Genevieve. "Tell him that papa—not I—You understand."

"Trust me!" He smiled, glanced appealingly at Dolores, met a frown, and started briskly away out the service-track.

"Wait," ordered Dolores. "I'll go, too. I've never been out on an unfinished bridge."

"You'll not. You'll stay ashore," interposed her mother.

"Oh fudge! Trot along, then, Mr. Scarbridge."

At her call, Lord James had halted and turned about, eagerly expectant. As, disappointed, he started on again, she addressed Mr. Leslie: "I'm not going back into that stuffy car, Uncle Herbert. Where's the place you call the office?"

He pointed to Ashton's quarters, and she skipped forward, past the engine, before her mother could interfere. The others followed her, wrapping their furs close about them to shut out the bitterly cold wind.

Dolores was still in the lead when the party reached

the office, but she paused in the vestibule for her uncle to open the door. When he entered, she stepped in after him, followed by Genevieve and Mrs. Gantry. Darting his glances about the office in keen search, Mr. Leslie crossed the room to stare concernedly at the litter of torn maps and papers on the floor in front of the desk. He hurried to the inner door and rapped vigorously. There was no immediate response. He rapped again.

The door opened a few inches, and Ashton's English valet peered in at the visitors with a timid, startled look.

"Well?" demanded Mr. Leslie. "What d'you mean, sir, gawking that way? What's the matter here?—all these papers scattered about—everybody out on the bridge. Who are you, anyway?"

"M-Mr. Ashton's m-man, sir!" stuttered the valet.

"His man? Where is he?—out on the bridge?"

"N-no, sir; in his rooms, sir."

"Tell him to come here at once!"

"Y-yes, sir, very good, sir. But I fear he'll be afraid to come out, sir. Mr. Blake—he ordered 'im to stay in, sir."

"Blake ordered him! Why? Speak out, man! Why?"

"He—he said the bridge—that it was about to fall, sir."

"Bridge—about to fall?"

"Yes, sir. So he pulled Mr. Ashton across the desk by 'is neck—manhandled 'im awful, and 'e told 'im—"

"What! What! Tell Ashton I'm here—Mr. Leslie! Tell him to come at once—at once! D'you hear?"

As the valet vanished, Genevieve darted to her father, her eyes wide with swift-mounting alarm. "Papa! Didn't you hear him? He said the bridge—it's about to fall!"

"He did! He did!" cried Dolores, catching the alarm. "Oh, and Jimmy's gone out, too!"

"'Jimmy'!" echoed Mrs. Gantry, staring.

The girl ran to the windows in the end of the room, which afforded a full view of the gigantic bridge.

"Hurry! Hurry, papa! Do something!" cried Genevieve. "If the bridge falls—!"

"Nonsense!" argued her father. "There can't be any danger. It's still standing—and all those men remaining out on it. If there was any danger—Must be some mistake of that fool valet."

"Then why are there no men ashore? Why are they all out there?" questioned Genevieve with intuitive logic. "Oh! it's true—I know it's true! He's in danger! And James— both! They're out there—it will fall! He'll be killed! Send some one—tell them to come ashore! I'll go myself!"

She started toward the door.

"No, no, let me!" cried Dolores, darting ahead of her.

"Stop!—both of you!" exclaimed Mrs. Gantry. "Are you mad?"

"Stop!" commanded Mr. Leslie.

Genevieve paused and stood hesitating before the vestibule door.

Dolores darted back to the windows.

A voice across the room called out: "That's—that's right! There's no need to go. It's all a fake—a pretence!"

Staring about, Mr. Leslie and the ladies saw Ashton beside the inner door. He was striving to assume an air of easy assurance, but the doorknob, which he still grasped, rattled audibly.

"You!" rasped Mr. Leslie. "What you doing in here—skulking in here?"

Ashton cringed back, all the assurance stricken from his face.

"You—you believe him!" he stammered. "But it's not fair! You've heard only his side—his lies about me!"

"Whose lies? Speak out!"

"His—Blake's! The big brute took me by surprise—half murdered me. He came here, drunk or crazy, I don't know which. Pretended the bridge was in danger."

"Pretended? Isn't it?"

"All rot! Not a bit of it!"

"What!"

"I tell you, it's all a put-up job—a frame-up. The brute thought he'd get in with you again—you and Genevieve. He schemed to discredit me, to get my place."

"Blake?—he did that?" eagerly queried Mrs. Gantry.

"Yes!" cried Ashton, and he turned again to Mr. Leslie. "Don't you see? He guessed that you were coming up. So he sneaked here ahead of you—took away my pistol and threatened to murder me if I left my rooms."

Genevieve looked the glib relator up and down, white with scorn.

"You lie!" she said.

"But—but—I—" he stammered, disconcerted. He stepped toward her, half desperate. "It's the truth, I tell you, the solemn truth! I'll swear to it! It was there, right at my desk. You see the maps, torn when he dragged me across—by the throat! Look here at my neck—at the marks of his fingers!"

"You're in luck. He had good cause to break your neck," commented Mr. Leslie.

"Herbert!" reproved Mrs. Gantry, greatly shocked.

"Papa! Papa!" urged Genevieve, running to grasp her father's arm. "You can't believe him! If Tom said the bridge was in danger— We stand here doing nothing! Send some one! If the bridge should fall—"

"Fall?" sneered Ashton. "I tell you it's safe, safe as a rock. Look for yourselves. It's still standing."

"Then he has saved it," snapped Mr. Leslie. "He's saved my bridge—his bridge! While you, you skulking thief—"

Ashton cringed back as if struck. But Genevieve dragged her father about from him. "Don't mind him, papa! What does that matter now? Send some one at once!"

"They're all out on the bridge already," he replied. "There's no one to send. Wait! I'll go myself!"

"Oh! Oh! The train has started on shore again—it's coming clear off the bridge!" cried Dolores. "It stopped part way, near this end. They'll be on it, they'll surely be on it. Yes, yes! There he is! There's Jimmy!"

She flung up a window-sash and leaned far out, waving her handkerchief.

Her mother turned to Genevieve, who stood as if dazed.

"My dear," she said, "do you not understand? Lord James is safe—quite safe!"

"Yes?" replied Genevieve vaguely.

"And Blake!" exclaimed Mr. Leslie. "He'll of course be coming, too. I'm going to meet him—learn the truth."

He cast a threatening glance at Ashton, and went out like a shot.

"Uncle Herbert, take me with you!" called Dolores, flying out after him.

"Blake!—coming here!" gasped Ashton. He ran to place himself before Genevieve, who was about to go out. "Wait, wait, Miss Genevieve, please! Save me! He—he said he'd smash me if I talked—he did! He did! Don't let him hurt me! He threatened to kill me—it's true—true!"

"Threatened to kill you?" repeated Mrs. Gantry. "Genevieve, call back your father. If the man really is violent, as Lafayette says—"

"Aunt Amice!" remonstrated Genevieve. "Can you believe this miserable creature for an instant?"

"But it's true—it *is* true!" gasped Ashton. "Mrs. Gantry, dear, dear Mrs. Gantry, you'll believe me! He will kill me! Take me aboard the car! Please, please take me aboard the car and hide me!"

"My dear Genevieve," said Mrs. Gantry, "the poor boy is really terrified."

"Take him to the car, if you wish," replied Genevieve. "He can leave it at the junction."

"Oh, thank you, thank you, Miss Genevieve!" stammered Ashton.

But Genevieve went out without looking at him. He followed with Mrs. Gantry, keeping close beside her.

35

THE FUTURE COUNTESS

AS THE FUGITIVE and his protectress passed out through the verandah and turned away from the bridge toward the car, they were relieved to see that Blake was not yet in sight. Genevieve was hastening out the track to where her father and Dolores and Lord James stood beside the heavily loaded bridge-service train.

Before Genevieve could reach the others, Lord James and Dolores came toward her, and Dolores cried out the joyful news: "It's safe, Vievie!—the bridge is safe now! Mr. Blake will be ashore in a few minutes."

"You're sure, James?" asked Genevieve. "Quite safe?— and he—?"

"Yes, yes, give you my word! Perfectly safe now, he said, and he'll be coming soon. Er—Miss Dolores, there's your mother going back to the car."

"And Laffi with her!"

"Quite true—quite true. I say now—you've left your muff in the office. You'll be chilled—nipping keen wind, this. We'd best go inside while we're waiting."

"Yes," agreed the girl. "Come back in, Vievie."

"No, no, dear. I'll come later. I'll wait here with papa."

"Ah, if you prefer," murmured Lord James. "But you,

Miss Dolores—really you should not stand out in this wind."

"Oh, well, if you insist," she acquiesced, with seeming reluctance.

"I do, indeed!" he replied, and he hurried her to the office.

When they entered, he led her to the big drum heating stove in the corner of the room, and went across to the inner door. He opened it, and called a terse order to Ashton's valet. He then closed the door and locked it.

Dolores started to edge toward the outer door. But he was too quick for her. He hastened across and cut off her retreat.

"No, no!" he declared. "You sha'n't run away."

"Run away?" she rejoined, drawing herself up with a strong show of indignation.

"It's—it's the very first opportunity I've had—the first time alone with you all these days," he answered. "I must insist! I—I beg your pardon, but I must find out, really I must! It seemed to me that—that just now you waved to me, from the window."

"To you? But how could I tell, so far off, that Mr. Blake was not on the train?"

"So that was it?" he replied, suddenly dashed. "Very stupid of me—very! Yet—yet—I must say it! Miss Gantry—Dolores, you've insisted on showing me your deepened dislike even since that evening. But you're so sincere, so candid—if only you'll tell me my faults, I'll do anything I possibly can to please you, to win your regard!"

"Ho! so that's it?" she jeered. "Because Vievie threw you over, you think I'll do as second choice—you think I'm waiting to catch you on the rebound."

"You?" he exclaimed. "How could that be? You've always been so frank in showing your dislike for me—how could I think that? But if only I might convince you how desirous I am to—to overcome your antipathy!"

"Lord Avondale," she said, "it is probable that you are laboring under a misconception. I am not an heiress; I am not wealthy. We are barely well-to-do. So, you see—"

"Ah, yes! And you—" he exclaimed, stepping nearer to her—"you, then, shall see that it is yourself alone! If I can but win you! Tell me, now—why is it you dislike me? I'll do anything in my power. Forget I'm my father's son—that I'm English. I must win you! Tell me how I can overcome your dislike!"

Dolores drew back, blushing first scarlet then crimson with blissful confusion. All her ready wit fled from her and left her quivering with the sweet agitation of her love.

"But it's—it's not true, Jimmy!" she whispered. "I don't— I'm not what you think me! I'm not sincere or honest—I'm just a liar! I've been pretending all along. It's not true that I ever disliked you!"

"Not true?" he asked incredulously.

She gave him a glance that answered him far more clearly than words. He started toward her impulsively.

"Dolores!—it can't be!"

She avoided him, in an attempt to delay the inevitable surrender.

"Ware danger, your earlship!" she mocked. "I warn you I'm a designing female. How do you know it's not the coronet I'm after?"

"Dearest!" he exclaimed, and this time he succeeded in capturing the hand that she flung out to fend him off.

"Wait—wait!" she protested. "This is most—ah—inde-corous. Think how shocked mamma would be. You haven't even declared your intentions."

"My intentions," he stated, "are to do—this!" He boldly placed his arm about her shoulders, and bent down over her back-tilted head. *"My* dear Miss Gantry, I have the honor of saluting—the future Countess of Avondale!"

Instead of shrinking—from him, as he half feared, she slipped an arm up about his neck.

With a blissful sigh, she drew back from the kiss, to answer him in a tone of tender mockery: "The Right Honorable the Earl of Avondale is informed that his—ah—salute is received with pleasure."

"Darling!"

"Wait," she teased. "You have it all turned 'round. You've yet to tell me the exact moment when. Vievie took second place."

"My word! How am I to answer that? Really, it's quite impossible to tell. You piqued my interest from the very first."

"But did you still lo—like Vievie when you proposed to her?"

"Er—yes—quite true. That was the day after our arrival from New York, y'know."

"Of course. But I wished to make doubly sure that you were sincere with her. Oh, Jimmy, to think I've got you, after all! I'm so happy!"

He promptly offered another salute, which was not refused.

The sound of quick steps in the vestibule startled them.

Dolores sprang away as Genevieve came hurrying in, too agitated to heed her cousin's blushes.

"Oh! I'm so glad you're still here!" she panted. "He's coming ashore. I—I told papa to tell him that—but not that I'm here! I must—I want to—"

"To play puss-in-the-corner with your Tom," rallied Dolores. "Oh, Vievie! who'd have thought it? You've lost your head! Hide over here behind the stove."

Greatly to her surprise, Genevieve instantly ran over and hid herself in the corner behind the big stove. Dolores and Lord James stared at one another. It was the first time that they had ever seen Genevieve flurried.

"Why, Vievie!" exclaimed the girl, "I actually believe you're frightened."

"No, I'm not. It's only that I must have time to—to think."

"Ah," said Lord James, with sympathetic readiness.

"I shall go out and meet him—detain him a bit."

"No, no. It's very kind of you, James. But there's no need. If only you and Dolores will wait and speak with him. I—I wish to hear how his voice sounds—first."

"Well, of all things!" rallied Dolores. "Can't you imagine how it will sound? He'll be hoarse as a crow, after shouting all his heroic orders to save the bridge. Ten to one, he'll have a fine cold, too—out there in this wind. Jimmy says it's really nawsty, y'know, with the beastly zephyrs wafting through the bloomin' steel-work, and the water so deuced far down below—quite a bit awful, don't y'know!"

"Don't tease, dear," begged Genevieve. "But you said 'Jimmy'! Oh, have you really—?"

Her face appeared around the bulge of the stove, flushed

with delight. But the sound of a heavy tread in the verandah caused it to disappear on the instant.

Blake came in slowly and with anything but an elated
look. It was evident that Mr. Leslie had refrained from
rousing his expectations. He stared at Dolores in surprise.

"You, Miss Dolores?"

"What?" she teased. "You surely did not think it would
be Vievie, did you?"

"Didn't think—"

"Yes—with Jimmy." She held out her hand to Lord
James, who clasped it fondly.

Blake caught the glance that passed between them. His
face darkened.

"Her?" he muttered. "Didn't think you were the kind to
play fast and loose, Jimmy!"

"Tom! You can't believe that of me!" protested the
Englishman.

"Couldn't explain matters out there among all your
men, y' know, but Genevieve insisted upon terminating
our engagement the very morning after. I had said nothing. She had already seen her mistake."

"Mistake?" queried Blake.

"You men are so silly," criticised Dolores, with a mischie-
vous glance toward the stove. "You ought to 've known she
loved you, all the time. Of course you won't believe it till
she herself tells you."

Blake looked about the room. Genevieve was close
behind the stove. He shook his head and muttered despondently: "Till she tells me!"

"Did you ever play puss-in-the-corner?" asked Dolores.

"You witch!" exclaimed Lord James. To divert her attention, he drew her to him and slipped a ring on her slender finger. "Ha! Caught you napping! It's on—fast!" She gave him an adorable look. "If it's ever taken off, you'll have to do it."

"That shall be—never!" he replied. Drawing her arm through his, he led her toward the door. "We're on our way, Tom. See you later at the car, I daresay. Must go now to break the news to 'Mamma.'"

"Won't she be surprised!" exulted Dolores. "It's such a joke that you and Genevieve didn't tell her! She's so sure of her methods—so sure. She'll find there are others who have methods, won't she, Lord Avondale?"

"Most charming methods!" agreed Lord James.

"S'long, Jimmy!" said Blake, gripping the other's carelessly offered hand. "Here's congratulations and good luck to you! Tell her—tell the others good-bye for me. I'll not come to the car. Tell 'em I'm too—too busy."

"Right-o! But we'll look to see you in town before a great while," replied Lord James, and he hurried Dolores out through the vestibule.

From the verandah the girl's clear voice sounded through the closed doors, free and merry, almost mocking.

36

THE OUTCOME

BLAKE STOOD WHERE the lovers had left him. Their sudden and seemingly indifferent leave-taking had added its quota of depression to his already sinking spirit. When he had come ashore and had been intercepted by Mr. Leslie he already had begun to feel the reaction from the strain and excitement of those interminable minutes and hours on the bridge—the frightful responsibility of keeping all those hundreds of men out on the gigantic structure, which at any second might have crashed down with them to certain destruction.

Now even the remembrance that he had saved the bridge could not stimulate him. Mr. Leslie's friendly praise, even his more than cordial hand-grip, seemed meaningless. The world had suddenly turned drab and gray. Her father had stated vaguely that some one was waiting to speak with him in the office. He had hastened in, half hoping to find *her*—and had found only them.

He had saved the bridge; he had found strength to do the square thing by Mr. Leslie and even Ashton. And now they were all gone, even Jimmy, and he was alone— alone!... *She* had come with the party. He was certain that some one had told him that. Yet she had not spoken to him. She had not even let him see her!

He went heavily across the room to the desk, and dropping into a chair, began methodically to gather up and fold the torn and rumpled blueprints upon the floor. But even an almost automatic habit has its limitations. A drawing slipped, half-folded, from his listless fingers. He groaned and leaned forward upon the desk, with his face buried in his arms.

Genevieve came out from her hiding place very quietly, and stood gazing at Blake. It was the first time that she had ever seen him give way to grief or suffering. Always he had stood before her firm and unyielding, even when most certain of defeat. It had never occurred to her that he could be other than hard and defiant over his own struggles and sorrows.

All the mother-love of her woman's nature welled up from her heart in a wave of tenderness and compassion. She went to him and laid her hand softly on his dishevelled head.

"Tom!" she soothed. "Tom! You poor boy!"

The touch of her hand had stricken his body rigid with suspense. But at the sound of her voice he slowly raised his head and fixed his eyes upon her in an incredulous stare.

"It is I, Tom. Don't you know me?" she half whispered, shrinking back a little way before the wildness of his look.

"*You!*" he gasped. He rose heavily. "Excuse me. I thought you were with them—on the car."

"Did not papa tell you?"

"He said something. I thought I had mistaken him. But you *are* here."

"Yes. I—I waited to speak with you—to tell you—"

"You told me that night all that's necessary," he said, averting his head to hide the look of pain that he could not repress.

"I was beside myself!" she replied. "You should have known that, Tom. How else could I have told you—told you—"

"The truth!" he broke in. "Don't think I blame you, Miss Jenny. Don't blame yourself."

"No, no, you do not understand!" she insisted. "Wait—what did you and papa do?"

"Made it up. So that's one thing less to worry you. He did it handsomely. Cracked me up for saving his bridge."

"Your bridge, too!"

"What! You know that?"

"Yes, and that you're to be partner with Mr. Griffith—finish your bridge, and build that great dam you invented, and—and if you wish, be partner in some of papa's business."

"That's too much. I told him I'd be satisfied with the credit for my bridge truss."

"Only that? Surely you'll not give up the bridge?"

"Well, 't isn't fair to kick a man when he's down. Ashton will have a tough enough time of it, I guess, from what your father said. He's to be allowed to resign, on condition that he acknowledges that he borrowed my bridge truss."

"Borrowed?"

"Yes. It seems that his father is one of your father's particular friends. So that's all settled."

She looked at him with radiant eyes. "Tom! You're even bigger—more generous—than I had thought!"

"Don't!" he muttered, drawing back. "It makes it so much harder. You don't realize!"

"Don't I?" she whispered, the color mounting swiftly in her down-bent face. "That night—that fearful night, I— Tell me—has James explained how we searched for you?—everywhere, all those days! We telegraphed all over the country. James searched the city, and papa had all his private agents— Where did you go?"

"South."

"South? Oh, and all this time—But that's past now—all the dreadful waiting and anxiety! Could you but know our delight when Mr. Griffith telegraphed that you were here!"

"What! Then you came because—"

"Yes, yes, to find you. Don't you see? We should have been here sooner, only the telegram was not delivered until after midnight, and I had to persuade Aunt Amice. She refused, until after I said I'd come anyway. But of course she doesn't know, even now. Oh, Tom! Tom!—to think you're over that dreadful attack and—"

"Attack?" he inquired.

"The one that started that night—through my fault— mine!"

"Your fault?" he repeated. "How on earth do you make that out?"

"I should have seen—understood! James had tried to explain; but I was overwrought. Not until you were going— But that is all past, dear! I've come to tell you that now you must let me help you. It is not right for you to fight alone—to refuse my aid, when I—when I—love you!"

"Jenny! You can't mean it? After that night—after what I did that night!"

"Yes," she whispered. "If you—if you'll forgive me."

"But—the drinking?"

"You can win! You proved it that night, when you crushed the glass. I no longer fear, Tom. All my doubt has gone. Even without my help I know that you—But I want to do my share, dear. If you're—you're willing, we'll be married, and—"

"Jenny!" He stood for a moment, overcome. Then the words burst from his deep chest: "Girl! Girl!—God! to think that I have that to tell you! Yes, it's true—I proved it that night—I won out that night! Do you hear, Jenny? I broke the curse! I proved it when I left you—went out into the night—after drinking all that whiskey—went down into the stockyards, past the worst saloons, all the joints. I went in and stood about, in all the odor—whiskey, beer— one after the other, I went in, and came out again, without having touched a drop. All the time I kept remembering that I had lost you; but—I knew I had found myself."

"Tom!"

"When I had made sure, I went to the freight yards, got into a fruit-car, and went to sleep. When I woke up, I was on the way to New Orleans. Been hoboing ever since."

"Oh!"

"Best thing for me. Put kinks into my body, but took 'em all out of my brain. About the drinking—it wasn't that night alone. I've kept testing myself every chance—even took a taste to make sure. Now I know. It's the simple truth, Jenny. I've won."

"My man!" she cried, and she came to him as he opened his arms.